SPIROS
& JENNY

SPIROS & JENNY

The Porn Star Brothers Series

L.J. DIVA

★ ROYAL STAR PUBLISHING ★

Chances is an imprint of Royal Star Publishing
www.royalstarpublishing.com.au

First edition paperback published in 2020
All Rights Reserved, Copyright ©L.J. Diva 2020

Trade Paperback ISBN: 978-0-6484864-3-5
Dust Jacket Hardcover ISBN: 978-1-922307-36-1
E-book ISBN: 978-0-6484864-2-8
A catalogue record for this book is available from the National Library of Australia.

Cover design: Royal Star Publishing and Odyssey Books
Cover photos: Greece - AlfioFinocchiaro/Shutterstock.com
Sydney - LeonidAndronov/Shutterstock.com
Typesetting in Minion Pro by Royal Star Publishing

Dedications

In 2014 a vague idea to write a book about a porn star came to me. In 2015 the idea brewed and grew and when my idol, Jackie Collins, passed away, the idea flourished with a vengeance.

Jackie Collins is the only inspiration in my life when it comes to writing. She had the passion, the brains, the ballsy rollicking attitude, and the kind of life that made me want to *be* her.

Without her, these books would not exist, for I would not have had the inspiration to follow in the same 'write whatever you want' league. Without her, I will continue trying to write the kind of books she wrote. Real, ballsy, and bonkbustingly good.

Jackie,

the Porn Star Brothers book series is dedicated to you as so many of my other books are. I thank you for the inspiration you have given me and hope you continue giving me, to go on and write more. I hope that you are well and having a good laugh wherever you are. I miss you and will continue doing so. Sometimes I think I feel you egging me on with my writing. Maybe that's true, and maybe it's just my rampant imagination; the same imagination that has given me the books I have written so far in my life. And sometimes, I really wished I could be you. You will forever be my idol and inspiration and I thank you.

RIP, Miss Jackie C.

And to the three Stefanovic brothers, Carlos, Pedro, and Tomas, without whom I would not have had names for my porn stars.

November 2018

"I now pronounce you, husband and husband." The minister closed his bible and stared at the two men before him. "You may now kiss."

Tomas Stephanopoulos and Roger Dencott faced each other in the Greek Orthodox Church in Armidale, Australia, lovingly smiled at each other, and kissed as husband and husband. It was the first time in forty-one years their marriage was actually legal. When they were done kissing, they turned to smile and wave at the wildly applauding family whistling and cheering them on.

The Stephanopoulos family had grown in numbers over the last forty-one years, with their grandchildren, bar Danté, married off and having kids of their own. They had hit thirty-seven members with three great-grandchildren being born that year alone.

Tomas, his beaming smile still in place, looked over his family, his brothers Carlos and Pedro with their wives Vivian and Angelina, and all of their children with their partners and children. His aunts and uncle who were left on his mother's side, his cousins and their families that were still surviving, or could attend, and finally, his gaze settled on his parents, now in their nineties, sitting in the front pew on his side. So incredibly thankful to his mama for standing up for him and his sexuality for the last forty years plus, he stepped over to her and her equally beaming smile.

Jenny Stephanopoulos, ninety, and the matriarch of the family, watched her son and son-in-law proudly as they kneeled in front of her and her husband, Spiros. "My baby." She gently laid her hand on Tomas's cheek. "My baby boy is finally *legally* a married man. Congratulations, my baby. I'm so proud of you." She kissed his forehead, and then gazed into his brown eyes. "I love you, always remember that. And Roger…" She turned her head to look at her son-in-law. "I know you will still look after him when I can't." Memories of her own wedding sixty-six years before had come bolting out of the blue and around her mind, infiltrating her heart with such sweet and tender moments.

"Of course, Mrs S," Roger murmured lovingly to the only real mother he'd had for the last forty years. His own parents had disowned him when he'd come out as gay in the 1960s, but he'd reconciled somewhat with his mother in 1981 when they'd been told they were dying of what had come to be known as AIDS. They weren't. It was a mistake made purely because so many diseases had the same symptoms and HIV hadn't even been known then. But, by a miracle, even though Tomas had died and been brought back to life, they had both continued to live very happy healthy lives, and at the ripe old age of seventy, Roger was still powering on due to great health and mental happiness, and an amazing family to be a part of.

"Dad."

Roger saw his son standing behind him, and getting to his feet, he took Simon, and his wife Deirdre, into his arms. He'd only found out Simon had existed in 2007 after Simon's mother had kept him a secret all those years. Before her death, Jan Metcalfe had told her son all about his father, who he was, and what he did. She'd said the Stephanopoulos family would take them in as their own. And they had.

"Congratulations, Dad," Simon said, hugging his father fiercely. He'd missed out on his dad's first wedding and was proud to be there for the second.

"Thank you, Simon." Roger kissed him on the cheek and grasped him by both arms. "It means so much to me to have you here. *Especially* this time. Not only is it legal, but Tomas can adopt you and make you fully, legally, one of our own."

Tomas heard his husband's words and pulled out of his father's arms where he'd been hugging him. The spitting image of each other, he glanced into Spiros's eyes, smiled, and stood tall, but kept a hold of his hand. "Yes." He gazed fondly upon Simon whom he'd come to know as a son. "I can now legally adopt you as my son, too. You'll officially be a part of the Stephanopoulos family." Setting his father's hand down gently, he hugged Simon. "Thank you for being here and for the happiness you've brought to Roger. I appreciate it so much."

"Well…it's brought a lot of happiness to me, too," Simon told him and gazed adoringly at his parents. "With Mum gone and no siblings, this has become the only family we have on my side. So…I guess it's brought happiness all round."

"It has." Roger hugged and kissed his grandchildren Stella, sixteen, and Liam, thirteen. "And I get to see my grandchildren grow up."

"Ah, I *don't* hate to interrupt this Dencott family gathering, but some of us actually want to get in for a hug," Cabot proclaimed and pushed through the family to get to his uncles. "Congrats, Uncle T." He threw his arms around Tomas's neck, held on tight while his big blue eyes crumpled and he willed himself to not cry. Tomas had been his biggest supporter during the last eleven years since he'd finally come out as gay and acquired HIV in 2007. And, except for his twin, Antonio, and his husband Tony, he was closer to Tomas than to his own father, or to his Uncle Pedro. The help they'd given him when he needed it the most was always appreciated, even in the last few years when he'd legally wed Tony in England and found a surrogate for their two children. Their son, Antonio III, was two, and their daughter, Jennifer, was six months old.

"Thank you, Cabot." Tomas hugged him back twice as hard, sensing the emotions skyrocketing around his nephew. For all the years he'd wanted children and never been able to have any due to the diseases he'd suffered from 1981, it was Cabot, the rebel of the family until 2007, whom he considered as close as a son could get. Even though he knew it drove his brother, Carlos, wild at the thought of his son being closer to his uncle, he also knew Carlos was grateful for all Tomas had done for his son. Tomas cast a curious glance at his brother who was standing next to the front pew and their mother, with a sour look on his face. Tomas grinned in delight.

Carlos saw the grin and scowled. "Yeah, yeah, T, we get it. And Cabot, you're not the only one who wants to hug Tomas, so get out of the way." He passed Roger with a pat on the arm, pulled Cabot from his brother's arms, and saw Cabot roll his eyes to which he scowled harder, making Cabot grin and slink off. "Come here, you." Carlos pulled his brother into his arms and kissed his cheek. "Congrats, little brother. You're finally legal like the rest of us."

Tomas's face lit up like a lightbulb. "We are. Only took forty-one years, but finally."

"Finally, my God." Pedro came up the rear and enveloped both of his elder brothers. "Forty-one bloody years to the day. How come you get two ceremonies and we don't?" He grinned at Carlos over Tomas's shoulder. "I feel left out."

"You always feel left out," Carlos returned. "Comes with being the baby of the family."

"You always did feel you were missing out on stuff," Tomas told Pedro. "But, in reality, it was me. At least in our twenties." Memories flooded back of the late '70s and early '80s and pain of recognition fled over his face.

Carlos saw it and hugged tighter. "We soon made up for it, though, with your wedding, and the holidays. All the things we did to make your time count." He didn't like remembering 1981, the year he'd lost and regained his brother, and forced those memories aside. "So, let's go make some more."

"Yes, let's." Tomas pulled out of his brother's embrace and hugged his way through the family who still crowded around.

As Jenny watched, a soft smile on her face, her left hand firmly in Spiros's, she noted how many had come and gone. Her parents were long gone, as were her older siblings and some of their children. Only her three younger sisters and younger brother were left. Most of their children were still alive, and half of them were there, plus some of their kids had come as had all of her own. She felt a tickling at her left ear and looked over her shoulder to see her beautiful golden-haired great-granddaughter. "Hello, Carys, my baby." She lifted her hand to tickle her cheek and got a giggling laugh in return.

"Gate-Gamma." The very cheeky four-year-old kissed her great-grandmother's cheek. "I love you, Gate-Gamma." Carys leaned over the back of the pew to kiss her great-grandfather. "Gate-Gampa."

"Hello, Carys, you've been a very good girl today," Spiros replied, a twinkle in his eye.

"I think she's getting antsy," Diana told them, struggling to keep her youngest in her arms as she tried wriggling herself free. "I might take her outside."

"Are we going, Mama?" Jaqueline, Diana's seven-year-old, asked. "Is there going to be cake at the party?" She'd had her fill at her grandma and grandpa's party, as well as Great Uncle Pedro and Aunt Angie's party, but could definitely go for thirds. Both girls were dressed in frilly dresses designed by Diana, and her cousin Alena, for *Haus of Stefan*, their fashion company. Ever since they'd started having children, children's clothing was all the rage at *HOS*, especially since there were more girls than boys being born.

"We'll go in a moment, sweetie," Jenny told her, getting a kiss from Jaqueline. She spotted Charles Kensington, Diana's husband, with their ten-year-old son Adam who was sitting quietly, and noted how all three of the Kensington children had the same golden-brown looks and blue eyes of their mother. Diana Villiers Stephanopoulos Kensington, was the daughter of her eldest son, sixty-five-year-old Carlos, and his wife, eighty-one-year-old former supermodel, Vivian Villiers. Glancing at the family, she readied herself to stand. At ninety, she was still fairly fit and spry, but did use a walking stick with a jewel-encrusted handle to help her. It also had a hidden implement in the handle, a sneaky little piece that her sons had found for her birthday. Spiros had a similar cane, but without the blade.

"Need help, Mama?" Tomas quickly moved to her side and helped her stand.

"I'm fine, my baby. This heat is doing my bones and muscles good. Although you might need to help your father." She watched Carlos and Pedro help Tomas get Spiros on his feet. At ninety-three, Spiros's age was catching up with him and hunching him over.

"I'm fine, my sons," Spiros told his boys. "Just a little creaky." He waited a moment until he was steady on his feet and then joined hands with his wife in the same place they had married sixty-six years previously. "But I agree with your mother, the heat is doing these old bones good." They moved slowly down the aisle and out into the sunshine. It was a beautiful November day in Armidale, New South Wales. A balmy twenty-eight degrees, there was not a cloud in the sky, and the scent of spring flowers drifted on the breeze that ambled aimlessly along.

The family had been in Australia for barely a week, having arrived on the first of November, and celebrated Carlos and Viv's, and Pedro and Angie's anniversaries first. All three brothers had married one after the other back in November 1977, and with it being almost one year to the date that gay marriage was passed in Australia, they had been planning this trip for a whole year. Back in 2017 when they'd celebrated their fortieths, they'd then watched in trepidation as their country had the referendum on whether or not to pass the law. They had, and so this trip was a year in the making, especially when they had thirty-seven plus family members in the same place at the same time in the same country. Not to mention Jenny's family.

Jenny watched as her grandchildren and their families, plus her siblings' families, boarded the buses she had hired to transport the majority of the family, and for those who couldn't take the buses, they had chauffeured limos. She carefully stepped into her and Spiros's limousine and watched her sons help their father. Carlos and Viv, Pedro and Angie joined them, while Tomas and Roger made sure everyone was safe and settled into their vehicles before climbing into the limo.

"You could have had your own car, my baby," Jenny murmured as they set off. "You didn't need to come with us."

"*Of course* we did, Mama." Tomas leaned over and squeezed her hand. "We're family. Where *you* go, *we* go. That's the way it's always been, and that's the way it always *will* be."

Jenny teared up. She'd raised her three babies to be mature, independent men, to love, respect, and honour themselves, their parents, and their partners. Her sons had done magnificently. Squeezing back, she took in her middle son, resplendent in his tuxedo, the spitting image of his father at the same age. His dark, grey tinted hair was slicked back as it always was, the silver-framed glasses enlarged his big brown eyes, and he had a smile that spread ear to ear.

Roger sat beside him, also in a tux. His brown hair had greyed through, and his dark eyes were soft with happiness. Pedro, her youngest at sixty-one, sat beside Roger in a black suit and shirt, while Angie sat opposite him in a black satin dress that flared around her stilettoed ankles. Viv was next to her in a soft blue chiffon creation from *Haus of Stefan,* and Carlos was beside her.

Her three boys had proved themselves to be the men she had raised, the men she would fight for until her dying breath.

"I can't believe the church we got married in is still standing." Spiros stared out the window at the changes Armidale had progressed through since they'd married in 1952.

"Neither could I." Jenny grasped his hand. "But it was. And since Tomas said he wanted the ceremony here, we started planning. Even the hall where we had our reception is still up and running, so we're headed there now."

"Will it be big enough?" Spiros asked, noting the warmth from his wife's hand.

"Absolutely." She smiled at her doting husband of sixty-six years. "They've added on over the decades, but since most of the family won't be there, there'll be more than enough room. Regardless of how many great-grandchildren we have now."

"Three more this year," Carlos piped up and gazed fondly at his mother. "Who knew Cabot was going to be a father. Antonio, too. It's weird…" He frowned slightly at the memories of the last four decades. "I always figured Diana would marry and be a mother, but somehow, with the way Cabot was going, I never really took him for being a husband, let alone a father."

"He's done a lot of growing up in the last eleven years," Tomas replied and leaned across in front of him to take Carlos's hand. "He's got great parents and uncles, and even greater grandparents who *all* pulled for him to get better and grow up. And he did."

"It took contracting HIV to do it." Carlos's comment had a tinge of snideness to it. Even though he loved his son, it still irked him that he'd been so blatantly disregarding of his sexual health that he'd contracted HIV, a disease he would never be free of.

"There's no point still clinging to the past, Carlos." Tomas saw the furrowed expression on his brother's face and knew he was not fully over the fact. "Cabot's more than proved he's matured far beyond any of *our* expectations. He's become an activist and advocate, helps out at the AIDS centres we have, does videos and books, and raises money for research."

"Yes," Jenny interrupted her son, making him look at her. "He has far exceeded our expectations. You need to let it go, Carlos. They have Antonio and Jennifer now, and both babies are HIV free. He's become the responsible son you always wanted."

Carlos let out a strangled sigh. "I know," he relented. "But…I still…" Unable to come up with a word, or phrase, to explain his feelings, he shook his head and sighed again.

"Hold anger towards him eleven years on for being stupid enough to contract it," Jenny supplied. She knew her son like the back of her hand because he was exactly like her, and there were still moments she wished Cabot didn't have HIV, and even the odd moment she wished Tony didn't have it either, or at least while he was with Cabot. But those ships had both long sailed, and nothing could change the fact her grandson and his husband had both contracted HIV via an assault from the same man one year apart. "The past cannot be changed, Carlos," she murmured, deep in thought. "If it could, there would be so much I *would* change."

"Mama?"

Jenny came out of her reverie to find all six of her children, and her husband, staring at her in surprise. A soft sigh escaped her as she prepared her next words. "So much has happened in our lives, *your* lives, *the kids'* lives. Not all of it good. There's so much I wish hadn't happened, I could change, I could relive, but then…" She took a deep breath, and her brow furrowed. "It wouldn't, maybe, make us as strong and close-knit as we are. Our foibles, our wrongs, our mistakes, choices, words and actions, they could've all been so different, so…" Her eyes closed and she breathed softly in thought.

"Mama? What's wrong? Are you okay? Are you ill?" Tomas's voice was soft as he held her hand. "What is it?" He knew the year had been tough for his mother. After turning ninety in May she had laid out her plans for her and Spiros's belongings, which children, grand and great-grandchildren everything would go to. She'd launched into a detailed instructive course with the grandkids for when it was time for them to take over the business, and had handed the reins of *Stephanopoulos Inc.* over to him, Pedro and Carlos, although she was still in charge in name and signature until her death.

"I'm fine, my baby," she murmured and opened her eyes. "Just… this year has been one for reflection of life and family, and who knows how long your father and I have left." She raised a hand to quieten their protests. "And thinking about it all, filling out the scrapbooks every year as I do, all of the people we've lost, we've gained…" Shaking her head at the memories, she went on. "I would change everything that happened to you boys in 1977. I would take away your illness from 1981," she glanced at Tomas, "I would take away the assaults on Cabot and Alexis, and Angie and Viv long before that, I would take away the kidnappings, and deaths, and poisonings, everything that everyone ever did to all of you, my babies." Jenny looked at each reflective sad face. "I would change all of it. Take away your pain and suffering, the pain and suffering of your children… but…in doing that…" Her eyes closed again and she breathed steadily. "It would more than likely change everything about us and who we are now. How close we are, how we've evolved as a family unit all because *of* those experiences we've had since 1977. We would be different. Not us. And *I like* us. I like who we are now and what we've become, and we've become that *from* the life experiences we've all had. We wouldn't be who and what we are without them. And regardless of how much you might still want to kick and scream about Cabot, Carlos," she said as she pointedly looked at her son, "we cannot change it. And, if it *wasn't* for that diagnosis, he might not have turned into the very mature and adult Cabot we have now."

"Oh…there are times he's still very much that brat from 2007," Carlos replied with a nod of his head. "You can see it in his eye, or when he stomps his foot when he doesn't get his way. That child is still very much alive in him. It likes to rear its ugly head every now and then."

"Steele Stefan." Pedro grinned. "I saw him pop out just last month when baby Antonio threw his shitty nappy in his face." Laughter flew around the limo.

Steele Stefan was the moniker Cabot had gone by in his modelling days. From fifteen to thirty, Cabot and his twin Antonio had been known as Steele and Phoenix Stefan. But, after Cabot's diagnosis at twenty-five, they'd slowed down on modelling and quit at thirty when they'd both got married.

"See what I mean, he's still very much a brat," Carlos managed through his tears of laughter at the image of Cabot and baby Antonio. The whole family had seen it happen. "And when he pops out, it reminds me of 2007 when he contracted HIV and the massive amount of crap he put us through."

"*But without that,*" Jenny went on, "he wouldn't be the man he is now. He and Antonio are both husbands with children and have matured beyond our expectations. As much as I'd love to change so many things in the past, it would change everything that is now. And *I love* what we have now." She nodded out the window. "And we're here. My, it has been expanded upon since our reception."

What used to be an average reception hall off the main street of Armidale, was now a massive two-storey building with multiple spires, rounded archways, disability ramps up either side of the larger set of stairs, a circular driveway, and a car park to the side. The owners had wanted to keep the original building, so it had been turned into the lobby and renovated.

The car pulled to a stop out the front, along with the others, and the boys, Viv, and Angie piled out.

"Papa, do you want your chair?" Tomas leaned down in the doorway. "It will save you walking all the way."

"Yes, my son," Spiros murmured. "I am feeling a little worn out."

Tomas and Roger quickly pulled the chair from the boot of the limo and set it up with the cushion and blanket. "Here you go. I'll help you out." Tomas helped his father from the car and into the chair that Roger held onto. Once Spiros was settled, Roger pulled the chair away and Tomas and Carlos helped Jenny out of the car.

Straightening her pretty blue and pink chiffon top with matching blue pants and slip-on flats, Jenny carefully walked up the stairs, with the help of her sons, and inside to join her husband and children. She watched as her family piled in, and then as her grandchildren, and their partners and children, managed to get themselves in with three prams and multiple strollers. The menagerie of her adult grandchildren trying to wrangle twelve children of their own made her smile. That smile turned into a chuckle, which turned into dainty laughter that echoed through the centre's large and luxurious lobby.

"What's so funny, Mama?" Angie asked, bemused by Jenny's sudden laughter.

"Your children." Jenny pointed at the mussed hair, frazzled expressions, and toddler taming that was going on. Except with Danté. At twenty-five, he hadn't yet got to the stage of marriage and children.

Danté shook his head at his siblings and cousins then noticed the amused looks his parents, uncles, and grandparents were giving them. He strolled over and casually slung his arm around his grandmother and kissed her cheek. "I'm so glad I'm not a part of that, yet. They all look utterly useless."

Jenny laid a hand against his chest. "Oh…you will be…one day."

"Not if I have anything to say about it," he quipped. "Look at them. Useless."

Smiling, Jenny looked up at her youngest grandson who'd grown to six foot one like his older brother Dominic. With his dark brown hair and brown eyes, he'd turned into quite a mature looking man for his age, and had girls and women fall at his feet when he DJd in the family's club. "It will happen for you one day, my baby. You'll know when the right one comes along, and then it will be on like Donkey Kong."

"Grandma!" Danté complained, a look of horror on his face that his grandmother still used such terms, much to the laughter of his parents and aunt and uncles. "I can't believe you still use that phrase. How old is it?"

"It doesn't matter how old it is, it's true. When the right girl comes along for you, you'll know. Don't you worry."

"I'm not worried." Danté gazed down at her still bright blue eyes. "Coz I've still got my favourite gal, hey!" His head flew forward and he looked over his shoulder to see his father. "What'd you do that for?"

Pedro had playfully smacked him up the back of the head. "Stop trying to charm your grandmother, you kids have always done that when you want something, and today's not the day to do it. It's Tomas and Roger's day, so help your grandmother inside so we can get on with the festivities."

"Who said I wanted anything?" Danté argued, but did as he was told when he saw the look on his father's face. "All right, all right, I'll help Grandma. I'm not after anything." He helped her into the reception room, that had the capacity for a thousand people, and led her over to the side where the tables and chairs were placed for their immediate family.

The room was cavernous, with a high ceiling, a stage opposite the door, a huge dance floor in front of it, and carpeted dining space around it.

The club supplied luxurious seating for Jenny and Spiros as matriarch and patriarch of the family, but Spiros chose to stay in his wheelchair while Jenny took the cosy velvet-covered throne style chair they had made for her.

As everyone found their seats at the tables placed around the dance floor, Jenny watched on fondly. Tomas and Roger were to her left, with Carlos and Viv, Pedro and Angie opposite them. The family sat in order at the tables with Simon and Deidre and their children at the next table with Diana, Charles and their children, followed by Cabot and Antonio with their families, and then Alena, Dominic and Alexis with theirs. Danté sat with his best friend Nick Gatos and his parents, Mike and Maggie, who were Angie and Pedro's best friends since

1977, his sisters, Summer and Melody who were Alexis's best friends, and Doctors Dan Ardent and his husband Derek Blaine who'd been integral honorary members of the family since 1981 when Dan treated Tomas for his AIDS symptoms. Jenny's siblings and their families were spread out at the tables that were placed around the dance floor until they were opposite the head table.

A late lunch was served and then speeches were made.

"I want to thank Mama and Papa, of course, for standing by us all these years." Tomas held his glass aloft. "Last year when we celebrated our fortieth wedding anniversary, it was tinged with some sadness." His eyes moistened at the thoughts he needed to turn into words, and blinking back the tears, he took a breath and continued. "We had watched for forty years, the continuing saga of gay marriage, and gay rights, not only in Greece, but America and here in Aus. And finally…" He looked down at his mother beside him and held the hand she offered. "Australia, last year, made gay marriage legal and official."

Cheers and applause flew around the room with a few whistles thrown in.

"Thank you." Tomas grinned, only waving three fingers of his left hand that held his glass so he didn't spill any. "Roger and I watched with a twinge of sadness in 2014 when our nephew Cabot was able to legally wed Tony in England." He glanced down the tables at his nephew who smiled and waved his fingers at everyone. A touch of Steele Stefan coming out as he primped at the attention. "And we wondered when Australia would follow suit. Well, four years after my nephew, and forty-one years after our first ceremony, Roger and I can now finally say…we *are* husband and husband." He held his glass up and the room cheered more. "So, without further ado," Tomas gushed. "Let the festivities begin…again!"

Waiters took away plates and refilled champagne glasses, and Pedro stripped off his jacket and headed for the stage where the DJ decks were still set up from the previous two nights for his and Carlos's anniversaries. He unbuttoned his shirt, rolled up his sleeves, put his headphones on, and set the needle on the first record.

"Everyone give a shout out to my brother Tomas, and his newly legal husband, Roger," he said into the microphone. "We're gonna rock all night, and celebrate until morning, with all the hits from the '70s, '80s and right through until today. At some point, Dom and Danté will take their turn, so you'll see they've still got it and can keep up with their old man, but for now, let's rock this joint, Armidale." He spun around and flung his arms in the air. At sixty-one, he still had what it took to be the best DJ in the world, and most certainly the best in Greece, still taking to the decks every Friday night in the family's club, *SB3*, on Mykonos. His sons ran the rest of the week and had been trained that year to run *SB3* and the family's music label, *Sync*. When it was time for Pedro to step down, the company would pass to his four children, with each running aspects of the family empire, particularly, the music side.

Pedro danced to his left and boogied to his right, all while watching his family hit the dance floor. He was the proud youngest son of the two most incredible people he knew, Australian born Jenny, and Greek-born Spiros. He was the proud youngest brother of the two most incredible brothers anyone could ever have, Carlos and Tomas. The proud husband of Angelina, and the proud father of the four most amazing children on the planet, Alena, Dominic, Alexis and Danté. And was now the proudest grandpa, after bragging to Carlos, of the five most amazing little human beings on the planet. Five-year-old Ava, and three-year-old Harper, the two most adorable little girls on the planet in their frilly pink and blue party dresses and shiny shoes, who giggled and held hands as they bounced around, and one-year-old grandson Hunter, all by his eldest, Alena. He watched the girls on the floor with their mother, looking just like Alena with their big blue eyes and dark curly hair.

Alena's husband, forty-three-year-old singer-musician, Luca Saint, had been married into the family for seven years. An Italian American, he was tall, dark, and devastatingly good looking, suiting Alena's looks as a couple. They had made music together on stage and off. He watched them dance together in a rhythm he shared with Angie, one of passion and fire, even after all these years.

His gaze wandered to his eldest son. Thirty-five-year-old Dominic, or Dom Stefan as he went by professionally. He was married to thirty-two-year-old Australian Greek Davina Smythe. They had met two years ago and hit it off instantly, and recently celebrated their first wedding anniversary. They had baby Christopher who was a healthy six months old and sleeping in his pram being watched over by Jenny and Angie. He saw Dom pull Davina into his arms and kiss her.

Pedro watched his eldest two children and memories of him and Angie came flooding back. His children were experiencing the love, passion, and fire they'd experienced decades earlier, and he was glad that the love his mama had instilled in him, he and Angie had instilled in their children. He gazed over the crowd for his other two and found Danté talking to Nick. "Always working," he murmured, proud of his son for starting up his *IT Web Solutions* business eleven years earlier at the tender age of fourteen, and making it a massive success. They employed many people in Mykonos and Greece and had built quite a business. Danté had grown into quite the young man at twenty-five, taking on maturity and adulthood, unlike Dom and Cabot who hadn't at the same age.

He lowered his eyes and saw his daughter, thirty-year-old Alexis, sitting at the table with her doctor husband, forty-year-old Marcus Wellcroft. They'd only met last year and quickly fallen in love and married earlier in the year. She was holding his youngest grandchild, three-month-old Marais, and a doting mother she was, gently rocking her baby back and forth. Her smile was electric with happiness and Marcus was a doting father, leaning over and gently rubbing his daughter's cheek.

Pedro's smile was soft as his gaze wandered down the room towards his wife who sat next to his mama. Both were watching him with soft smiles. His smile broadened at having been caught getting sappy about his family, and he blushed and glanced away. But, after a thought, he turned the music down and spoke into the microphone. "Has anybody ever said what an awesome family we are?"

The crowd looked up at him and all replied, "Yes," before breaking into laughter.

"Good." Pedro nodded. "Because we are, and I am so damn proud to be a member of it. I have awesome parents, awesome brothers, an awesome wife and sister-in-law, awesome kids and nephews and niece, and now even more awesome grandkids and great-nephews and nieces. We are all so damn awesome that I'm going to play this song." He stopped long enough to pop on *Everything is Awesome* from the *Lego Movie* soundtrack, and when the first beats of the song came on, the adults groaned, but the kids screamed in joy and jumped around holding hands. Ava and Harper were joined by Jaqueline and Carys, and three-year-old Izabella, Antonio and Maria's eldest daughter. He watched as two-year-old Antonio, and one-year-olds Valentina and Hunter bounced up and down as their parents held their hands, dancing with their cousins and siblings. His smile softened. Yeah, he was one damn lucky guy indeed.

"He's happy," Angie said as she watched her husband's face.

"He should be. He has everything anyone could ever want," Jenny replied, glancing from her son to her daughter-in-law. "Go and be with him. You don't need to watch the children all night." Her eyes turned to Christopher, still soundly sleeping, and she added, "You're both incredibly lucky. Just as your father and I are, and have been." Her eyes found Angie's. "Go on, join your husband. We'll watch Christopher."

"You sure?" Angie moved to stand, but thought better of it. At fifty-nine, the Stephanopouloses were the only parents she'd known since she was eighteen and had married into the family. Pregnant with Alena, and desperately alone after her father's death, her in-laws were a godsend in her hour of need and she'd taken to them as they'd taken to her.

"Go," Jenny encouraged, and managed to pull the pram around so it was in front of her and Spiros. "Or go and dance with your grandbabies, just as Spiros and I used to back in the '70s and '80s. Remember when Alena and Diana were young and we'd take them to *Studio 69*?"

Angie laughed. "How could I forget? They were the princesses of the ball."

"That they were." Jenny gazed at all of her grandchildren, grown-up adults having kids of their own. Her eyes teared over at the long-gone memories. There were times when they were happy for a few years and sad for the next few. The late '70s, and early to mid-'80s were a hell of a time as her whole life had been, but those years had seen a lot of upheaval in her personal and family life, all for it to settle down come the late '80s. The '90s and most of the noughties had been wonder-filled years, but reverted back to upheaval in the mid-to-late noughties when Cabot had gone off the rails only to be brought back from the brink of death with his diagnosis. The years following repeated the cycle they'd experienced three decades earlier. Weddings and babies as the grandchildren got married and had children of their own.

"The next generation is here and growing by the minute," Jenny murmured, her gaze wandering back and forth. She had three sons, three in-laws, seven blood grandchildren and one about to be adopted. Eleven blood great-grandchildren and three by marriage, with three being born that year. So far, her ninetieth year hadn't gone so badly, and they were planning on spending the rest of November in Australia and would probably stay until May at least to have a good long dose of Aussie sunshine and spend what could be the last time with her remaining siblings.

"Mama?"

It brought Jenny out of her memories and she took Angie's hand. "Go and dance with your babies while you can, my baby. Time is just too short."

Worried by her mother's words, and knowing that year had been tough on Jenny, Angie frowned and glanced at Pedro, who was too busy dancing to an '80s hit, so she looked out to the dance floor, longing for her grandbabies.

"Go, Angie," Jenny urged. "We're fine. And we have three doctors in the house if we need anything." Her eyes flitted from Angie to Marcus, to Dan and Derek. "All *very capable* doctors."

Angie's slow grin faltered. "I know. It's just that I sense something."

"What?"

Angie stared into her mother's eyes. "That you know your time is up and you're getting ready to leave us."

"Not for a good while, yet, I hope." Jenny squeezed her daughter's hand. "It was just time to prepare the family, that's all. It had to be done one day."

"I know," Angie rushed on, pushing her black hair out of her face and behind her ear. Even after all these decades, it was still straight and black, with the help of dye in a bottle, of course, just like Pedro's. "It's just I sense something, we all do, and we're not sure what." She kissed Jenny's hand.

"Don't fuss," Jenny reassured her, taking in Angie's big brown eyes, dainty features, and slim figure. "Go and be with your grandbabies while you can. Go." She gestured out to the floor and watched her great-grandbabies dancing around, huge grins on their faces, and lit up eyes. They were all beautiful and took after their parent's. "Go."

Angie sighed and watched her mother-in-law's twinkling eyes and smile as she stared happily at the children. "Okay, Mama. Yell out if Christopher needs help."

"We'll be fine," Jenny told her and watched as Angie slipped off her black heels and swished onto the dance floor in a sea of black satin. Her elegant evening party dress had been designed by Alena for *Haus of Stefan.*

"*Are* you all right, my love?" Spiros had seen the look on his wife's face and heard the tone of her conversation with Angie. He'd also sensed something was not quite right and wondered if something was going on that she hadn't told him. "What is it, Jenny?"

A soft sigh passed her lips and she turned her head to her husband. "Just memories, that's all. Memories of us, and how we came to be. Our life here in Australia, and then moving to Greece, our children, grandchildren, great-grandchildren, and how they've all come to be. The love and the loss…" Her voice trailed off and her brow furrowed. "So much…so many memories that we have, so much love for *and from* our babies. Why, just eleven years ago we were all doing that *Flair* magazine article on the family and how we'd managed to build a family empire, or dynasty, or whatever word was used." Jenny's lips turned into a grin. "That's what we've built, unbeknownst to us at the time, 1977, when I wanted Stephano's money for what he'd done to our boys—"

"Jenny, there's no need to mention his name," Spiros murmured, surprised that she had.

"I know, but where would we be without that money? Certainly not able to fly around the world on a whim, or start up businesses, or buy homes. What Stephano did to our boys made us all closer. And what happened to Tomas and Roger made us more so. We've grown from that." She grasped her husband's hand and smiled. "*We've* made us who we are, without *us*, we wouldn't be. Our kids and grandkids wouldn't be, and neither would theirs." She noted the tears in Spiros's big brown eyes. His hair was fully grey now, and thinning all over, but he still had the moustache she liked from the late '70s. He'd kept it all these years just for her. It was the one constant she had to look forward to every morning when she woke, and every night when she went to bed. Spiros and his tickly moustache. It was thin and grey as well, but he'd kept it just for her. Not that it did much tickling anymore. They hadn't made love in over five years, but they still kissed and cuddled every night, and the fires still burned brightly in both of them. "We have our family, because of us," she went on, leaning towards him as the music and lights surrounded them. "Our family is because of us and what we did with that money. What we turned it into and made of it. After we told the grandkids the story in 2007, it brought thirty years of everything to a close. The final chapter, if you will. And all of the kids have been able to move on with their lives, and meet and marry partners just as ambitious as them to start a new generation of Stephanopouloses just as we'd planned. Look…" She waved her somewhat withered hand over all before them and saw multiple generations of lineage along with her siblings' families. "Look at them. *We* made this. *We* created magic."

Spiros chuckled. "Yes, my love, we did. But you seem very melancholic. Is it all the planning you've done this year? Our estates and wills, signing over the company to the boys, deciding who will get what. Has all of that made you this way? In a weird mood none of us can put our finger on…" He worried for his family, his wife especially since she'd carried the burdens of the family for decades once they'd moved back to Greece in 1981 upon Tomas's illness. It was all hands on deck. *Stephanopoulos Meats* needed running, they'd built *SB3, Sync* and *S'Reel,* taken over *The Windmill Hotel* and multiple buildings, homes, and office spaces, plus businesses as the grandchildren grew. The family also had *Prologue Press,* their publishing house through which they published all of their books.

And even though they'd hired managers for each, Jenny kept her hand in it all until this year, whereas Spiros had retired from running his family's meat shop and from managing *SB3* back in 1995 at the age of seventy. Jenny kept on doing her weekly business meetings with her managers and accountant until it was time to hand it all over to their sons. She'd had been training them off and on for about ten years, but that year, it was time for them to step up and take on *Stephanopoulos Inc.* or *S.Inc.* as it was affectionately known. Not only was it time for them to manage the company as a whole, but to start training their children to run their parts of the business.

Carlos had *S'Reel,* his movie production company, and *Stefan Productions* with Pedro who had *Sync.* Tomas and Roger had *In Shape,* their gym and personal training business, along with three AIDS care homes in Miami which Simon and Deidre were helping out at. Cabot and his husband Tony DeLuca also helped out at the gym and with the care homes, and Cabot and Alexis had the *Mykonos Assault and HIV/AIDS Support Centre.* Diana and Alena not only ran *Haus of Stefan* and *Styled by Stefan* but *Villiers Style* that Viv had originally started in 1980. Danté had *IT Web Solutions* with Nick, as well as DJing with Dom at *SB3* and working at *Sync,* and Antonio was getting into documentary and movie making.

Every single one of the family was busy in some way, and it had been time for Jenny to pass it on, so they could have a few more years with some peace and quiet. Except…that hadn't happened…

Spiros glanced at each member of his family, smiling as memories came flooding back. All the years, all the tears, all the times that made it worth it.

"What do you think Mama and Papa are smiling about?" Carlos asked Viv as they danced on the floor with Diana, Charles, and six of their grandchildren. At sixty-five, Carlos still had the same golden-brown hair his mama gave him, and always denied he used hair dye to help it along. He was reasonably fit and healthy thanks to Tomas and Roger, and all the good food his mama and brother had made over the years. He was also an extremely successful movie writer, director and producer. He noticed the sneaky grins his parents gave each other and the quick set of kisses they enjoyed, thinking that no one was watching.

"Aw, I think it's sweet." Diana was happy that her grandparents were still happy and in love after sixty-six years of marriage. "I hope we're like that," she told Charles. At forty, she and Charles had been married for nearly eleven years, their anniversary being at Christmas, and had three children to show for it.

At fifty-one, Charles Kensington had been an author and the family photographer for the last decade. He'd been a famous photographer when he'd met Diana when she was the tender age of nineteen, and at their first shoot, he'd fallen in love. He had still been grieving the loss of his wife and daughter a year earlier and knew that love with the nineteen-year-old goddess was just not going to happen. Over the next ten years, his apathy for models and the world of modelling became maddening, and his obsession with Diana had heightened, but upon being kidnapped in a war zone in 2007, after spending a weekend with the beautiful Diana, he'd been rescued by Jenny's security team and found out Diana was pregnant and pining for him, just as he was pining for her. So, he had a lot to be grateful for thanks to his grandmother-in-law. "So do I," he finally replied, giving his wife a quick kiss.

"Gamma, dance Gamma," Carys called to Viv. She was dancing between her grandparents and holding hands with Vivian and Jaqueline.

Viv's laughter floated around them. "I remember when your mama would say that to *her* Gamma, it just seemed like yesterday." She glanced laughingly at her daughter. "It was just like yesterday when you were four years old and calling Jenny Gamma."

Diana giggled. "Wasn't it? My goodness. How many years ago was that? Times have certainly passed." She smiled at her mother, still so elegant at eighty-one. Her golden-brown hair swayed gently against her shoulder blades, her petite slim figure still cutting a rug on the dance floor. And even though Diana had inherited her mother's beauty, she'd inherited her father's and grandmother's famous blue eyes, and an assuredness about life and who she wanted to be. She glanced to her father, still the same Carlos Stephanopoulos she'd always called daddy, with his bright blue eyes that crinkled in the corners as he smiled at her. She smiled back and moved over to him, threw her arms around his neck, and kissed his cheek. "I love you, Daddy. You and Grandma are my rocks."

Carlos, teary from the unexpected moment, wrapped his arms around her waist and hugged back. "I love you too, my baby. You're my only daughter, and I'm *so* glad Viv and I had you." His eyes caught Viv's which were just as teary as his own, and he laughed lightly. "No time for tears, my baby, this is a celebration."

Diana had been watching her grandparents hold hands and kiss over her father's shoulder. "Look." She nodded in their direction. "They're still so happy and together all these years later. And you and Mama are still together and happy all these years later, and Uncle Pedro and Aunt Angie, and Uncle Tomas and Roger." Her eyes scanned the room, moving from person to person as she spoke. "I hope all of us are as happy and together when we get to our forty-first and sixty-sixth anniversaries." Her eyes lingered on her good looking husband, and her arm slid around his waist as his slid around her shoulder. "Do you think we'll still be together in another thirty years to celebrate our fortieth, or forty-first anniversaries?"

"Oh, I think I'll be able to manage that." Charles kissed her lips lightly. "Although, I'll be old by then. You'll have to look after me."

"Old! Pfft!" Diana exclaimed. "You'll only be in your eighties. Grandma's ninety and Grandpa's ninety-three; you'll be fine." Looking into her husband's sparkling green eyes, she noted the greying temples and odd streak through his brown hair. Charles had held up well the last ten years after recovering from the kidnapping, and he was fitter and healthier than ever, which was why their sex life was still explosive, even after three children, whom she loved and fiercely adored, just as her mama and daddy loved her, and her grandparents loved everyone, Something they'd all inherited from generation to generation was to love, protect, and honour each other, from siblings, to cousins, to parents, to grandparents. You love, honour, and respect, and protect where, when, and how you could, and they did that as a family unit. The closer they were knitted together, the better they could do it, and the more protected they were against the world.

"Dance, Mama, dance." Carys tugged on her mama's hand. At four, she was far from the youngest of the entire family, but she was the youngest of her own, and she knew that meant lots of hugs and kisses from everyone.

Diana looked down at her baby and saw the spitting image of her from that age. The memories bolted through her like a wild brumby. "Oh, my goodness, it's like I just went back in time to when I was saying that." Lifting Carys into her arms, she kissed her chubby cheek. "Having fun, my baby?"

"Yes, Mama." Carys's curly-haired cherubic head bobbed. "Lots of fun."

"Just like when you were four." Viv's memories took her back. "God, that was so long ago." She took her daughter and granddaughter into her arms and hugged tightly. "I love you, my babies."

"We love you, too, Mama," Diana replied as her father held them all.

"Aw, look at them." Tomas's smile was melancholic as he watched his niece, and brother and sister-in-law. "So sweet."

"And Carys and Jaqueline are just like Diana when she was little," Roger murmured against his lover's cheek. They were slow dancing to an '80s hit with a funky beat, but it didn't urge them to go faster. They slow danced to pretty much everything. It was what they did, what they do, slow dance in each other's arms to fully appreciate the moment together, and take those few moments to be fully *in* the moment.

"Yes, they are," Tomas agreed and turned his attention to his husband. "Can you believe we are finally *legally* married?" He tenderly pushed some hair back behind Roger's ear. "I love you."

Roger's grin slid ear to ear. "I love you, too. But you already know that, otherwise, we wouldn't have been together for forty-one years. You know..." His gaze swept over his husband's face, taking in the tanned skin, big brown eyes, and salt and pepper hair. "The legality never bothered me. We've loved each other all this time, stayed together all this time, and legal, or not, it never changed how I felt about you, not one iota."

"Naw, Roger." Tomas blushed. "I love you, too. Happy forty-first anniversary, and happy wedding day, since it's now officially legal."

"Happy anniversary, my love." Roger kissed him tenderly before pulling him closer. Regardless of the music, they had a few moments of peace before tantrums pulled them back to earth.

"No, Mama, no hold my hand." Harper Avery Stephanopoulos Saint placed her chubby little clenched up hands on her hips and frowned at her mother.

"Don't you no me, missy," Alena told her daughter as she flicked aside a wayward strand of hair in exasperation. She was holding her youngest child, Hunter, by the hands as he tried to stay upright and dance. Harper had started getting testy over something insignificant, and Alena had grabbed her hand to pull her close so she could warn her to stop the tantrum.

Harper was having none of it. "No, Mama! I'll tell you no all I like." Her big blue eyes stared defiantly at her mama, and her little red bow-shaped lips stubbornly pursed together. Her curly black hair, cherubic cheeks, and hands on hips stance made Angie burst out laughing.

"Now you know what I had to put up with when you were little," she told her daughter. "You didn't get this with Ava, but you're certainly getting it with Harper. And just wait another year, or two, with Hunter, then you'll know what I went through with *all* of you." She danced beside her family, marvelling at the gorgeous little girls she had for grandbabies. They were spitting images of Alena when she was little, and it made Angie relive more than a few memories on a daily basis. She grasped Ava's hands and watched her bounce up and down to the song currently playing. "Want to join in, Harper? Wanna hold Glamma's hands?" Glamma, something Angie had no problem being called since she was glamorous *and* a grandma, held out her hand and expected Harper to take it.

Harper, being the independently minded child she was, shook her head until her curls bounced in a rhythm of their own. "No, Glamma, no hold hands. Harpa no hold hands. Harpa no be told off by my mama, or anyone else." She crossed her arms and kept shaking her head. "No, no, no." Her foot stomped, and in a heartbeat, her daddy swung her into his arms.

"Stop all this nonsense at once, Harper Saint. I'll have none of it," Luca told his daughter. Meeting Alena on her 2010 European tour, he'd instantly fallen for the dark-haired beauty and more than happily joined the family in 2011 when he married her. And while not happy about the airtight prenup he had to sign, he knew he'd more than get all he wanted out of the most famous family in the world. He tickled his daughter under the chin and she burst into giggles.

"No, Dada, no tickle." Her laughter was contagious as she flung herself over his shoulder, eyes closed, enjoying the moment from her doting father. If anyone could get Harper out of a tantrum, it was her daddy.

"How come she does that for you and not me?" Alena asked, flustered and annoyed at her husband for being able to defuse the bomb that was her daughter. She watched her mother lift Hunter into her arms and smother him in kisses, then take a hold of Ava's hand.

"Because I'm her daddy," Luca stated simply, holding his daughter in his arms. "I don't tolerate her bad moods, or accept no for an answer. *And* I smother her in kisses." He blew a raspberry on his daughter's cheek, making her burst into a fit of giggles all over again.

"My Dada loves me." Harper kissed her daddy back. "Mama no love Harpa," she declared, eyeing her mother's surprised look.

"What the…?" Alena placed her hands on her hips. "Of all the—"

"Just like you," Angie cut in. "She's so much like you she may as well *be* you."

"I *was not* like that when I was four!" Alena exclaimed, waving a hand in her daughter's direction. "I *did not* act that way."

"Oh, *yes you did*," Angie quipped. "Wouldn't do a thing I told you to do, but burst into a fit of giggles if your father lifted you, or your uncle Tomas took care of you."

"That's because I'm a prince, don't you know," Tomas cut into the conversation he was overhearing. "May I have this dance, Princess Alena?" He half bowed and held out his hand to the laughs and giggles from the family.

Alena smiled, curtsied and took her uncle's hand. "Of course you can, Prince Tomas." She slipped into his arms and hugged him tightly; remembering back to the time at Disneyland when she'd first called him that. She was only three, a year younger than Harper, but the memories still stung. "I love you, Uncle Tomas."

"I love you too, my little A-ena." Tomas squeezed back, using the name she'd called herself when she was little because she couldn't pronounce her ls. "And don't worry about Harper; she'll grow out of it. You did."

"Yeah, at twenty-nine years of age," Roger murmured over Tomas's shoulder. "Took long enough."

Alena laughed and remembered back to 2007. "Yeah, it did, and took something pretty damn horrific to make me get over myself." She glanced over at her baby sister, Alexis, still sitting at the table holding her daughter and beaming with such happiness as she looked from her child to her husband. "She's finally happy after all this time."

"Yeah." Tomas was still melancholic as he and Roger looked Alexis's way. "She's with a man, in a solid relationship anyway. She was always happy. Just missing something."

"You think she found it?" Roger asked, gazing at his niece.

Tomas smiled at Alexis radiating happiness. "Better with Marcus than Lorenzo."

"Ugh," Alena groaned. "I'm so glad that's long over. It was so weird and awkward that my little sister was dating my ex-boyfriend."

Luca's ears pricked up and he listened in. He'd never known the full story of Alena's relationship with Lorenzo, or what Alexis had to do with it, and no one had told him.

"It would have been," Tomas said. "But you were all adults and moved on with your lives, and now Alexis is happily married with a baby girl of her own." His eyes teared up at his youngest niece holding her daughter and the trials and tribulations she had gone through after being raped back in 2007. She'd started dating Lorenzo six months later, a doctor whose way through med school his mama had paid for. Lorenzo had dated Alena years previously, but broke up a few months later. It didn't stop Lorenzo trying it on years later with Alexis and it had lasted five years. Now, Alexis was newly married and a mother, and Marcus seemed like a great guy. The family had only been introduced to him mid-2017 when he'd started working at the assault clinic Alexis had with Cabot. They'd started it up after their assaults and had made a huge success of it. Such a success, that Dr Marcus Wellcroft had moved to Mykonos especially to help out and had fallen in love in the process.

Tomas watched his nephew-in-law kiss his wife, saw her face light up like a Christmas tree, and saw her notice the family watching. She blushed, smiled, and ducked her head down.

"Yeah." Alena grinned. "She's happy."

Alexis giggled. "The family noticed." She rubbed Marais' cheek with her forefinger. Her baby girl was the most beautiful, best-behaved of the entire family.

"Noticed what?" Marcus glanced from his wife and child to his in-laws. Angie, Alena, Tomas and Roger were watching with beaming smiles, and just down the way, Jenny and Spiros were looking between them all. "I see what you mean."

At forty, Marcus was new to the family, and such a large one had shocked him at first. He'd heard about the clinic and Stephanopoulos family, met Dan Ardent and Derek Blaine in New York who'd also told him about it, and since he'd been looking for a sea change the year before, decided to pack up and move from Washington to Mykonos. He'd met Alexis first and family members soon followed. And after being invited to thanksgiving, he'd really seen the scope of the family tree and how large it was, especially when it was all in one room, or house, since they'd had it at Jenny's house. He knew there and then what he was getting into, but he didn't care. By that time he'd fallen madly in love with the beautiful doe-eyed Alexis and proposed on Christmas Eve, to which she'd squealed yes and they passionately made love for the rest of the night. Now they had beautiful Marais Angelique Stephanopoulos Wellcroft to start their family. Of course, he hadn't known Alexis was already pregnant when he proposed, and Marais came a little early into the world as a healthy, beautiful baby with big brown eyes and tuft of black hair. He watched as she peeked curiously over the edge of the blanket at the lights and all the people dancing, and not liking what she saw, clasped her hands and went back to looking up at her doting mother.

"Hello, Marais, my beautiful baby girl," Alexis cooed softly and watched her daughter's face move through a series of expressions. "Are the music and lights too much for you, Bubba?"

Marais' little eyebrows lifted, her eyes widened in wonder at her mama's beautiful face, and then her brows turned down at the intrusion of the music and her Aunt Alena.

"I love you, little sis." Alena kissed Alexis's cheek, surprising her before planting one on Marais' forehead. "I love you, too, my beautiful little niece." She rushed off, leaving them both stunned at the exchange.

Marais clenched her hands, screwed her face up, and cried out, burrowing deeper into the blanket and her mama's arms as her mama held her closer.

"It's okay, Bubba, it's okay, my baby." Alexis kissed her daughter's rosy cheek and nuzzled her, holding her to her chest for safekeeping. "It's okay, my baby. It's okay." Being a mother had come so naturally to Alexis that it had surprised her beyond measure. After being single for five years and busy at the clinic, she'd contented herself with nieces, nephews, and cousins as they came along, figuring, that at twenty-nine, she still had time to meet someone and have children. When Marcus had walked through the door of the clinic offering to help, she'd fallen madly in love with the good looking, brown-eyed hunk. Seeing him every day, dreaming of him every night, love had happened quickly, and she'd become pregnant their first night together in November last year. Thank God he'd proposed as she'd also told him she was pregnant, and they got married earlier in the year. Happy with her husband and three-month-old, she looked lovingly from her daughter to her husband. "I love you."

Marcus smiled softly. "I love you, too, Alexis."

"We can't interrupt them, they're having a moment," came whispering across the air.

"I can hear you, girls." Alexis laughed. "No need to whisper." Her two best friends, twins Summer and Melody Gatos, quickly sat down at the table. They had been best friends since 1988 when their mothers had given birth.

"We just wanted to see how tiny little bubba was doing," Summer said, gently pulling back the blanket to check on her honorary niece. "If you two want to go dance, we can watch her."

"Absolutely we'll watch her if you two love birds want to canoodle on the dance floor," Melody added. At thirty, the two girls were still waiting to have kids of their own, and so heaped all their love onto the kids in the Stephanopoulos family. And as lifelong honorary members like their parents and brother, they hung out with celebrities, musicians, movie stars, and that's how, finally, they'd met the two hunky twin brothers to whom they were now engaged.

"Speaking of love birds…" Alexis watched the girls inch their chairs closer to hers to coo over the baby. "When are the weddings?"

"Not until summer next year," Melody replied. "As much as we're twins marrying twins, that wasn't to say I wanted to share my wedding day. *But* the boys came up with the idea and we're running with it." She glanced unhappily at Summer. "Right?"

"Considering the family's paying for it, we may as well," Summer replied.

Two years ago they'd been working at the head office of *Haus of Stefan* in Athens on the *Stefan Productions* lot and had met the twin actor heartthrobs about to make a big name for themselves as action stars. With all American good looks, Thomas and Richard Morrow were the new actions stars in Hollywood thanks to Carlos putting them in the movies he produced. And they had long been fans of Steele and Phoenix Stefan, so took on new monikers of their own as some weird form of flattery towards their idols. Cabot and Antonio had thought it hilarious when they'd met the twins, and laughed about it afterwards, but To and Ro Morrow were not to be put off. They wanted to be the biggest action stars in the world and outdo Arnie, Bruce, Sly and Tom. And with Carlos directing and producing, they were on the fast track to doing so. The twins made sure they stayed on top by taking daily acting lessons, martial arts and weapons training, and were currently learning how to fly helicopters so they could make their action scenes more believable. And that was *after* learning how to ride stunt bikes, fly planes, and skydive. The boys were out to be the best at everything they did, but had fallen madly in love with the girls during the filming of a movie two years ago. Luckily, the girls were their biggest supporters and encouraged them to strive even higher.

"We are lucky." Melody sighed, happiness floating around her body, despite having to share a wedding.

"You are," Alexis agreed. "Took you girls long enough to find a guy, but to find twin brothers…kinda like my cousins…" She giggled softly, remembering back to when Summer and Melody had both said they wanted to marry Cabot and Antonio, having no idea that Cabot was gay and no longer interested in girls, only to set their sights on Dom instead.

"Oooh," Summer squealed. "Don't ever mention that again. *How embarrassing.*" She laughingly covered her face with her hands for a few seconds. "We were so young and stupid and childish."

"And in love." Melody laughed. "I had it so bad for Antonio."

"At least he's straight." Summer sighed. "I had it bad for Cabot and look how *he* turned out."

"He's grown since then." Alexis gently bounced Marais to keep her quiet. "*A lot* of growing up. *But* you also set your sights on my brother."

"Well…why not?" Melody cast a sly glance over her shoulder at Dom. "He's still *really* hot and shredded like a tiger."

"Ew, my brother." Alexis screwed her nose up. "At least you didn't go for Danté."

"Ew, Alexis," the girls simultaneously replied. "That's gross." They all turned to where Danté and Nick were sitting, talking about business no doubt.

"Ugh, the girls are looking," Nick scoffed and nodded in the direction of his sisters.

Danté peered over his shoulder and saw them giggling with his sister and brother-in-law. "Meh, girls are always giggling about something."

"Yeah, they are, but my babe's not a giggler. She's a serious freak gamer chick and I love her for it." At twenty-six, Nick had been dating for two years. He'd met Maddy James at a tech show he and Danté were attending for their business and had hit it off immediately as he'd been a gamer since he was a kid. Now he was trying to get Danté paired up. "When are you getting a girlfriend?"

"When the universe gives me one." Danté smirked and pulled his phone from his pocket. He was constantly looking at it 24/7, or at least when he was awake. It took a lot to run a business and DJ three nights a week, but he managed it by letting the company manager do her job, and not taking on so much himself. Not only did they run the family's websites for all of the businesses, but also set up and ran other people's. That was the whole reason behind *IT Web Solutions.* He and Nick ran the family's online businesses, so running everyone else's seemed the natural thing to do. After he ran the idea past his family at the tender age of fourteen, they had allowed him and Nick to slowly build it up while still attending school. Only once they'd graduated, could they take it on full-time, and that was seven years ago.

"Don't you want a girlfriend?" Nick pulled his own phone out to see if Maddy had texted him. When he found nothing, he went in search of her social media to see what she was posting about.

"When the time is right." Danté pocketed his phone and glanced at his best friend. "But I certainly won't be cyber-stalking her."

"Who's cyber-stalking?" Nick looked up, his face red. "Oh...I'm not..."

"You are." Danté grinned and peered around the room. He saw most of his family out there, but didn't feel the need to dance himself. Not that he didn't love it anymore; he did, but just when he was behind the decks on stage. He had no need to dance anytime other than when he was on stage feeling the vibrations throbbing through the floor and his headphones. He loved it, always had, always would, and he was itching to get his turn.

"Why *are* you still single?" Nick asked. "It's not like you're *not* good looking. You've had girls swooning over you for years. Remember when you started DJing at fourteen and all the girls from school would come to the club just to stand in front of the stage swooning over you? You've got the looks, man. You're stacked like a shredded ten-pack, six-foot-plus, you've got the charm, the money, the build." Nick gazed at his best friend, envy rippling through his body. At five-ten, he only averaged a two-pack on any monthly basis. "Why the hell are you still single?"

"Why the hell do you care so much?" Danté raised a brow at him. "I'm only twenty-five; love my music, my business. As Grandma said just before we walked in, when it happens, it will be on like Donkey Kong."

Nick cracked up. "She did not," he cried through tears of laughter. "Your grandma actually said that to you this afternoon?"

Danté replied dryly, "She did," and glanced at his grandmother who was still canoodling with her husband. "It runs in the family. It'll happen when it's ready and meant to."

"Yeah, but dude, that means you're not dating, kissing, having sex. And sex is *awesome*." Nick moaned, and his eyes closed in pleasure. "So awesome."

"So I figure, from the number of children my siblings and cousins keep having." Danté looked at his siblings, cousins, parents and uncles. "It'll happen when it happens. The DNA runs strong in this family."

"How strong?" Nick tapped on his friend's arm. "You haven't had sex, yet, have you?"

Danté turned his way and shrugged a nonchalant shoulder. "Do I need to? I haven't met anyone I've wanted to be intimate with, so why sleep around, or have meaningless one night stands with women just for the sake of it, or for the sake of not being a virgin anymore. Not that that means much to a guy. So what! I haven't had sex. I don't think Dom had at my age, or at least not much, and we all know that my parents and uncles certainly had. So had Alena, Alexis, Cabot and Antonio… I don't need to. It will happen when it happens." He absentmindedly rubbed his right leg, the one that had been bitten by the shark back in 2007. He'd had surgery on it the following year, and extensive physiotherapy, but every now and then, regardless of the working out he did in Tomas and Roger's gym to keep it strong, it still ached when he was inactive for too long, and he'd been inactive for too long. "I'm gonna go and replace my dad and hit the decks," he told Nick. "Go dance with some of my grandma's relatives. There are some pretty young things over there." He pointed to the other side of the room where some of his father's cousins' kids and grandkids were standing.

"Yeah, they're pretty." Nick flicked a smile at them. "But it's *you* they've been looking at."

"Hardly, we *are* related." Danté stood and stretched out his arms and legs, and ended with a back stretch. "See you when my shift's over."

"Yeah, just watch them run to the front of the stage and stay there," Nick called as Danté walked off towards the stage.

He bypassed Alexis and Marcus, giving Marais a tickle on the cheek, and kissed his grandma and grandpa before climbing the stairs and rolling up his sleeves. He popped open a few buttons for air, revealing the dark golden-brown nest of hair artfully splattered across his muscular chest. It was something his father didn't have, but his uncles, grandfather, and brother did. He checked over the playlist, waiting for his father to finish up with the song, and saw the girls from his grandma's side all rush toward the stage and start dancing. He raised a brow, as did his father who glanced at Danté and tilted his head in their direction.

Danté glanced at the back of the room to see Nick standing and madly pointing his arms in their direction as if to say, *I told you so.* Shaking his head and laughing, Danté grabbed the second set of headphones and was about to put them on when Pedro grabbed his arm and pulled off his sweat-covered ones.

"Looks like you've got some admirers. The family's famous here too, you know." Pedro winked at his son and grabbed a towel to wipe the headphones. "Make them weak at the knees, Danté."

"Ew, Papa. Don't say such things. We're related to them. *By blood!*" Danté emphasised the last two words. "Ew!"

Pedro shrugged, hung up the phones and wiped his face. "Yeah, but still…"

"Gross, Papa. Get off stage." Danté frowned, settled his headphones comfortably over his ears, and looked at the girls down the front. Glancing at Nick, who was still waving his arms around, he shook his head. He knew what it was like to have screaming fans front of stage, girls in particular. He'd had it since he was fourteen.

Watching his father walk up to his parents and kiss them both, his eyes followed as Pedro grabbed a jug of water from a passing waiter and drank from it. Once his thirst was quenched, he moved to the dance floor to join his wife and family.

A twinge panged Danté's heart, and a momentary frown crossed his face. Why a twinge? What was it about that scene that would twinge his heart? Regret at not having a wife and child? Regret at not having a family to call his own, even though he was still young? Why a twinge? Alexis had only just had Marais at thirty, and Dom was a first-time father at thirty-five, so he had a good ten years, or so, to worry about starting a family.

He caught sight of his grandparents and it hit him like a bolt out of the blue. That if he waited another five to ten years, longer even, then by the time he married and had kids, his grandparents wouldn't be there. That thought drove him back a few steps where he bent over, hands on knees, gasping for air. Ripping off the headphones, he thanked God the music was still playing. He hadn't had a panic attack in years, not since he'd got over his fear of the ocean after the shark attack, but this one was very real, and catching him by surprise.

He heard voices through the haze of rolling emotions, and through fuzzy eyes he saw his father, brother, and mother in front of him, reaching out to him, helping him, pulling him from behind the decks and curtains into the side of the stage.

"Danté, hey." Pedro gently slapped his cheeks, watching in semi-horror as his son gasped for air and stared at him through glassy eyes.

"Sweetie." Angie dabbed a cold wet cloth over her son's face and neck. "Calm down, sweetie, it's okay, it's okay."

"Here's a chair." Dom placed a chair behind his brother and helped him sit. "Danté?" He worried for his brother, having not seen Danté have an attack behind the decks before. Not on stage, not when it came to music. The water, yes. The stage, no. It had been years since the last one, and it was the last one Dom hoped to ever see.

For some reason, everyone had slowly turned to look at Danté when he was on stage. They had seen his eyes look at all of them, and then land on Jenny and Spiros. They had seen him frown, had seen the shock roll over his face. They saw him stumble back and heave over, and Pedro had flown past Dom, slapping him on the arm to catch his attention, Angie streaming behind them as they raced for the stage to find Danté having an attack.

"I brought some water." Tomas filed into the room with Roger, Carlos and Viv, and Nick and Simon trailing behind him.

"And I have more wet towels," Alena said as she and Alexis came backstage. "You okay, Little D?" She used the affectionate nickname the family had for him.

Danté, still in a dazed state, drank slowly from the glass his mother held to his mouth. His eyes moved from person to person as they stared down at him, his ears half deaf in that weird state like when you're floating in water and can't hear clearly. The reason for the panic attack came flooding back, and he pushed Angie's hand away and tried to hold back the tears that threatened to flood.

Diana, Cabot, and Antonio came through the door, looks of shock and concern for their cousin on their faces. "Danté, you okay, sweetie?" Diana asked softly, noting the worry on everyone's faces. They all knew he'd never received enough physiological help straight after the attack, he didn't want it, but then the panic attacks happened in the years after. He'd talked to Xanthe Metlos, the family's counsellor, and while it took him a few years to feel safe in the water again, and not have panic attacks, that wasn't what this attack was about.

Seeing the family's concerned faces, except for those two most important, the reason for the attack hit him again. The tears burst forth and he bent to his knees, head in hands, crying as he hadn't in a hell of a long time.

"Aw, sweetie." Angie fell to her knees in front of him, arms around her son. "It's okay, we're all here. We're not going anywhere." She looked up at Pedro, who looked down with an equally confused expression.

That just made Danté cry harder, and made everyone trade puzzled glances.

"We're all here, sweetie," Angie repeated, patting his back to soothe him.

"G-g-grand-ma," Danté stuttered between great gulping sobs.

"Someone call?" Jenny slowly stepped into the room with the help of Dan and Derek. "Took me a while to get here, and I figured with everyone traipsing in, you wouldn't need me for a while." She waved Angie out of the way so Derek could place the chair he'd brought in front of Danté. Sitting, she leaned on her cane and examined Danté's face. "Why don't you tell me what's going on, and the rest of you," she looked at her family, "can leave us to talk."

Danté fell off his seat onto his knees and his head landed in her lap. He sobbed even harder.

Jenny instinctively knew something was very wrong and it had nothing to do with his shark attack. She directed her family and looked at Dom. "Take Danté's turn on stage. Go." He nodded and left, and she turned her attention to everyone else. "You all go, too. Danté clearly needs to talk something through, and your father and the children need looking after. Go." She watched her children and grandchildren nod in confusion, but slowly turn and file out the door. Pedro and Angie were last and stopped to look back at their youngest child sobbing in his grandmother's lap.

Nodding, Jenny waved them on, then Dan and Derek, who left. She waited for the door to close and heard Dom introduce himself and the next song, and then stroked Danté's hair for a few moments. "Okay, that wasn't about your attack, so what *was* it about? I saw you watching everyone. Saw your expression change, saw you double over in emotional distress. So, spit it out. What is it?" She waited for him to lift his tear-stained face to her and then weep as he told her.

"Oh, Danté, my little Danté." Wiping his tears away, she motioned for him to sit in his chair. When he did, she took his hands in hers and told him what he needed to hear. "It doesn't matter if you are still single and not in love. It will happen when it happens. It will happen when it's meant to, and if that's after I'm gone, then so be it. And when it does, you'll know that it was me who sent her to you. So, don't worry." She wiped away the tears that fell from his eyes like waterfalls. "I will be watching over you, my little Danté, and sending you love each and every day, and will send her your way. You are destined for someone. There is someone out there for you. How do you think this family ends up married so fast? Because we all find our soulmates. I found your grandfather, your parents found each other, your siblings and cousins all found theirs, and one day, you will too. And you'll know when it happens. Because then it will be on—"

"Like Donkey Kong," Danté muttered, a small smile lighting up his lips.

"Exactly!" Jenny gently grasped his chin. "We will all be gone one day, Danté. And your grandfather and I know we don't have much longer. That's why I started the course this year; to make sure you all know how to run the business for when I and your fathers aren't here."

His bottom lip quivered. "I don't want you to die."

Jenny let out a slow sigh tinged with sadness. "Neither do I, my baby, neither do I."

*****

Back in the main room, everyone slowly got back to dancing. They knew Jenny and Danté would be a while, and children need to be taken care of. Jenny's family inquired after Danté and expressed their concerns. Stories of his attack all those years ago were retold, and everyone kept glancing at the door, waiting for them to come out.

Unsure of what else to do, Angie wandered around after her children and grandchildren, asking if they were okay and needed anything. She ended up with Spiros who was chatting to Davina about Christopher sleeping through it all.

When everyone else had rushed off, Davina had quickly gone to her grandfather-in-law's side to make sure her son was all right.

"Is he still sleeping?" Angie peeked under the hood of the pram to see her sleeping grandbaby.

"Still," Davina replied, a touch of British English coming through her Australian accent. Born and raised in Australia to a Greek mother and Australian father, giving her shiny dark brown hair, sparkling green eyes, and a creamy Mediterranean complexion, she'd spent ten years working in London television when she'd been sent to report on the hot DJ Dom Stefan, making his debut on the English stage. It was lust at first sight, and once she knew what all the Stephanopoulos men were famous for genetically, she never left his side, wanting in on *Sync* and *S'Reel* to pursue her TV talk show ambitions.

"He's such a good baby." Angie sat down next to her daughter-in-law and gently rocked the pram. "Sleeps a lot, like his dad did, but once we put music on, Dom would dance and move and wriggle just like his dad." She glanced over at Pedro to see him talking to his brothers and worried for her son. Danté's panic attacks hadn't happened in years, so what the hell brought this one on? She hoped Jenny could get it out of him.

"Your wife is boring a hole in you with her eyes," Carlos told Pedro. They were standing on the dance floor talking about Danté and the last three days of celebrations. The three of them glanced at Angie, but she didn't notice.

"Lost in thought, I'd say," Pedro replied. "Did you see Danté's face when he was on stage? That scared the absolute shit out of me. And when he gasped and bent over, my God..." He clutched his chest. "Just about gave me a heart attack."

"How many years has it been since he had one?" Carlos asked.

"Eight years, three months, two weeks," Tomas replied. "He was okay after a few years."

Pedro studied his brother's face. "You've been counting?"

"Death," Tomas said simply. "It does things to you. Makes you count the seconds, minutes, days, weeks, years. It didn't just happen to me. Danté was nearly taken by the shark and battled demons over swimming again for three years." His brows slid down in thought. "We nearly lost Alena in the crash landing of the jet on her tour years ago. Diana, Charles, and the kids when that avalanche hit close to where they were holidaying, Dom was caught up in that bombing in London, Antonio and Maria had their car accident on their honeymoon, Alexis had her rape, and then there was Cabot..." Their eyes turned to their son and nephew who was holding baby Antonio and throwing him up in the air while Tony held baby Jennifer.

Cabot caught sight of his father and uncles watching him and his blue eyes grew wide. "What? What have I done now?" He always felt as if he'd done something wrong when all three Stephanopoulos brothers eyed him off. "Should I not be throwing baby Tony in the air?" He glanced from them to his son who was wriggling and giggling.

"Nothing's wrong," Tomas told him. "You survived, that's all." His smile was always special for his nephew and Cabot knew what it meant.

"Aw, thanks Uncle T. You've been a better father to me than my old man, the great Carlo Stefan," he cheekily said, getting a scowl and retort from his father back.

"Watch it, boy, I can still backhand you, and I'm sure your grandmother could still slap you if you're aiming for another one," Carlos said. Cabot and Tony looked at him in shock, as did Pedro and Tomas. Scowling harder, Carlos stormed away to find his wife and calm down.

"What...the hell...was that?" Pedro asked a surprised Tomas.

Tomas shrugged and turned to Cabot, seeing his shocked expression. "You okay?"

"Ah..." Cabot's mouth gaped open and he couldn't say anything else. He'd actually thought he was getting along better with his father, certainly after he'd married Tony in 2012 in their commitment ceremony, and especially once the kids had come along. Looking from his uncles to his husband to his brother who had appeared at his elbow, he could say nothing.

"I've noticed Papa has been acting strangely this year," Antonio said. At thirty-six, he and Cabot still looked alike with their golden-brown hair and fit physiques, even though he'd filled out a little since quitting modelling. They weren't Steele and Phoenix Stefan anymore, so had no need to starve themselves to stay in shape. "I think it's what he's been doing with Grandma. Sorting out wills, the estates, who gets what, training us to take over." His pointed look was aiming for his uncles. "Grandma thinks she doesn't have long, Papa's freaking out, so he's probably freaking out about us, and if one of us is going to go first," he tapped Cabot's head, "it's you, considering your condition."

Cabot slowly comprehended what his twin was saying. "I don't have a condition, I have HIV, and I'm on meds and happy and healthy."

"Yeah, but the fact you contracted it in the first place still freaks him out eleven years later. *Especially*," Antonio raised a brow at his brother, "when Steele Stefan comes out."

"Naw!" Cabot complained, his face screwing up. "Only once in a blue moon. I'm still growing up, you know. He doesn't come out like he used to."

"Still," Pedro joined in, giving his nephew a soft smile. "You caused a lot of grief for a lot of years, and yes, you've come more than good this last decade, but your father still feels the effects of your actions. More so since they so closely resembled everything we went through with this guy here." He flung his arm around Tomas who looked at him in shock. "We basically relived every single death of every single person we lost, or nearly lost, when you tried to kill yourself and revealed you had HIV," he told Cabot who had enough decency to look embarrassed. "And while we're all happy that the two of you are alive," he looked from Cabot to Tomas and back, "it's your dad who took it hardest. First, he lost his brother, and he and Viv lost a whole bunch of friends, then they nearly lost you. We all relived it from twenty-six years previous to that, and if Antonio's right," he nodded at his nephew, "as his sons, he's expecting the two of you, *and* Diana, to be around long after he's gone. Because even though we don't want to think about it," he pulled Tomas close, "Mama and Papa may not have much longer."

"Don't say that!" Cabot cried, his pout jutting out, his brows furrowing. "I don't want to even think of her not being here." He held little Tony close as he squirmed.

"Neither do I," Antonio added. "But...*it will* happen one day soon." His gaze wandered over to their father sitting with his father, quietly joking about something and holding hands.

Cabot followed his gaze and felt torn. He loved his parents and grandparents, and desperately wished he had the same kind of loving relationship with either his mama or his father, that he saw good old Carlos have with *his* mother. It had annoyed him somewhat, the closeness he saw the two of them have and he wished he could have that with his father. He knew his actions from back then had long hindered that plan.

"It's not too late, you know." Antonio spoke in Cabot's ear. "The problem is you're closer to Uncle Tomas and Roger than you are to Papa. So, maybe that's okay instead since Uncle T doesn't have kids. And Simon's not his kid anyway, even once he adopts him." He peered over his shoulder at Roger dancing with Stella, and Simon dancing with Deidre. Their son Liam had been hanging around with Adam, or the kids from the other side of the family, just as Stella had been since they were closer in age. Antonio turned back to his brother. "I think it's time you had a real heart to heart with your father. Don't you?"

Cabot heard his brother's words and considered them as he stared over at his father. He wasn't sure what he was feeling still. Shock, dismay, pain. His father's words and expressions pained him, as did not having that emotional connected bond that Carlos had with Jenny. Yes, he'd been closer to Tomas the last ten years, and yes, got along better with him and Roger than with his father, but he missed *that closeness* with his father, even though they had been getting along better than they had when he was a kid. But...Antonio was right. Something had changed in the great Carlos this year, and they'd all seen something happen between Carlos and Jenny. Sentimentality, finality, whatever it was, Jenny was preparing for her eventual death, and Carlos hadn't dealt with it one bit. And so, maybe it was reflecting in how he treated Cabot.

"I'm fine," Cabot murmured, deep in thought. "I'm fine."

"Are you?" Tony touched a gentle hand to his husband's face and then managed to catch a squirming baby Antonio as he wriggled out of Cabot's arms. "Come 'ere, you." He lifted him into the air before swinging him onto his hip. "What'ch'ya doin'?" Tickling his son, he made him giggle. "What'ch'ya doin' Tonio, what'ch'ya doin'?"

Antonio DeLuca III was his son by blood. After finding a surrogate willing to donate her eggs, and going through multiple procedures to make sure no HIV would be passed on via his sperm, Tony and Cabot made plans for having children. Antonio came along in 2016, and using the same surrogate and her eggs, and Cabot's sperm, Jennifer Vivian Stephanopoulos had come along on May 21, 2018, making them both incredibly happy parents. And with Jennifer safe in her uncle's arms for the moment, Tony could spend a moment with baby Tony and Cabot.

Cabot's blue eyes focussed on his husband, the delectably tall Spaniard Colombian Brit, Tony DeLuca, whom he'd met in 2007 and fallen head over heels for. Tony had first proposed marriage while visiting his family's estate in May 2008, but Cabot wasn't ready for it then as he was still learning to be a mature adult dealing with HIV, and not some snot-nosed brat that made everyone hate him. He'd been a rampant sex addict, screwing everything that moved, but contracting the disease and meeting Tony had changed all of that. Their first ceremonial marriage was in 2012 at the DeLuca estate in Spain. Their legal one had been in London in 2014 after the country made it legal for gays to be married. And with Tony being British born and bred, they'd taken the whole family to England to celebrate. He clasped Tony's faced and kissed him. "I'm so happy you accepted me and helped me change for the better."

Tony's delectable lips curled up at the corners and his greeny hazel coloured eyes sparkled. "I'm so glad I came into your life, too." Those lips kissed Cabot. "And I'm glad we can be legally married and have children."

Cabot shyly tugged at Tony's shirt collar. "So am I," he managed before baby Antonio smacked him in the face. "Oi! What was that for?" Cabot's eyes widened as Antonio giggled and Cabot went in for the attack, tickling his son as revenge.

"I'm still surprised your brother could actually father a child, given he has HIV," Maria Van Star muttered casually to her husband, Antonio. They'd been married for six years like his brother since the wedding was the day after Cabot and Tony's at the estate in Spain, and they had their two beautiful baby girls, Izabella and Valentina. Maria was of fiery French Italian decent, huge in the modelling world as Cabot, Antonio, Diana and Vivian had been, but was continuing to model where the others had quit. With her heritage, she still looked thirty-three instead of thirty-nine and had agreed to live in Mykonos with her family as long as they travelled regularly to Rome, Paris and London. This trip was her first to Australia.

"So am I," Antonio replied, gently rocking Jennifer in his arms. Regardless of the fact Cabot and Tony were married, and both had legal parentage of baby Antonio, it was Jennifer who was his biological niece and the one he would be closest to. She was the cousin to his own daughters and Diana's children. Not baby Antonio.

"Is it not confusing to have so many Antonios in the family?" Maria pushed on. She'd always questioned why and how the family did things, didn't want to do them herself unless they benefit her in some way, and always riled the ire of her in-laws except for Jenny who always had a twinkle in her eye and would say, *'Oh, that Maria has a mind and will of her own. Good for her.'* And so, while she wasn't particularly close to any one member of the family due to her fiery nature, it was Jenny she got along with most. Jenny, who always encouraged her children and grandchildren to pursue dreams and ideas, and that encouragement included the in-laws and great-grandchildren.

Yes, Maria knew she'd hit on something big marrying into that family, and she planned on staying for as long as she could. Seeing her daughters play with their cousins and grandmother, Maria leaned on Antonio's shoulder and dropped her voice. "I'm still not sure it was a good idea for the two of them to procreate. What if the children end up contracting HIV?" Ever the rebel, Maria loved to drop bombs and stir people up with her own version of life and how it should be, and while she knew her husband was loyal to his family, she loved to get a dig in.

Antonio's temper flared, but he kept it in check. If it was one thing you didn't do in this family, it was attack a member because the rest would rally. "At the end of the day, Maria, it's none of our, *or your*, business. They've done it, and my niece and nephew are here. End of story *and* discussion." His warning tone and sharp glance were enough to make her back off, and he watched her pointed left eyebrow rise and fiery green eyes narrow.

She hated being told off by him, and he hated the fact she questioned everything his family did, but the little spats also resulted in fiery sex, and he felt his infamous eleven-inch cock rise to the occasion. He handed Jennifer to Cabot. "Here's your daughter, I need to have a private word with my wife."

Cabot grinned at his brother. "We all know what that means, you dirty dog."

"Not as dirty as you, Cabot," Antonio retorted and grabbed his wife's arm. He rushed her out of the room, down the hall, and opened the first door he found unlocked. Seeing the room was dark and empty, he pushed Maria inside and shut the door. His cock was out and being manhandled by his wife in seconds as she was as horny as him.

"Glad that was Antonio and not Cabot." Pedro grinned, seeing his nephew and wife seek out some alone time. He and Mike were walking back from the toilets where he'd changed out of his sweat-stained clothes and into another pair of pants and a shirt.

"Aren't those days long gone for Cabot?" Mike asked, knowing full well how Cabot had calmed down and stopped having sex after his diagnosis, and meeting Tony had helped him get on the right path as they had so much in common. Not to mention the extensive therapy he'd undertaken.

"Yeah, he has." Pedro was wistful after seeing his nephew go off for a tête-à-tête with his wife. He missed the days when he and Angie would sneak off and have sex, or make love in *Sync's* office when no one as around. Not that sex had died down, they still burned the candle at both ends sometimes, but it was calming down in ferocity and frequency.

"So, what's the problem then? The *actual* problem?" Mike grasped Pedro's elbow and brought him to a halt. "What *is* going on in your family this year?" At sixty-six, Mike had been Pedro's best friend since 1977 when they'd met while working at *Studio 69*, the hottest nightclub on the planet at that time. Pedro had run away to New York with Angie and got the gig as DJ in the club, and Mike was the bartender who ended up hooking up with Maggie. They started dating, moved to Mykonos in 1983, married in '85, with Pedro and Angie as their best man and matron of honour, and had been made honorary members of the family at the time. Their twins, Summer and Melody, came along and ended up being Alexis's best friends, and their son Nick was born the year before Danté, but that didn't stop them from being best friends. It clearly ran in the family.

"I have absolutely no idea," Pedro replied and ran a hand through his still-damp hair. "We're all starting to think it has something to do with Mama sorting out the business this year and handing it over to us. Carlos has gone weird, Danté just had his panic attack which hasn't happened in years, we're all getting weird vibes from Mama, and the conversation in the limo on the way over, my God. We're all worried on some level that something's happening, *particularly*, with Mama and Carlos."

"Could it be the fact Cabot actually became a father this year?" Mike asked, crossing his arms and thinking it through. "Cabot's passed on a legacy that might just backfire in everyone's face. Same with Tony. Do we all know for sure those kids won't end up with HIV, or AIDS, down the track?"

"The doctors are the top-notch specialists in the world. Their money saw to that." Pedro smirked. "But then Mama would have, too. So, we've all been reassured that the kids *will not* contract HIV at some point by some of the top specialists in the world, including *our very own,* Dan and Derek."

"But is that what Carlos is worried about, *or,* is it the fact your parents may not have much longer?"

Pedro's brows slid down in thought before he screwed his face up. "Bah! I don't want to think about Mama and Papa not being here, and Tomas and Carlos clearly don't either. It's been a very long year of learning the ropes and getting the kids into it, and they were all eager to learn and find out what they'd be taking over. *But* they also have their own kids to worry about, and three of them were born just this year, so…" Shaking his head, he shrugged. "It could be a couple of things. We can't pinpoint what. We can only guesstimate that it's Mama's estate planning."

"Well…I guess it had to be done," Mike said as they moved on. "We all have to think of it sometime." They entered the reception room and wandered down to the head table for Pedro to leave his bag. Jenny and Danté weren't back, and Spiros was still chatting with Carlos.

Pedro eyed his brother and father. "Yeah, I know, but who wants to talk about death when we have such a great family?"

"And you're lucky yours are still alive and together." Mike grabbed a drink from a passing waiter. "Maggie and I have both lost our fathers, so…"

"We're lucky," Pedro finished, his eyes still on his father. Wandering over, he stumbled on Angie's shoes that she'd taken off earlier. "Argh, Angie!" Righting himself, he settled into his mama's velvet chair next to his father.

"You called?" Angie had seen him trip and rushed over. "Sorry, thought they were out of the way." She kicked them under the table and kissed her husband. "Sorry, babe."

Pedro pulled her onto his lap and slid his arms around her. "We having fun?" he asked those around him. Maggie had come over to join Mike, and both nodded. Spiros and Carlos grinned, sharing a secretive glance. "You need to use the bathroom, Papa?"

"Yes, I think I might," Spiros replied. "Can you two help me? I don't want to disturb Tomas and Roger right now." They all looked over at the love birds slow dancing in the middle of the floor.

"Of course we can," Carlos declared and flicked off the brakes on his father's wheelchair and rolled him backwards. He and Pedro headed off with Spiros while the others chatted.

Nick rushed up to them. "Do you know how Danté is? He's been in there for over an hour."

"And he'll stay for another hour if he needs to," Angie said. "As far as I know, he hasn't had a panic attack in years, and then all of a sudden tonight he has one. *On stage*. The one place he loves most." She shook her head in bewilderment. "I have no idea what's going on, but if Mama can fix it, then great. Do you know what caused it? You two were talking before he went on stage."

Nick shrugged a shoulder. "I dunno. We were talking about girlfriends and when he was gonna get one. That everyone but him is married with kids. When was it gonna happen?"

Puzzled, Angie thought for a moment. "Well, I don't know why he would have an attack over that."

"Maybe it wasn't," Dan supplied as he and Derek stopped by. "Thought we'd come see if Spiros needed help, but I suppose Carlos and Pedro have it under control."

"More than likely," Angie said. "What do you *mean* maybe it wasn't? What else could make Danté have an attack on the one thing he loves most, the stage. He's never had an attack on stage. Ever!"

"And it probably wasn't about that. It could have been over something completely different. Something someone said, someone did, or didn't do, a weird blip of the radar out of the blue random thought he had." Dan's hand waved in the air to emphasise his words. "Until he tells us, we won't know what caused it."

Dan Ardent had been an honorary member of the family since 1981 when he'd treated Tomas and Roger in the hospital in New York, and further still in Jenny's home in Mykonos. He stayed for seven months before flying back to New York to take up his hospital job, but found he'd been replaced by Doctor Derek Blaine. It was love at first sight for both of them, and now at sixty-seven, green-eyed brunet Dan had been with blue-eyed brunet sixty-six-year-old Derek for thirty-seven years, and both spent their time between Mykonos with the family, and New York at the clinic, *The NYC HIV/AIDS Research and Support Clinic* that Jenny had helped fund since 1982. It was under the family banner of *S.Inc.* and kept him and Derek comfortable in the brownstone they owned thanks to a decent wage every week. Not to mention the house on Mykonos Jenny had gifted them with back in 2008.

"He'll be fine." Derek gently touched her elbow. "He's a Stephanopoulos, and Jenny's grandson. She'll get it out of him and help him through it."

"I know, I know." Angie brushed away the thought. "It's just, he's my baby—"

Nick raised a brow. "He's twenty-five, Aunt Angie."

Angie sent him a scathing look. "He's *still my baby. All four* of my children are, and I'll worry about them until my last breath. Just as Jenny worries about all of us and all of her grandbabies. She wants to make sure we're all okay." Her gaze had been wandering among the party-goers, picking out her children and grandchildren, seeing them all fit and healthy, except for Danté.

"He'll be fine, Angie." Maggie slipped over to her best friend and put her arms around her shoulders. They'd been best friends for so long they both considered themselves sisters, and at the same age of fifty-nine, they were still as close as ever.

While Angie had found out she had half-siblings by her father, Maggie was an only child, and so her friendship with Angie and the subsequent decades of being a part of her family made her feel as if she had more than enough siblings to go around, and a family big enough to help her out in times of need. Tearing up at the thought of losing more of her own family, she hastily brushed her reddish-brown hair out of her brown eyes, using that as a cover for wiping her tears away. She'd already lost her father and father-in-law and didn't want to lose any more members of her family. "Come on, let's get back to dancing and teach the girls the hair spin we used to do." She pulled

Angie onto the floor as Pedro and Carlos came in with Spiros.

Spiros was shuffling along on Carlos's arm as he'd wanted to exercise for a bit. Pedro wheeled his chair alongside, and Antonio and Maria came up the rear, holding hands and smiling like lovesick teenagers.

Dan and Derek waited for them and helped settle Spiros back into his chair.

"Dan, Derek, checking up on me?" Spiros chuckled and his gnarled hands helped pull the blanket over his legs.

"Of course we are. What do you think?" Dan said. "You okay?"

"A little puffed from all that walking, but it did me good," Spiros replied. "Got the old ticker moving, along with my circulation."

"That's good. A little exercise can do wonders," Derek said as Tomas and Roger rushed over.

"You okay, Papa?" Tomas helped straighten the corner of the blanket and tucked it around his father's legs. "You should have come and got us, Carlos." He sent a pointed look at his brothers.

"They are more than capable of helping me, Tomas." Spiros laid a hand on his son's shoulder. "You and Roger are celebrating. It is your day; you don't need to help me today as there are plenty of people who can."

Tomas kneeled in front of his father. "I know. It's just…Roger and I are the ones who promised to look after you and be your carers for the rest of your lives, and so we need to do that. When someone else does it, I feel we're not doing our job." He took his father's hand and kissed it. "I love you and Mama. You fought to save us, and now we'll repay that by helping you."

Spiros smiled, though memories of watching his middle son, his spitting image, die in front of him was a burden too much to bear, they had borne that burden as a family, and come through it as a family. He looked into Tomas's eyes. "I know, Tomas. I know. And you are, don't worry." His free hand stroked his son's cheek. "You've done more than enough to make your papa proud."

With tears falling, Tomas nodded and rested his head on his father's hand. "Yes, Papa."

Simon, seeing this, left Deidre's side and walked over to his father, silently putting a hand on his shoulder and looking into his face when he turned.

Roger hugged his son and sighed. "You okay?"

Simon slid his arms around his father's neck. "It must be hard knowing they're getting older. Don't have long."

"It must be hard for you, too." Roger pulled back and stared into his son's eyes. "You watched your mum pass."

Simon gasped in air and glanced at the ceiling trying to get a hold of his emotions. In his mother's last breaths, she'd told him who his father was and where to find him. She'd collected all sorts of ephemera on the family, and kept a scrapbook of Roger's deeds in the gay and AIDS communities. He and Deidre had packed up their two kids and flown to Mykonos to meet his biological father, a man he didn't know existed because his mother had never mentioned it. He'd been so desperate to meet Roger he'd turned up at Jenny Stephanopoulos's house at eleven o'clock on Thanksgiving night to meet him, only to have to take a DNA test the next day to prove Roger was his father. They'd spent the last eleven years getting to know each other and being a family.

"Ah...yeah, it's hard." Simon took a deep breath and his brown eyes connected with his father's.

"You look just like I did at forty-two," Roger said softly, wiping away his son's tears. "But there's a bit of your mum in you, too." He watched his daughter-in-law slide her arm through her husband's. "You both okay?"

"We're fine," she said. "This is just stirring up some memories for this one." She gently nudged her husband. "Old memories, new memories. We get to be a part of your wedding this time."

Roger's smile beamed across the room. "Yeah, you do, and I'm so glad you're both here." He enveloped them both into his arms; Simon Dencott, the son who stood as tall and proud as he, and Deidre Dencott, the cute, bubbly brunette who always urged her husband on and encouraged Simon and Roger to do things together. "Thank you both for being here. I appreciate it so much."

"Thank you for letting us be a part of your life," Deidre responded.

Letting go, Roger's smile shone at both of them then he looked over his shoulder at his husband, finding everyone around them staring with mushy looks on their faces. "Ah…everyone okay?"

"More than okay." Tomas got to his feet and hugged his husband from behind. "I'm glad you two found each other."

Simon smiled an exact replica of his father's. "So am I."

"Yeah, which is nice and all," Carlos drawled, "but it's nearly five and Mama's still not out with Danté, and tea, or dinner, or whatever the hell you people call it these days, is about to be served."

"What do ya mean, *you people?*" Chris Marsh, the boys' cousin, called out. "You're one of us, ya yobbo, or have you forgotten your roots?"

"Bahaha," burst out of Cabot and he quickly covered his mouth with both hands. But when everyone turned to look at him, he snorted and doubled over in laughter.

"Not *those* kinds of roots, dickface," Antonio told his brother. "The kind *you* know so well. He's talking *family* roots." Rolling his eyes, he watched Cabot laugh harder.

"Enough, Cabot," Carlos said sharply. "And as for you, ya yobbo…" He swiftly moved over to his cousin. "We never did get it on over Berry Wilder. Come on, put up ya dukes." He play punched his cousin and they tussled as they did as kids, wetting themselves laughing as everyone watched on and sniggered.

"Whatever happened to Berry Wilder?" Pedro asked, watching his red-faced brother and cousin. "Anyone know where she is, or what she does?"

"She's a high powered attorney with her own firm in Sydney," Cousin Hayden volunteered. "Works with a lot of feminist and anti-men organisations."

"I actually think she ended up a lesbian, didn't she?" Cousin Dean added. "We can all blame Carlos for that."

Guffaws from those old enough to remember their school days back in the '60s when Berry Wilder had a massive crush on Carlos, and Chris had a massive crush on her, went around the room. In 1967 when Jenny and Spiros moved the family to Greece, Berry had been inconsolable, and not even Chris could get an in with her.

"Hey, if she ended up a lesbian, that's not my fault," Carlos huffed and pushed back the golden-brown hair he got out of a bottle. There was no way the great Carlos Stephanopoulos was going grey.

Pedro checked his watch and then waved at Dom who nodded and looked to his left to see his grandmother and Danté still talking.

Jenny noticed and waved him backstage.

Dom made sure there was enough music on, then trotted down the stairs into the backstage area dripping in sweat. "Grandma, it's Danté's turn next." Grabbing a towel from the pile on the side table, he wiped his face.

"No, it's not. It's nearly five and dinnertime. Can you set that thing so it will keep playing by itself for the rest of the night, or until one of you gets back on stage?"

"Ah…" He glanced from her to Danté who sat with his head hanging, and his hands holding his grandma's. "Sure. Everything okay?"

"Fine. Just go and set the machine and change into something drier." She eyed the soaked clothing clinging to his body.

"Ah…okay." Dom went back on stage, set the decks to play music for the next eight hours and hurried back. He grabbed his bag and looked for a place to change.

"Just go behind the curtain." Jenny pointed to her right. "We won't see you."

Grinning, Dom moved behind the curtain and dropped his bag. DJing was hard work and he always worked up a sweat. At thirty-five, he'd filled out thanks to training with his uncles at their gym for the last seven years. He was broader, muscular, had a slight tan that glinted off the dark hair spread across his pecs and down to his eight-pack abdomen and tight lower stomach. It was the body Davina had been driven wild by, especially his manhood; the sizeable package that ran in the male side of the family.

After stripping off everything and towelling down, he pulled on fresh underwear and socks, yanked up mid-blue ripped jeans and old black biker boots. He buckled up his studded belt, and slid into an old faded black Black Sabbath t-shirt. He already wore his music clef ring, along with several others, on his right hand, and had a few black leather and stud bracelets on both wrists. A black studded leather banded watch accompanied them as they always did. They were items of jewellery he'd worn since his late teens. It made him a little different to his siblings and cousins, even though Cabot had copied his look over a decade ago. A rather large tattoo he sported on his upper left arm was another difference. He was the only one in the family to have one, and loved the fact it set him apart. It was the Greek symbols for love and family and he'd got it on his thirtieth birthday. He was also considering another tattoo to represent Davina and Christopher, but it had to be something he could add to when they had more children.

After spraying on deodorant and body spray, he flung back the curtain, and, drying off his still jet-black, slicked back with an undercut, hair, he asked, "You guys okay?" He threw his sodden clothes into his bag and zipped it up.

"We're fine." Jenny smiled at the young man she was proud to call her grandson. "Help me up and we'll go."

"You okay, Danté?" Dom laid a hand on his brother's shoulder before he could move. "You freaked us out before."

They'd become incredibly close in the last eleven years, but before that Dom couldn't bear to be around his younger brother.

"I freaked myself out." Danté stood and was eye to eye with his brother. Having finished growing, his brown eyes stared into Dom's blue ones. "But I'm fine. Now. Just needed to talk to Grandma." He helped her stand and slid his left arm around her waist, while his right hand held onto hers. Dom took the other side and they slowly made their way back out. Everyone turned to stare, but waited for them to arrive at the tables.

"I think everyone who needs to freshen up, should," Jenny called out. "Dinner is served any minute, so off you go." She watched members of her family rush off, and held her hand out to Angie. "I need to go as well. Do you mind?"

"Of course not, Mama." Angie took her hand and muttered to her son, "You okay, Danté?"

"I'm fine, just help Grandma." He smiled tightly and took off for the toilets.

"He'll be okay," Jenny told her as Viv joined them. "Just needed to talk some things through."

"Like what?" Angie was itching to know what had sent her son into a spiral.

"Like what we've been dealing with this year," Jenny said and let the matter drop. "I'm famished. I hope they start serving soon."

Angie traded a look with Viv behind Jenny's back and helped her the rest of the way. After the family was done, they converged back in the reception room and sat down to a luxurious dinner, followed by an equally luxurious dessert.

"Mmm, that was good." Jenny patted the napkin to her lips and turned to Spiros to see he'd only eaten half of his meal. "Not hungry?"

"You know I don't eat much these days, I just need a few mouthfuls." Spiros laid his spoon down and shakily wiped his mouth. "I fill up easily."

"Yes," Jenny murmured, "so do I, actually." She looked around the room at every face at every table, saddened by who was missing out by not being there, or not being alive. Besides her parents and older siblings, Spiros's parents were decades gone, and she knew she was lucky to still be there alive and kicking. Her gaze moved on from her younger siblings and their families to her own and all of the in-laws there now were. There were honorary members she thought of as children; Dan and Derek, and Mike and Maggie. And their kids were just as much her grandchildren as her own. She looked over her great-grandchildren, the grandchildren and their partners, and finally, her gaze took in her sons and daughters-in-law, ending on Tomas at her side. All three boys were her pride and joy, and she was damn proud of all of them, but Tomas most of all. With everything he'd gone and come through, he'd shown her, his brothers and father, plus his husband and sisters-in-law, that he not only had the physical strength, but the emotional and mental strength to get through it all and come out the other side fitter and healthier than he was before. And he had thrived. Oh, by God, how he'd thrived on his mama's love and support all these years to become the most amazing incredible human being she'd ever known. He'd far exceeded her and Spiros, and even his brothers. Oh, yes, Tomas Giorgio Stephanopoulos had far exceeded them all.

Tomas sensed it, and turned from his husband to his mother to see her soft loving expression. "Mama…" he whispered and took her hand. He knew that look, that expression so soft he knew she was radiating happiness for him. "I love you."

She squeezed his hand. "I love you, too, my baby," she whispered. "So much, with every fibre of my being, I love you."

"Mama." Tomas shifted his body, so he was fully facing her. "I love you." He was about to say more, but his mother interrupted him.

"You have made me so proud with everything you've done, and everything you do. And day in day out you exceed your limits and blow us all out of the water. You have achieved so much in your life, and I am so proud of you, my baby."

"Naw, Mama." Tomas's face crumpled and tears flowed. "That's not true and you know it."

"Poppycock!" Jenny squeezed his hand as hard as she could. "You know full well it's true and I will say it until my dying breath—"

"Don't say that," Tomas cut her off. "Don't say that. You *are not* going to die and that's all there is to it. *End* of story. *End* of discussion."

"It isn't," Jenny said. "And *you* know it, which is why we've done what we've done this year." Her eyes took in all of her children. They were watching her with furrowed brows and confused faces. "Isn't it time for more dancing?" she added, trying to change the subject.

The wait staff came in and cleared the tables, the family wandered back onto the floor, or finished feeding and changing children. The tables were moved and reset at right angles to the dance floor, so they weren't in the way, and Jenny and Spiros settled back for a quiet moment.

"You okay, Danté?" Angie stood by her son as he sat talking to Nick.

"I'm fine, Mama." He gazed up at her concerned face. "I'm *fine*."

"Ah, dude, I think some girls want some selfies." Nick pointed to Danté's second cousins who excitedly stood around the table.

Seeing them, Danté stood and kissed his mother. "I'm fine, *really*." Leaving her, he walked over to his relatives and took photos with them, after all, he hadn't done his set, so he felt he owed them something.

"Ah, why won't she stop crying," Cabot moaned. He'd fed, watered and changed his daughter, but she was grumpy, frowny and squawky.

"Maybe she has gas," Tony offered and watched Cabot shift her to his shoulder and pat her back.

"Maybe she just doesn't like you," Antonio replied, shaking his head at his brother's useless attempts at raising a child.

"I second that," Dom added, sitting on a nearby table and putting one foot on a chair. "I wouldn't, either, if I were her." He was holding Christopher in his right arm and the bottle in his left hand. It was the first time he'd been awake since getting to the reception hall and he was hungry.

Antonio guffawed and looked over his shoulder at his cousin. "Too true."

"Two against one isn't funny," Cabot whined at his twin and cousin. Dom was a year younger than them, but they'd all grown up together until he and Antonio left to model in New York.

"They're hardly against you, Cab," Tony soothed and settled baby Antonio on his feet. He watched him toddle off towards his great-grandmother. Jenny was the only great-grandmother Antonio would know since his own blood grandparents and great-grandparents were all long gone. Tony had lost his grandparents when he was only two, along with his father. His mother had died twelve years ago, so little baby Jennifer and Antonio only had the Stephanopoulos family, and Tony didn't mind one bit. He watched Antonio cling to Jenny's legs and noticed how quickly most of the other children gathered around. Aged one to sixteen, there was fierce competition among the younger ones for Great-Grandma's love, and he saw Cabot's siblings and cousins gravitate her way with them. It was as if Jenny was the sun and the whole family orbited around her.

"Cabot," Jenny called. "Bring her here."

Fed up with not being able to quiet his child, Cabot walked over to Jenny and placed her namesake in her arms. "I can't get her to stop. If you can, I'll love you forever."

"I thought you already did." Jenny raised a brow in amusement and saw him grin. She turned her attention to her great-granddaughter, named in honour for her. Jennifer Vivian Stephanopoulos, born on the same day as her great-grandma. "Jennifer, you stop this at once. You've been fed, you've been changed, you've been burped. There's no need to cry, so stop it now. You're a Stephanopoulos."

Jennifer stared into her great-grandma's face, saw the serious expression radiating out of her eyes, and promptly stopped crying.

"What the hell…?" Cabot's voice trailed off as he stood staring at his daughter. "How the hell…did you do that?"

"The same way I did with all of you," Jenny told him and watched him slump into the closest chair. "Quickly and efficiently." She gazed at all of her great-grandchildren gathered at her legs and her smile beamed at all of them. "Hello, my babies."

"Gate-Gamma." Carys held onto Jenny's leg and bounced up and down. "Tell us a storwy, Gate-Gamma."

"Do we have to have a story?" Carlos groaned and ran a hand through his hair. "We're supposed to be celebrating."

"That's usually Cabot's line," Antonio quipped, watching his daughters hug his grandmother's legs.

"Ah." Cabot sighed and brushed his hair aside, a reflection of his father. "I think I'm too tired to celebrate. The kids have worn me out." He lifted his feet onto the table in front of him and crossed his legs. Noticing Carlos staring at him, Cabot put his feet down, but his father kept staring, a weird, serious expression on his face.

Christopher finished his bottle and Dom passed it to Davina.

Danté stood by his side, peering over his brother's shoulder. One brow arched, his lips in a frown.

Dom saw him. "Wanna burp him?"

"Ugh, no." Danté shook his head. "You can do it." He took a step back and held up his hands, palm sides out. "Make sure there's no vomit, it stinks."

Dom smirked. "Like *you'd* know. Scared you'll have another attack?" He watched his brother's face flicker with emotion and something gripped his heart, making his chest contract, and his brow furrow in concern. "Danté?"

"I'm fine," Danté bit back. "And I wish everyone would stop asking."

Those around him went quiet, but most of Jenny's family were dancing on the floor.

Sighing, Danté jammed his fists in his pants pockets, clenched his jaw, and stared at the floor.

Tomas moved over to his nephew's side and propped his chin on Danté's shoulder. "What is it?"

Breathing hard, Danté frowned and looked at his uncle. "Death," he whispered.

Tomas teared up and rubbed Danté's back. "We've all dealt with a lot of that. Is it your shark attack?"

Danté shook his head. "No. It's stupid. I just realised that by the time I marry, or have kids, Grandma and Grandpa will be gone, and it sucks."

Sympathetic murmurs went through the family.

"We've all lost someone, kid," Pedro told him. "You never got to meet our great-grandfather, Giorgio, or our grandparents on Papa's side, and only barely met Mama's parents."

"And mine are all long gone," Angie added. "My mother died when I was ten. Daddy died when I was eighteen and pregnant with Alena."

"And my mom and grandparents and aunts have all gone," Simon said, feeling his heart gripped by pain. "Mom got to see her grandkids, but Dad nearly didn't." He glanced at his father who grabbed him by the shoulder.

"And you know all of mine are gone," Tony said. "The kids will only know this family. Who are pretty damn awesome, by the way."

"And we've lost our dads." Maggie slid her arm around Mike's waist. "They'll never see any great-grandchildren."

"Mine are gone as well," Charles added, wrapping his arms around Diana. "They got to see the kids before they went, though."

"Yeah, yeah, all right. I get it," Danté muttered, thinking back to his conversation with his grandmother and rubbing his aching forehead which was making him feel sick with grief and guilt. "I get it, but it just sucks. When the time is right, she'll come along regardless of *who* is still around." He smiled at Jenny through the aching. "And then it will be on like Donkey Kong!"

Guffaws went around the family and members pulled chairs over, so everyone could sit and chat.

"Tell us a storwy, Gate-Gamma," Carys repeated, unsure of what everyone was laughing at as she hadn't understood most of what everyone was saying. Her cousins, Ava, Harper, Izabella, Antonio and Hunter, plus her sister Jaqueline, and multiple children she didn't know from her gate-gamma's side of the family were all crowding around, all wanting to get on Gate-Gamma's legs, but she pushed them away. "No! Gate-Gamma's for me."

Harper pushed back with both hands, while the other kids looked on.

"Girls!" Jenny said sharply, drawing their attention back to her. "There's enough room for all of you. Now, sit down." She watched them try to take centre place in front of her. Carys took the prize position, even though Harper still tried pushing her out of the way.

"Stop it, Harpa," Carys crossly told her cousin and slapped her on the arm.

"Carys!" Diana exclaimed in shock. "We don't slap."

Carys glanced over her shoulder at her mama before bowing her head and blushing at the telling off. "Sowwy, Mama."

"Tell Harper that," Diana told her.

Carys frowned fiercely at her cousin, a black-haired replica of herself, not wanting to say it.

"Carys..." Diana warned, exchanging amused glances with Alena.

The frowning cherub glanced from her beautiful mama to her grinning cousin and forced out, "Sowwy, Harpa."

Harper poked her tongue out and blew a raspberry at her cousin, getting a telling off from her great-grandma.

"Harper!" Jenny frowned at her great-granddaughter. "*No more.* Apologise to Carys."

Harper, hating being chastised by anyone, especially her gate-gamma who had an unhappy expression on her face, bowed her head. "Sowwy, Cawys."

"So, what story are you going to tell, Jenny?" Rebecca, Jenny's sister asked and ignored the girls. "How about one not even *my* great-grandkids have heard?"

Looking at all of her family crowding around and pulling chairs close, Jenny contemplated what story to tell. After what Danté had just said, and the conversation they'd had earlier, and seeing Jennifer, her little namesake, in her arms, she knew there was only one story to tell. Looking into her husband's still sparkling eyes, she smiled. "I think it's time we told them the story of us, don't you?"

Spiros returned the smile, touched his left hand to little Jennifer's head, noted all of the grandchildren and great-grandchildren gathered around, and cleared his throat. Once he had everyone's attention, he started. "Our story goes all the way back to 1950 in Mykonos Greece…"

August 1950

Spiros Giorgio Stephanopoulos glanced up at the big white clock on the wall, saw it was five o'clock, untied his apron, and threw it down on the counter. "I'm off now, Papa. See you next week."

"Spiros!" Giorgio Stephanopoulos's imposing figure came to a stop in the doorway between the shop and the backroom of *Stephanopoulos Meats*. His tone made his son stop in his tracks. "I want a word."

Sighing, Spiros rolled his eyes and turned, spying two of his younger brothers, Matthias and Costas, watching him over his father's shoulder in the meat room. "Yes, Papa?"

"Step into my office." Giorgio moved past his son and into the tiny office at the back of the shop, waiting for Spiros to follow.

Looking at his youngest brother, Theseus, who was escorting the last customer out the door and turning around the closed sign, Spiros sighed again and walked into the office. He knew what these talks meant. The only time you were called into the office was for a lecture, either on how you needed to do more, or about taking over the shop one day. Not that his brothers received *that* lecture, only *he* did as he was the eldest of eight children. At twenty-five, Spiros knew he was being primed for taking over the business. In the Stephanopoulos family, as per the rules, everything was handed down to the eldest, usually a boy, and so on and so forth. So, when Giorgio died, Spiros would inherit and take over. But Spiros didn't want to take over. He wanted freedom and the right to make his own choices about where he worked and what he did, and right now, he wanted to head down to the beach for a swim with his friends.

Giorgio closed the door behind his son and walked around his desk to his chair. "Sit." He watched his son's deflated expression as he sat on a chair. "Spiros."

"Am I in trouble?" Spiros jumped in.

"No, no, of course not." Giorgio waved a dismissive hand. "I wanted to talk to you about the shop. Get you ready for taking over now that you're twenty-five." He watched his son's expression change and didn't like what he saw. "You *will* be taking over, Spiros."

"I do not want to, Papa," Spiros told him, that unnerving clenching in his gut holding on tightly. It was not that he was afraid of his father, but his father could impose an almighty wrath when he wanted to. He also knew he had to stand up for himself. "I have told you; I do not want to take over the shop. You are still young enough; we just work here. And you will be here for a long time. I do not need to take over."

"That is what is expected," Giorgio said. "You will now become the manager, just as I did when I turned twenty-five. Just as your son will at twenty-five. It is tradition."

"Not *my* tradition, Papa." Spiros thrust himself up and paced the small room. "I want to get out and see the world. Learn new things, *see* new things, meet new people. I want to know what it is like in other places. I want to see and hear and breathe new things." His fists were clenching in time with his words and he finally stopped and faced his father. "I do not want to be stuck here for the rest of my life, Papa."

"What? Like me?" Giorgio said in disdain. "You do not want to be like me? Is that it? Well, you need to know your place, Spiros, and it is as manager of *Stephanopoulos Meats*, and one day, the owner."

"No, Papa." Spiros vehemently shook his head. "I do not believe that. Not now anyway. Not at twenty-five. You have a long way to go, and maybe one day, but not now. Not while I am young. I want to see the world, and I will find a way to do it." He gripped the back of his chair so tightly it shook. "I will do it."

"No, Spiros. You will know your place. And that place is here." Giorgio had never thought about the fact his son might not want to do it. He had taken over after his father, as his father had before him. It was a tradition in the Stephanopoulos family that the eldest son automatically took over the store upon the death of the father after managing it from the age of twenty-five. Usually. He had received the store from his father as a business to run, so Giorgio senior kept the business *and his son* in the family. As for the tradition, Giorgio saw it as an honour, but Spiros clearly did not. "Are you dishonouring me, Spiros? I will not like it if you are."

"No, Papa." Spiros stood straight at his full height of five foot eleven and faced his father. "I just do not want to do it now. I want to know what the rest of the world is like while I am still young enough to enjoy it. See who I might meet, the life lessons I might learn. Right now, I do not want to be in Greece. I want to travel."

"You will do as you are told, Spiros." Giorgio thundered to his feet, standing an inch above his son at six foot. "You are the eldest. You will take over."

Spiros sighed and shook his head. "We are just going around in circles, Papa. I will see you on Sunday." Opening the door, he closed it on his father and his name being called. It had taken a lot of mental strength to do that because his father was not to be disobeyed. He walked into the back room, past his inquisitive brothers, grabbed his bag from the wall hanger, and left via the back door. After trudging along the cobblestone streets until he arrived at his tiny two bedroom apartment he shared with his best friend, Christos, he let himself in, pulled his bag from over his head, and dumped it on the two-seater couch in the tiny living room. Spiros dumped himself next to it and dropped his head into his hands.

He was twenty-five years old, had lived out of home since he was eighteen, and worked in his father's meat shop since he was fourteen, although he'd helped out before that. Ever since he and his four younger brothers were old enough, they'd been doing something involving the family's shop, while his three younger sisters were either at school, or at home helping their mother with women's chores until they were primed for marrying off. That was the way it was. The men and boys went out to work, while the women and girls stayed home and learned how to be homemakers and wives. They may have been on the island of Mykonos, but that didn't stop rules and regulations, or laws, or age-old traditions, from being carried out.

It had been very cramped in the Stephanopoulos household growing up. As each baby had come along, the family grew, but not the size of the house they lived in. It only had two bedrooms to share among eight children and two adults, and the boys had all bunked into one room, but eventually, they had been moved down to the basement, so the girls could have the second bedroom. Not that the basement had been that bad; it was only a place to sleep for the night and keep your stuff. And he'd been so desperate to get out of home that he'd organised to rent an apartment with his friend long before he turned eighteen.

Spiros leaned back and slid down a little. Finding a comfortable position, he heaved a sigh from the pit of his abdomen. As much as he loved his parents and family, he just didn't have the inclination to run the family business. He wasn't interested, at least for now. Not when he was young and alive and free to do what he wanted, *when* he wanted. Hauling his feet onto the ratty old coffee table in front of him, he glanced around at what he and Christos had. A small kitchen diner with a two man table was behind him, a small record player sat against the wall in front of him, a couple of single chairs to accompany the sofa, and a bed and wardrobe in each small bedroom. The rent was cheap, and the bills were low due to them not being home much, and there was a tiny bathroom which held the toilet, shower, and laundry. It wasn't much, but it had been theirs for the last seven years, and he'd managed to save a lot in those years, since he'd started receiving a legal wage from his father. Working at fourteen, you didn't receive a paycheque, but his father had given each of his sons a drachma, or two, a week for helping out, so, he'd managed to save quite a bit since.

The scent of raw meat drifted into his nostrils and he winced. "Damn it, I forgot about the boys." Moving quickly into the bathroom, he shed his clothes and left them on the floor to be washed later. He washed his face and hands and then changed into shorts and a shirt in his bedroom. Slipping into sandals, he grabbed his bag and wallet, making sure he had enough money for later. Friday and Saturday nights were the only ones he and Christos allowed themselves to spend some money on a good meal and a couple of drinks, otherwise, besides paying the bills, all in the bank it went. He left and rushed down to the small cove he and his friends hung out in all summer long and saw them waiting for him on beach chairs on the sand, sipping their ice-cold drinks, and chatting.

"Ah, here he is. I thought you had flaked out on us." Christos waved him over. "We have already been checking out the girls for an hour." At twenty-five, he'd been Spiros's best friend through high school, and like a lot of Greek boys, was on the lookout for a girl. Not that he had any trouble getting one. His jet-black hair, mahogany eyes, and tanned complexion saw to it. As did his five foot ten muscular frame with its dark hair spread in all the right places. No, Christos never had any trouble getting a girl with his charm and wit, but definitely had trouble keeping one due to his wandering eye…and hands.

"No, no." Spiros relaxed into a beach chair and glanced at all of his friends. "Papa wanted to talk to me after work, and then I went home and just sat thinking about it."

"Is he still on at you to run the meat shop?" Yannis asked. He'd been friends with Spiros and Christos for five years and they hung out every Friday night.

"Ugh, he is." Spiros ordered a drink from the bikini-clad waitress of the beach bar and watched her retreating figure as she walked off to make the order. Women didn't titillate him as he thought they should. Sure, they had nice curvy figures, and sure, he was a man who was attracted to the opposite sex, but he'd never had a serious girlfriend, or found a woman he wanted to marry. Marriage and babies were a long way off.

"So…what are you going to do?" Yannis asked, sipping his beer.

"I do not know." Spiros accepted his beer from the waitress, took a long drink, then set his head back. Closing his eyes, he waited for the sun to sink beyond the horizon before opening them. He noticed his friends had gone on chatting and ignored him, and listening in on the conversation about which restaurant they should eat at, Spiros mentally calculated the number of hours and years he'd be working if he kept on at the meat shop. Even if he lived to a ripe old age and kept on working to seventy-five, that would be fifty years of life spent carting meat around and selling it to the island, and he didn't want that. No matter how much family tradition had been pummelled into his head, he did not want to spend another fifty years in the family's meat shop. "God, I would be seventy-five," he murmured in disbelief.

"What did you say?" Christos asked, turning to his friend.

"I would be seventy-five if I worked in the meat shop for another fifty years." Spiros slowly shook his head. "Imagine that. Working in a job for fifty years. Longer, since I started working there eleven years ago. Sixty-one years in the same place, doing the same job, day after day after day. God…"

"I would be bored out of my skull," Xenos said. He was twenty-one, six-foot, and a good looking Greek boy. He'd been working with Christos for the last three years and regularly met up with them on a Friday or Saturday night.

"I think I would be too," Spiros agreed. "If I do not get out soon, or go and do something else, I am going to go out of my mind and die of boredom."

"Why do you not get another job?" Nicodemus suggested. At twenty-six, he was the oldest of the group of friends and had changed jobs four times.

"What? Like you?" Spiros raised a brow at him. "I often wonder why you cannot stay in a job. Besides, what else would I do? I have been in the family shop since I was a kid, working since I was fourteen. What else *would* I do? *Could* I do?"

"Anything," Nicodemus told him. "There are other businesses on the island; a lot of them have nothing to do with meat. Why not give it a go?"

"Because I do not know what else I would be good at," Spiros murmured, deep in thought, the idea of him leaving seeming better and better all the time.

"What about moving to one of the islands, or Athens? Plenty of jobs there," Yannis said. "You do not have to be confined to the island. The mainland would have plenty of jobs."

"The *world* would have plenty of jobs," Spiros muttered, liking the idea of him getting out of Mykonos for the big, bad world. "But where would I go?"

"Are you still thinking of actually leaving?" Christos asked. He'd also had a few chats with Spiros about moving to another country, but hadn't thought he was serious.

"Leaving where?" Nicodemus asked, checking his watch. "Can we continue this conversation over dinner? I'm starving."

The others agreed and collected their things, finished their drinks, and walked down the beach until they came across a restaurant they liked the look of. After finding a table, they sat down and looked over the menu. More drinks were served, and they got back to the conversation.

"So…where and when were you leaving?" Christos continued where he'd left off.

"I am not, at least, not yet," Spiros placated his friends. "We keep getting letters from our cousins in Australia. My aunt and uncle moved there two years ago and they keep saying how wonderful it is. And then some of Mama's family have moved to Italy, and some have moved to England." He shrugged. "I am just wondering if maybe I should spread my wings and move too. An exciting new life in an exciting new country. I can do anything."

"Except speak English, and do anything other than work in a meat shop," Yannis joked. Even though a lot of English speaking tourists came to Mykonos through the summer months, they had only picked up a few words themselves, as they hadn't learned English in school.

"That is true." Spiros set his beer aside as the waitress placed his plate on the table. It was heaped with steaming lobster pasta and was a meal he treated himself to every Friday night. "I do not mind taking on a new trade," he continued. "I do not know if I would need qualifications, but I am a fast learner and a hard worker." He stabbed a piece of lobster with his fork, placed it in his mouth, and let it slide down his throat. "It is just a matter of which country I would move to and that will decide what job I take on."

"It is not like you will be a world-class chef, or an artiste," Xenos joked and picked up his gyro. He took a bite from the heavily laden roll and juices dribbled down his chin. Chewing, he swallowed and licked his lips. "There is no way *you* could make something like this."

"I know meat, but I am not much of a cook. I know wood, but am not much of a builder. I know the ocean, but am not much of a sailor," Spiros told them. "The only thing I do, and have done, is work in a meat shop."

"Then maybe that is where your talent lies," Christos said. "Maybe you just need a change of scenery, not profession."

"Maybe," Spiros agreed and silently finished his meal. After another hour, he said goodnight to his fellow party-goers. "I am calling it a night." He flung down a couple of notes for his meal and rose to leave.

"You sure?" Nicodemus asked. "We are headed off to *Inferno* for the night. Probably be plenty of hot chicks there." The boys guffawed and elbowed each other as they walked out of the restaurant.

"No. I am fine. I just need a quiet one to get some thinking done." Spiros waved as he backed away. "Have fun, boys." He left them laughing, and elbowing each other, as they walked off towards the hottest nightclub on the island, and started trudging back to his apartment. But, deciding better of it, he did a u-turn and headed back to the beach, hoping the walk and sea air would do him good. Moving at a steady pace, he found himself on a hill with a view of the ferry dock, and finding a place to sit, watched the ferries bob gently in the water and people mill around the shops and restaurants below him.

The light summer breeze caressed his tanned skin and ruffled the soft curls in his wild jet-black hair. His mind wandered with dreams of ferry rides and working in Athens, or living there. What would he do? What could he be? He allowed his mind to go farther and imagined sailing the seas to another country. Italy, Turkey, Africa,

Spain, Portugal. Could he survive in English speaking countries with no English skills? Would he be welcome? Find a community with other Greeks who had sailed the seas in search of something else, something better, something new? Could he leave his family? His parents, brothers and sisters. Could he leave the island on which he'd been born and raised? The only place he'd known in his whole twenty-five years of life. Could he do it? *Would* he do it? And would he do it alone? What if one of his friends wanted to do it with him? He wouldn't be alone then.

With an overwhelming sense of excitement, he wandered back the way he'd come and hit the beach at a steady stride. He dropped his bag, removed his shirt and sandals, and ran for the cool flatness of the Aegean Sea. It was refreshing on his warm skin, and washed all of his trepidations about his future away, leaving him refreshed when he walked out. Carrying his bag and shirt, and wearing his sandals, he walked home feeling renewed. His gait was lighter, his smile higher. He felt good. The decision to leave felt right. It was just a matter of when.

*****

Sunday, after church, when every member of the Stephanopoulos family attended the local orthodox, they congregated at his parents' small abode on the third street back from the beach.

His four younger brothers were all married off with children, or children on the way, and his three younger sisters were being set up for future husbands by his parents. Yet, as oldest, Spiros had bucked that trend, that wanton need of his parents to marry off their children, and was still single.

It was very crowded at the Stephanopoulos dining table.

"Can someone pass the salt?"

"I need another drink."

"Does someone have the potatoes?"

"Spiros, when are you getting married?"

"When I find the right woman, Mama."

"He needs to become manager of the shop first."

The clattering of dishes stopped. So did everyone at the table.

Spiros sighed. "Papa, I told you, I do not want to be manager. Make Matthias the manager. He is married with children. A steady job will be good for him." He passed the potatoes to his sister and the salt down the table.

"It does not work that way, Spiros, you know that," Giorgio told him for the billionth time. "You know that it gets handed down from eldest son to eldest son. And *you* are the eldest son. The other boys get nothing. When I die, the meat shop is yours. If your mother and I are both gone, the house is also yours. Whatever money there is can be divided if you wish, but it will also be yours. They are the rules of the family. You know that."

Spiros glanced at each and every family member at the extended dining table in his parent's small dining room. His mother, Katyana, sat quietly on his left. His brothers sat to his right. All were silently eating, looking down at their plates. His sisters and sisters-in-law were opposite the men, also silently eating with their eyes down. It was solemn and disturbing.

"Papa, I understand the so-called rules; you have drummed them into us for the last twenty-five years, but why can they not be broken? Why do we have to continue such archaic nonsense?"

"It is not nonsense," Giorgio roared, slamming his fist on the table, making everyone, and every piece of crockery, jump.

Silence descended once more. An uncomfortable one at that.

"The tradition has passed from father to son for generations, and will continue to do so with *this* generation."

"No, Papa." A surge of strength and willingness to stand up for his beliefs fled through Spiros's body. "I am saying no. You may have married off my brothers, and are getting ready to marry off my sisters, but I am not yet ready to get married. And I do not want to be stuck in the meat shop for the rest of my life. Why can you not change the stupid family rule? Who made it, anyway? Why can you not change it, so all of the family get something instead of only the eldest getting it all? That is unfair to the rest of the family." He motioned at his brothers who refused to meet anyone's eye.

"Because, clearly, unlike you, Spiros, I stick with tradition," Giorgio spat, disliking his son's tempestuous nature. "And you will fall into line, or else."

Spurned by those words, Spiros frowned. "Or else what? What is so wrong with me wanting to do something different and not take over the shop? Why *can I not* do something else? Like travel, or work overseas? Live in another country, even. Why do I have to take over the shop? And *do not* say it is tradition because I am not buying it." No longer interested in his mother's lamb meal, Spiros pushed his plate away. "I do not want to be stuck on this island for another twenty-five years, getting fat with a wife who does nothing but pop out children. I want to do something productive and adventurous and different."

"Like what?" Giorgio scoffed.

"Like…like move to another country. Maybe I will do that." Spiros excitedly waved his arms around as he spoke.

"And leave us, your mother, your responsibilities here?" The frown on Giorgio's face was one of thunder.

"They are not *my* responsibilities, Papa. They are yours," Spiros reminded him. "And if I want to leave Mykonos, then I will leave Mykonos. In fact, the more I think about it, the more I like the idea."

"Then the more I will have to put my foot down, Spiros," Giorgio warned. "If you do not stay here and abide by the family's time-honoured traditions, and take over the shop as manager, then you will not be welcome in this house. You will not be welcome in this family."

The frown rolled over Spiros's face. "What? What are you saying?"

"I am saying, that if you choose to leave the business, the family, and the island, then I will have no choice but to disown and disinherit you."

Shocked expressions flew face to face as Spiros stared hard at his father's impervious stony one. "Pap…you cannot be serious? Just because I want to see the world…you would disown me?"

Giorgio's nod was short and sharp. It wasn't a decision he'd actually made. He'd thought it up on the spot in a hope of keeping his son at home. He wouldn't actually do it. But then, he didn't think Spiros would either.

"But I…" Spiros shook his head in shock, unable to comprehend the ferocity of his father's word. "You would not…would you?"

"If you have finished with your meal, then I suggest you leave now, so you can have a good think about your future decisions." Giorgio gestured towards Spiros's pushed away plate. "That has gone to waste. We do not waste food in this house. We cannot afford to."

Stunned, Spiros turned to his plate and slowly pulled it back. That too was one of the rules in the house, that you ate everything on your plate and didn't waste food, or drink. The family were not rich, and waste was abominable.

In silence, the meal was finished off, and after the dishes were done, Spiros bade his family goodbye and left. The stony silence was too much to bear, and he felt the weight lift from his shoulders as he walked down the streets, getting away from that horrendous cloud of anger. He'd never seen his father like that. It was more than upset, more than angry. It was some sort of…

Unable to put his finger on what vibe he'd been getting from his father, he considered his options, and one of them was to talk to his grandfather, Giorgio senior. Heading home, he was glad to see Christos wasn't in, and after changing from his Sunday best into shorts and a t-shirt, Spiros dialled his grandfather's home.

"Mr Stephanopoulos's residence, how may I assist?"

"Hello, it is Spiros Stephanopoulos, his grandson. Is he in? I want to talk to him."

"Of course, one momento."

Spiros could hear the noises in the background and then what must have been the extension being picked up.

"Hello, Spiros? To what do I owe the pleasure?" Giorgio Stephanopoulos senior was seventy-four years old and still fighting fit for his age. He got around without the use of a cane and had a full head of salt and pepper hair.

Sighing, Spiros told him everything that had happened at lunch. "I cannot believe he is serious. Can he really disown me, Grandfather?"

"Well, he can try," Giorgio muttered. "My estate will go to him upon my death, and to you upon his, depending on who goes first. So, he is just following tradition. It will all go to you upon his death, and so on and so forth. Your father is a stubborn man, Spiros. And it is obvious you are following in his path with that stubborn streak. He can try and disown you, disinherit you, etc, but my estate will still go to you via him, so there is no need to worry. Your father struck out on his own in a much similar way. He refused to live like a wealthy man, lives like a pauper struggling to make ends meet. That was his choice, and he has made a go of *Stephanopoulos Meats* just as he was determined to do. Would not let me help him in any other way except for the job in the first place. And while it may not be my most profitable business, he has still made it profitable." Giorgio senior was an incredibly *influential and* affluential man who had many a zero to his bank balance which he wanted to spend on his family, and since his son was the only heir left, his daughter having died childless many years earlier, the only family he had was Giorgio junior. But his son refused to spend his money, claiming his children could earn their way through life as he had to. And while Giorgio senior agreed, he didn't like the fact he now had great-grandchildren and couldn't do anything for them.

"So, what do you suggest, Grandfather?" Spiros wound the phone cord around his fingers then detangled them.

"Do whatever you want to do, Spiros," Giorgio told him. "Do you need money? I have plenty, and your father will not let me spend it on you all."

"No, I am fine. I have plenty saved up. But what if he disowns me?"

"I doubt he will. I know my son, and he may say he will, but, I doubt he will do anything about it in the long run. Life is too short, Spiros. Do what makes you happy."

Grinning, Spiros thought it was the best advice he'd heard all day. "Thanks, Grandfather."

*****

For the next week, Spiros worked hard in the shop for another wage, but started researching countries to which he could move and get work. His friends were equally excited and helped out, asking all manner of people they knew about the rules and restrictions of moving to another country and taking on jobs. By the end of the week, he had a list of countries that were potential new homes, and on Sunday, in the family home, the universe gave him another push. His mother had received another letter from her brother and his family about how great Australia was, how the local Greek community was thriving, and saying they were more than welcome to come for a visit. Spiros managed to scribble down their phone number and address without anyone knowing, and planned on making a call as soon as possible.

He did it that night.

Not knowing what time it would be in Australia, he rang his aunt and uncle, hoping he wasn't getting anyone out of bed.

"Hello, Stephanides residence."

"Hello, Uncle Nikos, it is Spiros. Katyana's son."

"Ah, Spiros, my boy, to what do we owe this pleasure?" Nikos sounded cheerful.

"I was ringing to find out about Australia. You suggested we come for a visit."

"Yes, yes, anytime, my son. We will put you up; you will stay with us."

"What if I…" Spiros took a deep breath. "What if I wanted to stay?"

"Stay?" Nikos asked. "You mean for longer than a holiday?"

"I mean…forever…maybe…" Spiros's nerves got the better of him and he started tumbling over his words. "What if I wanted to move there, start a new life, have a new life. What is it like? Is it hard to do? Where would I go first? Does everyone speak Greek? How would I speak English?"

"Calm down, Spiros," Nikos told him. "Everything is easy. The Greek community all speak Greek, and for those of us who also speak English, there are places you can learn it. It is a beautiful country,

Spiros. The beaches are wonderful, the nature is wonderful, and everything is so cheap."

"How did you go once you got there?" Spiros propped his legs on the coffee table. "Was it easy to understand everything? Everyone?"

"We already spoke some English and we quickly picked up what is known as Australian," Nikos said. "It is very easy and simple, and you will go far if you learn it. In fact, I think there is a free class at the local recreation centre you could take. Will you need a place to live? You can live with us until you are able to get your own place. And I can give you a job in the meat shop, or as the Australians call it, the butcher shop. Or one of my fellow Greeks could find you something. We all help each other here. Are you planning on moving? Have you made plans, yet? How are you getting here? *When* are you getting here?"

Spiros laughed lightly. "I have no idea, Uncle Nikos. I have only just been thinking about it recently. Papa wants me to take over the meat shop now I am twenty-five, but I do not want to. I want to *do* other things and *try* other things. Maybe live in another country, but my Greek would be a hindrance to me living in an English speaking society. I just wanted to know what Australia was like."

"If you are going anywhere," Nikos said, "come here. At least you will have us to support you and help you find a job and a house. Think about it." He glanced at the clock on his kitchen wall. "In the meantime, I must go. I am a very busy man these days."

"Okay. Thanks, Uncle Nikos. I will let you know either way what I decide. Bye."

"Goodbye, Spiros. Say hello to your mother, brothers and sisters for me."

"I will, bye." As he slowly replaced the phone in its cradle, Spiros contemplated things further. His uncle had a point. Moving to a country where he already knew people would be a bonus, especially when they already spoke and understood the English language, something he was yet to do, but would surely have no problems with if there were English classes being run for free. And he didn't know what the conversion rate from the Greek drachma to the Australian pound would be, but surely he'd come out the other end with more money? Right? Maybe he could make it work after all. His aunt and uncle were there, doing well from the sound of their letters. Maybe it would be a better place to be, the better place to go. Yes, it was far away on the other side of the world, and how he was going to get there legally was another matter. And something he would have to do research on.

*****

"So, what have you decided?" Matthias asked him at work Wednesday morning.

"About what?" Spiros hefted a carcass of lamb onto the metal chopping table in the middle of the back room of the shop.

"About whether you are taking over the shop, or leaving?" Matthias cast a furtive glance into the store to see if their father was listening, but he was busy serving a customer. He had waited until now to question his brother because he hadn't wanted to upset their father for fear of his wrath. Still, his curiosity was piqued, and he was desperate to know.

"I am not definite, yet," Spiros replied, smashing the cleaver through the carcass. "But my decision is getting closer, and I am leaning towards leaving."

"Where will you go?" Costa, his second brother, asked quietly as he passed behind them carrying a tray of fresh-cut lamb forequarters.

"Well…I am narrowing it down." Spiros glanced into the shop front, seeing his father ringing up the tab. "Australia is definitely one of the top three."

"Because of Uncle Nikos and Aunt Melina?" Anatole asked, gathering the pieces of lamb that Spiros was chopping and arranging them onto trays.

"Yes." Spiros slammed the cleaver for the last time and wiped his hands. "It would be very helpful because they are there, yes."

They busied themselves for a few moments as Giorgio came in for another tray of lamb chops and then got to work on the beef.

"Do you know when you will go?" Matthias asked, placing huge hunks of cow on the table to be chopped.

"No. I have to look at the best way to go about it. Uncle Nikos and Aunt Melina went by boat. They took two suitcases each and had enough money to buy everything they needed; the house and car, and a hefty deposit for the shop, which is now paid off. They own it all and are debt-free after two years. Our cousins have jobs and are working hard to build their own lives. And, from their letters, they all say they love it. So…" He shrugged. "Why would I not?"

"Do you think we should all go?" Theseus asked. As the fifth son and fifth in line of succession, he knew that *Stephanopoulos Meats* would never be his. So, maybe a life in another country would be an adventure. The problem was, he was recently married off with a baby on the way.

"Are you thinking of leaving, too?" Spiros asked him. "You only got married this year and have a baby due next year."

"Yes, I know," Theseus muttered. "But I am twenty-one, and if you are thinking about leaving, then why can I not?"

"Because you have a wife, and a baby on the way, you need stability," Matthias told him and shoved a tray of beef cheeks into his arms. "So you need a solid job to pay off your house and support your wife and forthcoming child. But for now, take these out to the shop." At twenty-four, he was the second eldest with a wife and two children of his own. Like his brothers, he'd been kicked out of home at eighteen into a home of his own that he had to pay off with his job at the shop. All the brothers were married once they turned twenty-one, except for Spiros. And while Matthias loved his wife and children; he also envied his elder brother the freedom he still had. Not to mention, it wasn't any of *them* who'd be getting the shop, or home, as an inheritance. There were times when he hated Spiros, mainly when family talk turned to the shop and who got what in the event of their father's death, but he also secretly hoped Spiros would take off, so their father would disinherit him and then he would, *or could,* possibly inherit instead. If Spiros wasn't there as manager, then maybe he'd get the top job instead. *And,* if Spiros did leave and did not come back, then that sealed the deal even more. Didn't it?

"What will you do?" Costas asked, getting an inkling of what Matthias was doing. As much as he wished he could leave with Spiros, he was more deathly afraid of what his father would do.

"I do not know. I am yet to put a plan together. It is already August, the end of summer. I would need to get legal papers, a visa maybe. I do not know." Spiros wiped his cold, bloody hands on a towel, and then wiped his arm across his forehead. "Is the cooling on? It is warm in here."

Matthias checked the thermometer. "It is. Must be you and your guilt."

Frowning, Spiros glanced at his brother. "Why would I be filled with guilt? And why would it make me hot?"

"God, Zeus, Ares, whoever, is making you feel guilty for making the choice to leave your family, and go against your papa's wishes," Matthias said.

Spiros snorted and glanced into the shop. "Hardly. I am hot because it is hot in here and I am cutting up hunks of meat and exerting my energy."

"Have you thought about the rest of us?" Costas asked. As the third brother and third in line, he'd long ago realised he would get nothing in the event of their father's death.

"The rest of you are grown adults who can make their own choices," Spiros muttered. "You all decided to abide by our parents' wishes and get married and do your duty. I did not. Your choices are yours. If you want to leave, leave. If you are too scared to, then stay in the same old job doing the same old things. But remember, once more children come along, you are stuck, unless you make the decision to further your own careers, or make the decision to move and do your own things. Grandfather lives in Athens, as do most of Mama's family. Why can we not? Why can *you* not?" Spiros asked each of his brothers. "Why can we not spread our wings, and live and work somewhere else, if it furthers our careers, or offers us opportunities for other work, or a better life?" He threw the towel down. "I am done with everything. This job, this life, this town. I want to see the world.

You lot may not, but I do."

"Still going on with this whimsical fantasy of yours?" Giorgio asked. His wide muscular frame blocked the doorway from the shop. "I thought you had forgotten about it this last week as you have not mentioned it." He was disappointed to hear Spiros's words to his brothers as he had hoped he'd got over his dreams to leave.

"It is not a whimsical fantasy, Papa." Spiros eyed the clock on the wall. He had five minutes left until closing, so he picked up the hose ready to clean out the sink.

"Then what would you call it?" Giorgio went on, intently watching his son.

"I call it a thirst for adventure and knowledge. A thirst to travel the world and see new places, and do new things. Why do we need to live all of our lives in the one place? In Mykonos? You were not born here; you were born in Athens. Grandfather lives there, and most of Mama's family does. So, why can I, *we,* not?" He pointed to his brothers. "Why can we not explore the world and do what is best for us, for *our* families? Why?" He watched the expressions fly over his father's face and knew he was thinking about it. "You only came here to work in this shop because your father gave you the responsibility of it. You met Mama and decided she was the one you wanted to marry and you did. *You* chose to live here, work here, so why do you expect your sons to as well?" Spiros walked around the table to his father. "*You* made the decision to move here from Athens, so then why can *we* not make the same decision to move from here to where *we* want? A place that will give us opportunities to grow as men, as husbands, maybe even as managers, or business owners. Why do *we* not get the same choice, Papa? Why are you taking that choice away from us?" He watched his father's face for any sign of backing down and thought, for just an instant, that there was a flicker of that.

Giorgio hardened. "I see your point, Spiros. I did make the choice to come here and take over the shop. It was one of my father's businesses and he offered it to me in exchange for not taking anything else he offered. That was a deal none of you needs to know about." There was no way that Giorgio was going to tell his children that their grandfather was a mobster who owned half of Greece by way of shipping, buildings and companies. He'd chosen to not accept handouts of dirty money and didn't want his children to either. "I also understand Greek tradition. A man's possessions are handed down to the next in succession. My father's belongings will be handed to me, just as mine will be handed to you. So, know this, this shop will be handed to *you*, Spiros. It *will* belong to you one day. You are my eldest, that is just the way it is." He held up his hand to stop his son's protests. "And while I understand if you want to live on another island, or move to another part of Greece for a few years, you will still inherit this shop upon my death. If you wish to leave for somewhere else then…" He sighed. "We will have an issue."

"So, Athens is okay, but not another country?" Spiros was confused as to what his father was actually saying.

"In Athens, your family can watch over you, mentor you, help you out. You are only a ferry ride away," Giorgio said. "You will be able to easily come back if you need to, or you can live there and still work here—"

"Papa," Spiros interrupted. "I do not want to work here for the rest of my life. I do not want to live in the same old drudgery for the next twenty-five, fifty years of *my* life. This is not my life, Papa, it is *yours*, and you are making all of *us* live it. You are making all of *us*," he turned and pointed to his brothers who huddled nearby, "live out *your* choice. Why can we not make our own? Like *you* did."

Giorgio's brow furrowed. He knew Spiros had a point, but he wasn't about to fight him on it. Tradition was tradition. "Spiros." His voice was low. "You can move to Athens, you can move to Santorini, or Naxos, or even Crete. At least they will still be in reach, but if you choose to leave Greece altogether for another country, if you choose to defy our family's traditions, then I will have no choice but to disown and disinherit you. Do you understand?"

"No, Papa." Spiros shook his head. "Not at all. You will allow me to move to Athens, or another island, as long as it is in Greece. But you will not allow me to see the world, or travel, or go and visit our relatives in other countries? Papa…that is…" The head shaking continued in disbelief. "Wrong on so many levels, not to mention contradictory." The blood in Spiros's veins boiled and bubbled along. "You will only allow us to move to another part of Greece, but not make the choice to travel, or move to another country, or make our own way through life?" He took a step back and stared hard at his father. "Why would you be so contradictory, so hypocritical, so… so…dictatorial?" Spiros waved his arm around trying to emphasis and explain. "Grandfather gave you a choice, *you chose.* So, why can we not?" He looked from his brothers back to his father. "They may not have the balls to stand up to this monstrous stupidity, but I do. I have spoken to Grandfather. He told me to go and encouraged me so. I have spoken to Uncle Nikos in Australia, and he says they have a great Greek community, plus, he bought his house and car, and his business was paid off in two years. Why can I not do that? *We…"* He swung his arm to encompass his brothers who stood by with heads bowed. "Why can *we* not do that? Why is life restricted for us *by* you? I just do not get it. Why are you doing this to us?"

"I gave you work. I gave you jobs; you earn good money working here," Giorgio roared as he advanced on his son. "And you repay me by leaving. By running away from family tradition and responsibility? No. No son of mine will run away from tradition." He surprised Spiros by gripping his shirt and hauling him off his feet. "You will not defy me, Spiros. As eldest, you will stay here and become manager, and then owner of *Stephanopoulos Meats."* His eyes bored into his son's shocked brown ones. "You will not defy me. *Not* you!"

Spiros managed to breathe in a ragged breath. "And if I do…?

"Then you are no son of mine." Giorgio let him go and Spiros slumped to his feet. "If you choose to leave Greece, Spiros, then you are no longer my son. I will disown you and disinherit you. Do you understand me?"

Breathing just as hard as his father, Spiros found the strength to back away. He grabbed his bag from the hook by the door. "Yes…" He barely breathed. "I get it, Papa. I understand you perfectly." Knowing that tears were ready to flow, he turned from his family and walked through the open back door. Trudging home, he took the long way and detoured off to the beach to watch the ferries come and go. Waiting until dark, and many a tear was shed; he finally made his way back to his apartment. His father certainly hadn't minded kicking his sons out at the age of eighteen to take care of themselves, to live and breathe on their own, and all of them had loved it. His two brothers after him had shared an apartment for a year before marriage and babies made them move out, but thanks to help from their in-laws, they had nice homes to live in while he was stuck in a dingy two-bedder with barely a stick of furniture to his name. But that had been his choice, so he could save money, and he didn't yet need a family home for a wife and growing brood. No, he had no idea when that would happen. Maybe in his new homeland…when he found one that was.

Australia was looking better and better all the time, especially now his father had been adamant about disowning him. *Surely he cannot be that serious*, he thought as he hefted himself over cobblestones to arrive at his apartment building. Climbing the outside stairs, he wondered if he'd be welcome at work the next day, or Friday. He'd wanted as much money as he could get for when he left.

Walking through the door, he found Christos was already home.

"About time you got here." Christos excitedly waved a piece of paper in Spiros's face. "I think I found your answer."

"Answer to what?" Spiros frowned as the paper was shoved at him. He took it and read the flyer. *Australia needs you!* It stated in Greek. *Are you willing to travel to Australia for an easier life, better wages, and a new job? Then we want you!*

The flyer detailed the travel arrangements, and where and when the next boat would be leaving.

"Well?" Christos asked, wondering if his friend would take the bait.

Dazed that the universe had given him the answer to his prayers, Spiros looked at his friend but said nothing.

"When does it leave?"

"Monday," Spiros finally replied.

Christos grinned. "We had better throw you a going-away party, then."

*****

On Thursday, Spiros reluctantly showed up for work. He hadn't wanted to, but knew that their wages were received on Friday afternoon, and he needed that week's pay.

Silence greeted him as he walked through the back door and hung his bag on the hook. Three of his brothers wouldn't look at him and busied themselves with sorting meat. His father was in the shop dealing with customers, along with Theseus. Not sure how his father would respond to him being there, and with fear and trepidation in his heart about what would happen, he set to work doing his daily chore of cutting up the sides of lamb for the day.

It was an hour before Giorgio stepped into the back room for more meat and noticed Spiros working silently, head bowed, eyes down. His gaze moved past all of his sons and he saw the same morose expression on their faces. He knew he was being harsh with them and that he didn't really have the right to dictate what they did and where they worked, but he also wanted to keep his children close. He was the only son of Giorgio Stephanopoulos, and, after his sister had died, the only child. His mother had died long ago, and he and his children were the only Stephanopoulos heirs. Not that he wanted them getting into the business that his father was in.

He knew more than enough about his father's past life as a crime boss, and knew, after a conversation many a year ago, that his father used to carve up humans in that shop, particularly gangsters and criminals that did him wrong, and he wanted his children to have none of it. So, maybe, in that sense, Spiros was right. He'd chosen the meat shop before he'd known about the human carcasses that had once hung in the walk-in freezer, but his children didn't need to. He contemplated his life and his family. Five boys, four of which were married off with children, and three girls who weren't yet of adult years, or marriage age, but whom were prearranged into marriage anyway, as their sons had been.

Except for Spiros. Spiros had bucked every which way at the thought of marrying at twenty-one and settling down with children, and he'd thrived once he'd been shunted out of home at eighteen.

Giorgio had watched his eldest grow and learn and become a free-spirited man just like he'd been at that age. But…he'd also had a new wife and a shop to take on, and yes, taking on the shop was his choice and his alone. Sighing, he picked up what he needed and walked back into the shop.

Spiros stopped chopping for a moment and breathed a sigh of relief. All he needed to do was stay out of his father's way for another day and a half, keep his mouth shut and his head down, and finish work, then have lunch at home on Sunday with church in the morning, and he was done. He got on with his work, but there was an uncomfortable silence for the rest of the day.

And Friday was no better, but at least he'd made it to the end of the week and had another pay cheque in his hand. His friends took him out that night to celebrate and hear his final plans.

"So, what is happening? Are you leaving on Monday?" Christos asked, downing his first beer of the night. They were at the *Napoli* restaurant bar and grill for their last meal together.

"Yes." Spiros nodded slowly, letting out his anxieties from the last week. "I think I am."

"Told your parents, yet?" Nicodemus asked. He was itching for an adventure and was considering going with Spiros.

"Well…" Spiros closed his eyes for a moment and breathed slowly before opening them. "Considering the arguments we have had about it this last week, I am thinking, that he is thinking, that I have either forgotten all about it, or I am still planning to do it. And while I know it will cause issues in my family if I go, if I stay I will just be unhappy for the rest of my life."

"You are going then?" Xenos urged, wondering if he should join him.

Nodding his head slightly as he thought, Spiros's brain finally stopped on the one answer. "Yes," came out in a rush and adrenaline pulsed through his body as excitement followed. "Yes. I am going. I am going."

"Hear! Hear!" his friends cheered, and they clinked their glasses in celebration.

"When are you leaving?" Yannis asked.

"Ah, it will be Sunday night. I head over to Athens Sunday night, and the boat leaves from Athens port on Monday." Spiros had read and re-read the flyer Christos had given him a thousand times and had rung the number on it for more information. He'd written everything down and gone over it a million times trying to formulate the plan in his mind and what he would do.

And how he would tell his parents.

He still had fear in his heart, tons of it, about actually telling his family, especially his father. He knew his mother would be a mess, and would more than likely not say much at all. His mother was a typical Greek housewife who stayed home, bred, and kept house. She didn't have an opinion around her husband, but Spiros had once seen her at an after church tea service put on by the women and she had been gung-ho. Couldn't stop her talking about her husband, or family. It had surprised him; how feisty his mother was in that situation. But then, she was surrounded by other women in the village and not the men. The men she was quiet around and did what the dutiful housewife did. The contradiction in his mother had delighted him. Knowing that she was not kowtowing in every aspect of her life was good. Underneath the black-clad exterior of his mother, was a woman who still did what she wanted in the privacy of the women's groups she belonged to, and it wasn't just all about his father.

"I am thinking of coming with you," Xenos blurted out, surprising those at the table.

"What?" Nicodemus was stunned. "You too?" Everyone looked at him, and he looked back and grinned. "Why not? As Spiros pointed out last week, I cannot keep down a job, and maybe Australia will be a riot. New country, new people, new women." The grin grew larger as he sat back in his seat and tossed a lock of hair off his forehead. "*Lots* of women."

"Is that all you would go for?" Yannis asked, wondering how many more people he knew were going to flee. World War II had created a mess, and the Greek government were only now trying to sort it out by offering their citizens a way out by travelling to countries like

Australia for a better life. He'd already had aunts, uncles, and cousins leave.

"Not just that," Nicodemus replied. "We could all have a better life than here. Even though Mykonos is great, all of Greece has suffered these last ten years. We are lucky to have the jobs we have, but with so many people leaving for better countries, what will we have left? We would probably be better off leaving, too."

"True. The war did wreck Greece. Many of us are barely surviving," Yannis agreed. "But I will stick it out and hope that good old Mykonos builds itself back up again. The tourists are starting to come back in summer."

"They are, but as you have both said, the war made a mess, and that is why Uncle Nikos and Aunt Melina left with their children," Spiros told them. "They took their money, what they had left anyway, and have made a real go of it. So, if they can do it, so can I."

"And so can I," Xenos added. "A lot of my family have fled. I will too."

"And so will I," Nicodemus said. "I am out on my own. I can probably make better money somewhere else and can help my parents. Maybe even move them over at some stage."

That comment made Spiros frown. His parents would more than likely refuse to set foot outside of Greece, let alone move across the world to another country that spoke a different language. His parents and siblings didn't speak English either, so there'd be no way they'd move to Australia. A deep sigh left him and he wandered off in thought.

"Spiros…you still with us?" Christos flicked him on the head.

"Mmm…what?" Spiros came out of his reverie.

"What were you thinking about?" Yannis asked, finishing off the last of his baklava.

With a deep breath in, Spiros said, "The fact my parents would never move outside of Mykonos. Neither, maybe, would my siblings. Although, I think I put some thoughts into my brothers' heads this last week. I have a feeling a few of them may end up leaving, at least to Athens to see how they can get along there." He drank the last of his beer and slowly set the glass on the table. "I do not like the fact that my father might disown me if I go. I do not know how my mother will cope. With any of it."

Christos watched his best friend's face flutter with emotions. "Would she go along with your father and abide by his decision if he disowns, or disinherits, you?"

Sadness stopped Spiros's face cold. "Yes, she probably would."

"That sucks," Xenos said, sympathy flooding from his voice. "How will you cope with that if it happens?"

Spiros shook his head and looked at him. "I do not know how I will, except to put all of the pain it might cause behind me, and just look forward to the future and what it holds. Just keep remembering that I am doing it for me and not for them. And then…maybe one day…" a shrug of a shoulder, "we may make up and they will forgive me. One day…"

"Yes, maybe they will. Are you going to tell them before you leave?" Nicodemus waved to a waitress and ordered a bottle of ouzo.

Taking a deep breath to quell his anxieties, Spiros slowly let it out. "On Sunday, after lunch."

"Ouch, at a family lunch." Xenos grinned. "You are game."

"Have you told yours?" Spiros watched as the waitress placed the bottle and five glasses on the table.

"I only just made up my mind tonight, so, not yet. But I do not think they will mind. They might want to join me," he said.

"Well, I propose a toast." Christos poured five glasses of ouzo. "To Spiros and his new life in Australia." He raised his glass and the others followed suit. "May your journey be safe, may it be short, and may you accomplish all that you dream of."

"Hear! Hear!"

They knocked back the ouzo and poured another round, drinking until well into Saturday morning.

*****

Sunday morning, after recovering from his hangover, Spiros attended church with his family, sitting in the pew behind his parents, shame, pain, and guilt flushing his face red. He was uneasy around his father, and his grandfather for some reason, who had come over from Athens to join them, and couldn't look him in the eye, couldn't stand near him, could barely kiss him hello when he'd arrived at the church. He knew what was to come. Knew it would lead to an argument, another round of 'if you leave I'll disown you'. Knew that it could destroy his family into a billion pieces. But, he'd also been raised to stand by his convictions and his choices, and he'd made the choice to leave Greece for Australia tomorrow. He just needed to take the ferry over to Athens that night.

Crossing himself, he followed his parents and grandfather down the aisle and out into the sticky heat of summer. It had been sweltering in the church since there was no cooling except for multiple fans going throughout, and everyone had been fanning themselves with what they could. At least outside there was a breeze that helped dry off their sodden clothes. Removing his jacket and tie, Spiros pulled at the top buttons of his shirt for relief and saw his brothers do the same as they followed their parents back to the family home for the usual Sunday family lamb meal and whatever stilted conversation followed.

His pulse quickened, and in turn that quickened his breathing. It wasn't just the ten-minute walk to the house; it was the fact he was yet to tell his parents he was leaving. Yet to feel the wrath of his father, and yet to feel the unspoken anger, hatred, whatever, of his siblings and mother. If his mother sided with his father, it would kill him, although he'd understand. He wouldn't back down, not now that he'd packed up his clothes and meagre belongings, and organised with the landlord for Yannis to take over his half of the lease and live with Christos.

Finally, they arrived and piled in through the door. The house was small, with small rooms that barely accommodated all of them around the dining table in the small dining room. The air was warm and stuffy, and everyone quickly opened the windows facing the sea for a hint of breeze. The oven was lit, the table was set, and forty-five minutes later, amid Giorgio senior raving over his grandchildren and great-grandchildren, they sat down to eat.

Spiros had been silent the whole time, watching his father and grandfather with the kids. Watching his brothers with each other, watching his sisters and sisters-in-law helping prepare and serve the meal. The last meal he would have in that house. The last meal of his mother's, the last meal with his family.

It pained him, struck him in the heart as if the lamb shank bone had been sharpened and stabbed through his chest. He felt himself giving in, backing down, believing in the rules and regulations his father had so defiantly set for him the last twenty-five years. The years of being told he would take over the business, the shop, the house when they died. He'd never liked being told that. As a child, it had scared him out of his wits. That his parents could suddenly drop dead and he'd have to run a shop he knew nothing about as a five, ten, fifteen year old. He'd suffered nightmares for years, thinking that his father would die and he'd be left in charge. As he'd got older and started working in the shop and learning how things worked, the nightmares had eased off and ceased altogether when he'd left home at eighteen. He was eighteen; he could do what he wanted. He had his own place and knew more about running the shop. It still wasn't enough. He wanted more, and at twenty-five, he was striving for it, and all it would need, all it would take, was the price of a ticket aboard the boat taking him from Athens to Australia.

Was he scared? Absolutely. But underneath that fear was excitement and wonder for a new adventure, a new land, a new life. He just didn't know why his father couldn't accept that. Tuning in to the conversations around him, he slowly ate his mother's lamb. It was the last meal, *her* last meal, and he wanted to savour it until the last bite. He listened to his father and grandfather talk about the business and money, and his ears pricked when Giorgio senior asked his son if he wanted any more of the family business.

"No, you know the deal. The shop was all I wanted," Giorgio junior replied, scraping up the last of the mint peas on his plate.

"Well, I have a proposition for your children, then," Senior went on, a twinkle in his eyes as he glanced at each surprised face down the table. His gaze landed on Spiros. "Since your eldest son has reached twenty-five, and the other boys are now adult age, I want to offer them the same deal I offered you. The chance to manage one of my businesses, either in Athens, or here on Mykonos, or any of the islands I have businesses on."

All five boys stared at him in shock, but his brown eyes twinkled back. "I gave your father the chance, now I am offering it to you. *All five of you*," he emphasised, his eyes still on Spiros.

"You cannot do that," Junior told him.

"Why the hell not?" Senior asked. "They are my only grandchildren; you are my only son. The business will have to go to you, or Spiros, one day, but that does not mean I cannot offer my grandsons the same I afforded you. They *are family*, Giorgio. *You* are the only family I have left." He was sitting to the right of his son and laid his hand on his arm. "You are my only family. Your sister is gone and she left no heirs. You and your children are all I have."

Giorgio junior's eyes scanned his father's face, looking for some kind of ulterior motive. His gaze moved on to the shocked faces of his daughters and daughters-in-law down the right side of the table, the shock on his wife's face at the other end, and the suspicious expression on Spiros's. His other sons were hiding their excitement, but barely. "They work at the shop; it is not called *Stephanopoulos Meats* for nothing. It is a family business."

"Yes, because you chose to bring your sons into it," Senior reminded him. "Before that, it was me working in the shop, owned by my father, and his before him. The name is from *my* forebears, *your* forebears. You did not start it to run as a family business, you took it over from me as it was the only business that was actually started by the Stephanopouloses. All the rest were started by me. They do not need to all work there. I can offer them businesses just like I offered you. If they are interested, that is." He'd come up with the idea after speaking to Spiros and had organised some of his companies to be ready if they took him up on the offer. He was hoping to ease the burden of Spiros leaving.

Giorgio junior sighed, leaned his elbows on the table, and crossed his hands in front of his face. He was seriously considering the proposition, especially if it meant keeping Spiros in Greece. Although, from the look on his son's face, he wasn't buying it. "Okay." He glanced from son to son as he spoke. "You may offer each of the boys a job, or business, of their own." His eyes darted to his father. "But it cannot have anything to do with the reason we made our deal over. Do I make myself clear?"

Senior nodded. "Absolutely, I have already thought about what parts of my business the boys could be good at. I do have several meat shops in Athens if you want to manage and take over one, and they have no connection to the one here," he told his son. "I also have a lot of businesses in shipping, or construction, if that pleases you. It is hard work, and you would work from the ground up, but you would be managers, and maybe owners, one day. I do have a few other interests, but it will be up to you what you want. And you can take your pick here on Mykonos, another island, or Athens."

The excitement exploded and four of the boys chatted in tandem.

Drowning out the noise, Spiros quietly watched his father and grandfather, wondering what was really behind this decision. It wasn't one he'd be involved in; he already knew his destiny was waiting for him in Australia, and that meant being on the boat tomorrow. He cast a glance at his brothers and their wives. His sisters looked excited for them, but they knew they wouldn't be on the receiving end of anything, not unless their grandfather offered their future husbands the same deal. His eyes landed on his mother who sat to his left at the end of the table.

While she was silent, her eyes sparkled in excitement for her boys, and disappointment for her girls. She was training them to be wives and mothers, just as she'd been trained by her mother, so she knew this offer was only good for the men in the family. Her eyes connected with Spiros and she placed her right hand on his. "Good news, Spiros. Why are you not excited?" She noticed no happiness on his face, or in his eyes. For in its place was a very serious frown. "Are you not happy at this offer?"

Spiros breathed deeply, trying to keep his mental strength, and squeezed his mother's hand. "It is a good offer, Mama. A very generous offer. But I will not be accepting it."

Every single person in that room, one by one, went silent, and all eyes turned to him.

Katyana looked at her husband in surprise before her eyes darted back to her son. "What do you mean, Spiros?"

Spiros's breathing grew rapid along with his pulse. "I have made my choice, Mama…" He almost couldn't say the words, didn't *want* to say them, but needed to, otherwise, if he left without telling them, it would be worse than death. "I am leaving Greece," he forced out.

"What…?" Katyana reeled back in shock. "What do you mean, you are leaving Greece?"

With all eyes on him, Spiros quickly explained. "I have decided to leave Greece and move to Australia. I want adventure, to see the world, another country, learn about other cultures."

"Are you still on about that fantasy?" Giorgio junior yelled and banged his fist on the table making everyone jump and remain silent. "I will not tolerate your childish fantasies any more, Spiros."

"They are not, Papa," Spiros yelled, and forcefully pushed his chair back to stand up. "I am leaving tomorrow for Australia. It is *my* choice, *my* decision, *my* life. It *is not* a fantasy. *It is* happening."

Giorgio junior roared to his feet. "Then you will no longer be welcome in this family, this home. If you choose to leave then you will be banished. I will disown and disinherit you."

"Giorgio." His father tried to stop him.

"No! Papa." Junior flung off his father's hand. "My sons do not disrespect me, this household, or this family. I have told you, Spiros, your place is here."

"No, it is not," Spiros defied. "Not anymore, Papa." He turned to his stunned mother, took her hands in his, and bent to kiss her cheeks. "I will call and write, but do not tell Papa," he whispered in her ear. Placing his chair under the table, he glanced at each member of the family until his eyes landed on his father. "I *need* to do this, Papa. Why you cannot understand that, I do not know. But *I* need to do this for myself. Adventure is calling me and I am going to run towards it with open arms. Why can you not be happy for me?" He stepped towards his father, but stopped when Giorgio threw up his hand.

"Because he did not take a chance himself," Giorgio senior said quietly.

All eyes turned toward him and he felt the burning coming from his son. "Spiros is right. He *has* the right to travel and live where he wants, just like you did. And *you* chose to be here, in Mykonos, and that is where you have stayed, and that is where you *will* stay because *you* made that choice for yourself. Do not force your choices onto your sons, Giorgio. I never forced you. You cannot force them. You cannot make them do what *you* want, cannot make them be like you. You need to let them go, so they can be the men *they* are meant to be."

Junior's eyes burned into his father's. "Did you know about this? Did he tell you what he had planned? Did you know? Are you helping him?" He glared at his father who shrank back.

For all of Giorgio senior's fearsome seven decades, his son actually made him fear for his safety.

"You!" Junior's arm flung towards Spiros. "Get out of this house. Get out of this family and never come back. You will not be welcome. You will not be wanted, and for all of your insubordination, your brothers will no longer have the choice of a job because you," he turned to his father, "have been in on this from the beginning. And if you want to see your grandchildren and great-grandchildren again, then you will not side with Spiros. Do you understand?" He gripped the table to try and control his rage.

"Oh, I understand perfectly well." Giorgio senior stood and faced off against his son. "You are being as stubborn and mule-headed as I was at your age. As Spiros is at his. You do not dictate to me, Giorgio, because I can destroy you in a flash." He clicked his fingers in his son's face, making him flinch. He turned to his grandsons. "Spiros, you are free to do whatever you like, as are the rest of you boys. My offer still stands. Do not let your father stand in the way of a potential career, or happy life. If staying here is it, fine. If moving to Athens is it, you all have my number. As for the rest of you," he glanced at his granddaughters, "you are old enough to call me for help if you need it." Turning back to his son, he went on. "I know, right now, that choice will get me banished from this family as well. Am I right, Giorgio?" He watched his son's face flicker with emotion. "Are you going to banish me *and* Spiros from this household? *This family?* You may not like what I am doing, or have done, but you will not stop me from seeing my grandchildren."

"I can try," Giorgio junior muttered, fury dripping from his words.

"Yes, I suppose you can," Senior muttered in return. "But that is the one thing, the *only* thing, because at the end of the day, Giorgio, you do not have control over, own, or dictate to any of us. I am your father, you have no say in my life, but it certainly did not stop you from taking a business from me to call your own. Did it?" There was a warning behind his tone that only his son knew about.

And Giorgio junior picked up on it. "Do not threaten me, old man. You made your choice, and I have made mine—"

"And now your sons can make their own," Senior interrupted. "*We* made *our* choices, Giorgio, now let them make theirs."

Fuming, Giorgio junior clenched his jaw so hard he thought he heard teeth crack. "My sons will make the choices I give them to make—"

"No, Papa," Spiros interrupted. "We are grown men. My brothers have wives and families to worry about, and take care of; it is time *we* made the choice for us."

"You," Giorgio junior bellowed and turned around. "You are no longer welcome in this home if your idiotic fantasy is to leave for somewhere else."

"Uncle Nikos and Aunt Melina moved to Australia, why can I not?" Spiros asked. "Lots of Greeks are moving to Australia for a better life. The war devastated our country and we are doing nothing but picking up the pieces."

"And if that is all you think of this country then you can leave, too." Giorgio junior advanced on his son. "Leave. Leave this house, this family, this country. Leave and do not come back. You are not my son. You are a traitor." He spat on the floor at Spiros's feet. "Get out of my house and do not come back, you filthy traitor."

Seeing the hatred in his father's eyes, Spiros took a step back and glanced at each member of his family. All had bowed heads, except for his grandfather who stood defiantly by. "Mama, Grandfather, everyone." He sighed in dismay at the way it had ended, knowing that even his grandfather might turn against him in the vain hope of still seeing his grandchildren and their offspring. Nodding at his grandfather, he said, "I'll understand."

Senior nodded in return. "I know you will, my son."

With a last glance, Spiros turned and left the family home, trudged back to his apartment to meet up with his friends, and together they gathered their cases and bags and made their way down to the dock to catch the ferry to Athens.

Stepping onto the ferry, Spiros looked over his shoulder at his home. The island he'd known for twenty-five years. But things had changed. He was leaving and had no idea if he'd ever be back, or ever see his family again.

October 1950

"Jenny, are you still going down to the wharf on Saturday to help with the new boatload of immigrants?" Sarah Marsh asked her daughter as she carried the large casserole pot from the kitchen to the dining room and sat it at one end of the table. She wiped her hands on her apron and made sure the plates and cutlery were laid.

"Yes, Mum. I'll be going down with a friend as we're on the welcoming committee. Why?" Jenny asked as she scurried around the table setting napkins. At twenty-two, Jennifer Marsh still lived at home with six of her eleven siblings and had been working at a typing firm for local business, getting their excess paperwork typed up and sorted out.

"Just wondering." Sarah hurried back into the kitchen of her two-storey red brick home and quickly pulled two more casserole dishes from the oven.

"Wondering what? Why?" Jenny stopped behind her mother and peered over her shoulder at the sizzling veggies in the dishes. "Mmm, yum. Smell those." She moved on to gather glasses for their drinks and set them on the kitchen counter as she spoke. "Is there something wrong? Do you need me on Saturday?"

"No, no." Sarah turned off the oven and placed the lids back on the dishes. She saw another of her daughters standing at the table waiting for something to do. "Rebecca, can you take these in please, and get your brothers and sisters for tea. It's ready."

"Sure." Rebecca carefully carried a dish into the dining room and started calling for her siblings.

"It's just that I was having a conversation with Mrs Stephanides from next door today, and she said that her nephew, her husband's nephew, and some of his friends were coming on the boat that arrives on Saturday." Sarah tucked her tea towel into her apron and pulled out two jugs of homemade lemon drink from the fridge. After setting them on the kitchen table, she closed the door and continued. "I told her I thought you were going down there this weekend, and maybe you could keep an eye out for him and his friends."

"Oh." Jenny looked at her mother in surprise. "Does he speak English? I don't know Greek except for the odd word I've heard the Stephanides say, or Effie has taught me. What does he look like?" Jenny helped her mother by carrying the glasses into the dining room and setting them around the table.

"I have no idea." Sarah placed the jugs in the centre of the table. "You'll need to have a chat with them before you go."

"Mmm," Jenny murmured. "I'll try and remember to do that." She had been helping out for the last four years down at the wharves in Sydney with her family, helping migrants who came each year by boat. Thanks to the government's immigration policies, Australia was taking in more migrants than ever before. And since their own ancestors were immigrants, the family felt it was their duty to help others to their country. There were small thriving communities of Greeks, Italians, Europeans, and Asians in the local Armidale district. Several hours from Sydney, Armidale was a thriving population all of its own.

"Matthew, teatime," Sarah called to her husband who was busy listening to the local radio station and reading the newspaper. "Kids, take your places." She bustled to the end of the table and waited while her husband lumbered in from the lounge room to sit at the head of the table.

"And what do we have tonight?" He lifted the lid of the casserole dish in front of him. "Ah, apricot chicken, my favourite."

"There are two, as usual, so enough for everyone, and two side dishes of vegetables," Sarah told her family as they joined hands to say grace.

With bowed heads they murmured, "Amen", after their father, and started dishing out chicken and vegetables, handing plates of food down to the other end of the table as they went.

"So, how will I know who he is?" Jenny asked her mother, continuing the previous conversation as she sliced into her meat to cool it off.

"You'll have to ask them for a photo if they have one." Sarah popped a piece of roast carrot into her mouth and chewed and swallowed before continuing. "She only mentioned it because they know we've helped out over the years. After all, we helped them when they first came here. They had a phone call and letter from the nephew about which boat he'd be coming on. They've been waiting for the news that the boat is here on Saturday. That's why I mentioned you to her. Either pop over and let them know you're going, or wait for them to catch up with you."

"Okay. I'll be going with Effie, my Greek friend from typing school. She speaks English better than most and can help me out with the language, at least. So, I'll try and catch up with them before Saturday, but don't know if I'll be able to as I've had to bring work home this week and will be extra busy."

"It's going to be extra warm this weekend," Faye said, pouring herself a drink and passing the jug to Barbara. "Unseasonably so for late October."

"Well, we are coming into spring soon, and the weather does get warm come November," Barbara replied, pouring herself a glass of drink. "Anyone else?" she asked.

"I'll take it." Big brother Ned stood up and leaned over the table to take the jug. "We're going to the roller derby on Saturday if anyone's interested." He poured drinks for himself, his father, and two brothers before setting the jug back on the table and sitting down.

"Make sure you don't hurt yourself, dear," Sarah told him and moved on to her chicken.

"And if *I* wanted to go to the derby?" Faye asked, slyly glancing at her mother.

"Don't even think about it," her father warned. "It's a man's thing, not a woman's."

"Dad!" Jenny exclaimed. "That's so incredibly sexist." She looked from her father's surprised face to her sister's. "If you want to go, Faye, go." She heard the guffaws coming from her right. Her three brothers were trying to contain their laughter at the thought of a girl at the derby. "What are you three sniggering at? If I wasn't busy, I'd go myself." As the oldest girl left at home, Jenny had no problems sassing her brothers. Ned and Arthur were older; Philip was younger, as were her sisters. But, unfortunately, even in 1950s Australia, sexism was rife.

"You!" Philip snorted so hard lemon drink came out his nose, and he quickly set his glass down and picked up his napkin to wipe his face. "What would *you* know about derbies?"

"What would *you* know about manners at the table," Jenny retorted and popped a green bean into her mouth. She chewed with her mouth closed and swallowed. "At least *I* have manners." Cocking a brow at her brother, she turned back to her father and sister. "Dad, stop being so sexist, and Faye, you do what you like. If you want to go, go. As for me, I've already promised I'll be at the wharf on Saturday, so I have to be there, and I have so much work to do this week because it's busier than usual. We have to bring home what we don't get done during the day."

"As I said, it was only mentioned in passing," Sarah repeated. "If you have a chance to speak by Saturday, then you do. How are the rest of you going?" she asked her children and one by one they talked about their day.

Rebecca was training to be a nurse. Barbara worked as a receptionist in a magazine company. Faye was the typist at the law firm Ned was working at as a lawyer. Philip was hauling lumber on building sites, and Arthur was training as a mechanic and working in the local petrol station.

After eating, they washed and dried the dishes, and sat out on the porch to take in the warming weather. The boys threw a football around the large green backyard, and the girls chatted about the local dance coming up, except for Jenny, who got back to work typing up that day's documents ready for tomorrow. She shared a room with

Rebecca, as the oldest girls, and had set her typewriter up on the small desk between their two beds. Quickly and efficiently, she did her work and completely forgot about the neighbours, tumbling into bed just after ten-thirty.

The next two days were exactly the same, and on Friday night she took a call from her friend Effie.

"You're still going to pick me up tomorrow, aren't you?" Effie's English was perfect for someone who'd only been in Australia for five years.

"Of course," Jenny replied. "We'll have to go early; I need to drop my sisters off in town before we get there. They're buying dresses for that spring dance next month. They'll catch a ride back with a friend."

"That's okay. The head of the committee said the boat won't arrive until about ten and then they'll take a couple of hours to unload everyone, so we can take our time," Effie told her. "What are you wearing? It's been so warm this week that I've pulled out my dresses early."

"Same here." Jenny wound the phone cord around her fingers. "I'm thinking that pink dress with the light blue print. The one I got in town at that autumn sale, but haven't worn."

"Oooh, I like that one. Maybe you'll meet the man of your dreams as he walks down the gangplank," Effie teased.

"Don't be silly," Jenny chastised. "I'm only twenty-two; I'm not ready for that, yet. I'm not planning to get married until I'm at least twenty-five—"

"But that doesn't mean the man of your dreams can't come along," Effie butted in. "Don't you want to meet your soulmate? He could be on that boat." Her laughter tinkled down the line. "And so could mine."

"Funny ha-ha." Jenny smiled. "Since they're Greek immigrants, they'll be more up your alley than mine."

"Who said I wanted a Greek boy?" Effie asked. "I don't have any problems with dating Australian boys. I quite like them."

"Don't your parents want you to marry a good Greek boy?" Jenny remembered back to a conversation they once had.

"Yeah, they do." Effie sighed. "Although, at the rate I'm going, I think they'd be happy with any boy marrying me."

"Oh, I don't think so." Jenny thought back to more stories from Effie. "You're their only daughter. They want the best man possible for you."

"*That's* the problem," Effie complained. "*They* want the best man for me. They don't care who, or what *I* want. Just what *they* want."

Jenny glanced at the clock and saw it was already ten. "We'll chat more on the way tomorrow. It's late, and I need a good sleep."

"Okay, see you tomorrow."

Jenny placed the phone in its cradle and sighed, thinking back to what Effie had said; *maybe you'll meet the man of your dreams.* "Hardly!" she muttered and wandered upstairs to lay out her clothes for the next day and get ready for bed, finding Rebecca doing the same. "Got your shopping list ready?"

"Sure have." Rebecca snapped her handbag shut and set it on the floor next to her shoes in front of her wardrobe. "You sure you don't want to come? Don't you need anything for the spring dance next month? Then there's the summer dance after that in December. Plus the Christmas dances and New Year dances, and then more summer dances, and the Valentine's dance."

"Okay, I get it." Jenny laughed lightly. "I bought a whole bunch of things in the after summer sale this year, don't you remember? I've barely worn any of it." Opening her wardrobe, she took in all of the winter clothes still hanging there and then reached for the large boxes sitting on top. Gently setting them on her bed, she lifted the lids, pulled back the tissue paper, and carefully rolled back dress after dress. "See, none of them have been worn yet, and I can take them in, or re-fashion them if need be. All I need are coloured accessories to change them from say, a Christmas dress to a Valentine's dress." She glanced at her sister. "And Mum has that huge trunk full of material that we could make something out of. She made me my twenty-first dress and will probably make yours too."

"I know, we're already planning it." Rebecca grinned. "But I'm hoping to get some winter clothes if they're throwing them out. And I do need a new pair of boots."

Jenny pulled out her shoe boxes from the bottom of the wardrobe and flipped the lids up. "Looks like I need some, too. I've only got the one pair, but my good party shoes still look like new."

"Well, lucky you." Rebecca threw her bed covers back and pulled her nightie from under the pillow. "I'm going to change, see if I can get to the bathroom before anyone else." She left the room and saw Faye just closing the bathroom door. "Drat, I'll have to wait." Banging on the door, she told her sister to hurry up and leaned on the wall to wait in line.

Smiling to herself, Jenny pulled out her bright pink dress with the pale blue embroidered flowers and birds, slid it onto a hanger, and hung it on the side of her wardrobe. She closed the boxes and put them back, then laid her shoes in front. Closing the doors, she turned to her small dresser and got her blue accessories ready to put on the next morning. Hearing Faye come out of the bathroom and Rebecca go in, she got her bed ready and waited her turn, but all the while Effie's words rumbled around in her head. *Man of your dreams, you might meet the man of your dreams.* Her smile growing bigger, she allowed herself to fall sideways and drift off.

*****

The alarm went off at five and Jenny breathed in. She heard her sister yawn and hit the clock to shut it off, and was prepared to go back to sleep in the peace and quiet.

"Rise and shine, sleepyhead." Rebecca shook her awake. "Time to rise and shine."

"Mmm." Jenny rolled onto her back and realised she was in bed. "Did I?"

"Yes." Rebecca slid into her dressing gown and slippers. "You fell asleep waiting to use the bathroom. I tucked you in. No point waking you."

"Ugh, thanks." Jenny stretched her arms above her head and realised there was no point waiting in line for the shower, so slid out of bed, donned her dressing gown and slippers, and went into the bathroom to wash her face, even though her sister was showering. There were times when they had to share in tandem while everyone took turns. She headed downstairs to get breakfast started, and found her mother already there, also in her robe and slippers.

"You're father's sleeping in, and Ned, Philip and Arthur are using our bathroom, so you girls aren't so jam-packed." Sarah set the kettle on the stove top and gathered cups for their morning coffee. "Do you want a big breakfast?"

"Not yet." Jenny popped two slices of bread into the toaster. "Maybe just a piece of toast for now, and a coffee when it's ready."

"You're not hungry?" Sarah pulled out all the condiments, milk, and juice from the fridge.

"No. I'm normally not up this early." Jenny leaned against the counter and watched her mother set about making breakfast at the kitchen table. She cracked eggs into bowls and whisked them, sliced up tomatoes, and unwrapped bacon slices, and then the kettle finally boiled. She watched her mother pour five cups of water and then refill the kettle and set it back on the stove. Watched her add teaspoons of coffee from a tin to the cups and give them all a good mix. Watched her pour milk into two cups and hand one to her.

Jenny carefully took it and smiled before setting it down beside the plate she had next to the toaster. The toast popped and she put it on the plate and handed it to her mother who buttered both slices and handed one back.

"I think I better put the toast on the grill; it will be quicker and make more at one time." Sarah took a bite of her piece and turned to the grill. "What are you smiling about?"

Caught, Jenny picked up her coffee and took a sip. Strong, just the way the family liked it. "Were you always like this?"

"Like what?" Sarah got the other stove top burners going and added pans of lard on top.

"This." Jenny waved a hand at all going on in front of her. "Domesticated."

Sarah's laugh was soft. "I trained myself around everything else I was doing. As you know, I studied nursing, just like Rebecca, and continued to work when I could as all of you came along. It was hard, mind you." She added the eggs to one pan, and the bacon to another. "I did it all while having and raising twelve children. Once Barbara was of school age, I could work for longer hours and earn money to look after all of you. Times have been tough these last thirty years, but we've managed."

"And you still manage to get up at the crack of dawn and feed us all," Jenny went on. "I don't know how you do it."

"With help from all of you," Sarah said as Ned and Arthur came through the door. "Once you were all old enough, you helped out with the younger ones and that was a bonus." She quickly scrambled the eggs, flipped the bacon and tomato slices, and pulled the first lot of toast from the grill. "Boys, help yourselves." She laid out the food onto plates and let the boys make their own toasted sandwiches.

Rebecca and Faye walked through the door and the procedure started again.

When breakfast was finished, the kids helped clean up before getting ready for their days out, and Sarah fixed breakfast for her and Matthew who had finally come down. He knew better than to expect breakfast early on the weekends, so he waited until the kids were fed and he could spend time with his wife.

After her shower and getting dressed, Jenny thought about Effie's words, and what she had seen her mother go through that morning, on her way downstairs. What if she met the man of her dreams today? Was she ready for domesticated bliss? Ready to get married and settle down to raise a brood of kids? What if it didn't happen at all? What if she didn't meet a man and fall in love? Never married, never had children? What if she were gay like her two uncles on her mother's side? Or ended up a spinster like two of her mother's sisters? What if...what if...what if...

Signing, Jenny slid a light coat over her dress as there was still a chill in the air at that time of the morning, and considered how her life would be if she ended up single and childless for the rest of her life. An icy dagger pierced her heart and slid through until it hit her back. The cold spread through her body and she almost heaved a sob.

The thought of never falling in love and having babies nearly destroyed her. She was only twenty-two, but some people considered that old. And while she knew her limit was twenty-five at the least, giving her three years to meet a man and fall in love, it was entirely possible that *none* of it could happen.

Jenny choked and covered her mouth with both hands. Looking into the hallway mirror, she was shocked to see such despair on her face. She was pretty enough, with her golden-brown hair held back by combs and curled. The pink of her dress brought a glow to her rosy cheeks, and the blue of her accessories brought out the blue of her eyes even more. With a slim medium frame, she was attractive to many a young man in Armidale, but the way she looked now, staring at herself in the mirror, it looked as if she were about to burst into tears.

"Are you ready, Jenny?" Sarah stopped at the bottom of the stairs before heading up and saw her daughter's stricken face. She went to her side. "Jenny?"

"Oh, Mum," Jenny sobbed and burst into tears.

Sarah took her distraught daughter into the good lounge room that was only for entertaining visitors and shut the door. Looking around for tissues, she dug through her dressing gown pockets and found some fresh ones. "Here, love, don't ruin your make-up now. You'll be leaving in a minute." She expertly dabbed at her daughter's face and fixed the few smudges already made. "Now, without crying again, tell me what's wrong." She listened patiently while Jenny told her of Effie's words and her own thoughts that morning. "Oh, love, you're only twenty-two, there's no rush for you to get married. You only graduated from typing college last year and got your first job. One thing at a time, hey."

"But what if I never fall in love?" Jenny sobbed. "What if there's no one out there for me and I'm left a spinster, or an old maid, or whatever we're called these days." She blew her nose and dabbed at her eyes.

"What if, what if, what if. Jenny." Sarah took her by both arms. "You're *only twenty-two*, anything could happen at any time, but sitting here sobbing about it won't make it happen any faster, or at all.

Dry your eyes, fix your make-up, and go about your day like it's any other. You hear me?"

With a small nod, Jenny's lips turned up at the corners. "Okay, Mum. I'll go about my day like any other."

"Good, because your sisters are waiting, and I'm sure Effie is, too. Go and clean yourself up and off you go." She watched Jenny hurry off to check herself and then rush out to the car where her sisters were waiting in the cold. The four girls shared one car just as the boys shared one, and her mother and father had theirs. With seven children at home, they'd had to save every cent to afford them, but the kids had pitched in with money saved from their wages, and so shared in each car. It was just a matter of who got it and when.

"What took so long?" Barbara asked as Jenny hurried out. "We were supposed to be gone fifteen minutes ago." She watched as her sister got behind the wheel and they climbed in behind her.

"I know, I'm sorry. I got caught up talking to Mum about something." Starting the engine, she checked her mirrors and backed out of the drive.

"Everything all right?" Rebecca asked from beside her. She knew her sister well and could tell when something was bothering her.

"No…yes…I don't know." All Jenny could do was sigh as she drove to Effie's place on the other side of town.

"About time you got here. You're late," Effie called as Rebecca got out and into the back, so Effie could have the front seat.

"Sorry, I was talking to Mum," Jenny apologised and quickly took off. "Besides, I thought we didn't need to be there until ten or twelve."

"Twelve is when they start unloading the passengers," Effie reminded her. "But we should be there by ten."

"And we wanted to be at the shops by nine," Faye added. "So we wouldn't miss any of the seasonal bargains."

Jenny managed to glance at her watch before turning onto the highway heading out of town and directly towards Sydney. "It's still early. We should make it." Checking the petrol tank, she was glad she'd topped up the night before.

They made small talk on the way, gossiping about boys and what the locals were doing. Barbara and Faye already had dates for the upcoming spring dance, Rebecca was considering her options as three boys had asked her to accompany them, and Effie had a string of suitors. As did Jenny, but her mind wasn't on them at the moment. She liked the boys in town, just as her sisters and friends did, and had gone to school with most of them. She just wasn't interested in them in any way other than as friends. Her soul was singing out for someone new, someone who made her want to sing with happiness, someone who would love her for her, and want to share the ups and downs of life together, marry and have kids, someone who made her heart sing with love. She heaved a sigh.

"You okay, Jen?" Effie asked, noticing her friend's grimace. "You're not ill, are you?"

"No, no." Jenny brushed the concern aside. "Just…thinking about the future."

"Pft! God, what?" Effie laughed. "*How far* into the future? Later today, tomorrow, next week, next month, next year?"

"Next couple of years and further, actually," Jenny said, taking the exit for Sydney.

Effie watched her friend's face. "Has no one asked you to the spring dance, yet?"

Rolling her eyes, Jenny shook her head at the teasing Effie was heaping on her. "They have, but that's not what I was thinking of."

"Personally, I think there's no point worrying about anything but today and tomorrow because everything else you can't do anything about." Effie nodded authoritatively. "No siree, you can't do anything else about it, so just live for today."

They quietly chatted until they reached the city and Jenny dropped her sisters off near the main shopping hub for their expedition.

"Make sure you get your ride home, and you have enough money for food and phone calls," Jenny told them out the window.

"Yes, Mother." Rebecca grinned. "Don't worry; I've kept money separate, so it doesn't get spent. Bye, see you tonight."

"Bye, girls, stay safe," Jenny called and drove off for the main wharf of Sydney Harbour. "So, I'm sticking to you like glue, today."

"Me? Why?" Effie rifled through her purse to make sure she had money for food and then set it aside and turned to Jenny.

"Because you speak Greek, I don't, except for the odd swear word you've taught me, and the few Mr and Mrs Stephanides…" The realisation hit Jenny and she slammed the wheel with her fist. "Darn it! I forgot to talk to them about their nephew. Oh, shoot!"

"What about their nephew?" Effie pointed to the sign on the side of the road. "Turn here."

"Mum told me on Wednesday that the next-door neighbours, Mr and Mrs Stephanides, had a nephew coming on today's boat. Mum told them I'd be here, and Mrs Stephanides asked if I could find and help him. But I never got back to them because I've been so busy."

"Busy wondering who'll take you to the spring dance?" Effie sniggered.

"Oh, stop it!" Jenny chastised. "Busy at work, just like you. You know it's a busy month; all the businesses want their documents typed up."

"It is. I've been taking paperwork home with me. Pull in here." Effie pointed to a car park close to the entrance.

"Exactly." Jenny pulled the brake and turned the car off. "Are we ready?" She looked at her watch and found it was only nine-forty-five. "Isn't the boat coming in soon?"

"If it hasn't already." Effie jumped out of the car and excitedly waited for Jenny to lock up. "Come on, we might see it."

They hurried into the terminal and towards their fellow committee members. Their job was to work on the dock and direct the passengers to the closest booth inside where more members would speak to each and connect them up with a family member, or someone from the local community to help get them established.

They lined up against the windows in excitement and watched the liner slowly manoeuvre its way into the harbour and dock at the wharf. Watched as the government ministers, and people from immigration, moved towards the walkway as it was attached to the boat, and then ascended to shake hands with the captain before disappearing inside to speak to the passengers.

Knowing there would be another two hour wait, Jenny and Effie helped set up the booths and refreshment tables in case anyone needed a drink, or food, in the unseasonably warm October weather.

Jenny paused to wipe her brow, and deciding to shed her coat, she was unable to find a place to put it, so checked her watch to see how much time they had left. "I'm just dashing out to the car," she told Effie. "It's warm, and I don't want to leave my coat lying around."

"Can you take mine?" Effie slid it off and handed it over. "I'll wait near the door, but hurry, there are only a few minutes left."

Jenny was back in ten minutes and waiting with Effie when the girls were sent outside to the dock to await the passengers' descent.

*****

"And so, ladies, gentlemen, children, welcome to Australia," the Greek community leader told the passengers on board. "When you descend, you will be greeted and sent to a booth where you will be matched with your family member, or members of the Greek community who will help you get settled into your new home. Kalós ílthate stin Afstralía. Welcome to Australia."

Spiros and his friends Xenos and Nicodemus were itching to get their feet on dry land after two months on board. While accommodations hadn't been bad, they weren't *The Ritz* either. There were very basic hygiene matters, toilets and showers, and a laundry for clothes washing that the passengers did themselves. And while it had been quite boring on board, they had tried to learn a little English from the English speaking crew members, and made up games to not only keep themselves entertained, but also the kids on board.

Seeing that families were being sent off first, they wandered over to the deck facing the harbour.

"It is beautiful, no?" Spiros told his friends, his excitement building.

"Very," Nicodemus agreed, glad that he had changed into a clean set of clothes and had a shower. "I hope we will meet girls here."

"Is that all you are thinking about?" Xenos cuffed him around the ear. "There is more to Australia than just girls. We learned about it.

Beaches and water, people and places, mountains and massive rocks."

"It is indeed beautiful." Spiros breathed in the salty air and stared at the arched bridge in the distance. "Even the bridge is beautiful."

"It is. We do not have one on Mykonos," Xenos joked and leaned over the railing to stare into the water. "Is the ocean the same?"

Nicodemus shrugged. "Same water covers the whole planet, just called something different." He turned around to see how many people were left and noticed only a few in the main room. "Come, it is time to go."

After an arduous journey where they had spent many a night wondering if they'd ever make it in the stormy seas, they collected their cases and bags, and slowly filtered out the door as the last passengers to arrive. They saw the excited faces of people waiting on the dock to greet them, others waved Greek flags from the sidelines, and a banner was strung across the door of the terminal that had *Welcome To Your New Home* in Greek and English.

After throwing his duffel bag over his left shoulder, and taking his case in his left hand, Spiros dug into his pocket for his uncle's address. He wasn't sure if they were coming to collect them, or if they'd have to find their own way to Armidale, but he hoped it wasn't too far away as he wanted to see more of the beautiful city they were currently in.

Stepping onto the gangplank, Spiros carefully walked down and stared at the faces pointed towards him. There, in a bright pink dress with blue accessories, was the most beautiful girl he'd ever laid eyes on. Her golden hair glowed in the sun, and her smile made the world seem brighter. His friends were elbowing him in the ribs.

"Get a load of those girls." Nicodemus had spotted Effie. "*She has to be Greek.*"

As if knowing she was being talked about, Effie turned from the people they'd just been helping, to the three young and extremely good looking men descending the walkway last. "Blimey! Get a load of them."

Jenny's smile never wavered as she turned her head to the left and laid eyes on the tall, dark-haired, beautifully exotic man who was staring back. Her heart thundered in her chest and her soul sang.

Unable to tear his gaze away, Spiros stepped onto the dock and stood looking at the beautiful woman in front of him. His friends were already speaking Greek to her companion, but it was the golden-haired beauty with the magnificent smile that had captured him *and* his heart. "Ah…hello…" he tried in broken English. "I am Spiros."

Jenny breathed in, all aflutter. "Oh…hello Spiros…I am Jenny."

"Jen…nee," Spiros tried to repeat.

Effie helped him out in Greek. "Her name is Jennifer Marsh, but everyone calls her Jenny. She's twenty-two and single." Her eager eyes noticed the two of them were unable to take their eyes from each other. "And you are?"

"Spiros Stephanopoulos. Twenty-five and single." Nicodemus nudged his friend to speak.

Spiros blushed. "Ah…yes…I am Spiros Stephanopoulos," he told Effie in Greek.

Effie translated for Jenny. "He says his name is Spiros Stephanopoulos, he's twenty-five, and single."

"Oh…Effie!" Jenny blushed nervously and extended her hand. "Hello, Spiros. I'm Jenny."

Spiros went to shake her hand, but the moment their hands met the electricity flew through them and instead, with a pounding heart, he turned her hand and kissed it instead, not once taking his eyes from hers.

"Oh…" Jenny breathed, unable to tear her blue eyes away from his brown ones.

"Wow, you work fast," Effie told her. "Got him eating out of the palm of your hand already." She turned to the other men, finding Nicodemus quite attractive, and conversed in Greek. "Where are you off to? I need to direct you to a booth."

"Spiros's aunt and uncle's place," Xenos said, noting how attractive both girls were. "He has the address. Armidale or something."

"Oh." Effie arched a brow at the young, creamy complexioned, hunk. "They wouldn't happen to be Mr and Mrs Stephanides, would they?"

Nicodemus shook Spiros, who came out of his dreaming of Jenny, to look at his friend.

"What?" Reluctantly letting go of Jenny's hand, he grabbed for the paper with his uncle's address.

"Where does your uncle live?" Xenos asked him.

Spiros held the piece of paper out for Jenny and Effie to look at and the address was one Jenny knew.

"Oh, you're Mr Stephanides' nephew," she gushed, shyly glancing at the hunky Greek in front of her. "They wanted me to look for you and get you back to Armidale."

Effie translated everything and the boys became excited. Spiros in particular.

"My aunt and uncle know you?" he asked in Greek. "Do they live near you?"

After hearing Effie's translation, Jenny replied, "Yes, I know them; they live next door to us and are our neighbours."

Effie told him and his face lit up like a Christmas tree.

So did Jenny's when she realised what that meant.

Effie took charge. "Okay. You'll need to come this way then, so you can get yourselves marked off." She led them inside to the booth where they told the committee member they'd be taking them to Armidale as they were staying with Jenny's neighbours, and after the paperwork was signed, she let them know what was happening in Greek and then let Jenny know in English.

"Oh, I don't know if we should take them," Jenny fretted. "I'm not sure we can fit everyone and their luggage in the car."

"It will fit, don't worry," Effie told her. "Come on." She led the way outside to Jenny's car and helped pack their luggage into the boot while Jenny made the car tidy and wound down windows.

"Boys, you can get in the back." Effie slid into the front and turned sideways to face Jenny, so she could easily talk to them over the seat.

Jenny got behind the wheel, put the key in the ignition and adjusted her mirrors. Her eyes caught Spiros's reflection as he'd sat behind her so he could be close to her. "Oh…" she murmured and glanced away. The blush rose from her neck to her face, and she worried it would be unbecoming. Then she worried she was being silly for thinking it was unbecoming, and what was she worried for when she didn't know him at all whatsoever, so why was she gushing over him? *Oh, stop it!* she silently chastised herself and started the car. *What are you doing?* "Are we ready?" she asked out loud.

Three excited, but broken English, yeses came from the backseat.

"Okay, onto Armidale we go." Pulling away from the terminal she added, "Effie, care to play tour guide?"

"Of course." In Greek, Effie explained all about Sydney as they drove. The different shops, the different communities, and how Australia was becoming a multicultural country. Once out of the city, she went into more casual conversations about Greece and how it had fared, and what they planned on doing in Australia.

While Xenos and Nicodemus willingly conversed with their attractive tour guide, Spiros remained quiet, content to just watch Jenny over the seat. Her eyes flickered to the mirrors every minute, or so, so he counted the seconds until he saw her blue eyes light up in the reflection. Saw her blush and look away. Wondered why his heart was still racing in his chest, wondered why and how he knew she was the one for him. He relaxed back in his seat and let the breeze from the open window ruffle his woolly hair. It needed a cut; two months on a boat at sea had made it wild and untamed just like his heart. She was the most beautiful girl he'd ever laid eyes on. The way her golden curls gently brushed her elegant neck, and softly swayed against her shoulders, made his fingers want to brush it aside and kiss the white of her skin. The way her hands expertly manoeuvred the car around bends and curves made him want those hands on his own bends and curves to expertly handle him. The way her eyes lit up when they saw *his* reflection in the mirrors. He wanted them to only look at him. For there to be no other man that she looked at, or lit up for, or blushed for.

Was he falling in love with the very beautiful Jennifer Marsh?

Damn straight he was!

Jenny noticed the dreamy faraway expression on Spiros's face when she checked the rear-view mirror. Effie and the other two men didn't even notice that Spiros wasn't talking. And she was busy concentrating on the road and those deep chocolate brown eyes that were staring at her every time she looked in the mirror. Oh, God, how they were doing things to her. Making her insides quiver in anticipation. Of what, she didn't know, just that her stomach was a mess of knots and they were trembling. Her tongue darted out to lick her lips and she rubbed them together hoping her lipstick was still in place and she wasn't a mess. Not that it mattered if she was, but she was on the immigration committee and had a standard to uphold. She had to look her best at all times, no matter what was happening, or what she was doing; she had to keep herself together. It was 1950; women had to look presentable and well kept.

The exit for Armidale came up on her left and she indicated, smoothly leaving the highway and heading for home. Keeping her eyes on the speedometer and petrol gauge, she checked her watch to see they were making good time, and tuned back out of the Greek conversation going on beside her. Thinking it through, she realised that she was taking them to her neighbour's house. That's where they'd be living, presumably, especially Spiros, since he was their nephew, and that would mean she would see him every day.

I wonder if he has a girl back home, she thought, wondering if what Effie had told her was true. A flare of jealousy fled through her at the notion of him having some lucky girl back in Greece. *Oh, don't be absurd. Even if he does, it's none of your business. He's probably promised to some nice young girl who'll he marry on her twenty-first, or twenty-fifth birthday. But hang on, didn't Effie say he was twenty-five. So, wouldn't that mean he'd already be married off?* She had no idea what age Greeks were married off in Greece, but in Australia, it wasn't too dissimilar. Effie still wasn't married off and she was twenty-four. Mr and Mrs Stephanides' children weren't married off, although the eldest son had been dating a friend of hers for two years. So, would that mean Spiros would be married off to a Greek girl in Armidale, or Sydney, or would he be open to the possibility of marrying an Australian girl?

Now, why would I be thinking about that? She blushed, and mentally kicking herself, she drove into the outskirts of Armidale.

Spiros noticed the blush when she'd last glanced in the mirror, and wondered if she was thinking about him the way he'd been thinking about her. Oh, yes, for the last God knows how many miles he'd been thinking about nothing else except for the gorgeous Jenny Marsh. Questioned whether she currently had a boyfriend, how many she'd had, whether she'd be interested in a Greek boy with next to no English skills, and the fact he'd be living right next door to her. *That fact,* he loved. The fact that he could look out a window and possibly see her, or go out the front of the house and possibly see her. The fact that he'd have every reason to run into her every day because she lived right next door to his family. *Oh, God, how lucky am I?* he thought, his eyes never leaving the rear-view. *How lucky am I to be living right next door to the most beautiful girl in the world? How in Zeus's name did I get so lucky to meet the most beautiful girl in the world right off the boat, the moment I set foot on dry land in Australia,* on *Australia, I meet the most beautiful girl in the world?*

"Almost there," Jenny told them, turning down her street.

Effie translated, telling them they were nearly at Spiros's aunt and uncle's house.

Jenny pulled into their driveway, honked twice, and turned off the ignition. "We're here." Stepping out of the car, she came face to face with Spiros. "Oh…we're here…at your aunt and uncle's home."

"Spiros?"

Spiros turned from the beautiful Jenny to see his aunt and uncle come down the front porch steps. "Uncle Nikos, Aunt Melina." He ran over to them and rapid-fire Greek followed.

Jenny and Effie pulled the luggage from the car, but when Jenny grabbed a suitcase the handle broke, it went tumbling down to the ground, and the lid flew open. "Oh, no," Jenny cried and quickly grabbed at the case to set it right side up. She straightened the clothes and her hand brushed against something sharp. "Ouch!" Pulling her hand away, she saw her finger was bleeding.

"Everything all right?" Nikos asked, leading everyone around to where Jenny was sucking blood from her finger.

She looked up, red-faced. "I'm so sorry. The handle broke and it opened up and fell. I tried to fix everything, but cut my finger on something."

Spiros saw what had happened, and kneeling down next to Jenny, took her hand in his and gently wrapped his clean handkerchief around her finger. He apologised in Greek and his uncle translated.

"He says he's sorry about your finger. His case is old and broke on the journey over." He watched his nephew dig into his case and pull out a framed photo of his family. The glass had broken, which would have been what cut Jenny's finger. He kept translating as Spiros spoke. "This is my family. My mother Katyana, and father Giorgio, my four brothers, Matthias, Costas, Anatole and Theseus. And my three sisters, Agathe, Damara, and Phaedra, and this is me." He watched his nephew smile at Jenny, and Jenny very shyly, but alluringly, smile back. "He likes you, young Jenny. And by the look of it, you like him too," he said in English.

Jenny tore her eyes away from Spiros. "What! Oh…what…no… I just…" She quickly stood and smoothed her dress. "Need to get Effie back home and have things to do. Um," she gulped, "you ready to go, Effie?"

"Sure," Effie said slowly, watching her friend blush, and the strong strapping Spiros sort out his case. When he was done, he shut the boot and turned to his uncle.

"They need to go," his uncle explained in Greek. "We should get you into English classes as soon as possible, so you can start conversing with Australians." Switching to English, he added, "Thank you, Jenny, for bringing my nephew and his friends home. I know it was a long trip. Say goodbye, Spiros."

"Good…bye…" Spiros managed and reached out for Jenny's hand.

She thought he meant to shake it, so extended her hand. But once again, he kissed it instead. "Oh…" The blush rose up her neck to her face.

"My nephew *definitely* likes you, young Jenny." Nikos grinned. "Maybe you can teach him English, but in the meantime, we'll let you go. Come, Spiros." He led his nephew and his friends into the house, and once they were inside, Jenny finally came to her senses, breathed, and climbed into the front seat.

"Ah…what was that all about?" Effie slid into the front seat and cast a glance at her very red friend.

"Nothing at all." Jenny tried inserting the key into the ignition, but fumbled due to the kerchief around her finger. "Oh, bother. I forgot to give him back his handkerchief." She unwound it to see her finger had stopped bleeding.

"You can run in and return it to him now," Effie slyly suggested.

Seeing the bloodstain, Jenny frowned and folded it up. "No. I'll give it a wash first to get the blood out of it. I can't hand it back bloody, it might be the only one he has, and I don't want to ruin it, or I'll have to buy him another one." She started the car and slowly backed out of the drive.

"Well…" Effie got a sly look in her eyes. "Christmas *is* coming up; you could pretend the blood didn't come out and replace it with a nicer one anyway."

"Oh, you!" Jenny moaned, exasperated with her friend's matchmaking.

November 1950

The spring dance in November came around quickly and celebrated the last month of the season. Jenny's sisters and friends had dates, even her brothers, who had worked up the gumption to ask girls out, had dates, and Effie had a date with Nicodemus, Spiros's very good looking friend. Effie had the balls to ask him to the dance herself, and he'd said yes.

It had been a month since Spiros and his friends had landed on his uncle's doorstep. A month since Spiros had sailed into Jenny's heart and she into his.

They'd seen each other every day. In the morning when she went off to work, he was getting ready to go out for the day with his aunt and uncle, or cousins, to explore his new hometown. Or, in the evening, when she came home he would be waiting on the front porch, pretending to casually converse with whoever was sitting with him. But, in reality, he just longed for her, for the sight, the touch, the smell of his Jenny. His uncle had enrolled him in the local English classes at the recreation centre, along with his friends, and Effie had been a big help by taking his friends out and helping them get used to their new way of life. But Spiros yearned for Jenny and studied hard at English so he could ask her to the spring dance. He just had to work up the nerve for it and waited until the day before to do it.

Watching over the low chain wire fence that divided the driveways of the two properties, Spiros waited until she pulled into her driveway, nervously got to his feet, and walked over to the fence.

Jenny alighted from her car, turned to shut the door, and noticed him over the roof. "Oh, Spiros, hello." She walked over to the fence. "Hello there, how is your English class going?" Her mother had given her all the details as she spoke to Mrs Stephanides every couple of days over the fence, so she knew Spiros and his friends had been taking the classes.

"Ah…hello…Miss Jenny." Spiros spoke slowly, unable to take his eyes from her. "My English, I think, is good going."

"Oh." Jenny hid a giggle behind her hand. "Sounds as if it will take some time for you to get the grasp of it." She watched the blush rise up his neck and flush his cheeks. "I could help you…" popped out of her mouth without her brain thinking about it.

Spiros lit up. "Yes, may you?" Nodding eagerly, he prepared himself for what his uncle had coached him on. "Miss Jenny…ah…are you… going to the…dance of spring tomorrow?" His palms were sweaty so he wiped them on his pants leg, but his mouth had suddenly turned drier than a desert. He'd never asked a girl out before, never kissed one, held hands with one, dated one. And he wasn't sure if he was doing it right.

"Am I…?" The heat rose up from Jenny's loins to flush her face to what must have been the same colour as Spiros's. "Oh…you mean the spring dance…tomorrow…" While many young men had asked her out, she hadn't yet picked anyone, hoping against hope that she somehow would be able to go with Spiros. Of course, he had to ask, and, of course, she had been waiting for him, but now, here he was in front of her, asking. Staring into his chocolate brown eyes, she fell. Her heart collided with her chest in triple time, and her blood sang as it sped around her body. Staring at his lips surrounding even white teeth, she noticed the creamy smooth texture of his skin, the thick rich blackness of his neatly trimmed hair, the height of his muscular lean frame with manly muscular arms and legs. Her gaze moved from his face down over his muscular chest to the sizeable package bulging through his grey pants. "Oh…" slid out of her mouth and the throbbing between her legs beat in double time with the butterflies in her stomach.

"Miss Jenny…?"

The sound of her name being spoken made her raise her eyes to his. "Oh…" She flushed, realising what she had been looking at. "Ah, oh…" Flustered, she added, "Oh, I'm so sorry. Oh, my gosh." Unable to look him in the eye, she dashed inside.

"Miss Jenny, wait," Spiros called. Unsure of what had just happened, he stood there staring at the house next door, a depression befalling him that she had not said yes, but run away from him as if he were a leper. "Miss Jenny?" he mumbled miserably.

"Oh, my gosh, how embarrassing." Jenny ran up the stairs and into her room, throwing herself on her bed. *How could I be so stupid,* she thought, knowing she had made an absolute fool out of herself by staring at him that way. *And oh, my, gosh, I think I licked my lips when I looked at his crotch. Oh, my gosh, how could I? What a fool he must think I am.*

"Jenny…what's wrong?" Sarah came through the door. "What happened? Did you just get fired from your job? Don't worry, sweetie, you'll get another one."

"No, Mum." Jenny rolled over to see her mother, sitting beside her on the bed.

"Then what is it?" Sarah patted her arm. "What could have happened that would leave you so mortified and lying face down on the bed?"

"Oh…" Jenny buried her face in the pillow. "It's so embarrassing," she mumbled.

"Did it have to do with that Spiros boy from next door? I saw him standing at the fence looking quite disappointed."

"Disappointed?" Jenny pulled the pillow away. "Why would he be disappointed? I didn't say no."

"No to what?" Sarah asked.

Jenny sat up and swung her legs around to sit on the side of the bed. "Why would he be disappointed when I didn't say no to going to the spring dance with him?"

"Well…did you say yes, though?" Sarah had been told a lot of things by Mrs Stephanides, including that her nephew had a crush on Jenny.

"Well…I…um…" Jenny bit her lip and frowned. "No. Oh, no!" she wailed. "He must think I'm such a fool. I just stood there looking him up and down, marvelling at how muscular he was and I ended up staring at his…" She glanced at her mother, blushed and continued in embarrassment. "Um…parts I shouldn't be looking at."

Sarah laughed. "You can say it, dear. His crotch. Which is perfectly natural when admiring the male form. Are you attracted to him?" She hadn't seen her daughter flustered over any boy, or man, before, and wondered if this was the beginning of her first crush. Or love.

"Oh…" Jenny gulped. She had been acting like a lovesick fool over him for the last month, wondering how his name was spelled, if he'd learn enough English in time to go to the spring dance. Whether he even knew *how* to dance. "I…like him," she managed, unsure of how much to say. Even if it was her mother, that didn't mean she was going to tell her everything.

"So we've all noticed." Sarah chuckled. "If you like him, get to know him. If he asked you to the dance, you'd better go and say yes before he asks someone else in your place. It's what you've been hanging out for this last month, isn't it?"

Jenny gaped at her mother. "How could you possibly have known…?"

"You've been lovesick." Sarah got to her feet. "If you didn't say yes before, go and say yes now, before he changes his mind. I think he's sitting on the front porch next door like a lost lovesick puppy."

"What! Oh, my gosh. I…" The fluster came back. "How do I…? When do I…? Should I apologise?"

"No need, child, just go and tell him, yes, you'll go to the dance with him." Sarah left her to it and waited to see how long it would take.

Not long at all.

Five minutes later, after freshening up, Jenny raced downstairs and out the door, having decided on the quick and simple approach so her nerves didn't get the better of her. She flew to the wire fence dividing the two properties and saw Spiros hurry towards her. Taking a deep breath, she gushed, "If you're still interested in taking me to the spring dance, I'd love to. You are still interested in taking me, aren't you? I'm not too late with my answer? Oh, silly me, of course, I'm not too late, you only just asked me fifteen minutes ago, it's not as though you've had the time to ask anyone else since you asked me, unless I wasn't your first choice. Oh, how silly of me—"

"Miss Jenny," Spiros interrupted her, shaking his head in confusion, having not understood most of what she'd said. "Will you say yes to dance of spring?"

"To the spring dance…" Jenny gazed dreamily into his eyes.

He nodded, unable to tear his gaze from her. "Are you say yes?"

"Yes," Jenny breathed. "Oh, yes. Yes, I will go to the spring dance with you." And then embarrassment overtook her and she raced back inside.

"She said yes," Spiros muttered in Greek and fist-pumped himself. "She said yes." All he needed now was to make sure his new suit was ironed and ready for tomorrow.

*****

At seven p.m. Saturday, there was a flurry of activity in the Marsh household. The boys were tying their ties, while the girls were putting the finishing touches to their hair and make-up, and then the doorbell started ringing.

"Oh, no, they're here," Rebecca cried and glanced out the window to see Faye and Barbara's dates out front. "Girls, your dates are here."

Faye and Barbara quickly sprayed on perfume and hurried downstairs where their father was opening the door. They came to a halt at the bottom of the stairs while their dates said hello to Mr Marsh.

"Take care of my girls, boys. We will be there, so will be watching."

"Yes, Mr Marsh," the two lanky twenty-year-olds said in unison, both nervously rubbing sweaty palms on their pants.

The girls giggled and rushed out the door, and Matthew had barely closed it when Ned and Arthur came rushing down the stairs.

"Gotta go, we gotta pick our dates up," Ned called out and rushed out the door his father reopened. His brother followed. The boys were sharing their car for the night and double dating.

Matthew saw another car pull up outside and the driver alight. He waited until the man approached. "And who are you here for, young man?"

"Rebecca, Mr Marsh." He held out his hand to shake. "I'm Nathan Beauregarde."

"Nice to meet you, Nathan," Matthew shook his hand and turned to call out to his daughter. "Rebecca, Nathan's here."

"Oh, Dad. Why does he have to yell?" Rebecca slid into her dance shoes and hurried down to meet her date who escorted her to his car and opened the door for her.

Watching, Matthew closed the door and turned to his wife. "Only two more."

"Gotta go." Philip ran down the stairs, throwing his suit jacket on as he went. "I gotta pick up my date and—"

"You also have to double date with Jenny and Spiros," Sarah quickly reminded him. "And since it's *her* car and *she's* driving, you'll wait for her."

"Naw, Mum!" Philip stomped a foot and pulled a face.

The doorbell rang and Matthew opened it a fourth time to see Spiros standing in a light grey suit and white shirt, holding a corsage. While they hadn't got to know each other well in the last month, he had spoken on the odd occasion to Spiros and been told everything by his uncle.

"Mr Marsh?" Spiros inquired. "I am here for Miss Jenny."

"Of course you are." Matthew nodded and called for his daughter. "Won't you come in?" He gestured for Spiros to enter and waited while he carefully stepped inside. "This is my son, Philip," he told Spiros and watched them shake hands.

"Mr Philip." Spiros nodded. "I am Spiros."

"Yeah." Philip nodded a return greeting. "I've seen you around."

"And here's Jenny, looking pretty as a picture." Matthew held out his hand and moved over to the stairs.

Jenny gracefully floated down in her knee-length chiffon party dress in a shade of blue that made her eyes glisten like brilliant sapphires, with a wide sash in a darker shade tied around her waist into a large bow at the back. Her kitten heel dance shoes matched her dress, and her golden-brown hair was done up into a fashionable French twist. She kept her jewellery simple, a small pair of sapphire studs, and a sapphire pendant necklace to match. She grasped her father's hand and finished descending the stairs.

Spiros had never seen any woman as beautiful as Jenny Marsh, and he was absolutely speechless.

Blushing, and averting her eyes, Jenny smiled shyly and noted the corsage he held. "Is that for me?" Seeing his dazed expression, and fearing he didn't understand, she pointed to it. "Is that for me?"

"Oh." Spiros looked down in surprise. "Yes…corsage?" He offered it to her, unsure of what to do with it. He'd spoken to his cousins in great detail along with other young Greeks in the area about the traditions of dances. And while it wasn't necessarily a Greek thing, his uncle had suggested a corsage to make an impression on his first date.

"Yes." Jenny smiled brightly. "That's right, a corsage." She took the plastic box and carefully pried it open with the help of her mother, and saw it was on wrist band. Sliding it over her left hand, she adjusted it until it sat perfectly on her dainty wrist. "There."

"Can we go now?" Philip whined and rolled his eyes. "This slop is pathetic."

Matthew cuffed him round the ear. "You will be polite since your sister is driving you there, because one more word like that, and *we* will bring you home."

Scowling, Philip skulked out the door and waited by the car.

"We shall go, yes?" Jenny indicated to the door and led Spiros outside, explaining the situation to him. "We are double dating with my brother and his date, but must pick her up first. You can sit in the front passenger seat." Pointing to the other side of the car, she saw him nod and move around to the door. Carefully climbing into the driver's seat so she didn't crush her dress, she waited until Spiros and Philip were settled. "Okay, Philip, where does your date live?" She started the car and he gave her the address, then she backed out of the drive. Five minutes later they picked up her brother's date, and ten minutes later pulled to a stop in a car park next to the Armidale recreation centre. "We're here."

They alighted, and while Philip and his date, Ann-Marie, hurried inside, Jenny smoothed her dress and turned to Spiros. "Are you ready?" She watched him button up his jacket and nervously hold out his arm.

"I…escort…you?" he asked uncertainly.

Blushing, she accepted and slid her right arm through his. "Yes, you may." They entered the lobby and stopped behind a line of others waiting to enter the main room, and heard the band in full swing through the double doors. People were mingling about, chatting, sipping cool drinks, or taking a respite from the crowd inside.

Making it through the doors, they stood to the side and watched the band for a few minutes. Jenny tapped her foot in anticipation of a night of dancing and excitedly turned to Spiros. "Do you dance?"

"Dance," he mumbled, dazed by the noise and large crowd. "Oh… yes, dance."

"Oh, good, come on." Jenny led him onto the dance floor in front of the stage and waited for him to take her in his arms.

Spiros stood still, watching her and all the other couples, not quite sure what he was expected to do since he'd never danced with any woman other than his mother or sisters. And it was Greek dancing at that.

"You *do* dance, don't you?" Jenny asked, stepping closer and watching his expressions, one almost of horror.

"He's just not used to dancing with women he's not related to." Nikos junior, his cousin, rescued him as he danced close to them with his date. "Hello, Jenny, Spiros."

"Nikos," Jenny replied warmly. "Delores, how are you?"

"Good, Jenny," her half Greek, half Australian school friend replied. She'd been dating Nikos since he'd arrived two years ago.

In Greek, Nikos quickly explained, once again, how to dance with a woman. While they had given him and his friends lessons in all things Australian, they had only briefly gone over dancing. "Just follow my lead." He and Delores danced beside them, and Spiros took Jenny gently into his arms and started moving.

Jenny gasped at his touch. "That's it." The burning of his handprint on her back, she just knew, would be there permanently. "You're getting the hang of it."

They followed Nikos and Delores around the room and danced for a couple of hours before stopping for a breather and a cool glass of punch.

"You picked that up easily," she told him as they chatted out in the cool quiet of the lobby.

"I can follow…if I watch." Spiros's English needed a lot of work, and he was more relaxed and at ease talking in Greek, but he knew he needed to learn the language better if he was to converse with his fellow Australians. Especially Jenny. His eyes skimmed her up and down, and his heart started pounding louder than the bass drum in the band. "You…are…beautiful…Miss Jenny."

"Oh…" Jenny flushed bright red. "Um…thank you." Quickly taking a sip of drink for something to detract the attention, she saw the corsage right in front of her eyes. "It's very pretty." She pointed to it when he raised a questioning brow. "The corsage is very pretty."

His eyes glanced from hers to the corsage and back. "*You* are very pretty."

"Smooth, man, real smooth." Two young men Jenny knew from the local neighbourhood approached them. "Is this who you chose to come to the dance with?" one asked. His cocky, out for trouble attitude made Jenny's hackles rise.

"Yes, Jeremiah Clarkson, it is. And you have no need to be so rude. This is Spiros Stephanopoulos. His aunt and uncle live next door to me. And this," she told Spiros who had turned his head to her when she'd said his name, "is Jeremiah Clarkson and Richard Mayson. Two young men I know who happen to know my older brother Ned."

Spiros hadn't caught most of what was said, but he held his hand out to shake. "Hello, I am Spiros."

Jeremiah and Richard sneered at the hand. "Couldn't do better than a wog fresh off the boat, Jenny? You had us to bring you to the dance. Hell, you would've had half the men in Armidale bring you to the dance, so why did you pick a bloody woggy little Greek shit?" He slapped Spiros's hand away.

"How dare you!" Jenny exclaimed, the fire burning in her belly. "How dare you be so rude and so mean to not only a new immigrant but the nephew and cousin of people you know, *I* know, my next-door neighbours. *How dare you*, don't *ever* expect me to *ever* date either one of you ever again. And *neither* will my sisters. I'll make sure of that."

"Something wrong?" Ned asked. He had run into Nikos junior on the way out the door and was looking for the bathroom when they'd come across Jenny and Spiros fighting with two of his friends. "Jenny?" With the way he was raised, he'd side with his sister and her fighting spirit any day over any one of his friends.

"Your so-called friends were being incredibly rude to Spiros and me. They called him a bad name, and slapped his hand away when all he wanted to do was shake theirs."

Spiros had quickly explained in Greek to Nikos who got the gist of it.

"Wog, huh?" Nikos said to the two boys and took a menacing step towards them. At six foot and broad-shouldered, he could punch on any day of the week and win over some of the pathetically built boys in Armidale. He was also the champion of the local boxing club. "Is that what you call my cousin? The same thing you called me two years ago, and probably the rest of my family, except for my sister who you dated and whose pants you tried getting into. Wog, huh." He moved another step and Jeremiah and Richard backed off, putting their hands up in defence.

"Well, that's not nice now, is it?" Ned said to them. "What would make you two boys go and call a new arrival *that?*" He watched them closely, waiting for their answer. "Well…I'm waiting."

"Because he is," Jeremiah spat and pointed to Jenny. "She's willing to date him and not us. She turned *us* down for the dance, all for what?" He waved an arm around and his face screwed up in anger. "Some filthy piece of woggy shit?"

Nikos pulled his arm back and fired on all cylinders, letting his arm fly towards Jeremiah's face. His fist smashed into his jaw, and

Jeremiah sprawled backwards on the floor. "What did you say?" He leaned over Jeramiah who scuttled backwards.

Ned held Nikos back. "Easy there, Nikos, the olds are coming." They looked towards Ned's parents, other adults, and Nikos senior coming up the rear.

"What happened here?" Matthew Marsh demanded, seeing his son holding Nikos back, and his daughter's shocked expression. "Jenny?"

"Um…" She shook her head to clear the confusion of the last few moments. "They were being mean to Spiros and me, and said awful things to both of us, and Nikos um…" She glanced from him to her brother, unsure of how much to say.

"I punched him for what he called my cousin," Nikos replied, daring anyone to argue back. "I defended my cousin." He stood his ground at his full height.

"What was it he called Spiros?" Nikos senior asked, coming to stand by him as the two boys were helped up.

"The term, *some filthy piece of woggy shit* was used," Nikos told him quite loudly so all heard. Murmurs went through the adults.

"Right, I suggest you two boys leave," Matthew said and pushed Jeremiah and Richard towards the door. "We have no need for that kind of language here. And best you don't ask my daughters out anymore." He cast a quick look at Ned. "And maybe don't hang around my sons anymore, either. Off you both go."

"Why should we go?" Jeremiah complained, pushing back. "He's the one who's come to our country. They're the ones taking our girls."

"Enough," Matthew roared, and pushed the boys out the door. As head of the town's council board, he had more say than others *and* more respect. "No more, now leave." He watched the boys scuttle backwards, swearing and flicking their fingers up before turning to his son and daughter. "Is everyone all right? Jenny?"

"Fine, Dad," she said. "Just a little shaken by their rudeness. I *cannot* believe how mean they were."

"Not the first time," Ned told her. "I noticed it a couple of years ago, but it didn't last long. Now they've been doing it again in the last month since we had new arrivals." He looked at Spiros. "Sorry about that."

Nikos senior had translated everything for his nephew, and Spiros nodded and thanked Ned for his kind words.

"Well," Nikos went on. "Now that that is sorted, let's get back to the party, shall we?" He laid a hand on his son's shoulder and muttered something in his ear. He led his son back into the main room, and the others followed, leaving Spiros and Jenny alone again.

"Oh…my…" Jenny breathed out in relief. "That should never have happened. I am so sorry that you had to experience that."

"I'm sorry…" Spiros replied, trying to find the words to finish the sentence.

"Oh, no, don't *you* apologise," Jenny told him. "That was horrible, what they said."

Spiros gently laid a hand on her arm and she gasped. "I'm sorry… for what they say to hurt you. You looked…" He struggled to find the word and made an angry scowl instead. "Thymós, anger."

"Oh, you mean angry?" Jenny supplied, thinking she really should be teaching him English because clearly, the classes weren't doing that well.

"Yes, yes, anger." Spiros nodded.

"Yes, I guess I was," Jenny murmured. "It was horrible what they said to you, and they shouldn't have said anything." She looked at him and saw beads of sweat on his forehead, and worried that she didn't look so fresh herself. "Why don't we freshen up?" Taking his arm, she led him down the corridor to the bathrooms. "Freshen up?" She pointed to the sign on the door to the gents. "I need to freshen up, too." Pointing to the ladies, she stepped over to the door, a coquettish look on her face as she peered over her shoulder at him. "I'll be back in a minute."

Spiros watched her go in and pushed open the door to the gents. Seeing the urinals, he smiled. "Ah, ouritírio, urinal. I go." He freshened himself up, wiped the sweat from his brow, and used the hand dryer to dry the sweaty armpits of his shirt. Once dry, he walked outside and waited for Jenny who came out a moment later, looking as fresh and glowing as when she arrived.

"Here we are. Let's get back to dancing, shall we."

They walked into the room and accepted glasses of punch, standing by the sidelines watching the older patrons dance to a classic tune. After fifteen minutes, the band changed tempo, and everyone on the floor exited for the younger generation to have another go.

"Come on." Jenny took their glasses and set them down on a side table, grabbed his hand, and led him onto the floor. They followed the lead of their relatives and friends, and soon Spiros got the hang of 1950s dancing in Australia. After an hour, they made their way off the floor for the older patrons to dance again, and for the rest of the night, the generations took turns. In between, Jenny taught Spiros new words and phrases in English, finding he picked them up quickly.

When the night ended, they found Philip and his date and proceeded out to the car. Jenny dropped off Ann-Marie and drove home, coming to a stop in their driveway. They climbed out, and she waited for her brother to let himself in before turning to Spiros. "I had a lovely night." She walked around the car and stood by him. "Thank you for the corsage and the dancing. You picked it up quickly."

"Dancing, yes, I like dancing," Spiros said. He also liked Jenny. A lot!

"Yes, dancing," Jenny repeated. "You're very good at it."

"Thank you. But no Greek dancing?" He was confused as to why there had been none that night. "Why no Greek dancing?"

"Oh, I don't know," Jenny said. "Probably because that happens in the Greek Club. Have you been there yet?"

They were interrupted by her sisters' dates bringing them home. Giggling, all three girls kissed their dates goodnight and got out of the cars. Seeing Spiros and Jenny, they giggled more and rushed into the house holding hands.

"Philip's inside," Jenny called and watched them go in before turning back to Spiros. "My sisters. All younger than me. So is Philip, whereas Ned and Arthur are older. And we have three older brothers and two older sisters as well, but they're all married off and don't live at home. Have you spoken to your parents, or brothers and sisters since arriving here? They must be so excited that you came?" She knew she was gushing, but couldn't help it; being around Spiros made her nervous.

"No…" he muttered a hint of sadness on his face. "Not talked to them."

"Oh, I'm sorry," Jenny murmured. "Did they not want you to come here, or have you just not contacted them, yet?"

"Both," Spiros said, not wanting to talk about his family anymore. He stepped closer to Jenny, but was interrupted by the arrival of a car.

Ned beeped his horn, and he and Arthur got out, giggling at the scene before them.

"Stop being so childish," Jenny called. "Everyone else is inside except Mum and Dad." Hearing the giggles turn to laughter, she added, "Grow up, you two." They went inside and closed the door. "Ah…" she sighed. "Siblings."

Spiros smiled softly and remembered back to the days he and his brothers would tease their sisters. They were good times he would never have again.

"Thank you for asking me to the dance." Jenny stepped closer. "I… was hoping you'd ask me…" Gamely, she took his hand in hers. "I'm glad you asked me to the dance." She wasn't sure what she was hoping for, but whatever it was, was interrupted by her parents arriving home.

Parking behind their children's cars, Matthew and Sarah caught sight of Spiros and Jenny in their headlights. Exchanging amused glances, Matthew said, "Now…what do we think of this?" before getting out of his car. "Jenny. Spiros." He closed the door and waited for Sarah to come to his side, and then they headed into the house. "Don't stay out too long, Jenny. Tomorrow's Sunday, we have church in the morning."

He opened the front door, and as his wife passed she said, "I think it's sweet." They shut the door to find the rest of the kids on the upstairs landing, giggling their heads off. "To bed, you lot," Sarah said, and ushered them away. They left the front porch light on for Jenny.

"Oh, my…that was embarrassing," Jenny murmured, blushing at the thought of her parents seeing her holding Spiros's hand. Oh…she was holding Spiros's hand. Glancing down, she saw their fingers had entwined. Now when did that happen?

"Church…you go?" Spiros asked surprised since he hadn't seen them at the local Orthodox Church his family went to.

"Yes. Catholic church, on Sunday mornings," Jenny said. "And you? Do you go to the Orthodox like your family?"

"Yes." He nodded. "Greek church."

"Well, I guess you would." Jenny shuffled closer. Waiting. For what, she wasn't sure. But a kiss goodnight, or something, would be nice. And, oh, how she wanted the hot looking Greek in front of her to kiss her. She blushed harder and shyly glanced away.

"I walk you…to door?" Spiros asked and pointed in the direction of the house.

"Oh, um, sure." Jenny stepped back and turned around so she didn't break the connection they had with their interwoven hands. They walked up the porch steps and stood under the light.

"I enjoyed tonight," Jenny said, waiting.

"Me too," Spiros replied, wondering if he should kiss her or not. After contemplating the fact her parents and brothers were inside, and the fact that this was their first date, he decided to keep things proper. So, he brought her hand to his lips and kissed it, pressing the soft flesh of her hand to the soft flesh of his lips, his face, his cheek.

A sigh escaped out of her and she felt hazy and relaxed.

Reluctantly, letting go of her hand, he said, "Good…night, Miss Jenny."

A soft smile lit up her face. "Goodnight, Spiros."

He nodded, a smile beaming across his face, and left, but instead of walking down the drive, he ran over to the fence and jumped over it in happiness.

"Oh, careful," Jenny cried out and saw him fall. "Oh, are you okay?" She rushed over to find him jumping up and laughing. "Are you okay?"

"I okay." He nodded, the smile still in place. "I very okay."

"Oh." She giggled. "Okay then, goodnight."

"Goodnight, Miss Jenny."

"You *can* just call me Jenny." She hadn't moved, didn't want to, just stood there gripping the top bar of the low chain wire fence.

"Just call me Jenny," he joked and grasped the fence as well, his hands on the outside of hers, almost touching.

"Yes." Another giggle. "Jenny. I am Jenny."

"Jenny. You are Jenny," Spiros murmured, coming dangerously close to her.

"And…you…are…Spiros." Jenny melted into the deep pools of chocolate that were his eyes. Breathed in his scent.

"I…Spiros…" He breathed in hers. "You…Jenny…" She was as exotic to him as he was to her. "Jenny…" His face was so close he could see her eyes glitter like diamonds in the moonlight.

"Spiros…" she whispered before their lips met.

Fireworks, thunder, balls of lightning, sirens all sounded, and the earth trembled and shook where they stood.

Several moments passed before they parted, panting lightly from the spectacular light show they had just witnessed in their intoxicated state.

"Oh…" She breathed in. "Oh…oh…" Realising what had just happened, she blushed. She'd never been kissed by a boy, or man, before. And while she'd had dates, she'd never kissed them because she hadn't wanted to. "Oh…I…ah…need to…" Stumbling backwards, she turned and raced for the door, slamming through it as if wild hounds were after her. "Oh."

"Jenny," Spiros murmured, a huge grin on his lips. "My Jenny." Happy, he danced all the way inside and fell asleep dreaming of her.

*****

After church service the next morning, Jenny's sisters all wanted to know the gossip from the night before, so they gathered in Jenny and Rebecca's room, discussing the dance detail by detail.

After Jenny told them what had happened with Jeremiah and Richard, the girls agreed that they would never date them again.

"I suppose it's just as well Ned and Nikos came along," Rebecca said as she sorted out her accessories drawer. "Since Spiros doesn't understand English, yet, it must have been hard for him to comprehend what was happening. At least he had Nikos to explain and defend him."

"Yes," Jenny murmured, lying against a pile of pillows and tucking her feet under her. "What they said was horrible, and I couldn't even repeat the words they used to try and explain it to him. I'm just glad Dad told them to get out."

"What did he have to say about it?" Faye asked. They'd heard the commotion, but hadn't gone to investigate.

"Not much. Once he threw the boys out, he asked if we were all right and went back to the dance." Jenny contemplated telling the girls about the kiss from Spiros, but figured they'd know anyway.

"How *was* Spiros when you came home?" Barbara asked, perched on the end of Jenny's bed, swinging her legs back and forth. At eighteen, she was the youngest Marsh and had only been allowed to date after her birthday.

"He was fine," Jenny said, a small smile playing on her lips. "He didn't seem too cut up about it, thanks to his lack of English, I suppose. He was quite happy when I left him and came inside."

"I bet he was, considering you'd just kissed him." Rebecca slyly glanced at her sister.

Jenny blushed and hid her face for a moment. "Yes, I had assumed you'd all be looking. Have fun, did we?"

The three girls traded glances and grinned. "Yes."

"Oh, do tell us, Jenny," Faye urged. "Was it like all the other boys you've kissed? Is kissing a Greek different from kissing an Australian boy? We want all the details."

"Well…" Jenny started, but then stopped and thought about it. Her sisters had all kissed boys and she hadn't. Was there something wrong with her to not *want* to kiss boys? She wondered if her sisters had gone further. Obviously, Harriet and Joanna had since they were married off with children, but for the seven Marsh siblings left at home, none of them were ready for that. Yet.

"Well," Faye prodded. "He kissed you. What was it like?"

"Everything I could have wanted from a first kiss." Jenny's eyes glazed over dreamily at the memories.

"What? What do you mean…*first* kiss?" Barbara asked. "Have you never kissed a boy before?"

The blush crept up Jenny's neck to her face and she said nothing.

"What? Are you for real?" Faye added, surprised at her sister. "You've *never* kissed a boy?"

Embarrassed, Jenny couldn't look at any of them. "Well…so what if I haven't?"

"Why not?" Rebecca left her accessories drawer hanging open to sit on the bed and face Jenny. "Why haven't you kissed a boy? You're older than us and we all have."

"Oh, well…hooray for all of you," Jenny said snidely and then frowned. "Sorry, didn't mean that. *So what* if I haven't? There are no rules to say we have to. Besides, I haven't come across a boy I've *wanted* to kiss. I've been much too busy."

"It's okay if you haven't," Rebecca hastened to add, seeing her sister's discomfort. They had always been told by their mother to not kiss boys unless they were special. And if Jenny hadn't met anyone special until now, then that was okay and Jenny's business. "What was it like? It *was* your first kiss after all."

Memories flooded back and Jenny's blush grew deeper.

"Must've been pretty good if it makes you blush like that," Barbara teased.

Without a moment's hesitation, Jenny burst out with the whole story.

"Oooh," Rebecca murmured. "If you heard, or saw, all of that, he must be very special indeed."

"I know," Jenny gushed. "It just felt so right. As if I'd waited my entire life for it. I'm so glad I waited because that was perfect." A dreamy sigh escaped from between her rosebud lips, and her eyes sparkled.

"So…it was worth it then?" Faye asked, nudging Rebecca who was beside her. They exchanged a glance and giggled. "The fact you've been lovesick and pining for him all month, and now you've had a date."

"I haven't been pining," Jenny chastised. "Just biding my time. He's new to the country and has been learning English, although he could definitely use help on that front. I didn't know whether he'd even want to ask me, and even though other boys have, I just didn't feel like dating any of them again. I've been dating them since I was eighteen. Been there, done that. Why should I keep going back to something that didn't work? They're nice enough to dance with, or have a luncheon with, but other than that, I've just been bored with the boys here in Armidale. We've even dated the same ones."

"True," Rebecca agreed. "But that doesn't mean because they weren't right for you, they wouldn't be right for another girl. Maybe Spiros is the one you've been waiting on."

"Maybe." Jenny pulled her feet out from under her and slid them into a pair of flat shoes. "It's nearly lunchtime, let's go help Mum."

*****

In the Stephanides household next door, there was a lot of Greek and a little English going on as Spiros told them about the dance over lunch.

"Sounds like you've got it bad, cuz." Nikos junior laughed. "You've got the hots for little Miss Jenny next door?"

"The hots? What is the hots?" Spiros broke some bread apart to dunk into his meal. "What does that mean?"

"It means you're sweet on her, like her, *really, really* like her," Maria, his cousin, told him. She was the only daughter in the Stephanides family with two older and two younger brothers. "She looks as if she likes you, too. I saw her today when we first came home from church, and she was gazing longingly over this way. I think she has the hots for you, too."

The heat rose to Spiros's face and he quickly downed his beer. He had been dreaming and thinking of Jenny Marsh since the day they'd met, and wondered if she had a boy she was sweet on. But he'd asked her to the dance only the day before it, and she'd said yes, so that meant she hadn't said yes to anyone else. Had she been waiting for him to ask? He'd waited until he knew enough English to ask her, and she'd said yes. Little Jenny Marsh from next door had said yes to going to the spring dance with him. And that had thrilled him down to his toes. So much so, when they'd come home, he'd fallen down and ripped his pants jumping over the fence. But that was okay, he'd rip more than his pants for his Jenny any day.

"Thinking about asking her out again?" Vasili asked. As the youngest Stephanides, he wasn't allowed to date girls as he wasn't eighteen. "I can't wait to ask out girls. I'm hanging out for it."

"And you can keep hanging out for it." His father waved a piece of bread at him before popping it into his mouth. "The girls in Australia do not date until they are eighteen, or have their parents' permission."

"So, when are girls allowed to get married?" Spiros asked.

"Thinking of proposing already?" Nikos junior grinned. "Jenny *must* be special."

The creeping redness hit Spiros's hairline. "I not ask, no, my sisters are being prepared for marriage once they turn twenty-one, just as my brothers were expected. What is the age limit here?"

"Girls need their parent's permission to marry here," Nikos senior told him. "But over the age of eighteen, which Jenny is, she is free to choose. Once they marry, they must stop work to take care of the babies that come next."

"Just like Greece?" Spiros murmured in thought.

"Just like Greece," Nikos senior replied. "If you are interested in dating Jenny Marsh, remember to use your manners and ask."

"There are a couple of summer and Christmas dances coming up you could invite her to," Maria added. "Then there's the New Year's dance, another summer dance in January, the Valentine's dance, the St Patrick's dance, not to mention all of the Greek celebrations you could invite her to."

"Would she go to Greek dances?" Spiros asked, wondering how much it would all cost and whether he needed to get a job immediately. You couldn't date, or marry, unless you had a job.

"I don't see why not," Melina said. She'd become quite friendly with Sarah and her daughters, and all were willing to congregate with other nationalities.

"Will I need to get a job to buy more suits? I cannot wear same one," Spiros continued and then became a bit panicky. "I did not have much to bring with me. Do I need new clothes?"

"You will if you keep ripping them." His aunt laughed. "At least I was able to mend the split in your pants. Try not to jump any more fences."

"Will I need them anyway? And should I buy Jenny a Christmas present? I had not thought about presents when we came. I will need to buy all of you something as well."

"No, no." Nikos senior waved a hand to dismiss him. "Do not bother about that. Just worry about next year. We are giving you and your friends a reprieve until next year when you can start work and pay rent and board, unless we look for a place for you to live. Keep the money you brought with you for you and what you need right now, such as clothes and dating young Jenny. If you want to work somewhere else, we will look for you and help you get something. Meanwhile, concentrate on your English."

"I am not sure I want to work in another meat shop." Spiros finished off his meal. "Papa and I had many an argument over me becoming the manager of the family store. I wanted to travel and see the world, or move to another country. He wanted me to stay and do my duty as firstborn. Would it not be a slap in the face to him if I take the job here, but did not take it there?"

"Well…" Nikos senior stroked his chin in thought. "It could be. How about this? You look for another job you could do in the next month, or so, and if you don't have anything by New Year, you come and work in the shop? It's not as though my sons do." He gave his second eldest, Zenon, a light clip around the ear.

"I don't work there because I like cars too much, and building motors. I got a good job in the local mechanics," Nikos junior proudly told Spiros. "I can build an engine from the ground up and then take it apart and build it again. If you ever need your car fixed, when you get one that is, let me know and I'll do it. I fix Jenny's car when she needs help." He gave him a wink.

A bolt of jealousy speared through Spiros at the thought of his cousin getting under Jenny's bonnet. "Is that *all* you do?"

"Aaaahhh, someone's jealous." Nikos junior saw the scowl on his cousin's face. "Don't worry, my friend. I have Delores. She's more what the Australians say, my cup of tea. You can have Jenny. Unless your friends want her?"

"Nicodemus has fallen for Effie." Spiros calmed down a little. "And Xenos is just enjoying being single."

"I haven't seen much of them around," Melina said and started gathering plates. "Where have they been hanging out to?"

"The Greek Club." Spiros handed her his plate. "Effie's been a big help introducing us to people her age, as has Nikos."

"Especially the girls." Nikos junior grinned. "Not that Spiros needs help with that." He nudged his cousin in the ribs. "He has Miss Jenny Marsh."

"Hardly." Spiros stood and stretched his back. "Can I help with anything?"

"No, no." Nikos senior waved him away. "Housework is a woman's work. Why don't you go outside and pine for your Jenny?" He chuckled. "She might be waiting for you, too."

Embarrassed, Spiros followed his cousins out to the back yard for a lazy afternoon. His gaze immediately flew next door to see if Jenny was outside, and found that she was watching her siblings kick a ball around.

Enchanted, Spiros leaned against the porch pole and stood staring at her as she sat reading between watching goals that her brothers scored.

Sensing that someone was watching her, she glanced at her family and then to her left, seeing Spiros standing there. He waved, and, after a moment, she waved back. Walking over to the fence, she got up on the railing and looked over. "Hello."

Spiros leaped off the porch and over to the fence, staring up at her spectacular face. "Hello, Miss Jenny."

She smiled brighter than the sun. "You don't have to call me Miss Jenny, Spiros. Jenny will do. How are you?"

"Very good. Dance very good last night." The kiss was still very fresh in his mind.

"Yes, it was, except for those horrible boys," Jenny agreed. "You picked dancing up very quickly."

"Yes, I try," Spiros murmured, gazing dreamily up at her.

Ned bounced onto the fence and saw everyone in the backyard. "You lot want to play football?"

The Stephanides kids glanced at each other and nodded, and instead of walking down the drive and around to the neighbours' backyard, they just jumped the fence and joined in.

"Oh...am I...?" Spiros was confused as to whether he was supposed to do the same.

"No, no, it's okay," Jenny told him. "Walk down and I'll meet you." She pointed to the driveway and climbed down, meeting him at the chain wire fence. "Hello."

"Hello, Miss Jenny." Spiros beamed and carefully climbed over. He saw the book in her hand. "What is book?"

"Oh." Jenny held the book up. "It's just *Pride and Prejudice*. The English might be too hard for you. How *is* your English coming along?"

"Okay." Spiros nodded at her. "I learn English."

Jenny's laughter floated along on the breeze. "Yes, I know. But I was thinking, maybe I should help you learn. Those classes are all well and good, but I could help you, too. What do you think?" Her heart thundered in her chest and she wondered if he could hear it.

"You learn me English?" he asked, unsure of what she'd just said.

"Yes, I can *teach* you English," Jenny said and had a thought. "Wait here." She raced inside, leaving him questioning why she had run off, only to come back out a moment later and beckon him over to the porch. "Here, sit." Pointing to the bench, she sat and waited for him.

He sat beside her and wondered what she was up to.

"Here." Jenny placed an open book in his hands. "Read from here." Her finger pointed to an animal. "Cat. A cat makes the sound meow." The family still had baby books lying around the house from when they were little, and just in case the grandchildren came over. Jenny thought they should be easy for Spiros to pick up.

Spiros glanced at her elegantly long finger with its pretty pink nail polish. His eyes moved from the picture to her. "Cat," he repeated.

"Yes, that's right," Jenny urged. "A cat makes the sound meow."

"A cat makes the sound meow." Spiros watched her face, not the book.

They sat there reading until the sun went down and everyone was called in for tea.

"Well, I think that's been very good for today, Spiros." Jenny gathered the books. "You did very well."

"I did very well," he repeated, excited that it had been so easy, but then, it was Jenny teaching him.

Hearing her name called, Jenny stepped towards the door. "I have to go in now. We could continue this tomorrow, after work and tea, if you like. A couple of hours each day. Would you like that?" She so desperately hoped he'd say yes.

"Yes, yes." He nodded like an eager puppy, desperate to spend more time with her, and that led him to the desperation of asking her. "Would you go to next dance with me? Summer?" Unsure if he'd said it properly, he added. "*All dances* with me?"

Surprised, Jenny's eyes grew wide. "You mean…*all* of the dances we have coming up, such as the Christmas and New Year's, and Valentine's and St Patrick's, and *all* the others?"

"Yes." His head bounced up and down. "*All* dances. I ask you so no one takes you…" Noticing her expression, he hastened to add, "Is that wrong to do?"

"Oh." Jenny blushed. "No, no, in fact, I think planning ahead is very smart. Um…let me check my diary to see if I can make it to the summer dance and I'll let you know tomorrow. Okay?"

"Okay." Spiros beamed. "Tomorrow."

"Yes." Jenny retreated back towards the screen door and opened it, unable to take her eyes off him. "Tomorrow. Goodnight."

"Goodnight, Miss Jenny." Another nod and he watched her beaming smile disappear behind the door. Smiling himself, he descended the stairs, and running over to the wire fence, launched himself over it, this time without falling and ripping his pants.

*****

After tea, Jenny checked her diary for December and found that she was indeed free for all dances for the month. Smiling, she marked them off with love hearts and Spiros's name to remind her she was already taken. There were three dances in December, but she had no idea if there were any Greek ones. She called Effie, and asked what the Greek community was doing for Christmas and New Year.

"We generally have Christmas our way," Effie told her. "But we have a couple of other things this month as well."

"What about New Year's in January? And Valentine's and St Patrick's?" Jenny pushed on. "Do you celebrate those things?"

"We celebrate everything; we don't turn down a party." Effie laughed. "Anything for a good time, we're up for it."

"When are your next dances for?"

Effie gave her the dates for up to New Year's. "Planning on asking Spiros?"

Jenny paused before answering. "Actually, he already asked me. To all of them."

"What!" Effie had been lying on the floor next to the phone, but that news made her sit up. "You're kidding? When?"

"Today, or technically, this evening after I gave him an English lesson, and before I got called in for tea."

"Oh, my God!" Effie exclaimed, only to be told off by her mother for taking the lord's name in vain. Rolling her eyes, she leaned against the wall. "You're kidding, right?"

"No. He was very nervous about it, but managed to ask me to the summer dance, and then he said *all* dances. When I asked him to clarify if he meant all including Valentine's and St Patrick's next year, he said yes."

"Wow." Effie was more than stunned. "It's fairly obvious that he's liked you since he met you. We all saw it. Even saw that you liked him right back."

"I guess," Jenny murmured demurely. "And I don't mind one bit."

"Has he kissed you yet?" Effie pushed for an answer. "Come on; tell me, did he kiss you last night at the dance, after the dance, during the dance?"

"Oh, for goodness sake, Effie," Jenny chastised. "The dance wasn't all about that. It was about spending time together and getting to know one another."

"Well, you certainly did that." Effie raised a brow. "We all saw you two dancing."

"Yes, like every other couple there. Just like you and Nicodemus. Have *you* kissed *him,* yet?" Jenny tried deflecting the conversation back to Effie.

"I certainly have, and I liked it very much," Effie said. "In fact, I think he may be my personal partner for all dances. So, it looks like me and Nicodemus will have to double date with you and Spiros. What do you think of that?"

"I don't see why we can't, especially if it's to Greek dances. I've only been to a couple of Greek celebrations with you, but felt a bit…" She frowned while trying to find the right words or phrase. "Like the odd one out."

Effie laughed and tangled her long black hair around a finger. "Well, you were. You were the only Australian at both parties. We'll teach you our ways, yet." She was interrupted by her father telling her to get off the phone. "Bah! I gotta go. My patéras is telling me to get off the phone. Gotta go. Call me tomorrow and let me know what happens. Bye."

"Bye." Jenny heard the dial tone and replaced the phone in its cradle. Going back to her diary, she decided to make a list of all the dances and celebrations she knew would be coming next year, and counted twelve as they had them every year. And that wasn't including any that Spiros might want to take her to at the Greek community club. "Oh dear, it's not as if I have a lot of clothes to wear, although I do have all of those pretty dresses I bought earlier this year. We may have to restyle them, or…" A thought came to mind. "I could raid my sister's wardrobes and restyle their dresses." It wasn't as if the four girls hadn't done that already, and they even had some of their older sisters' dresses and unwanted items from when they'd not been able to return to their former sizes after having children. Maybe she could even restyle those to suit her. The more she thought about it, the more excited she became, and the more she thought of Spiros and attending the dances with him, the more her heart pounded in double time, and the more her blood raced and zipped and flashed through her veins. Smiling, she made a list of clothes she had and what she could wear to each dance to see if there was anything she needed. She might not be the most fashionable belle of the ball, but she was going to try her damndest to be.

December 1950

The next few weeks were busy for Jenny. With full days typing up documents, and two hour sessions every night teaching Spiros English, not only did they find time to fit in the summer dance, but church on Sundays, and volunteering in the local community until, finally, it was December twenty-third and time for the Christmas dance.

Spiros knocked on the Marshes' door at seven-twenty p.m. in his new two-piece summer seersucker white suit and shirt. With the money he'd saved in Mykonos, he'd managed to buy many versatile pieces for all occasions with his aunt and uncle helping him with designs and fabrics for what suited the Australian summers and winters, and he'd also managed to buy Jenny a Christmas, Valentine's, and birthday present way ahead of schedule. He had seen them in the jewellery store in the main street when shopping with his aunt, and she'd helped him speak to the store clerk. He had the other two presents tucked away in his wardrobe, and the first in his pocket as he planned on giving it to Jenny that night.

Jenny hurried to open the door and saw him standing there looking very cool, yet smart. "Hello. Come in." Holding the door open, she waved him in.

Spiros entered and offered the corsage. He'd given her one before every dance and wasn't about to stop. He also had a huge bouquet of roses ready to be delivered to her tomorrow for Christmas.

"Oh, another corsage, how sweet. You *are* thoughtful." Jenny took the box, took out the red roses, and slid it over her wrist. "It's so beautiful, and matches my dress."

"Yes, red for Christmas," Spiros told her. "You said you were wearing it when I asked, so I could match colours." He took in her sleeveless, knee-length satin, red and green poinsettia print party dress with its sweetheart neckline. She had pinned roses and baby's breath into her hair, and wore red dancing shoes that accentuated her legs as the dress gently swished around them. Red netting under the skirt helped pouf the dress out.

"You are beautiful...Jenny..." Spiros couldn't take his eyes from the woman in front of him, and, oh, how he ached to do more than hold her hand, or hold her when they danced.

"Hello, Spiros. Jenny, you look lovely," Matthew told his daughter as he and Sarah came downstairs. Most of the town would be at the dance even though it was a warm summer night.

"Mr and Mrs Marsh." Spiros nodded in greeting. His English had become better with Jenny teaching him the alphabet and words. She said it was the same technique used in schools to teach children how to read and write, and he'd gone home each night and practised until after midnight, so he was doing well indeed. "How are you? You are coming to dance. Yes?" He saw they were both dressed up and made the assumption.

"Yes, Spiros, we are," Sarah said, noticing how lovely her daughter looked. "Are your aunt and uncle coming?"

"Yes, they are. They left when I came over," Spiros said. "Are we going?"

"Of course," Jenny said. "Just have to wait for the girls. We have to take them with us. I hope that's okay?" She hadn't yet asked him if he minded, but then she'd only found out a couple of hours ago.

"That is okay. No problemo." Spiros smiled brightly, wanting to show his Jenny that everything was okay, and he would be okay with everything as long as he was with her.

"Oh, that's good." She heaved a sigh. "Girls," she called, while her parents walked out to their car. "Time to go."

Rebecca, Faye, and Barbara came rushing from their rooms and downstairs.

"Make sure your lights are off," Jenny reminded them and flicked off the lounge room lights. The Christmas tree lights were still on, so she rushed over and turned them off at the socket. "Okay, let's go." After locking the door behind them, they settled into the car and followed her parents to the recreation hall where the Christmas dance was being held. They found a park, made their way in and found their table, which happened to be next to the Stephanides' table.

Half the town was there to celebrate Christmas, and a big feast had been cooked up for those who wanted to eat. There were chickens, turkeys, hams, salads and vegetables, and after everyone had gathered a plate, they sat and enjoyed a delicious meal while Christmas music played.

Jenny's brothers were sitting with their dates nearby, and her sister's dates had joined them at their table. They popped Christmas crackers, wore the paper hats they found inside, and told the silly jokes to each other. At eight p.m. the band strode on stage and took their places. Many a Christmas song was played throughout the night, and Jenny only danced with Spiros.

"You're really getting the hang of this," she told him. With her right hand in his and her left arm draped from his right shoulder, she felt at home in his arms. They'd had multiple dance parties, and each time he got better and better at dancing. Each time Jenny felt more and more relaxed and at home, as if she belonged in his arms. And she liked it. *Loved it,* even. As if she were his girl and no one else would, or could, ever come close to making her feel alive when she was with him. *He* was the only one she wanted to date, and she hoped he felt the same way about her. He'd only been in the country for two months, and she'd thought more than once that he might want to date other girls. But since he'd asked *her* to all of the dances, then she'd tried to keep her doubts in check.

"The hang? What is the hang?" Spiros asked, looking down into her sparkling eyes. At five feet eleven, he was several inches taller than her, but her heels brought her closer to his height.

"Oh." She blushed at his eyes boring into hers. "Um, it means you're learning how to dance fast. Getting the hang of it." Her eyes flitted all over the place, one minute they looked into his, the next over his shoulder, or over hers, or at his lips, or down. They couldn't look at him for more than one moment in case he saw how she felt about him.

And what was it that she felt…?

"Yes, yes. I get the hang of it." Spiros twirled her around unexpectedly and she laughed. "See? I get hang of it. Dancing, yes?"

"Yes." She was sure she was as red as her dress. "You've definitely got the hang of it."

They danced to several more up-tempo numbers before the band slowed down and played Bing Crosby's *White Christmas.*

Spiros pulled her closer and they slowly moved in circles.

Acutely aware of the looks they were receiving, Jenny tried to keep the tone of conversation light. "Um, do you have white Christmases in Greece?"

Spiros shrugged a shoulder. "Not so much. Most of Mykonos is white anyway."

Unsure of what he meant, she asked, "You mean you have snow all year round?"

"What? Snow? Oh, no, I mean Mykonos is white. All of our buildings and windmills are white." He shook his head in confusion. "Is that not what it meant?"

A soft laugh came from Jenny. "White Christmas means a snowy one. Does it snow in Mykonos at Christmas?"

"Oh, white means snow. Yes, sometimes. It can get cold. Brrr." He shook his shoulders to indicate he was cold. "But snow, not so much." Twirling her again, he elicited a giggle from her.

"Oh, well, as you can tell from our weather, we have summertime over Christmas, so no white Christmas for us. Our winter is in the middle of the year and it can get very cold. And sometimes, we have snow, too." Gazing up into his chocolatey eyes, she wondered what it would be like to visit Mykonos with Spiros playing tour guide. "Do you miss home?" she asked softly, watching the range of emotions fly across his face.

Spiros's expression dropped. "Yes. I miss Mykonos. I miss family. This will be first Christmas without them." His brows furrowed. "Some friends still there. I sent them all letters and some things from here, like koalas and kangasroos, but I do not know if they will get them, or even keep them." He hadn't mentioned his father's last words to him, or the knowledge of his grandfather being forbidden to have contact with him. He'd rung the day before to wish them Merry Christmas, and his grandfather had told him what had happened since his departure. Giorgio junior had forbidden his children from leaving Greece, but did not mind if they took up their grandfather's offers to work in Athens. Three of Spiros's brothers had jumped at the chance and moved their families there already. His fourth brother was being kept back until his baby was born and old enough, and because he felt guilty about leaving his mother on her own. His sisters were still being primed for marriage to good little Greek boys, and Giorgio senior had been told no contact with Spiros, or he would not see his grandchildren and great-grandchildren. But, since half of them lived in Athens now, Giorgio didn't take his son's threats that seriously. And Spiros's friends, whom he'd left behind, were dating, so they wished Spiros well and thanked him for their presents and letters.

"Oh…how sad. Why wouldn't they keep them?" Jenny asked. She had been waiting for Spiros to open up about the life he'd left behind, but so far, he'd only told her good things about Mykonos and his childhood. She'd overheard a conversation her mother was having with Spiros's aunt and wondered what sort of people would disown their son for seeking new adventures and horizons. But she would wait for Spiros to tell her in his own time as trust in any relationship was important.

Relationship?

They weren't in a relationship!

Jenny blushed at the thought and tried not to show her discomfort at thinking so far ahead of herself.

Not wanting to tell her too much too soon in case it warned her off, Spiros shrugged lightly. "They did not want me to come, did not want me to leave family. I was expected to stay in Mykonos with family, get married and raise family, like my father and brothers. But I wanted to see the world, to see new places, and people. Like you, Miss Jenny Marsh." He pulled her a little closer and gazed into her sparkling eyes. "I wanted to meet new people, and if I had not left, then I had not would have met you." He knew he'd stumbled over his English, but saw that she'd understood his intentions.

"That's very sweet, Spiros." She smiled brightly at him. "At least you have family here to be with. You're not alone, and your friends have taken to Armidale very well, as you have." Unable to tear her eyes away from his, she added, "And I'm glad you came, because then I wouldn't have met you, either. And I'm very glad that I did."

He swished her around the floor as if they'd been dancing together all of their lives, both comfortable in each other's arms. "I am very happy I did, Miss Jenny Marsh."

They ended the evening at midnight when everyone helped pack up the unused food for the local charity shelter, and stored the tables and chairs against the walls. Jenny drove Spiros and her sisters home and parked behind her brothers' and parents' cars. Waiting for her sisters to go inside, she slid an arm through his and gently guided him into the shadows and away from prying eyes. "Thank you for tonight. I enjoyed myself."

"Thank *you*, Miss Jenny," Spiros replied. "I enjoy very much."

"And your English is getting better, with my help."

"Yes, very much it is. I still get, how you say, the hang of it."

Jenny's giggle gaily drifted along on the summer breeze. "Yes, you are getting the hang of it." She whispered, "I guess I should go in."

"I will walk you." Spiros walked her to the front door where he nervously fumbled in his pocket. The present had sat there all night as he hadn't found a good time to give it to her. "Here, Miss Jenny, for you." He handed over a small, brightly gift-wrapped box.

"For me?" Her heart thundered in her chest as she eyed the box and slowly took it from him. "I…I didn't get you anything." She'd already replaced the bloody handkerchief with a box of pretty new ones in masculine colours, but hadn't thought of a Christmas present as she had no idea what to get him.

"That is all right, Miss Jenny. This is for you, for Christmas." He urged her to open it and watched as she hesitantly untied the bow and opened the box. Inside was a small velvet box which she gently pulled out and turned around to flip up the lid.

"Oh, Spiros, they're beautiful." The small gold, heart-shaped stud earrings glittered brightly under the porch light. A ruby heart sat in the middle and little emeralds surrounded them. "Oh, I…" Speechless, she didn't know what to say, or do, so she compulsively kissed his cheek. "Oh…oh…" Realising what she'd done, she pulled back. "Oh… oh…thank you." Unable to look at him, she stared down at the glistening studs in the box. No one had ever bought her a present so beautiful, certainly not any man. All she'd ever got from her dates were flowers and a creeping hand on her knee. But Spiros had not tried that, and after being so polite and well-mannered with her, she really should have got him something as a thank you, if she hadn't been lost for ideas. "Thank you," she murmured. "They're beautiful."

"Just like you, Miss Jenny Marsh." Spiros's fingers gently tipped her chin up so he could stare into her eyes. "You are beautiful, Miss Jenny Marsh. Most beautiful girl I have ever met, and you deserve beautiful jewellery. Yes?"

"Oh," came breathlessly out of her. "I…"

"Deserve beautiful things for beautiful woman." Spiros nodded. "You are beautiful, Miss Jenny Marsh." And, ever so gently, he placed his lips on hers and kissed her for the second time since they'd met.

And what seemed to last for an eternity in Jenny's mind, only lasted a few moments in reality as the front door was opened by her mother.

"Time to come in, Jenny. Say goodnight. Goodnight, Spiros, thank you for escorting our daughter to the dance this evening." She watched them, how they'd sprung apart at the sound of the door, how they stood staring at one another while she had spoken, and she noticed the twinkling box in Jenny's hand.

"Um." Jenny swallowed the lump in her throat. "Yes, um, goodnight, Spiros. Thank you for my present, they're beautiful." Glancing down, she hoped the break in connection would spur Spiros to move.

Sarah opened the screen door as motivation. "Goodnight, Spiros."

Spiros politely bowed to Sarah, remembering his manners at all times. "Mrs Marsh, goodnight and Merry Christmas." Stepping away, he turned back to add, "Goodnight and Merry Christmas, Miss Jenny." Smiling, he walked down the driveway and into his uncle's yard, waving as he approached the house.

"Oh…wow…" Jenny had trouble catching her breath, and her mother had to lead her inside, closing the door behind them. "Wow."

"They're very pretty." Sarah looked at the earrings. "But it's time for bed. Off you go." She watched her star-struck daughter float upstairs and turn right for her bedroom. Smiling, she wandered into the living room to usher her husband along. They'd waited for their last child to enter the house before turning in themselves.

"He kissed her, didn't he?" Matthew asked as he took his wife's hand and flicked off the light on the side table.

"He did. Bought her a pair of very pretty earrings, too."

"Mmm, think it's going too fast?" They reached the top of the stairs and noticed the light under Jenny and Rebecca's door.

"I don't think it's fast enough for Jenny's liking." Sarah's smile grew bigger. "But at least he's a very polite young man and uses his manners. His parents have taught him well, and Mrs Stephanides told me that she and his uncle have taught him about our culture, so he understands what it takes to be in our society when it comes to dating our girls. They taught their sons the same thing and expect other boys to treat their daughter the same way. I don't think we have too much to worry about when it comes to Spiros." They entered their bedroom and closed the door.

"Is she interested in any other boys?" Matthew asked and flipped back the bed covers.

"No," Sarah stated matter-of-factly. "I'd say Spiros is the one, and I think Jenny knows it."

*****

On New Year's Eve, the town of Armidale gathered in the main street, which had been blocked off for the celebrations, and partied from lunchtime onward. Tables and chairs were set up in the street outside of cafés and restaurants. Christmas decorations were still strung across from store to store, and a huge stage was set up in the middle of the street so people at either end could hear the band play at different times throughout the day. But come seven p.m., the lights came on in a burst of colour, and everyone congregated to celebrate another year. Families mingled and helped serve food and drink when stores closed for the night. There were vendors selling fairy floss on sticks, or in bags, ice cream parlours thrived and were full to capacity as the townspeople wandered up and down, or sat and enjoyed the band, or music, coming through the loudspeakers.

Spiros had invited Jenny and was escorting her up and down the street. Dressed in his blue summer pants and matching shirt, he was smart, yet casual next to Jenny in her cool blue cotton dress and medium heels. Her hair was twisted up into a curly ponytail which was decorated with flowers.

"You look very lovely, Miss Jenny," Spiros told her as they walked.

She blushed, as she always did when Spiros paid her a compliment. "Thank you, Spiros. You look very nice, too. It's been very warm today," she deflected.

"Yes, it has. As warm as Mykonos in summer." Spiros thought back to the summers back home and was glad he'd been in the cool comfort of the meat shop on hot days.

"What is it like?" Jenny asked, having only read a little about it in books, and heard a little more from Spiros in the last few months. "Mykonos, I mean."

A small smile played on his lips. "It is very…how you say…we very tightly knotted together." His hands gesticulated with his explanation. "We all know each other, like here." He motioned at all in front of and behind them. "Mykonos is island, like Australia, but sometimes the town of Chora is also called Mykonos Town. I am from there. We have ferry boats to take us from island to island, to Athens. We have windmills, many windmills. We have water in front of homes and businesses, and we all know each other. You would like it, I think." He boldly stared at her. "I would like to take you back one day, Miss Jenny, to see my Mykonos."

Surprised at such a statement, Jenny came to a halt. "What?"

"I would very much like to take you to my home, Mykonos, one day, so you can see it." Spiros nodded in excitement. The thought of taking the beautiful Jenny Marsh home to show her off, and show her his island, thrilled him.

Jenny had seen pictures of Greece, and the Greek islands, in books, and while they looked incredibly beautiful, she could never imagine having enough money to visit there.

"I…don't know what to say…" Glancing around for a distraction from his gaze, she added, "It's a lovely idea, and I'd love to see it one day, but it's a pipe dream."

"Pipe dream? What is pipe dream?" Spiros asked as they continued walking.

"Oh, well, it's a dream that's too wonderful to possibly ever come true, that's a pipe dream," Jenny explained as they passed her sisters and their dates.

"Why would it never happen? I come from Mykonos to Australia. Why can we not go back to Mykonos? Why can I not show you my home?" He laid a gentle hand on her arm and pulled her to a stop. "Why can we not go back? Why can I not show you Mykonos?"

"Oh, well…" Jenny, unable to come up with a good enough reason especially since they weren't a couple, so she didn't want to push it, finally shrugged. "I don't really know why you couldn't, it just seems too fantastical, that's all. How would I ever get to Mykonos? How much does it cost? When would it happen?"

"I do not know, Miss Jenny." Spiros smiled. "But one day, maybe. Yes?" He hoped against hope that it would happen one day.

The blush deepened, and Jenny became embarrassed, so she moved them on. "I guess one never does know what the future holds. You just never know." Leaving it on that note, they chatted with neighbours and people they knew, ate delicious delicacies from Greece, and traditional foods from Australia, sampled the fairy floss and toffee apples, and had ice cream parfaits for dessert.

"Oh, did I thank you for the roses?" Jenny remembered. Spiros had not only sent her the bunch on Christmas Eve, but another earlier that day as well.

"Yes, Miss Jenny, you did." Spiros would have sent her a bunch every week if he could afford it, and he'd been seriously thinking about his future in Armidale and how he could afford to give her nice things. Maybe even provide a home for her there.

"Oh, good. They really are beautiful, and you really didn't need to…" She shyly glanced at him. "But I'm glad you did. It was very sweet of you." She also hoped it meant he was sweet on her because it was fairly obvious to all that she was sweet on him.

"I am sweet." Spiros beamed his happiness. "They are beautiful, like Miss Jenny."

"Oh, Spiros," she murmured. "You really need to just call me Jenny."

"Ladies and gentlemen, it's only five minutes until the new year, get your party hats and streamers, and make sure to be looking to the west end of the street for the fireworks," boomed across the loudspeaker.

There was a flurry of activity as everyone jostled for a good position, and managed to come to a halt thirty seconds before New Year.

Spiros stood to Jenny's left, his right arm gently, but casually, around her waist, and she shivered at his touch despite the warmth of the night.

"Ten, nine, eight, seven, six, five, four, three, two, one, happy new year!"

The fireworks exploded in the night sky, lighting it up with every colour of the rainbow, and every face was turned up to watch, mirroring the colours above them.

After five minutes of watching, Spiros glanced at Jenny's excited face and leaned in to whisper in her ear. "Happy new year, Miss Jenny."

Startled, Jenny looked over her shoulder at him, her lips close to his. She breathed in his cologne, he breathed in her perfume, both breathed in the musky hot scent of attraction, and his lips closed over hers for a brief tender kiss.

"Oh…" came out as whispered breath from between her lips. If it was one thing she wanted, it was more of that, but she was still aware of the people around her and who would be watching. "Happy new year, Spiros." Reluctantly, she pulled back and turned to finish watching the fireworks which lasted another ten minutes.

Once done, the festivities wound down as shops were shut for the night, and tables and chairs were packed away. Slowly, the crowd thinned as party-goers left, either walking home, or going off to find their cars down side streets, so they could drive home.

Spiros had driven to town with Nikos and his cousins, while Jenny had driven her sisters, so they met up with family and bade each other goodnight, but, upon arriving home, Jenny found Spiros waiting on his uncle's front porch.

Once her family was inside, Jenny wandered over the wire fence and waited for Spiros to join her. "I thought we had said our goodnights." Keeping her voice low, she glanced over her shoulder to see if anyone was watching.

"We did. But I wanted to say it again. Happy new year, Miss Jenny Marsh." He presented her with a bouquet of carnations tied with ribbon. "It is January 1951. New Year, new home, new Spiros. Flowers for January."

"Oh, Spiros, you didn't have to get me another bouquet, the roses are enough." Jenny lifted them to her nose and breathed in their scent.

"I know, but I want to. It is a new year. New times to look forward to. Yes? Much dancing to look forward to, parties and good times. New job. I am very excited by prospect of new year, Miss Jenny, and what I may bring with you." He nodded excitedly. "You are part of my life now, Miss Jenny." Shyness overtook him as he stared at her glittery blue eyes. "You are my life now, Miss Jenny."

In awe of the words that had just flowed into her ears, Jenny stood unmoving, her brain working overtime to comprehend the meaning, her heart ramming against her chest, her blood singing in her veins. He had just said that she was his life now. No boy, or man, had ever said that to her, said anything even remotely close to that to her, and it made her feel as if she was the only girl in the world. The only girl for Spiros Stephanopoulos. "Oh…I don't know what to say to that,

Spiros, it was beautiful, thank you."

"Beautiful, like you, Miss Jenny," he murmured and watched her delicate features blush. "We will spend more time together, yes? Over summer?"

"Um…yes, yes we will," she agreed. "There are lots of things to do. The local pool and park, dances at the rec centre, we volunteer as well, so lots to keep us busy if you're willing, or able, to join in."

"Yes, yes, I am willing to do anything you do, Miss Jenny," Spiros said.

"Jenny, time to come in now," Matthew called from the door.

"Oh." Her head flew around. "Just a minute." She watched him shut the door and turned back to bid Spiros goodnight. "Um, I'll see you tomorrow, then. I mean…later today." Smiling, she held the flowers tighter. "Thank you again for the roses and for these."

"Thank *you*, Miss Jenny." Spiros leaned over the fence and gently laid his lips on hers.

Jenny melted into them, her lips moving in time with his. A moan escaped her, and like lightning, her eyes flew open and she pulled back. "Oh…oh…I…ah…"

Spiros's lips curled up. "Goodnight, Miss Jenny. Girl of my dreams." With a little wave of his fingers, he backed away. "Goodnight, Miss Jenny." He walked backwards until he hit the porch and then turned and went inside.

"Oh…" came out of a dizzy Jenny Marsh. "My gosh, I…" Spinning around in circles, she danced across the yard to her own front door and floated up to her room.

January 1951

Through the heat of January, everyone tried their best to stay cool; either in the cooling comfort of the rec centre, or under sprinklers come evening time. Games of soccer, cricket and football were played at night on the weekends, Jenny continued teaching Spiros English every night, and attended church every Sunday.

Spiros finally conceded that the only job he was good at was being a butcher, so he took his uncle up on his offer and accepted the job at *Stephanides Meats*, while Xenos and Nicodemus got jobs in local shops in town.

Glad to be making money again, Spiros started saving in earnest. His uncle didn't charge him all that much for rent and board, and he didn't have a car, or home, to call his own, but if he was going to continue courting Jenny Marsh, then he needed to figure something out. He couldn't keep relying on her to drive them around town in her car; he had to have his own. So, that was the next step in his plan.

February 1951

It was Wednesday the 14th of February, 1951, Valentine's Day, and Spiros was all set to make a big deal out of his first Valentine's in Australia with the beautiful Jenny Marsh. First, he put on his best summer suit, borrowed his uncle's car, and drove next door so he could do the gentlemanly thing. He knocked on the door to the Marsh household and waited.

Sarah answered the door to a beaming Spiros holding a huge bunch of red roses. "Oh, hello, Spiros, please come in. Jenny will be just a moment." Opening the door wide, she waited for Spiros to step through before calling her daughter. "Jenny, Spiros is here." Turning back to her daughter's date, she added, "And how are you, Spiros? Keeping cool this hot February day?"

"Yes, Mrs Marsh. Very cool. I have been in the butcher shop all day, but now I am here to take Miss Jenny out for Valentine's Day." He held out the flowers to show her. "I bought her roses."

"And they're beautiful." Jenny descended the stairs in her bright red and white summer party dress. The ruby heart earrings he'd given her for Christmas sparkled in her ears. "They're beautiful."

Stunned by her beauty, Spiros extended his arms. "So are you, Miss Jenny. So beautiful."

"Oh." Blushing redder than the roses, Jenny took the bouquet, buried her nose in them, inhaled deeply and sighed. "I love roses, and they're perfect for Valentine's, thank you. Mum, can you put these in a vase for me?" Relinquishing them to her mother, she turned to Spiros. "So…where are we going?"

"Ah, you will have to wait and see, Miss Jenny. After you." With a smile wider than the Harbour Bridge, he opened the door and escorted her to the car where he helped her into the passenger side before running around to the driver's seat. They chatted about their days while he drove into town and parked at the local Greek restaurant. When he held her door open, she alighted, and he took her arm and escorted her inside where they were seated.

"I haven't been here before," Jenny remarked, looking around at the décor. Traditional Greek attire, flags, and memorabilia adorned the walls, and Spiros pointed them out with a brief explanation.

After the wine came, the food was served and they enjoyed their three-course meal ending with an incredibly sweet baklava.

"Oh, this is delicious," Jenny murmured. "I've only had it once before when I went with Effie to the Greek Club ages ago." Sliding the spoon into her mouth, she savoured the last bite, closing her eyes around the flaky honey pastry concoction. Swallowing, she removed the spoon slowly; making sure every last tasty morsel was devoured. Her eyes drifted open and she licked her lips, seeing Spiros eyeing her hungrily as if she were a tasty baklava. The candles illuminated the hunger in his chocolate eyes, the full parted lips, the creaminess of his skin.

Jenny stared, barely breathing, unable to contain the desire welling up in her from her loins to her throat; it was overwhelming and making her want to do things with Spiros that she'd never done with any other boy, or man, making her want to do more than kiss him; a kiss she hoped her parents didn't stop.

"Jenny," Spiros murmured raggedly. "You are so beautiful. The most beautiful woman I have ever met." He drowned in the glow the candlelight set around her. Her hair, twisted up into a chignon, added to the golden glow as light reflected off it. Her skin was creamy white and blemish-free, her figure slim and alluring, her lips red and inviting, her eyes sparkling with desire and lust and love.

The moment was interrupted by the waiter bringing more coffee.

The spell broken, they both drank and avoided eye contact until a few minutes later when Spiros paid for the bill and they left. He escorted her to the car and then drove to the lookout above town where he parked and turned off the ignition.

"Miss Jenny. I have…a present for you." Removing the small box from his pocket, he presented the red-wrapped gift. "I hope you like it."

With a pounding heart, she smiled and took the gift. "I'm sure I'll love it." Lifting the lid and pulling out the velvet box, she opened it to reveal a small gold heart pendant with a ruby heart that had emeralds around it. "Oh, Spiros, it matches the earrings you gave me. How beautiful."

"May I?" he asked, pointing to the necklace.

"Of course. Here." She held it out to him and then turned, so he could clasp it around her neck.

He nervously managed to do it up without dropping it and waited for her to turn around.

Jenny adjusted it to sit just so on her breast bone. "It's beautiful. You obviously bought it at the same time as the earrings. Thank you for both of them." Impulsively, and because of the unfamiliar flaming in her pelvis, she moved forward and kissed him on the lips.

He responded gently, surprised she had made the first move.

With no parents around to stop them, Jenny wanted more, she shifted her body so she was closer and kissed him harder. Having heard stories from her sisters and friends about kissing and the different styles of it, and how many of Armidale's boys would try and shove their tongues into the girl's mouths in a style known as French kissing, Jenny decided to be different. With a hunger rising in her stomach for more than just the lip pressing they were doing, she started opening her lips as they kissed, and a few moments later her tongue peeked out and slid across Spiros's lips.

Surprised, he pulled back and stared at her with wide eyes. "Jenny?"

"Do Greeks not…do it that way?" she panted, her hands against his chest, her face in his. She wanted him more than she'd ever wanted any boy in her whole entire twenty-two years, eight months, three weeks and three days of life.

Spiros gently held her by her arms. "Yes, we do. Do Australians?"

"Some…of us," she murmured, staring into his eyes. "I want you, Spiros. Kiss me." With no hesitation, Jenny planted her lips on his mouth and set her tongue free to mate with his, which was strong and willing. They probed, not too far, for not too long. Her hands flattened on his chest, feeling the wild beating of his heart beneath them. Her body pushed itself up against him, and he wrapped his arms around her as she wrapped hers around his neck. The burning in her pelvis made her ache for him, and when her leg fell between his, it was left with the imprint of his desire.

Hard and full, aching for his Jenny. *His* Jenny. No one else's. *His* Jenny Marsh.

All time disappeared and they barely came up for air, but finally, they pulled apart, panting, wanting, needing each other.

"I love you, Spiros," Jenny gasped, watching his face for emotion. "I love you."

He beamed back at her. "I love you, too, Miss Jenny Marsh. I think I have since I first saw you when I got off the boat." Brushing a strand of her hair aside, he lovingly cupped her face. "I love you, too, Jenny."

Jenny's smile reflected his. "You finally called me Jenny."

"Yes." His eyes glittered brightly with love. "*My* Jenny."

Her heart thundered. "Your Jenny?"

"Yes, *my* Jenny," he murmured. "Will you be *my* Jenny?"

"Yes," she almost screamed. "Oh, God, yes, Spiros, yes." She smothered him in kisses until her mouth landed back on his and she pushed her tongue in. The kiss lasted long into the night when they finally pulled apart.

"Does this mean we are now, how you say, going steady?" Spiros asked, his sizeable manhood aching at the thought of his Jenny's body on his.

"Oh." Surprised, she sat back, having thought for a moment it had been a proposal. "Um, yes…yes, I guess it does." Fixing her hair back in place, she took the moment to calm herself down and flicked on the internal light to check her watch. "Oh, no," she gasped. "It's past my curfew. We must get going, or my parents will kill me *and* you and not let us see each other. Quick, let's go." She flicked off the light and settled into her seat.

"Curfew?" Spiros started the car. "There is curfew? What is curfew?"

"Oh, it's a time when young ladies need to be home by. It's a work night, and I always need to be home by ten-thirty at the latest and it's *well* after eleven. Quickly, we need to get home."

Driving quickly, but safely, Spiros got them on their way. "What is curfew for weekends?"

"Midnight, unless it's a celebration, or dance. Then we can be a little late."

"Is this not celebration?"

That brought a smile to her lips. "I guess Valentine's is a celebration. But since I'm out late, my parents may not be happy, and may not let me out again."

Within ten minutes they arrived in Jenny's driveway and she quickly wiped her lips to make sure there was no smeared lipstick.

Spiros alighted and opened her door, escorting her to her porch. "Goodnight, Miss Jenny. My Jenny. See you tomorrow for our next lesson." He gently kissed her hand then watched her lips fly into a smile.

"Goodnight, Spiros, my Spiros. I'll see you tomorrow." Opening the door, she quietly went inside and shut it behind her.

"And what hour do you call this, young lady?" Matthew asked from the lounge room. He'd heard the car in the drive and knew it could only be them.

"I know, Dad. It's an hour after my curfew. We lost track of time. I'm sorry, it won't happen again." She kept moving as she talked, hoping she could make it upstairs without too much hassle.

"Jenny." His tone stopped her. Hauling himself to his feet, Matthew walked over to her and took her by the arms. "You've never been late for curfew before."

"First time for everything." She raised her brows in hope.

He noticed the necklace and nodded at it. "A present from Spiros?"

"Yes," she gushed and then calmed down. "A Valentine's to go with the earrings he bought me for Christmas." She hoped he didn't make a big deal out of it.

"It's very pretty. He must like you a lot. Do you like him?" It wasn't the first time he'd had to deal with an infatuated daughter.

"Yes." She fidgeted, wanting to get away to the safety of her room.

"A lot?"

Blushing, she added, *"Yes."*

"Do you think he's the boy for you?"

Looking her father straight in the eye, she said, "Yes, I do. And tonight he asked me to be his Jenny. We're going steady because he's the only boy I want in the whole of Armidale. The whole of New South Wales, Australia, and the world. He's the only boy I want, and I'm now his girlfriend and he's my boyfriend. Will that be a problem for you and Mum?" she asked defiantly.

"As long as you don't do anything stupid, or foolish, no," he said. "It's about time you found yourself a steady boy to date. We've been wondering when it would happen."

"What...?" She saw the twinkle in his eye and relaxed. "You mean...you don't have a problem with me dating Spiros?"

"Why would we?" Matthew flicked off the hall light and led her upstairs. "We know his relatives, he's proved himself to be a polite, well-mannered young man, and you haven't run around with many boys, so, we don't have a problem if you date him steadily. Just promise me you won't do anything stupid and won't break curfew again."

Jenny was weak with relief. "I won't, I promise. Night, Dad."

"Night, Jenny."

*****

The next day, when Spiros turned up after tea for his English lesson with Jenny, he wanted to talk to her parents first.

"Ah... Mr and Mrs Marsh, may I have word, please? Yes?" He nodded and smiled hopefully.

"Of course, Spiros, what's it about?" Sarah was pouring cold drinks for them and she watched him fidget. Her husband had told her all about the night before, and while she wasn't surprised that it had happened, she was surprised by how quickly it had.

"Um…it seems Miss Jenny and I are, how you say, going steady," he said. "I had not meant to ask last night, I was waiting until her birthday to ask her, so had not had a chance to ask permission *to date,* Miss Jenny." He shifted nervously from foot to foot, unsure of how they would take it.

Matthew eyed him up and down. "What do you mean; you hadn't meant to ask last night? Do you not want to date Jenny?"

"Oh, yes, yes, I do," Spiros hastened to explain. "I had plans to ask Miss Jenny to go steady on her birthday. But, last night when I gave her the present, it came out, and I asked last night before getting permission to do so." While his family had told him about the best way to present himself when asking for permission, he still felt very awkward and hoped they didn't say no. "So, now, I must get permission to date Miss Jenny and go steady." His palms were as sweaty as his mouth was dry, and he hoped against hope they would say yes.

"Are you serious about my daughter, Spiros?" Matthew crossed his arms and leaned against the kitchen counter.

"Yes, Mr Marsh. Very serious. Maybe serious for lifetime, but for now, we date. Yes?" He searched their faces for any kind of answer, and watched as they exchanged glances, small smiles on their lips. "Yes?"

"Yes, Spiros, you have our permission to date Jenny." Matthew saw Spiros's eager grin. "But there are some rules."

"Yes, yes, rules, yes." Spiros beamed with happiness.

"No more having her out past curfew unless you have permission," Matthew told him. "No disrespecting us, or our daughter, and no proposals, at least not this year. You will spend some time getting to know each other and dating, and you will work hard to provide for any kind of life you want to give my daughter. Do you understand? They are the rules."

"Yes, yes, rules. I understand. I have permission to date Miss Jenny." His smile said it all. "I have permission to date Miss Jenny."

"Yes, Spiros, you have permission to date Jenny." Matthew straightened and held out his hand which Spiros shook excitedly.

"Thank you, thank you, so much. I date Miss Jenny."

"Yes, Spiros, you're dating Miss Jenny." Sarah handed him two glasses of icy lemonade. "Take these and go practise your English. Jenny's waiting."

Carefully grasping the wet glasses, and still nodding in excitement, he rushed out to the front porch where Jenny was waiting.

"So, do we think he's worth it?" Sarah asked and handed her husband a glass of lemonade.

"I think *Jenny* thinks he's worth it. And as long as he proves it and does right by her, then that's all that matters." He chuckled. "Eager young pup, isn't he?"

May 1951

The next three months sailed by in a flurry of birthday parties, celebrations, dances and activities that kept everyone busy.

Spiros's English was improving all the time. He worked hard, saved harder, and only spent money on Jenny, especially when it came to her birthday in May.

"Flowers for my Jenny," Spiros said when she opened the front door.

"Oh, Spiros, they're beautiful." Jenny took the huge bouquet of roses and waved him through the door. "It's just a few more minutes and then we'll go. I'll pop these in some water."

He followed her through the house into the kitchen, watching how her shapely blue chiffon and satin party dress swished around her very shapely calves that were accentuated by her mid-heel blue party shoes.

She wore the sapphire earrings and necklace set that was a twenty-first birthday present from her parents, along with the matching bracelet from her siblings, plus a small gold watch from her father's parents, and a sapphire ring from her mother's parents. But, since it was her twenty-third, she wasn't expecting too much, if anything. The family was, however, all meeting at her favourite restaurant for tea.

Jenny quickly filled a vase and arranged the roses into it. "They're beautiful, Spiros. I love them." Turning, she bumped into him, laughed, moved the vase out of the way, and kissed him. "And I love you for it."

"I love you too, my Jenny." He followed her out of the kitchen and waited at the bottom of the stairs while she dashed up to leave the flowers in her room.

"So, Spiros, got a great present for my sister?" Ned asked as he pounded down the stairs to stop right in front of his potential future brother-in-law.

"Yes, Mr Ned. Very special for my Jenny." Spiros watched Jenny float down the stairs and stop on the bottom step next to her brother.

"Not being a pest are you, Ned?" She swatted him on the shoulder. "When are you moving out?"

"When I get married," he replied, and swatted her right back. "But with the way things are going, you and Spiros here will make that happen before any of us." Not that Ned was single, by any means. He had his fair share of girls swooning over him, as did his younger brothers. At six-foot, and twenty-five, he was prime meat for all the young girls in town. But he wanted to be a lawyer and get a good head start in the profession before thinking of getting married and raising kids as his older siblings all had. With his piercing blue eyes and mop of golden-brown hair, he knew he was a looker and that another few years of waiting wouldn't hurt his chances any.

"Ned," Jenny chastised, thoroughly red from the mention of marriage. "Any girl would be lucky to have you."

"Of course, don't I know it," he replied not so modestly. "That's why I know I've got time."

The rest of the family came downstairs and they donned their coats before stepping outside into the cool autumn air.

Spiros held out Jenny's coat while she slid her arms in, and he kissed her cheek before letting go.

She smiled and took his arm, so he could escort her out to his uncle's car which he had borrowed for the night.

Her sisters slid into the backseat of their parent's car, and her brothers took theirs.

They arrived at *The Cherry Blossom* restaurant to be greeted by the rest of the Marsh family; older brothers Edward, Dudley, and Lawrence with their wives and children, and older sisters Joanna and Harriet with their husbands and children. Effie and her date, Spiros's friend Nicodemus, were also there waiting.

After greetings and hugs and kisses from her nieces and nephews, they settled down to a lavish meal of delicate prawn cocktails in a rich sauce, roasted chicken with vegetables lightly sprinkled with lemon and herbs, and decadent chocolate cake and raspberry chiffon pie for dessert.

"You've gone all out, really, this is too much for a twenty-third birthday," Jenny told everyone as she glanced down the long table at them. She sat at the head with her parents to her left, and Spiros to her right.

"It's just a fancy dinner, love." Sarah patted her hand. "We have them all the time." She was glad that all of her children could make it, even though her two eldest daughters and two of her daughters-in-law were pregnant.

"I know, Mum. It just seems so much for a non-significant birthday," Jenny went on.

"Which is why we only bought you non-significant presents." Rebecca laughed. "You know how it is. Only what we need, not what we want."

"Speaking of," Faye cut in. "Can you open them now?" She motioned to a waiter who brought the two presents over to the table and sat them down in front of Jenny.

"Oh, goodness!" she exclaimed. "What could these possibly be?" Feigning surprise, she lifted the smaller square box and shook it. "My, it's very heavy. What could it possibly be?"

"You won't find out unless you open them," Arthur remarked and took a swig of beer. "Are we *really* going to do this with every birthday?"

"Oh, hush, you," Jenny joked and stood so she could open the box. "Oh, the boots I wanted. I did need a new pair." She held the black leather lace-up boots aloft to show everyone and read the card. "From my siblings I see. Thank you all." Placing the shoes in the box, she set it aside and opened the larger, rectangle box below it. "Oh, my goodness, it's beautiful." She held a three-quarter sapphire blue wool coat up high. It had sparkling buttons, faux fur cuffs and collar, and a matching blue satin lining. "Oh, Mum, Dad, this is gorgeous. I'll wear it forever. Thank you."

She set the coat down and kissed both her parents' cheeks, then ran around the table kissing her siblings in the same manner until she came back to her seat. "Thank you all so much. I needed both so much, and the coat is amazing." She slid it over her arms and wrapped it around her. The colour made her eyes sparkle, and she flipped up the collar to feel the warmth of the fur. "Oh, it's beautiful."

A smattering of applause went around the restaurant making Jenny blush when she realised it was for her.

"Oh." She quickly slid off the coat and folded it back into its packaging. "Thank you all, so much." Embarrassed, she sat down and had a sip of her wine.

"And what's your present for Jenny?" Nicodemus nudged Spiros in the ribs. "Gonna give it to her?" His English hadn't progressed as far as his friend's, but then he wasn't getting the extracurricular lessons Spiros had received.

"Oh…I do not know." Spiros glanced nervously around the table. "I had hoped to do it in private." He noted the serious expressions on her parents' faces.

"And you can." Jenny reached out and grasped his hand warmly. "You can give it to me later when we leave. You don't have to do it now."

"Good, good, later, yes." Spiros cleared his throat and drank the last of his coffee, his left hand still encased in Jenny's. He saw her family exchange glances and wondered if everything was okay, or whether they had a problem with him not wanting to give her the present.

After another hour, everyone stood up to leave and slowly made their way out to their cars.

"We'll take your presents home, love." Sarah picked up the larger box and handed it to Ned. "So you don't have to worry about them."

"Thank you. We'll be home later." Jenny held the door open for her mother as she carried the smaller box out.

"You know your curfew?" Matthew asked, buttoning up his coat against the chilly air.

"Yes, Dad. Eleven-thirty because it's a work night, but also my birthday. We'll be home by then." She kissed his cheek and waved goodbye to everyone before settling into Spiros's car.

Spiros drove to the local lake and parked alongside, so they could watch the moonlight dance across the ripples in the water. It was a chilly night, for May, and they cuddled together under a blanket he'd put in the car before picking her up. They also kept warm by getting all hot and heavy under that blanket.

"Oh, Spiros," Jenny sighed and put her forehead to his cheek. "I love you, so much. I want to do so much more than just kiss. I wish we could do so much more." On a recent trip to a local town, Jenny had stopped in at the local bookstores and library to see if there were any books on sex, or at least being in relationships, or having children. She'd only found one, and barely had time to look at the pictures before the eager eye of the store attendant cast a critical eye over her, but had seen enough to know the feelings she was having was love and lust and desire. That her womanhood was aching for his manhood, and she wanted to join in the act of sex. But not being married, she couldn't, at least, not if she didn't want to get pregnant out of wedlock. And, as far as she knew, protection was not available for unmarried girls. Another sigh left her. "I wish we could do so much more than just kiss."

"So do I, my Jenny. So do I." Spiros kissed her forehead and gazed into her eyes. "I love you, my Jenny. I cannot stand not doing more. But it is a must. We must not do any more than kiss. We will both be in trouble. A lot of trouble."

"I know," she murmured against his lips. "But I love you, and I want to do more with you."

"And we must get to know each other. And I must work hard and save money for a car and home one day. We must take our time and do things right, so we have your parents' blessing." He tore his lips from hers. "That is why I bought you this..." He dug into his jacket pocket and pulled out a gift box. "For you, my Jenny. For your birthday."

"Oh, Spiros." She opened the box and found a small velvet box inside. Pulling at the lid, she saw a gold heart-shaped ring with a ruby heart centre and small emeralds around it. It glittered in the moonlight coming through the windscreen. "Oh, it's exactly like the earrings and necklace." She hoped against hope it was an engagement ring, but waited for him to say it.

"It is promise ring," Spiros told her. "I was going to give it to you today and ask you to be my Jenny with promise of love and commitment, but we were eager on Valentine's and ended up going steady then, so we jump gun. The ring matches the set. You like?"

Disappointed that it wasn't an engagement ring, she smiled as brightly as she could. "*Of course* I like it. *I love it.* Will you put it on for me?" Holding out the box, she waited while he took hold of it and slipped it onto her right ring finger.

"Miss Jenny, will you go steady with me and be my Jenny, with the promise that I will be faithful and date only you, my Jenny, and that you will only date me."

Jenny's smile softened at his words and she glanced from the ring to Spiros. "*Of course* I'll be your Jenny. *Of course* we'll go steady, and, *of course*, you'll be the only boy I date. I love you, Spiros Stephanopoulos."

"I love you, Jenny Marsh."

Their lips locked, and when eleven-twenty rolled around they reluctantly pulled apart and drove home with Jenny snuggled up beside Spiros under the blanket. He walked her to her door and kissed her again. "I love you, my Jenny."

"I love you, Spiros." She flung her arms around his neck and passionately kissed him, barely hearing the door being unlocked and left open. "Ugh…" Reluctantly, she pulled away. "I'll see you tomorrow after tea for your lesson. We'll be reading *Pride and Prejudice.*"

"Ah, we finally get to read that?" Spiros murmured against her lips.

"Yes." She kissed him and let go. "See you tomorrow, my Spiros."

"Tomorrow, my Jenny." He kissed her hand and skipped back to the car.

Giggling, she went inside and closed the screen door, waving at

Spiros in the headlights as he backed out of her drive and drove into his. When she couldn't see him, she closed and locked the door.

"Have a good night, love?" Sarah asked as she walked out of the lounge room to escort her daughter upstairs. "I've left your presents at the end of your bed, and have it ready with a hot water bottle."

"Thanks, Mum." They ascended the stairs arm in arm. "I had a wonderful night and look…" She held out her hand. "He gave me a promise ring. Said he was going to ask me tonight to go steady with him, but we got ahead of ourselves at Valentine's. It matches the earrings and necklace he gave me."

Sarah was happy for her daughter. "It's very pretty, Jenny. He loves you very much." She saw the beaming smile as Jenny looked down at the ring.

"I love him, too, and we are now promised to each other. Do you and Dad like him?" She'd never stopped to ask if her parents liked her choice in a date. A foreigner, at that!

"We like him just fine, love. But now it's time for bed. Goodnight." She kissed her daughter's cheeks and watched her float off to her room.

October 1951

Winter in Armidale was cold, so Spiros's lessons continued inside the Marsh residence under her parents' watchful eye as they often stopped reading to kiss. But come spring, and with Spiros's English being perfected, they celebrated his first year anniversary of having arrived in Australia, with his friends who were renting a small flat together, in the backyard of his uncle's house with a big barbecue and lots of ouzo.

"We are all here to celebrate the one year anniversary of Spiros's arrival in not only Australia, but Armidale as well," Nikos senior said loud enough for all to hear. Not only was Jenny and her family there, but many other neighbours as well. "I know I not only speak for me, but my entire family," Nikos waved a hand at them, "when I say, we have had a great time having you here and am glad that you decided to come. And we don't mind if you still live at home because we know it keeps you close to young Jenny Marsh." He lifted his glass while everyone laughed, cheered or whistled, making Jenny blush and hide her face in Spiros's shoulder in embarrassment, while he tightened his arm around her. "So, put your hands together, for Spiros—"

"And Xenos and Nicodemus," Spiros cut in, pointing at his friends nearby.

"And Xenos and Nicodemus," Nikos went on, "and their first anniversary here in Australia."

Cheering went around the crowd and someone started playing Greek music on the record player.

Knocking back another shot glass of ouzo, Nikos waved everyone to stand up and get in a big circle for the Greek kalamatianos dance.

Laughing, Jenny tried to tell Spiros no while he pulled her into the circle, but she relented when Effie grabbed her hand and danced beside her.

"Did I tell you, yet?" Effie asked as they danced to the right.

"Tell me what? I haven't seen you in ages." Jenny swung to the left and danced back to the right.

"I'm engaged," Effie burst out and let go of Jenny's right hand to hold up her own. "See. I have a ring."

Jenny's head spun around and she came to a halt. "Oh, Effie. How exciting for you. When did it happen?" She hugged her friend and grabbed her hand to look at the narrow gold band with a tiny speck of a diamond.

"This evening, when he came to pick me up for the party. He asked my parents and they said yes. Then he asked me and I said yes." She excitedly jumped up and down. "I'm getting married."

"Married?" Spiros asked. "To who?" He came to a stop beside them and then noticed Nicodemus lurking behind Effie. "Nicodemus, you old dog. You did this?"

Nicodemus grinned. "Yep. Figured I'd better get myself a wife while I could. Not getting any younger. Neither are you. When are you proposing?" He slung an arm around Spiros's shoulders.

"When I am ready," Spiros replied and glanced at the ring. "When is the wedding?"

"Christmas," Effie said, a hand moving to her stomach. "May as well get it over and done with, right?" A slightly sick expression came over her. "I need to freshen up. Come with me, Jenny?" Grabbing her hand, she pulled her into the house, found the bathroom, and pushed Jenny ahead of her. She shut the door and leaned against it, letting out a deep breath.

"You okay, Effie?" Jenny studied her friend's face and mannerisms. "Are you—"

"Pregnant," Effie burst out and quickly covered her mouth with both hands, scared that someone had heard.

"Oh…my gosh, Effie. That means you and Nicodemus have been…" Not wanting to say the words *having sex*, Jenny made hand gestures. "You know."

"Doing weird hand gestures?" Effie smiled wryly. "You mean having sex? Yes, we have. Ever since my birthday two months ago—"

"Which means—" Jenny cut in.

"I'm anywhere up to two months pregnant."

"Were you not…using…?" Jenny blushed, being the good Catholic girl she was, she didn't like to talk about such things. "Protection," she whispered.

"You're kidding, right?" Effie frowned. "Here in Armidale?" She scoffed and started pacing. "I only found out a few days ago, and that means I'll be up to four months come Christmas, hence, the wedding."

"Do your parents know?" Jenny's heart went out to her friend, but they'd all heard the sermons at church and had all been warned from other girls who'd gotten themselves in the family way.

"I just said I found out a few days ago, so, no, I haven't told them. They'll go xiroi karpoi. Nuts!"

"Then how come Nicodemus chose today of all days to propose?" Jenny's quick mind calculated dates. "Does he know?"

Grimacing, Effie didn't answer, but she did dry heave into the toilet.

Screwing up her nose, Jenny found a clean cloth and rinsed it under the cold tap. After wringing it, she laid it around Effie's neck. "You told him."

"The day I found out," she muttered, slouching onto the floor. "He's the one who suggested we get married. Oh…" Taking the cloth, she patted her face. "How could I be so stupid?"

"Oh, Effie." Jenny carefully kneeled down beside her. "Mistakes and accidents happen."

"Not to you, Miss Goody Two Shoes," Effie replied scornfully. "They don't happen to you, oh, no, not to little Miss Goody Two Shoes, Jenny Marsh. Oh, no, she doesn't have sex, so she's not going to get pregnant out of wedlock. Oh, no!"

"Effie, stop it!" Jenny demanded. "You and Nicodemus made the choice to be intimate outside of marriage. You knew full well what the consequences would be, and now you have to deal with it."

Glumly, Effie sighed. "I know. And I know it's not your fault. I just feel so stupid. I'm not ready to get married, let alone have a baby. Oh…" She sat up straight and became animated. "Maybe I could, you know, not have it at all. I know some girls who got in the family way and then they weren't. I could get the name of the people who helped them."

"Oh, Effie, no. That's so dangerous," Jenny told her. "Why would you put yourself at risk like that? Of never being *able* to have children ever again. You know that's what happened to Olivia Mandell two years ago. She did that and ended up in the hospital with an incredibly bad infection that resulted in her having a hysterectomy at twenty-three. She'll never be able to have children, and was so distraught by the whole thing she broke off her engagement and moved goodness knows where to become a nun. She gave up life because of what happened. Oh, Effie, please don't do that," she pleaded with her friend. "If you don't want the child, give it up for adoption, or to a foster home, but please don't put your life at risk by doing that. *Please.*"

"Then what else do I do?" Effie asked, scared out of her brain. "I have no idea about *being* pregnant, let alone giving birth. And I certainly know nothing about looking after a child. What am I going to do, Jenny?" she pleaded. "What am I *supposed* to do?"

Worried for her friend, Jenny tried to come up with something. "You know for an absolute fact you're pregnant?"

"Yes, the doctor told me." Effie grasped her friend's hand in a death grip.

"Oh, Effie." Jenny shook her head. "Besides giving the child up for adoption, I have no idea what else you *can* do. Just *please, please* don't go to one of those people to do that. Please."

"So, I be a woman who can't have children because of that, I become a wife and mother, or, I have a bastard child and give it up." Gripped with despair, Effie burst into tears.

"Oh, Effie." Jenny took her into her arms and held her while she sobbed. "Please, just don't do the worst thing you could possibly do. You could lose your life."

"I would rather lose my life than be pregnant and unmarried," she sobbed on Jenny's shoulders.

"Please don't say that. You're twenty-five years old, more than old enough to have a child. And Nicodemus is nice, and he's Greek. Don't your parents like him?"

"They like him, well enough, but if they find out I'm already pregnant, they'll kill me." Wiping her face, Effie pulled some paper off the roll and blew her nose. Throwing the crumpled wad into the toilet, she flushed and climbed to her feet.

Jenny stood and smoothed her dress. "Are you okay?"

Shaking her head, Effie heaved a sigh. "No. I have no idea what I'm going to do, but if my parents find out, they'll make me marry anyway as to not bring shame to the family. So…" She glanced around the powder blue bathroom absentmindedly. "It looks as though I'm getting married and having a baby."

"Oh, Effie." Jenny rubbed her arm in support. "I'm so sorry."

"Will you be my bridesmaid?"

"What?" Surprised, Jenny could only stare at her. "Are you sure?"

A sad smile crossed Effie's lips, and a desolate expression crossed her face. "I don't want to die, Jenny; so, I guess I'm getting married and becoming a mother."

"Don't you want to?" Jenny asked softly, wondering what was actually going on.

"I did, one day." Effie washed and dried her hands. "The big Greek wedding, the perfect husband. I figured I had time to wait. That it wouldn't happen yet, and I'd have fun until it did." Frowning, she stared at her ring and moved it back and forth. "I don't think I'm ready."

"You're twenty-five, Effie. Most girls get called old maids if they live past that and don't get married. It seems to be the cut-off point around here for marriage. Even my older sisters were married by that age."

"And pregnant, if I recall," Effie said, smoothing back her ponytail and checking her face in the mirror. "At least my make-up's okay. So…will you?"

"Be your bridesmaid?"

"Yep."

"If you want me to be."

Effie hugged her. "Thanks, Jenny. Let's get back to the party. They'll think we've left."

Arm in arm they left the bathroom and made their way back to the party where Spiros and Nicodemus hurried over and kissed their cheeks.

"You two okay?" Spiros asked, looking from a grim Jenny to an even grimmer Effie.

"Not feeling well is all." Effie forced a smile onto her face. "I think I ate too much before. But I did ask Jenny to be my bridesmaid."

Spiros's face lit up. "Good, good, because Nicodemus asked me to be best man."

"One of them," Nicodemus said. "Xenos is the other. Figured since we came here together they should be by my side when I get married. I already asked him."

"We will be together, my Jenny, at Effie and Nicodemus's wedding." Spiros kissed Jenny's cheek and got a beaming smile in return.

"Yes, we will." Her smile grew wider as he slid his arms around her. "When is it, exactly? You said Christmas?"

"Well…" Effie couldn't match Jenny's smile. "Maybe we should do it before Christmas. Like a good couple of weeks before. Maybe the *first* of December." She looked at Nicodemus and barely managed to curl her lips up. "As soon as possible, I guess. My parents will do everything since I'm their only daughter, and it will probably be at the local Orthodox Church anyway, and the reception at the Greek Club."

"Which is just as well since I haven't managed to save much money," Nicodemus said. "Guess I'd better get onto that."

"You'll need to, for when we have children," Effie muttered, annoyed that he was so nonchalant about it. "If I'm expected to stay home and have babies, not work to bring money in, then you'd better start saving, or start working harder." She wasn't happy, and it was obvious to those with an idea. "What about a honeymoon?"

"If your parents are paying, then we have a honeymoon." Nicodemus shrugged, happy that his potential in-laws were well off.

Effie heaved a deep sigh and stared straight at Jenny. "Guess I'd better start planning my wedding."

Jenny picked up on the very unhappy vibe emanating from Effie and said, "I'll help you, Effie. I am the bridesmaid after all. Who's the other one?"

"Um…" Effie shook her herself out of her mood. "I don't know. We only just got engaged today, I hadn't thought about it. I don't have a sister, and you're my best friend, so…"

"What about your cousin?" Jenny asked.

"Athena?" Effie said. "Yes, yes, I guess I could. I'll go around there tonight and ask her. I wonder if my parents have told everyone by now. They probably have." She started laughing. "The whole town probably knows by now." The laugh became hysterical and people started to look. Even Spiros and Nicodemus were looking at her strangely.

"Why don't you come over to my place," Jenny suggested, reaching out and taking her hand. "I want to show you the new dress I bought." She quickly led Effie next door and up to her room where she comforted her friend for the next hour before cleaning her up and taking her back to the party. "Ah, there you are, my Jenny. Is everything all right?" Spiros kissed her cheek and watched as Effie went over to Nicodemus, a tight smile on her face.

"Everything's all right, Spiros," Jenny said and slid her arms around him. While upstairs, Sarah had come to see where the girls were and heard the whole horrid story. After a pep talk about sex, babies, and childbirth, and all of her options, Effie felt better enough to go back to the party with plans for the wedding and something to look forward to. Knowing that the whole community would be there to help her gave Effie a sense of relief, and all she needed to do was make sure no one else found out she was pregnant.

With everything she'd just dealt with, with Effie, it made Jenny start thinking about the possibility of marriage to Spiros and being pregnant herself. She knew that when it happened, she'd have her parents and siblings to support her, and that was more important than anything else. So, if her family would be there for her, then she intended to be there for Effie, especially so she didn't do anything stupid like have a backyard abortion. Shuddering, she couldn't imagine going through something so barbaric, and snuggled into Spiros's arms, her eyes on Effie, her smile for Spiros, and the love she had for him. Because that love would make her go above and beyond for the man she loved.

December 1951

Summer came, as did December, and that meant a month of celebration.

Effie and Nicodemus's wedding was on the first which started the festivities off. Jenny and Athena wore simple blue frocks as Effie's bridesmaids and watched as Effie was married wearing a bouffant hairstyle and an even bigger dress. Her parents had gone all out for the wedding of their only daughter, and every Greek and Australian in town was invited.

Effie was unhappy through the whole wedding and into the reception that was full of dancing and alcohol.

Jenny had to keep reminding her to cheer up, that it wasn't the end of the world.

But it was for Effie, who hadn't even imagined getting married so young, regardless of being twenty-five. By Christmas Day, she was starting to show, causing a bad reaction from her parents. However, they accepted that they couldn't do anything about it, and continued on as if she wasn't pregnant.

The town celebrated New Year the way they always did, by closing off the main street and turning it into a funfair. 1952 arrived in a blaze of fireworks and passionate kisses from Spiros. They had been dating for over a year and steadily dating for ten and a half months, and Jenny was incredibly happy with everything in her life.

February 1952

January passed into February, and Valentine's Day came around.

"I'm taking you out, my Jenny." Spiros presented Jenny with a huge bouquet of red roses when he picked her up for their Valentine's dinner.

"Oh, Spiros, you really need to stop spoiling me with flowers." Jenny's melodic laughter floated into the air as she took them from him. "You must keep the florist in business." She walked into the kitchen to fill a vase with water, with Spiros following.

"Anything for my Jenny," he said, watching her shapely figure in the red and white Valentine's dress with its sweetheart neckline and rose print pattern. "They match your pretty dress."

Arranging the roses in the vase, Jenny beamed in happiness. She'd picked out that dress especially, knowing it would be perfect for Valentine's, and she was hoping, after a year of going steady, that tonight was the night, so she wanted to look extra special for him. "They do, don't they." She set the vase on the table and kissed his cheek. "So, where are we going?"

Spiros took her into his arms. "We are going to the Greek Club for Valentine's."

Disappointed, but trying not to show it, Jenny's smile wavered. "Okay. We should go then." They walked into the hall and gathered their things. "We'll be home later," she told her parents and waved goodbye as they walked out the door. With Spiros escorting her to the car and helping her in, she hoped the dinner would be more romantic than it sounded.

Smiling to himself, Spiros drove off, not saying anything lest he spoil the surprise. He'd seen Jenny's lack of enthusiasm, but hoped that changed when she saw what he had planned. It had been months in the making.

Driving into town, he pulled into the car park of Jenny's favourite restaurant, *The Cherry Blossom.*

Surprised, Jenny's head swivelled towards him. "You said we were going to the Greek Club."

"We are, my Jenny. After dinner. Come." He alighted and opened her door, and giving her his arm, escorted her inside. "Special table for two please," he told the maître de. "Mr Spiros Stephanopoulos."

The maître de checked the register and nodded before leading them to a corner table for two overlooking the small garden at the side of the restaurant.

"Oh, Spiros. Well, you certainly surprised me," Jenny said as he held out the chair for her. She sat, settled her dress neatly around her legs, and placed her clutch on the table beside her plate.

"A surprise for my Jenny on Valentine's." Spiros sat opposite her and whipped his napkin across his lap. "Surprise!"

Smothering her giggles with her hand, she glanced around the restaurant and noticed others dining out for the special occasion. "You certainly did. Thank you for this. It's lovely. And one of the best seats in the house."

"Yes. Next to the beautiful garden. For my beautiful Jenny. You are very beautiful tonight, my Jenny. Just like every night."

"Oh, Spiros," she murmured, embarrassed by his compliments. "You always know what to say." She was wearing her studs and necklace he'd given her and the promise ring had been firmly on her right hand since her birthday last year. She couldn't imagine herself with anyone else and had been hoping since Christmas that he'd propose this year.

"It is not hard to compliment you, my Jenny. You are beautiful every single day." Spiros knew that the present he had for her was burning a hole in his pocket and he couldn't wait to give it to her.

"Oh, Spiros." She blushed and turned to look at the garden which had pretty coloured lights around it and through the water. She'd thought long and hard about a Valentine's present for him. Christmas and birthdays were easy enough when they were ties, hankies, or books, things that he needed. But Valentine's was special, and she hadn't gotten him anything last year, so wanted to make up for it now. She chose the one thing she could think of, even though it wasn't romantic. A watch.

The waiter came and took their order and they chatted until the first course arrived; a light tangy barramundi served in a citrus dressing.

"Mmm, that was refreshing," Jenny said as the plates were taken away and she dabbed at her mouth. "Did you plan all of this?"

"Yes, my Jenny." Spiros took a sip of wine and tried to control his nerves. He'd planned it to a T and hoped nothing went wrong.

Smiling at him lovingly, she said, "I loved it. And I love you." She sat back while the main course was placed before her; a lightly grilled filet mignon, with a mushroom and cheese sauce, and artfully piled spring vegetables.

"This looks lovely." Slicing through the meat, Jenny saw it was cooked just how she liked it, and placing a piece in her mouth, she closed her eyes to savour to taste. "Mmm…"

Spiros watched her, a secret smile on his lips. They were halfway through and almost there.

Making small talk, the conversation turned to Effie and Nicodemus.

"Have you seen them?" Jenny asked. "I saw Effie last week. She's six months pregnant and complaining about everything."

"I have seen Nicodemus." Spiros set his cutlery down to take a sip of wine. "He is working for her parents and uncles in their construction business."

"Oh, that's good." Jenny scraped up the last of her steak and wiped the gravy from her knife onto it. "A good steady job is important when getting married and having children." She popped the last morsel into her mouth and set her cutlery on the plate.

"Yes, it is," Spiros agreed. "I am glad I have an uncle to work for. If it was not for him, I would not have a steady job for the last year, and so no money to save hard for all the things I want. Like buying my Jenny bunches of roses and presents. I like spending my money on my Jenny."

Giggling softly and going bright red, Jenny patted her lips with her napkin and lifted her wine glass. "To Effie and Nicodemus, to having a good job, and to good futures ahead."

"To good futures." Spiros clinked her glass with his and downed the last mouthful of wine.

The waiters removed the plates and refilled their glasses, then brought out pieces of raspberry chiffon pie while they continued chatting. When dessert was over, the waiter cleared the table one last time and placed a plate in front of Jenny with a small red envelope on it.

"What's this?" Jenny asked, intrigued.

"Open it," Spiros urged and got ready.

Sliding her finger under the envelope flap, she popped it open and pulled out the card that had red and white confetti pour from it. "Oh, how cute." She sprinkled the card over the plate and opened it. There were two words written inside.

Will you…

With her heart in her chest, she could barely breathe. "Oh…" Glancing at a grinning Spiros, her eyes flicked up and down from the card to him. "Will I what?" she barely managed.

Sliding out of his seat and down on bended knee, he opened the small velvet box in his hand to reveal a gold ring with three sparkling diamonds all in a row, with the middle one sitting higher than the other two. "Will you marry me, my Jenny?" The love pouring out of him made it obvious to anyone watching that he was as serious as can be about Jenny Marsh. "Will you marry me and be my wife?"

"Yes," she whispered, staring from his eyes to the ring and back. "Yes, oh, yes, *of course,* I'll marry you, Spiros, *of course,* I will."

With a smile from ear to ear, he lifted the ring from the box and went to place it on her right ring finger.

"Oh, no, Spiros." She giggled breathlessly. "We're in Australia, we wear them on our left-hand ring finger."

"Oh, of course." He nodded and slid it onto the hand she held out.

"I love you, Jenny Marsh. You will be my wife, yes?"

"Yes, Spiros, yes I'll be your wife." She smothered him in kisses as he stood, and kept kissing amidst the applause that fluttered around the restaurant. "I love you, so much," she mumbled against his lips. "I can't wait to be your wife. Oh…" Gasping, she pulled back. "Do my parents know? Did you get their permission?"

"Yes, my Jenny." He calmed her. "I asked your parents for permission weeks ago. I told them it would be a Valentine's proposal and they said yes."

"Oh…yes…they said yes…" She leaned against him. "I'm glad they said yes. I don't know what I would've done if they'd said no. Oh…it would've been horrible."

"But they did not," Spiros told her. "They said yes, and now you have, too. My Jenny is going to be my wife." He kissed her cheek and hugged her. "My wife. Jenny Stephanopoulos."

Sliding her arms around his waist, she grinned. "Jenny Stephanopoulos. Wife of Spiros Stephanopoulos. I can't wait. Oh…" She pulled back. "Are we going to the Greek Club, or not? I can't wait to tell everyone and show them my ring." Gazing down at it, she tilted it back and forth so it caught the light. "It's beautiful, Spiros. I love it."

"Three stones, one for you, one for me, one to signify us," he said and kissed it gently. "I have saved hard, my Jenny, so we can have nice things, but at Greek wedding, all relatives help out by pinning money to wedding dress, or throwing it on the floor at the bride and groom's feet, so money will come in handy. Yes?"

"Oh, I don't know if I want that to happen." Jenny had only been at one Greek wedding and that was Effie's last year. She'd asked why relatives were pinning money to Effie's dress and been told that's what happened at Greek weddings. And Effie had been grateful for the money as Nicodemus had none and expected her family to pay for it all.

"We both have money and have saved hard," Jenny continued. "I don't know if I could accept money from your family."

"It is tradition, and yes, we have saved, but weddings cost money, and we will need a car and a home."

"Well…I have my car, even though I share it with my sisters. We could buy them out and they could buy something for themselves," she suggested, but was interrupted by the waiter handing them two glasses of champagne.

"Compliments of *The Cherry Blossom*, ma'am."

Jenny accepted her glass and said, "Oh, thank you, that's so sweet."

The manager led the other diners in a round of applause before it was time for them to leave, and on their way to the Greek Club, they chatted some more.

"I could save money by making a wedding dress and not buying one," Jenny said. "We have plenty of material at home, or I could buy some. We all know how to sew, so could easily do it. We could also make the wedding cake, we all know how to bake, or my aunts could do it. They run the bakery in town. My other aunts are hairdressers, so they could do our hair. Oh, we could save money on so many things."

"I could wear my best black suit instead of renting, or buying another one," Spiros suggested. "But I know my uncle and the Greek community will want to help out. That is what we Greeks do." He pulled into the car park of the Greek Club and turned off the engine. "We could have the reception here, or at the main hall in town. Where would we get married?" He knew Jenny was Catholic and he'd been raised orthodox, and expected her to be the same.

"Oh, I hadn't even thought about it," Jenny said, knowing full well that was a lie and she'd been doing nothing *but* thinking about marrying Spiros Stephanopoulos since Valentine's a year ago. She had the church, the reception hall, the types of flowers for the bouquet, the style of dress she wanted, all picked out. It was just a matter of executing everything with military precision.

"Would you marry in the Orthodox Church?" Spiros asked, wanting her reply before opening his door.

She gazed at him, loving every millimetre of his face, his hair, his eyes. Oh, God, how she loved him. "I don't know. I guess we'll have to talk about it."

Nodding, he got out and ran around to open her door.

She kissed his cheek and waited for him to lock the car before walking arm in arm into the club.

"Congratulations," everyone yelled, throwing streamers and confetti.

"Oh, my goodness." Jenny put her hands up to protect her face, and saw her whole family there along with her parents' families, her friends, Spiros's family, and townspeople she knew. "Oh, you couldn't have all come for us? How did you all know?" She was enveloped by her parents and younger sisters.

"When Spiros asked for permission and said he was asking on Valentine's, we decided to set this little shindig up," her father told her.

"But how did you know I'd say yes?" Jenny was astounded by the number of people who'd come.

"Oh, love, we knew you weren't going to say no." Sarah cupped her daughter's face. "You've been waiting for this for a year."

Blushing, Jenny hugged her way through family and friends, coming to a very pregnant Effie.

"Hey, you." Effie managed to get out of her chair and hug her best friend. "I wasn't going to miss this for anything."

They hugged, and Jenny gently touched Effie's bulging belly. "How are you, Effie?"

A desolate expression flitted over Effie's face. "I'm okay. Not liking being pregnant, but it goes with the territory. Right?"

"We're all here for you, Effie, just as we helped our other friends when they got married and pregnant. We'll help each other. Yes?"

Effie huffed sarcastically and crossed her arms over her stomach. "Yeah, sure, Jenny Marsh Stephanopoulos-to-be will be here to help me…little old Effie. Can't imagine you'll be asking me to be your bridesmaid to return the favour. I'm only six months pregnant and huge already. So, unless you're planning it for next year, there's no way I'll be in your wedding party."

"You could be matron of honour," Jenny suggested, wondering where the hatred was coming from. "If the wedding's soon, you could still be in it."

"Yeah, because you really want a big fat blimp in your bridal party." She sat heavily in her seat and kept her arms crossed. Looking away, she added, "Go ask your three skinny sisters. They'll be able to fit into dresses and not upstage the bride."

Disappointed in Effie's behaviour, Jenny's shoulders slumped and a gloom settled over her. "I don't know what you're going through, Effie, but I'd say something serious is wrong and I hope we can get past it." Getting no reply from her friend, Jenny sadly moved on.

"Spiros, congratulations. Syncharitíria. About time young Jenny made an honest man out of you." Nikos senior slapped his nephew on the back. "We helped out with this little shindig. Yes? When the Marshes told us they'd given permission, we got together and set this up for you and Jenny."

"Thank you, Uncle." Spiros slapped him on the back and hugged him. "Thank you for suggesting I come to Australia. Thank you for putting me up for more than a year, and thank you for giving me a job, so I could save hard for the day."

"You're very welcome, Spiros. Now, we need a speech."

"Speech, speech, speech," the crowd chanted.

Laughing, Spiros and Jenny made their way to the front of the crowd and addressed them. "Thank you, so much, to everyone for coming. We did not know this was happening, and did not expect it. I just thought we would spend the night dancing and having fun," Spiros said, looking over the crowd of excited faces.

Jenny stood beside him, clutching his hand between both of hers, blushing and giggling like a newly engaged young woman. She had waited for *that* moment from the moment she'd met Spiros. The potential new beau, the possibility of a life partner, a marriage and children, and while it scared her and thrilled her at the same time, she had never been happier. Listening to him finish up his thanks, Jenny smiled at her family and friends. Here was an engagement party she didn't need to worry about. Tick that off the list.

"*And* since I do not know when the wedding will be, I will leave that up to my Jenny," Spiros ended. "But for now, let us celebrate."

Cheers went through the crowd and they mingled with everyone there, chatting about what dress she'd wear, how she wanted her hair, and what Spiros was going to do, well past midnight.

*****

On Saturday, all of the women gathered at the Marsh home to start planning the wedding of Spiros and Jenny.

"I want everything to be perfect," Jenny told them and started talking about her wedding dress. "I'm just not sure whether to waste time looking for one to buy, or simply make it so I get what I want."

"It would be easier to make it. Oh, Jenny, let us do it for you," Rebecca eagerly looked at all of her sisters and sisters-in-law who nodded their consent. "That will be our present to you. Your dress. We'll do it exactly how you want it, and can work on it every night. It will be done in no time."

"Oh, girls, that's so incredible of you," Jenny cried and ran around hugging them all. "That would take a weight off my shoulders."

"And we'll do your hair, love," her aunt Matilda told her. "Just show us a picture of what you want, and we'll get to perfecting it."

"Oh, thank you, so much." Jenny pulled a picture she'd ripped out of a magazine from her wedding book and handed it to her two maternal aunts.

Sarah's older sisters, they ran the local hairdressing salon and discussed the hairstyle and how they'd do it while Jenny moved onto the food.

"I have no idea what the menu will be. Probably our favourite foods, which you know is roast chicken for me, and chocolate cake, or raspberry chiffon pie."

"What about Spiros? What does he eat?" Sarah asked, making notes as each item was brought up.

"Oh, I don't know, something Greek, I guess. But he eats a lot of Australian food, too." She paused and touched a finger to her chin. "Guess I'd better ask him."

"Yes, love, you'd better," Sarah said and made more notes.

"Okay, so what have we done so far?" Jenny called out.

"The dress," Rebecca said.

"Your hair," Matilda added.

"Half the menu," Sarah ticked off the list.

"So…we need my make-up, shoes, unless I wear my white going out shoes with the dress, the venue and the date." Jenny thought about it.

"The invitations," Melina Stephanides added. "How many are you inviting?"

"Oh, the guest list." Jenny flounced into a seat at the dining table as everyone sat on every other chair, or the floor. "I completely forgot."

"And the food," Barbara piped up. "You may have a menu, but who's doing the cooking?"

"Oh, the catering," Jenny gasped. "I had thought of asking *The Cherry Blossom* if they'd do it. It is my favourite restaurant, after all."

"Bernard is a personal friend of ours," Henrietta, her aunt, said. "We could ask him if he'd consider, but he'll need to know how many."

"Oh, I don't know." Jenny was becoming a little exasperated. She didn't want to *not* invite anyone, but couldn't afford to invite *every*one. "How many should I invite? I don't want to put anyone out."

"Well, you could invite everyone to the wedding, but invite only a select few to the reception," Sarah suggested. "But that could still put people out. At the end of the day, it's up to you, love, as it's your wedding. Your father and I are paying for the reception, but I suggest you keep it limited to just those you want."

"That would be family, and close friends and neighbours," Jenny said, mentally ticking off people. "That will be a lot."

"Then I'm going to suggest you keep it to one hundred people," Sarah recommended.

"One hundred, oh, goodness, I don't even think I know that many people." Jenny checked the guest list she'd already made up a year ago. It came to fewer than one hundred and consisted mainly of family.

"Does Spiros's family know he's getting married?" Faye asked as she and her sisters pored over bridal magazines they'd picked out the day before.

Jenny glanced her way. "Oh...I don't know... I guess he would have called, or wrote them a letter that it was happening. But I doubt they'll care. From some of the stories he's told me, his father disowned him for wanting to leave Greece and come to another country. For *defying* his father and not taking over the meat shop his father runs. It's all very sad indeed."

"Oh, how horrible," Matilda murmured while Henrietta tsk-tsked.

"How could one do that to their child?"

"Giorgio Stephanopoulos is a very strict man when it comes to his family." Melina nodded in their direction. "My husband is Spiros's uncle, his mother's brother, and we saw what Giorgio was like before we moved here. He did not want his sons to leave Greece, wanted them, especially Spiros, to take over the family meat shop. And from the letters Katyana has sent us, it seems Giorgio has disowned Spiros and does not want him back. Spiros's brothers have fled to Athens to take up jobs their grandfather offered them, but they are forbidden to leave Greece."

"Oh, how horrid for Spiros," Jenny murmured, a frown darkening her pretty face. "It must be so horrible for him."

"I think it is made better by you, young Jenny," Melina continued, watching her future niece-by-marriage-in-law with newfound love and affection. "He is in love with you and is so glad he came to Australia after all. He is very happy."

Jenny's shy smile slowly lit up her face. "I'm in love with him, too. And I'm so glad he came here and we met. I hope I can make him happy enough that it takes away the hurt his family have caused him."

"Probably not," Melina told her. "That kind of pain caused by family cuts very deep. It will probably never go away, or be healed."

The fact that she could not help Spiros on that level hurt Jenny deeply. She wanted to make him happy. Marry him, give him children, but if she couldn't make *that* hurt go away, she didn't know what else could. Sighing, she picked up her list of guests and considered cutting some, but at the end of it, everyone on her list were who she wanted at her wedding, and many included Spiros's family and friends in Armidale. She considered writing to his family to invite them, but figured she'd talk to Spiros first, and had better figure out what day they were getting married. Picking up her calendar from the table, she flipped through the months and then turned to her diary. There were many dances, festivities and celebrations happening all year, and she wasn't sure when they could fit it in. "Should we wait, or get it done quickly?"

"Depends on how fast you want to be married," her sister, Joanna, said. "You might want to pick, so we know how long we have to make the dress." All five sisters and three sisters-in-law would be chipping in money and time, but with her and Harriet being pregnant, they didn't have long.

"I guess I should make some calls to see when the church is free," Jenny muttered, and marked off free time that she had in her diary. "And what about the honeymoon? Where would we go?"

"Would Spiros take you to Mykonos?" Sarah asked.

"I'm sure he'd love to, but I don't think so." Jenny bit her lip in thought. "What about a week in Sydney? He hasn't seen it since he got here."

"You'd have to spend the night here and then drive down the next day, or take the train and spend money on taxis," Rebecca said. "Have you picked out a design for your dress yet?"

"Oh, sorry. I should have given you the picture." Jenny pulled out a magazine page from her wedding folder and handed it over. "Think you can make this?" It was a white satin bust with three-quarter sleeves and a chiffon skirt all the way to the floor. Embroidered rosettes with sequins dotted the skirt and the veil which drifted gently down the back of the model wearing it. "I love the veil so much I ordered it, but I'd like the dress changed a little to suit me better."

Looking at the photo, the girls conferred. "Shouldn't be too hard," Joanna said. "A pinch here, a dart there. How much do you want it changed?"

"Just the bust. I'm not sure of the style, but the skirt part's lovely. Maybe I should order the dress to save you girls having to embroider it all by yourselves, and then you'll just have to remake the bust."

"It says here, the chiffon skirt is an overlay," Faye read the description. "So it's technically not the skirt. Why don't we buy it, and make the actual dress to suit you and fit the overlay and veil to the dress?"

"Oh, that's a fabulous idea, girls," Henrietta said. "Matilda and I will help you out with cost and time if you need help getting the dress together."

"Thanks, Aunt Hetty." Faye started making sketches of dresses she thought her sister would like.

"So…what date were you thinking, Jenny?" Sarah brought the conversation back to the date as she watched her daughter flip through her diary.

"I have no idea." Jenny heaved a sigh and sat back. "There is so much on this year I don't know when to make it for, and then I need to know whether Spiros and I can get time off work for the day and our honeymoon. I'd better talk to Spiros first and then make a list of everyone we need to call before making that final decision."

That night, after a boisterous dinner with her family, Jenny spoke to Spiros. "Do you think your uncle would give you time off, and any idea when?" She had her diary and the calendar in front of her at the dining table.

"I have not asked, my Jenny, because we do not have a date yet," Spiros replied, watching her flip pages in thought. "Do you know when you want to get married?"

Signing, Jenny distractedly moved back and forth between the months. "I don't know. It all depends on when the church is available, when the reception hall is available…"

"Do you want to get married in the Orthodox Church?" Spiros asked, knowing she'd more than likely want the Catholic Church.

"Well…" She ran through a million and one things in her head and tried to sort them all out. "We could, you know I go to church every Sunday, as have you, but which would we go to once we're married?" She didn't like conflict, and certainly didn't want God to be angry because she chose Greek Orthodox over Catholicism.

"We could go to both, my Jenny." Spiros laid his hand over hers. "Your church in the morning, mine in the afternoon, or evening."

"Yes, I guess we could." Jenny considered it. "That is a good idea, or we could alternate. I thought of having the reception in the main hall. It's used by a lot of brides for their reception as it has a fully stocked kitchen."

"I could pick the church, and you could pick the reception hall?" Spiros suggested, wanting things to be as easy as possible.

"Yes, I guess we could," Jenny murmured and gazed into his eyes. "I love you."

Spiros's smile lit up the dining room. "I love you too, my Jenny."

*****

On Monday, Jenny made multiple calls to see when they could have both the Orthodox Church and the reception hall on the same day, and with to-ing and fro-ing, everyone finally settled on a date.

May the 23rd. Two days after Jenny's birthday. And a Friday!

Annoyed at the timing, but happy she finally had a date to tell people, and they could have the day off, invitations were made, calendars were given a final lock-in, and everything was set.

They just had three months and one week to get it all done.

May 1952

Since Jenny's birthday was two days before the wedding, they decided to combine her birthday and bridal shower with an early dinner at her favourite restaurant and then have the shower at the Marsh home.

"Oh, I'm so glad everyone can make it on Friday," Jenny told her guests as they nibbled on sweet treats and tea and coffee. "I was worried everyone wouldn't be able to get time off."

"Thanks to you making it an afternoon wedding, most were able to get the afternoon off," Rebecca told her and poured more tea for several ladies.

"Yes, I figured with it being a Friday, something I'm still not happy about, that it would make it easier for everyone to have it close to teatime, so they could head straight to the reception after the wedding. With luck, not too many bosses will fire their employees for taking a couple of hours off. But it will be chilly; it certainly has been the last few days."

"It's supposed to be warming up a bit," Matilda said, savouring the last bite of her tiny chocolate mousse cake. "It's about seventy-seven on Friday."

"At least that's something," Jenny murmured, happy that every little detail was finally finished. Her sisters had made her dress, the veil and overskirt were stunning, the cake was done, the menu catered for, and all she had to do was wake up Friday and get married.

"Are we opening the presents now?" Faye hurried over to the side buffet and picked up a small gift bag. Presenting it to her sister, she added, "For you."

"Oh, really, girls, you shouldn't have. The dress was already enough." Jenny pushed aside the tissue paper and pulled out a silky white full-length nightie. "Oh, girls…" Jenny's face slowly turned red. "You shouldn't have."

"Had *you* thought about it?" Joanna asked. "We figured since you'd be slipping the dress *off,* you'd need something to slip *into.*" She glanced at her sisters who all blushed and giggled behind their hands.

"I…" Jenny's face flared up with all shades of red. "Oh…"

"And here, love." Matilda handed over her and Henrietta's present. "The matching gown to go with it."

Jenny opened the box and put the two pieces together. "Oh, thank you all, they are beautiful, and honestly, I hadn't even thought about what I'd be wearing on the night. I've been so busy planning everything I'd forgotten about what comes after."

"How could you forget about that?" Gertrude Mason, Jenny's grandmother, said. "That's how we all got into the messes we have. The wedding night is how you're all here." As Sarah's mother, she herself had popped out thirteen children.

Burning with embarrassment, Jenny quickly put the nightie and gown away and opened the other presents. She'd told everyone to combine birthday and bridal presents together, if they liked, to make it easier and save money. She received multiple pieces of nightwear, and many gorgeous accessories for her honeymoon.

"Do you have your travel outfit ready?" Sarah asked. "You'll be leaving Saturday morning for Sydney."

"Yes. I spent all weekend making last-minute decisions. At least two outfits a day, one casual for sightseeing, and one for night-time. All of these accessories will help add to them. I'll get everything finished off by tomorrow night, and then pack it all Friday morning, so there are fewer creases." Jenny lay aside all of her presents into a couple of boxes to make it easier to carry upstairs later. "Thank you all, so much. The presents are beautiful. My dress is beautiful. *Everything* is beautiful."

"We'll be decorating the reception hall tomorrow." Henrietta glanced at her sister, who nodded. "We've got the committee onto it and it will all be done for you."

"And then we'll decorate the church on Friday morning," Matilda added. "It's the orthodox, so not much needs to be done, just some simple things for the ends of the pews."

"Seriously, I cannot thank you all enough." Jenny looked from face to face and saw sisters, friends, aunts, mother, and grandmothers. "I know we do this for each other's weddings, and for friends, but when it's your own, it's a little different."

"A little crazy," Matilda offered.

"A little hectic," Henrietta said.

"Yes." Sighing, Jenny sat down and looked at all around her. "All of the above."

"Have you gone to see Effie?" Joanna asked her. With four children already, she knew what it was like to be overwhelmed by the first, and silently thanked God for in-laws who were helping to look after the kids over the next few days.

"No, not yet." Breathing in and letting it out slowly, Jenny contemplated her future.

Effie had given birth just days before, so was unable to attend the wedding, or reception, and Jenny hadn't wanted to interrupt her rest. But it got her wondering if in nine months' time she'd be in the hospital giving birth to her and Spiros's first child. She also wondered if her and Effie's friendship was coming to an end. They'd been friends for six years, but in the last year, they had slowly moved apart. Unhappily married and pregnant, Effie had been morose most of the year, but Jenny hoped now that the baby was here, things would be different for Effie and she would get better.

"I was planning to go tomorrow. I haven't spoken to her in a month, or so. She got angry that I'd picked May because she'd be giving birth and unable to come. Accused me of setting the date on purpose, so she wouldn't be there. I don't know, but..." Jenny mentally looked for words to grasp. "I think she's really unhappy with her life. I don't want to say depression, or that she'd do something to herself, or the baby, but I really think she regrets how things have turned out."

"She wouldn't have been the first unwed woman to give birth and give up a child, if that was her decision, but she chose to get married." Sarah had spoken to Effie multiple times since she'd found out that Effie was pregnant last October. She had tried to coach her for what was to come, but had definitely sensed some panic and depression about what had befallen her. She was clearly scared about being pregnant, and what it represented on the other side.

"I know. But being Greek, it would have brought shame to her family, and she would have possibly been shunned." Jenny shook her head sadly. "I just don't think she was emotionally ready for it."

"That's what happens when you have sex without protection," Sarah went on. "You end up with a child, or a husband and a child. If she wanted to give it up, she could have. Many unwed girls and women do."

"I doubt her parents would have wanted that," Jenny cut in. "And she wasn't a girl when she and Nicodemus had sex and she became pregnant. She was twenty-five. Old enough to know better."

"Then she had to deal with the consequences." Gertrude tsk-tsked. "Having sex is how babies are made, and you'll be in the family way soon enough, Jennifer."

"Grandma." Jenny blushed. "That's not something I wish to talk about until it happens."

"Then I guess I'd better have that chat with you about baby-making," Sarah told her daughter, making her blush even harder at the chuckling she received.

*****

Next door at the Stephanides house, Spiros's bachelor party was in full swing. After Jenny's birthday dinner, the men had returned for their own party.

"Come, Spiros. Drink," Nikos senior encouraged, and poured another round of ouzo for the guests. Jenny's brothers, brothers-in-law, father, grandfathers and uncles were all in attendance, as was his own family, friends, and Nicodemus and Xenos.

They downed the shot glasses of ouzo, and the Australians shook their heads, or screwed up their faces, at the taste.

"I think I'll stick to beer," Matthew said, and quickly sculled half a glass to chase away the taste left in his mouth.

"Ouzo *is* an acquired taste." Spiros grinned. "Most of us are raised on it."

"But you do have good Australian beer." Nicodemus raised his glass in the air. "Beer is good." He knocked back his full glass and burped loudly. "Another for the new father."

Spiros was surprised to see his friend drinking so much so fast and led him out into the hallway. "Nicodemus, are you okay? Should you be drinking so much? You have a wife and new baby to look after. How *is* Effie?"

"How would I know?" Nicodemus muttered and drunkenly leaned against the wall.

"Have you not been to see her? Your child?" Spiros asked, wondering what was going on with his friend.

"No, I have not. Why would I? She is just the little woman who got pregnant and went to hospital to pop out a bastard child. Why would I care?"

"Because it is your son and your wife." Spiros was astounded by Nicodemus's unkind words. "You married Effie, willingly took what her parents gave you, and now you have left her to fend for herself in hospital?" He shook his head in disbelief. "I cannot believe you are so cold-hearted, Nicodemus. I cannot believe you could do that to your wife, to Jenny's best friend. Why did you marry her if you were not interested in being a husband and father?"

"Ohhh." Nicodemus leered drunkenly at him. "Do you not know? The bitch was already pregnant. That is why I proposed. Figured I had better, so I could set myself up."

"That is just nasty, Nicodemus. I never took you for that kind of man." Spiros could not believe the difference in his friend in two short years. He had changed, and not for the better. Looking Nicodemus up and down, he didn't know whether he still wanted to be friends or not. "If you cannot be sober for the wedding, or reception, please do not bother coming. If you can control your drinking, then you are welcome. If there is one ounce of trouble out of you at either, I will throw you out myself. Do you understand me?"

Nicodemus sneered back in his drunken state. "And who do you think you are to tell me that, Spiros?" He poked him in the shoulder, shoving him back. "Think because you have an in with the councilman it makes you a big boy?" Another push.

"Nicodemus," Spiros warned, putting a hand up to stop his friend.

"What?" Nicodemus continued. "Think you are a big man about town because you are marrying the councilman's daughter?" He shoved with both hands, but Spiros managed to stay standing. "Well?" Another shove. "Think you are better than me, Spiros Stephanopoulos?" Another shove. "You got the councilman's daughter, and I got the town whore."

"Enough!" Nikos senior commanded from the lounge room doorway. "You have had too much to drink. Nikos, you and your brothers take Nicodemus out into the back yard and hose him down. He clearly needs cooling off."

Nikos junior nodded and grabbed Nicodemus by the arm. With his brothers' help, he tackled him out into the back yard and shoved him to the ground, then hosed him down for a full minute.

"I am sorry, Uncle Nikos," Spiros muttered, watching from the kitchen window. "I have no idea what has got into him."

"Life," Nikos replied, watching a soggy Nicodemus sit up and wipe his face. "He apparently does not like marriage, or the thought of being a father, so he's been drinking and lost his job. Effie's parents are helping them by getting him another one, but he does not want to work."

"Didn't he work at their construction company?" Spiros asked, wondering why Nicodemus would risk losing such a great job.

"He was. But after coming to work drunk one too many times, they told him to stop, or lose his job. He didn't stop, so he lost the job."

"But her parents are still helping them?" Spiros was surprised they hadn't pulled him into line.

"She is their only daughter, so of course they are. They don't want to see her broken any more than they want to see her a single mother."

Spiros shook his head at all of the information. "I had no idea. But surely, if he is going to continue this way, a divorce would be better?"

"Not only is Armidale very Catholic, it's very Greek. We don't do divorces." Nikos pointed out the window at Nicodemus. "He needs to learn how to be a man and provide for his wife and child. I hope you don't turn out the same."

"Me?" Shock rolled over Spiros. "I would not even dream of mistreating my Jenny. I *am not* like Nicodemus." His eyes turned from his uncle to his friend and he frowned. "I do not know what happened to him, and I certainly would never think of behaving that badly. My parents taught me better."

"Good, good, Spiros." Nikos slapped him on the back and watched Nicodemus stand up and shake himself off. "Let's hope he can do the same as you."

"I will do better." Spiros nodded with confidence. He would treat his Jenny like a queen for all of their married life.

They watched the boys come in, and Nikos junior collected a towel for Nicodemus to dry himself off, and then went back to the party.

"Come, Spiros, I want to make a toast," Matthew called from the lounge room. He waited while a smiling Spiros entered the room and stood beside him. Clapping him on the shoulder, Matthew cleared his throat. "Now, when my Jenny first met Spiros, she couldn't stop talking about him. When he asked her to their first dance, she couldn't stop floating on cloud nine. I think we knew then that our Jenny had found the man she wanted to marry. She dated no one else, thought about no one else, talked about no one else. So, I'd say we learned early on that her heart was set on the new Greek boy in town, Spiros Stephanopoulos. I'd also say we learned that he was going to be the one that married our Jenny. Especially when he asked permission to go steady with her." A few guffaws floated around the room and Spiros turned a deep shade of red. "As we have always seen, Spiros has been nothing *but* polite and extremely gentlemanly with our Jenny. That's something we ask of all future sons-in-law when they ask for our daughter's hand in marriage." He eyeballed his two sons-in-law, knowing they knew he kept a strict eye on them. There was no way Matthew Marsh would tolerate any man abusing his daughters, and his sons-in-law knew it. So did his sons. All six of them had been raised to be men and treat women with respect and dignity, from their grandmothers to their mother and aunts, to their sisters, wives and daughters. He turned to his future son-in-law. "Spiros, you have shown manners, decency, and respect for our Jenny, and we thank you for it. We will be proud to call you our son-in-law." He raised his glass in a toast. "Congratulations."

"Syncharitíria."

Beaming at such kind words, Spiros raised his glass and toasted before clearing his throat. "Thank you, Mr Marsh, for the kind words. Thank you for allowing me to marry my Jenny. And thank you to everyone for coming and celebrating tonight, thank you, and thank you, Uncle Nikos, for letting me have two weeks off for the wedding and honeymoon." He toasted his uncle who just waved a hand as if to say, it was nothing, but then waved everyone on to cheer for him.

"Well, you haven't had a holiday since you started working for me," Nikos said. "You have worked over a year and a half with only public holidays and nothing else. You deserve two weeks off work."

"Thank you, Uncle Nikos." Spiros raised his glass.

"Did you let everyone at home know?" Xenos asked. Unlike Spiros and Nicodemus, he hadn't yet found a girl to marry and settle down with.

"I wrote to them," Spiros told him. "Received a letter from Christos and Yannis the other day, but nothing from my family."

"That father of yours can be stubborn." Nikos shook his head. "My sister would be going along with him just to keep the peace. Has she not written to you? I wrote to her when you became engaged and she wrote back, but completely ignored what I'd written. Just went on about what your siblings were doing."

"And how are they?" While Spiros had hoped for a reply, he waited for news from home in the letters his mother sent her brother.

"They are all doing well." Nikos poured another round of drinks. "Your brothers moved to Athens with their families, as you know, so has the youngest, Theseus, and two of your sisters are married with children on the way."

"Yes, that was the plan." Spiros sighed and thought back to before he left. "My youngest brother was newly married with a baby on the way, and my sisters were being primed for marriage when I left."

"It is the Greek way." Nikos handed him a beer. "We marry off our children when they are of age. Except for you. You bucked against it."

"That is because I did not feel ready for it. I did not feel that my future wife was there for me. I wanted to sail the ocean and see new places and meet new people. And I did that," Spiros told everyone. "I sailed the ocean, and on the way here, I saw new places when we stopped for food and fuel. I met new people, and found the woman I want to marry." Unable to find the right words for what he wanted to convey, he waved a hand and finally said, "I am happy. I have found my Jenny. My forever, gia pánta."

Cheers and whistles went around the room and the celebrations continued.

*****

On Thursday morning, Jenny went to the hospital to see Effie, taking a present, consisting of a basket of baby items, with her. Entering the ward, she found Effie sitting beside the bed looking out the window, and set the basket on the roller table over the bed. "Hello, Effie. Congratulations. How are you?"

Dazed, Effie stared up at her and took a few moments to register who she was. "Oh…look…Miss Perfect Jenny Marsh. How do you think I am?" She pulled the blanket around her and went back to staring out the window.

"Oh, Effie, don't be like that. I've done nothing to you except be your friend and try and be here for you. You're the one who shut me out." Jenny pulled a chair over and sat beside her friend. "Ever since the wedding you've shut most people out. That's not my fault."

Effie's head turned in Jenny's direction, a scowl on her pale face. Her hair was an unruly mess of curls, knotted and dark, her pallor pale and sickly. The dark circles under her eyes were pronounced, and the white of the hospital gown and blanket were doing nothing for her complexion. "Oh, no, because perfect Miss Jenny Marsh never does anything wrong. It's not as if you were there for me through the whole thing."

"That's because you shut yourself away," Jenny butted in. "You asked me to be your bridesmaid and I was. We saw each other at Christmas and New Year, and you were okay. But after our engagement party, you were just mean and hid away from everyone."

"What do you expect? I was six months pregnant and married, and then I found out my best friend was getting married and I knew there was no hope in hell of being her bridesmaid unless she waited six months for me, but, oh, no, Miss Jenny Marsh had to have it her way and to hell with what anyone else wants."

Stung, Jenny could only frown at her friend's fiery expression. The anger and hatred that spewed forth shocked her, and she didn't know what to say, let alone do.

"Jenny Marsh gets everything she wants," Effie spat. "Doesn't give a flying fat rat's about her friends and what *they're* going through."

"Stop it!" Jenny exclaimed. "I *am not* responsible for your actions, Effie. *You* chose to have unprotected sex with Nicodemus on your birthday, and *kept* having sex knowing full well you would end up pregnant. It was *your* choice to get married, and *your* choice to keep the baby. *All of that* is on *you, not* me. I didn't make you do anything. I just tried to be a good friend and help you through it. *You* chose to back away and hide from the world, *not me.* How dare you pin this on me? I am not to blame, *you are.*" Gasping for air, Jenny clutched her handbag tightly and shook her head in dismay.

The frown on Effie's face grew deeper the more the words sank in, and the more they sank in, the more depressed she became. She burst into tears.

"Oh, Effie." Jenny quickly pulled her chair over and held her while she sobbed. "It *cannot* be that bad. You have your mother, your aunts and cousins, me, my mum and sisters. We can all help you."

"I don't know what I'm doing," Effie stuttered between her sobs. "I don't feel good, it hurt like hell pushing it out, and I'm sore down there. It was horrible."

"So I've heard," Jenny muttered, gently rocking back and forth. "I have all of that to look forward to, you know. It doesn't mean it will be any easier for me."

Effie sniffed and pulled back. "It hurts. A lot. And you're so sore down there that even when you pee it burns. I don't want to do it again."

"If you have sex, you know you'll end up pregnant again," Jenny told her.

"I know. I've thought of refusing. Sex hurt like hell the first few times because I was a virgin and all, but after that, it felt *really* good." Looking into Jenny's eyes, she whispered, "Sex is *really* good once you get into it. You won't want to stop. But then you get bigger, and positions get awkward, and it doesn't always work right, and then you have the kid and it hurts even worse." Sitting back in her chair and wiping her face, Effie went back to staring out the window. "I don't know if I can do it, Jenny. I don't know if I can be a mother. I don't think I have it up here." She tapped her temple with two fingers and let her hand fall back into her lap. "I just don't know."

"Oh, Effie," Jenny murmured, rubbing her friend's arm. "Your family will help you through it. And mum and I are here for you. We'll all help you."

Sighing was even too much for Effie who was drained of all energy. "I need to go to sleep now, Jenny. I need to sleep." Her head rested against the back of her chair and her eyes closed.

Rubbing her forehead at the ensuing migraine, Jenny quietly got to her feet, tucked the blanket around her friend, kissed her on the cheek, and left the ward. All the way back to the car she thought about nothing *but* Effie and the downward mental spiral her friend had taken. Reaching out to unlock the driver's door, she stopped, had another thought, and then walked back inside and up to the nursery.

Looking at each crib, she found the one with Nicodemus's surname and stood watching him.

He was a baby boy wrapped in blue, with a head of black hair and dark eyes. He wiggled a little as he looked back at Jenny, his tiny forehead wrinkling, his mouth opening and closing.

She wasn't sure how long she stood there staring down at him, at *all* the babies. Twelve in total. But a million and one thoughts raced through her mind. In nine months she could be in there, in a ward, in pain, her baby lying here in a crib wrapped in blue, or pink. She wondered if she'd have a boy, or girl, first, or second, or third, and considered what that tiny new person would look like. Would he, or she, have black hair or brown? Blue eyes or brown? What would they weigh? *How* much would they cry? Would it be a long labour? Tearing up, she wiped away the trickle that slid down her cheeks. A part of her so desperately wanted to be a wife and mother, and hold a child in her arms; a child that was half her and half Spiros. Sighing, she inhaled deeply, said a silent prayer for Effie and her baby, and left. She had her life to begin.

*****

On Friday, the festivities started early. Jenny was treated to breakfast in bed by her mother and sisters, and then luxuriated in a hot bubble bath, making sure she smelled good and felt good. She finally packed her bags for the honeymoon, her aunts came around to do her hair, and her manicure was touched up. Her make-up was expertly applied by her sister, and her dress was taken down from the hook for her to step into. The chiffon overskirt was attached, as was the veil, which hung gently down Jenny's back. Everyone stood back to admire their handiwork while she slipped into her satin heels.

"Well...how do I look?" She stood staring at her mother, grandmothers, aunts, sisters and sisters-in-law, as well as her future aunt-in-law.

"Oh, Jenny," Sarah murmured through her tears, dabbing at her face with a tissue. "You're beautiful."

Beaming, Jenny tried holding back her tears. "You'll make me cry, stop it."

Matthew came into the lounge room to see what all the fuss was about and stopped short at the sight of his daughter. "Oh…Jenny."

"Dad?" She turned to him and twirled. "How do I look?"

A multitude of expressions crossed his face. "Like a princess, my girl. And I am so proud of you."

"Aw." She moved into his arms and hugged him, careful not to crush the satin bodice with its three quarter lace sleeves and sweetheart neckline. The embroidered veil and overskirt made her as pretty as a picture.

"It's time to go, my darling." Matthew looked from her to everyone else. "Off you go. Spiros and the boys have gone, so he won't see you, but everyone else needs to leave before us."

The family gathered their coats and purses and rushed out to their cars. Rebecca, Faye and Barbara, who were bridesmaids in simple blue frocks and matching jackets with seed bead and sequin detail so they could be worn again, climbed into their aunt's car so they could get there first.

Matthew and Sarah escorted Jenny to their car, which had been detailed and decorated with white ribbon, and helped Jenny inside without crushing her gown. Sarah climbed in next to her, and Matthew got behind the wheel. They slowly drove to the church and continued around the block, so the girls had time to prep everyone and be ready.

"Nervous, love?" Sarah reached out and held her daughter's hand. It was ice-cold and shaking. "Jenny?"

"Very nervous," Jenny gasped, trying to control the butterflies in her stomach. "Yesterday and now, I am a single woman, but in half an hour I will be a married woman. It's absolutely nerve-racking."

"You can pull out if you're not ready. I can keep driving and take you back home." Matthew glanced in the rear-view to see her bright blue eyes staring back.

"No, no, of course not." Jenny shook her head. "I love him. I want to marry him. It's just…oh…it's becoming more and more real. And I'm nervous, and excited, and scared, and happy, and a million different things all at once." The day before when she'd come home from the hospital and told her mother about Effie, and seeing all the babies and thinking about her own, Sarah had given her the talk. The birds and the bees. What to do during sex, that it might hurt for a day or two, and what having a baby was like. She had described everything in such detail it had left Jenny wanting to remain single and a virgin for the rest of her life.

"Was it the talk yesterday, love?" Sarah asked. "Maybe I went a bit overboard."

A small smile came to Jenny's lips and she grasped her mother's hand. "In part, but the other part is that I'll be a married woman. A wife, a partner in life within the hour, and it's exciting and nerve-racking. I'll be Mrs Spiros Stephanopoulos. Not Jenny Marsh anymore."

"You'll *always* be Jenny Marsh," Matthew said, pulling to a stop outside of the church. "First and foremost. You'll *always* be Jenny Marsh. *Our* Jenny Marsh."

Smiling at his reflection, Jenny said, "Thanks, Dad. We can go in now."

He gestured to her sisters who opened the door for their mother and Jenny to alight, and once she was out, they straightened the dress and pulled her veil over her face.

Matthew held out his arm. "Ready, Jenny?"

Taking a deep breath, holding onto her bouquet of red roses, and her father's arm for dear life, she nodded. Her mother rushed inside, and her sisters lined up. Walking in to the entrance, they heard the music start up and a clamouring as everyone got to their feet. With the girls walking down the aisle first, Jenny and Matthew soon followed until they reached the end of the aisle and he presented his daughter to a stunned Spiros.

From the moment he'd seen her enter the church; he'd been stunned into shock. She was beautiful. More beautiful than ever before, and he was the lucky one she was walking towards. "Oh…my Jenny…you are beautiful," he whispered, seeing her eyes light up behind her veil. With a pounding heart, he turned to the priest and the ceremony began.

It had elements of both Greek orthodox and Australian Catholic.

The stefanas were waved above their heads, they circled the altar three times, the priest blessed the rings, and they heard passages from the bible, especially Corinthians, which Jenny loved. They exchanged wedding rings and spoke their vows, and then Spiros presented her with an eternity band, surprising her as he pledged his love for eternity. The ceremony was soon over, and Spiros lifted her veil.

Her eyes were stunningly blue and showered him with so much love that he could barely breathe. "My Jenny," he managed before gently kissing her.

After the kiss, she breathed. "My Spiros."

Applause broke out in the church and they turned to see everyone on their feet, showering them with confetti and rose petals as they hurried down the aisle holding hands, laughing and beaming in happiness to come to a stop outside on the church steps, so they could thank their guests as they came out, and photos could be taken.

Guests ushered by, and the families gathered around them. Roll upon roll of film was snapped, including many from the guests and other family members, and, since it was late afternoon, they finished up and left for the reception hall with Sarah and Matthew driving them there.

The hall was beautifully decorated, with flowers as centrepieces on blue linen cloth-covered tables. Streamers, balloons, fairy lights, and vines of roses and baby's breath hung from the ceiling, and everything was coated in pink and blue, Jenny's favourite colours, making the hall look like a wonderland.

"Oh," Jenny gasped. "This is beautiful. Everyone did such a good job of decorating." As they made their way, hand in hand, to the head table, she pointed in delight at everything. "It's perfect." They came to a stop behind their seats and looked from one another to the sea of people around them. It was perfect. *Everything* was perfect. Her family were there, her friends were there, and everyone else that loved them and wanted them to be happy was there. Except for Effie, and Spiros's family.

Jenny turned and gazed into her husband's eyes and the world slowed down around them. "I'm sorry your family weren't here to see this. That must hurt."

His smile wavered, but never fully disappeared. "It does. But I have my uncle and his family, and now my new family. My wife, Jenny, and her family."

She beamed at the word *wife*. "And I have my new family, my husband, Spiros, and his family."

His lips curled back up at the word *husband*. "My Jenny." Gazing deeply into her magnificent blue eyes, he brought her hands to his lips and kissed them. "My Jenny. My wife. Jenny Stephanopoulos."

Jenny leaned in and kissed his lips. "Spiros and Jenny Stephanopoulos."

"Spiros and Jenny." He kissed her back.

"All right, you two, let's get on with this shindig," Ned yelled, sick of all the lovey-dovey stuff. Not that he didn't like kissing; he'd done it a lot, but he just didn't want to see his sister and new brother-in-law doing it.

Laughing, Spiros pulled out Jenny's chair and helped her be seated, and then sat beside her for the festivities to begin.

Dinner was served and was a combination of Jenny's favourite meal from *The Cherry Blossom* restaurant, and a popular Greek dish for those who wanted to try it. She'd consulted Melina and her daughter over the menu, and had them added in to make Spiros feel more at home. She'd been taking cooking lessons from his aunt, had learned to make simple Greek dishes, and had been practising with good old Australian roasts and casseroles that her mother had taught all of her girls to make.

Dessert was Jenny's favourite chocolate cake, with an array of chiffon pies and baklavas. Champagnes, wines, beers, and ouzo were passed around, and toasts were made.

"To our darling daughter, Jenny, and her new husband, Spiros." Matthew held his glass aloft. "May your marriage be happy, may it be fruitful, and may it be long. We hope it brings you many, many blessings. To Jenny and Spiros."

"Jenny and Spiros."

"Aw, Dad, thank you," Jenny called and watched as Nikos stood on the other side of the hall.

"To my nephew, Spiros, and his new bride, Jenny. I have watched you grow into a young lady, as with your sisters for the last four years. Your family helped us immensely when we moved here and we are forever grateful. We witnessed your help when it came to my nephew, Spiros, who had travelled the world with just two friends in tow, to land here in a country where he could not speak the language. You helped him with his lessons, so he could speak English, and all the while the two of you fell in love and dated and now…" He raised his glass to his nephew and new niece-in-law. "You are married. Our two families have become one, and anytime you need help, do not hesitate to ask. To Spiros, you are incredibly lucky, to young Jenny, so are you. To Spiros and Jenny."

"Spiros and Jenny."

The couple's faces beamed their happiness across the room and someone called out that it was time for the first dance.

The small band they'd hired stepped onto the stage, took their places, and started playing music for their first dance.

"Oh, goodness," Jenny cried and reluctantly got to her feet. It was not that she didn't want to dance; she just didn't want to be the only couple dancing on the floor. And she wasn't exactly fluent in the wedding dance.

Spiros escorted her to the floor and took her into his arms. "Are you ready, my Jenny?" He'd been taking lessons in the lead up to the wedding. While he had been learning how to dance with Jenny, the wedding dance was different. He didn't want to mess it up and had asked her sisters for help.

They waltzed around the floor with Jenny gazing lovingly into her new husband's eyes. She couldn't believe that she was married. That the day had finally come when Jennifer Melissa Marsh had gotten married. And not to an Australian boy, but a Greek boy, no less. Jennifer had never done things normally, always bucking the trend, doing things her way, and marriage was going to be no different. She was going to do it her way, and that's all there was to it.

They swished around the floor as other couples finally joined in, and spent the next hour dancing under the fairy lights hanging from the ceiling. It was a magical wonderland and she was lost in the atmosphere.

Finally, taking a breather, they stopped by the refreshment bar for a cooling punch.

"That was so much fun. I keep forgetting this is a wedding, *my* wedding at that." Jenny laughed. "I keep forgetting it's *our* wedding. It's just like one big party." She leaned in for a kiss and got it.

"Yes, my Jenny. It is one big party, and that is how we are going to live our lives. Like a big party. Full of fun and adventure. We will do so many things together as a married couple." Spiros had spent the last hour while they were dancing just staring at her in wonder. He had a wife. Jenny Marsh was his wife, and he was so happy he'd been floating on cloud nine.

"Like what?" Looking up at him, she couldn't help but give her brightest smile.

"We will have adventures and travel and see Australia," Spiros told her. "We are going to Sydney for our honeymoon, yes? We can go to Brisbane for our first anniversary, or for a family holiday when we have children. Yes?"

"Yes." Jenny agreed. "We can. We can see *all* of Australia."

"Yes." Spiros nodded in happiness. "Spiros and Jenny can do anything."

"How about dance Greek style," Nikos roared across the hall. "Let the Greek music begin." The sounds of *Zorba the Greek* floated across the room, and looking at each other in surprise, Spiros decided to pull Jenny into the circle dance happening on the floor.

"Oh, no, Spiros. Really?" She had only done the Greek dance twice and wasn't very good at it.

"Come, my Jenny. It is not so hard." Spiros held her hand the whole time, and after another half an hour of dancing, they laughingly collapsed into their seats at the bridal table. "Was that not fun?"

"Yes, yes, I guess it was." She gasped and reached for the punch the waiter poured. She didn't want to fill up on alcohol as she wanted to remember her wedding night and not feel sick, or have a hangover in the morning, but she also wanted to relax a little and not be so stiff and petrified when they went to bed later.

"Have I told you how beautiful you look, my Jenny?" Spiros

tenderly linked the fingers of his right hand with those of her left. He wore his wedding ring on his right hand, being Greek, while Jenny wore hers on her left.

Giggling, Jenny looked at her beautiful Greek husband. "As nice as it is to be called my Jenny all the time, you can just call me Jenny now. I am your wife, *now*. Jenny Stephanopoulos. Oh, that reminds me, I'll have to change my name when we get back." She'd forgotten all about the legalities of marriage.

"What do you mean, change your name?" Spiros inquired. "Is it not already Stephanopoulos from us getting married?"

"No, it isn't. I'll have to change it legally," Jenny informed him. "I can get that done when we get back from our honeymoon, and then I will *legally* be Mrs Jenny Stephanopoulos, *wife* of Spiros Stephanopoulos." She left a lingering kiss on his lips.

"Wife of Spiros." Spiros sighed and gazed deep into her sapphire eyes. "I do love the sound of that, my Jenny."

"Maybe I should call you, my Spiros." She giggled again, feeling the effects of the alcohol set in. "What are we doing now?"

"We could dance more, eat more, mingle more," Spiros suggested. "It is still early. Have we spoken to everyone, yet?"

"No, I don't think we have," Jenny murmured, and accepted a glass of champagne from a passing waiter. She sipped it as they wandered around the hall. They chatted with every guest, thanked them for coming, and hoped they were enjoying themselves. They spoke with the Stephanides family before coming to the Marsh family and in-laws.

"You look beautiful, Jenny," Margaret, her sister-in-law, told her. She was married to Jenny's oldest sibling, Edward. "And so happy, you look radiant."

"Thank you, Margaret, that's so sweet." Jenny kissed her cheek. "Thank you so much for coming. The kids with their grandparents?"

"Yes, luckily." Margaret smoothed her soft pink A-Line skirt. She didn't come a pinch near Jenny's natural beauty, but was considered handsome for a woman. "It means we've had the night to celebrate, but back to the grindstone tomorrow. You'll be right there with us soon, in about…nine months, I'd say." Margaret and Edward had been married for six years and had four children already.

"Oh, goodness, I don't know about that." Jenny giggled and reached for another glass of champagne from a waiter. "I'll have to see how things go first. Thanks for coming, Margaret." She kissed her brother's cheek and moved on to her other siblings and their families, or dates, finally coming to her parents. "Thank you so much for this." She spun around and waved her arms at everything before her. "For the wedding, the honeymoon, the being the best parents in the world. I love you both, so much." She flung her arms around them both, feeling light-headed and giggly.

"Sounds like you're very merry," Matthew told his daughter and patted her on the back. "You might want to rein it in for a while."

"Oh, I don't think I've had enough," Jenny muttered and pressed her lips to her mother's ear. "I don't want it to hurt. How much will it hurt?"

Sarah pulled back and looked into her daughter's worried eyes. "Just a little, and maybe some tomorrow, and things will be a little awkward until you find your own rhythm together, but it will be okay after that, so don't you worry. I don't want you drinking so much that you're sick on your honeymoon. You might want to make that your last, and make sure you have water before bed and a good strong coffee for breakfast."

Nodding slowly, as the room was starting to spin; Jenny noticed her eyelids begin to droop. "Yes, Mum. I'm starting to feel tired. Maybe we should go soon. It's been a long day."

"Did I hear you say you're going?" Nikos stopped by Spiros's side. "I have your wedding present outside and waiting. Are you ready to go?"

Spiros looked to Jenny for confirmation and Jenny picked up her father's arm to check his watch. "Oh, it's nine o'clock already. But yes, I'm getting tired and think we should go."

"Then let's get you sent off in style, come, come." Nikos led the bride and groom outside to the hall steps and waved an arm. "Your wedding present."

A crowd of guests had gathered around as Spiros and Jenny looked to see a four-door sapphire blue sedan with a white ribbon tied from the bonnet ornament to the windows, and a trail of streamers hanging from the back bumper.

"A car!" Jenny gasped, her hand flying to her mouth. "Oh, Mr Stephanides, this is too much, way too much."

"Please, young Jenny, you are now married to Spiros, you can call me Uncle Nikos. And don't worry, it is not new, it is just my old car done up and painted. Young Nikos did the work. It is a present for the two of you since you are now a married couple. I had it transferred to your name, Spiros." He slapped his stunned nephew on the back. "It is now yours since I upgraded."

"Thank you, Uncle Nikos...I do not know what to say..." No one had ever given him a car before. Secondhand, or not, and it rendered Spiros speechless that his uncle had even considered giving them something so big, let alone so valuable. He knew cars were not cheap, but for his uncle to afford a new one, and to be able to do up his old one, so they could have a car, was unbelievable.

"Oh...what will we do with my car?" Jenny asked. "We don't need two."

"We'll buy you out, Jenny," Rebecca told her. "We'll save the money and buy your share, and then you don't need to worry about it."

"Oh, that's a wonderful idea," Jenny said and turned to her family. "Should we go now?"

"If you like, love." Sarah hugged her. "We brought your luggage with us, so you'll just need to get it before you go."

"Ned, Arthur, go and get your sister's luggage from our car." Matthew tossed the keys to his sons. "And make sure it's locked."

Grumbling, the boys scampered off to retrieve their sister's bags.

"And mine is in Uncle Nikos's car," Spiros said, looking to his uncle for the keys.

"Young Nikos can get it." Nikos gave his son the keys to the new car. "Do not scratch it, Nikos."

Watching the scene before her, and seeing the guests crowding on the steps, Jenny called out, "Thank you, everyone. It's been so wonderful with all of you here to celebrate. Who knew that I'd ever get married?" She hugged her way through the crowd as their luggage was placed in the boot, and finally climbed into their new car.

Spiros started the engine, honked the horn, and slowly pulled away.

"Goodbye, thank you, see you in a week, I love you all." Jenny leaned out the window to wave madly at all she loved. Once on the road, she settled back into her seat, heaved a sigh and deflated. "Who knew weddings could be so tiring?"

Spiros laughed and drove them to their hotel for the night with Jenny snuggling up beside him. When they arrived and checked in, they carried their luggage into their room and freshened up before standing and facing each other. Even though both had had the talk, neither knew what to do.

"So…" Jenny pursed her lips together. "I guess we should…" She nervously glanced around the room, it was the honeymoon suite in the best hotel in Armidale, but that didn't matter one iota if they didn't know what to do next.

"My Jenny," Spiros said softly, seeing the fear and nervousness in her eyes. "We do not have to rush this. This is all new to me, too. I have never…" He looked away in embarrassment. "Never been intimate with a woman. You will be my first."

"And you will be mine," Jenny whispered, taking a step closer to him. "All we've ever done is kiss, and even though we've wanted to do more, we've restrained ourselves. So…um…" She reached up and pulled on his bowtie. "I guess we should take things slow and one step at a time." Sliding his jacket over his shoulders, she hung it on the back of the desk chair. "Better not forget that tomorrow." She laid the tie on the desk and carefully unpinned her veil and set it next to the tie. Her jewellery came next; the heart studs and necklace from Spiros, and the pearl bracelet from her grandmother.

Spiros came up behind her and carefully helped release her hair from the curled updo, so it cascaded down her back in waves and curls.

Turning to face her husband, she removed his watch and cufflinks, so his hands were free to run through her hair.

"Oh, my Jenny," Spiros murmured. "You are so beautiful. I love you, so much. I am so glad you became my Jenny. I am so glad you wanted me, Spiros, as your husband. My Jenny." His fingers slid through her golden curls and revelled in its silkiness.

Jenny leaned against him, looking up at him with her big blue eyes, loving his hands in her hair. "My Spiros." She breathed in his cologne, his musk, she felt the desires start to burn her body, and her eyes closed against the heat. "I love you, Spiros."

"I love you, Jenny." His lips found hers and mated with their new life partner.

Jenny responded by wrapping her arms around his lean muscular torso. They continued slowly, not rushing, taking their time. She unbuttoned his shirt to reveal the white singlet underneath; he unbuttoned the back of her dress. She unclipped the overskirt and laid it over the chair, sliding her dress off to reveal her white slip and stockings, she left it with the skirt. Stepping out of her satin heels, she faced her husband.

"Oh, my Jenny." His fingers slowly slid up her arms. "You are so beautiful."

Blushing, Jenny moved back into her husband's arms and pressed her lips to his, pressed her body to his. Felt the burning warmth of him against her. Felt the rising urge to do more than kiss.

His lips moved across her cheek to her neck, buried themselves in her hair, felt her body sag against his, moved on to her chest, and sliding her hands through his hair, she gasped.

In one swift motion, he picked her up, and kneeling on the bed, gently laid her down. He kicked off his shoes and slid his hands up her side.

She gasped and shuddered as her body lit on fire and her lips found his. Her hands found the material of his singlet and pulled it up, revealing his tanned torso. Jenny shoved the top over his head and kissed him as he lay on top of her. She wanted him, oh, how she wanted him. Her body compulsively moved, bucked up under him, her legs pinned together in fear, but her breasts wanting to be touched. Reaching down between them, she pulled her slip up, wriggling as he helped her pull it over her head. She was wearing a white satin brassiere and panties, plus suspender belt and stockings. Moaning against his lips, she pulled at his pants button and zip.

While he pushed them down, she managed to pull the bed covers down and crawled backwards as he slid back on top of her.

"Ugh," she gasped, his flesh burning her with its passionate heat. "Oh, Spiros."

"Ugh…Jenny…" he muttered, on fire and hard against his lover to be. "Oh, my Jenny…" His hands burned their way down her virginal body and slid under her leg. "Oh…Jenny…"

"Spiros." She pulled away from him to help unclip her suspender belt from her stockings, and he carefully slid them down her legs. Wriggling out of the belt, she slid her legs under the covers, pulling them over their bodies as Spiros came back to her.

He reached over and flicked off one of the bedside lights, leaving only the one light on in the room so he could see his Jenny. Leaning up on his elbows, his body full out on hers, his legs on the outside of hers, he gently swept the hair back from her face. "My Jenny," he whispered.

"My Spiros," she replied just as softly. "I want you, but go slow."

With a slight nod, he brought his lips to hers and kissed her deeply, his tongue probing, his hands caressing, as were hers as they explored his lean body and the heat it was exerting. Lips trailed down her neck and found their way to her breast bone. Hands joined them and gently kneaded her breasts.

"Ah…" escaped from Jenny as her bosoms heaved in desire. She pulled the straps down and kept on pulling, setting her firm high breasts free from their confines for him to ravish. "…Spiros…"

His mouth enveloped her left nipple, kneading it with his tongue.

"Ah…" Jenny had never experienced such burning desire rip at her body; she knew that this wasn't yet the act of sex, but the lead up was more than worth it and something she wanted again. "Ah…" His hands gently moulded her right breast and she bucked up under him.

"Oh, God…" she cried, not realising she had taken the Lord's name in vain in the throes of passion. "Oh…"

His lips moved down, and she ground her head into the pillow, thrust her breasts to the sky, and clamped her legs shut between his. She was possessed by passion and didn't know what to do about it except ride the storm out. Fumbling, she managed to unlock her bra and throw it away.

"Oh…Jenny…" Spiros tenderly kissed her stomach, knowing that within a year it would be full with his child. Hands held onto her slim waist and slowly, slowly, he pulled her panties down to reveal a thatch of hair as golden-brown as the hair on her head. "Oh…Jenny…" He kissed across her abdomen, kissing the outline of her hair.

Her hands tangled in the hair on his head as his lips devoured her.

His hands slid the material down her legs, flinging them to the floor. He quickly pushed down his own underwear and they went the same way. "Jenny…" Spiros lay beside her, a hand resting on her stomach. He tried not to let his penis touch her, not yet, anyway. He knew it was bigger than other boys', had seen his friends naked enough to know he was not normal, and that any woman he married would have to bear the brunt of twelve inches. He didn't want to hurt his Jenny; she was too special to him. "My Jenny," he breathed against her cheek. "There is something I need to tell you."

Groggily, she blinked a few times and pulled the covers up to cover her bare breasts. "Have we… We haven't, yet, have we?"

"No, my Jenny. But I need to tell you something, so you know, and so we can be careful as I do not want to hurt you."

"I know you won't hurt me, Spiros," Jenny murmured, looking up into the face of her lover, her husband. "But it will hurt the first few times. That's just the way it is. Mum told me what happens. It's okay." Her hand caressed his face.

"No, my love." He captured her hand and kissed it. "Listen, Jenny. I have known for some time…" Glancing away a moment, he continued, "That I am not normal. I have seen other men, my brothers, and I am not like them in the downstairs department. I may hurt you because of it. That is why I will understand and insist we take things slowly until you are able to accept me into your body. It may take a while."

"Spiros…" Panic started to set in. "What are you saying? That you are not normal like other men?" A myriad of images and thoughts flew through her mind and she wondered if he was man enough.

"Oh, my Jenny." He lay on his back and closed his eyes.

"Spiros?" Jenny rolled onto her side and laid her hand on his heart. "What is it?"

Sighing, he opened his eyes and looked into those of his wife. "Jenny. I do not want to hurt you, but I fear I might because…because…" He stopped and his eyes closed a second time.

"Because?" she urged. "What is it? Do you not want to make love to me?"

His eyes grew wide at the thought. "*Of course* I do, my Jenny." He rolled onto his side to face her. "It is just that," blushing, he kissed her hand, "I am bigger than normal men." He left it there and waited for her response.

"What do you mean…bigger than normal men?" She was quite confused with the way the conversation was going and just wanted to get on with making love.

Biting the bullet, he went on to explain. "My…penis…is longer than normal, my Jenny. I am afraid it will hurt you."

"Oh…" came from her, and shock at the word penis, and shock from hearing he was larger, knocked her onto her back. "I…"

"I do not want to hurt you, my Jenny," Spiros moved on. "I think we should take things very slowly, and if it hurts, or you cannot accept me, then we will stop. Yes?"

"Oh…um…yes…I suppose…" She looked into his eager eyes. "If it hurts I'll tell you. But it will hurt anyway because I've never been intimate."

"Then we will go slow. Yes?" Spiros kissed her gently.

The fires burned in Jenny's stomach. "Yes."

Facing each other, they started kissing, stoking the fires and turning them into a raging inferno. He rolled her onto her back and slowly inched his way over. First, his left leg slid between hers, and when she pulled him on top, his right leg.

She gasped at the package between his legs, knowing what it was, but not sure if she was ready. As much as she wanted it *and* him, she was scared.

"It is okay, my Jenny. I will stay here awhile, let us just kiss," Spiros encouraged and moved his lips back and forth on hers.

Their tongues mated and she relaxed. Her hands made their way over his muscular back and he shifted, the nest of hair on his chest setting her breasts and nipples on fire.

"Ah…" slid from her and his mouth enclosed around her right nipple, sucking it to attention. She writhed, thrusting her chest up towards him, and he took it, one hand on one breast, his mouth on the other, and slowly, slowly his erection probed the delicate entrance of Jennifer Marsh Stephanopoulos. "Ah…" Her nails dug into his shoulders, her legs spread themselves apart, and his hand lifted her, guided her, guided him in slowly while she cried out in momentary pain and he slid in as far as he could, stopping to give her a moment to adapt to him, his length, his fullness.

"Ah…" Jenny pushed her head back into the pillow, her eyes shut tight, and her face ran the gamut of emotion, fear, shock, pain, passion, desire, and a surprising feeling she'd never had before. Relaxing a little, her eyes opened, and she felt the pounding inside of her, but all she saw was the ceiling.

"Jenny?" Spiros appeared above her. "Are you hurt? I can leave you?"

"No…" she mumbled dazedly, digging her nails in. "Go slowly. *Very* slowly."

"Okay, my Jenny." With delicate thrusts, Spiros slowly slid back and forth, pausing between each movement. "You okay, my Jenny?"

Pain was mixed with the most exquisite feeling, a pleasurable feeling, one she couldn't describe if she tried. "Yes, I'm okay, keep going, don't stop."

He moved on, watching her face for any sign that she was in pain, or wanted to stop. The one thing he never wanted to do, *vowed* never to do, was hurt the love of his life. *His Jenny Marsh.* He watched, wondered what the expressions on her face were about. Was she enjoying it? Was he hurting her? He slowed, even though he felt the power of his desire surging to the fore. He knew this was his seed, had experimented with his penis to see what it could do, and knew the end was coming.

Jenny was in agony and ecstasy. While the pain of that initial entry was fading, the pain from such a long penis was doing damage to her nerves, especially the one that was causing so much pleasure. She wasn't sure where it was, or how it was happening, but every time he slid back and forth it was rubbed and sent an electrifying wave of pleasure through her. "Ah…" Her head pushed into the pillow, and her eyes closed against the onslaught. Her legs moved, bringing her knees up beside his hips. Her hands dug into his back and her breasts ached at the coarse chest hair teasing them. "Ah…"

"Not much longer, my Jenny. I am almost there," Spiros muttered through clenched teeth. A few more thrusts and he came. "Jenny, oh, Jenny." A few grunts and he was done. Panting, he set himself up on his elbows and waited for his wife.

"Ah…" Jenny saw stars and fireworks and felt his body resting against hers. "Ah…" she sighed, her body coming down from its rollercoaster ride.

"Jenny?" Spiros gently kissed her face, brushing her golden curls away and watching her lips curls into a soft smile.

"Spiros…" she whispered, knowing he was still inside. "Spiros…" Her chest heaved for air and she slowly opened her eyes to see her husband. "Spiros."

"My Jenny," he murmured and kissed her lips. "My Jenny."

"Spiros." She wrapped her arms around him. "I love you."

"I love you, too, my Jenny. Do you want me to slide out? Are you okay?"

"I'm okay." She breathed in. "It's okay." Even the motion of him sliding out was a mix of pain and pleasure. "Ah…"

He lay by her side, taking her into his arms, holding her while their breathing evened out. "Oh, my Jenny. Did I hurt you?"

"It hurt a little. But I think that was normal." She rested her head against his chest. "I think we should wait a few days to try that again. Just so everything is okay inside me. I don't want to make it worse."

"Okay, my Jenny. We will wait a couple of days," Spiros murmured against her head. "You sleep, my Jenny. *My* Jenny. My wife, my lover, *my* Jenny."

A soft smile lazily spread across Jenny's lips as she fell into a deep and happy sleep.

*****

They didn't wake until after eight the next morning when Jenny remembered she was now a married woman and had finally had sex. Smiling happily, she kissed her husband's chest and rolled over to check her travel clock. She winced at the pain. "Ow."

"You okay, my Jenny?" Spiros placed a hand on her back. "Are you sore?"

The warmth from his hand radiated through to her heart. "Yes. But I knew I would be. I just didn't expect sharp pain."

"Why do you not rest, and I will call room service and have a shower. Yes?" He kissed her shoulder and then her cheek.

Grinning, she kissed him back. "I'll have Eggs Benedict, juice and coffee."

"And so will I." Spiros made the call and hurried to take a shower. He was dressed and helping Jenny sit up in bed when the breakfast came.

They took their time enjoying it, savouring their first breakfast as husband and wife, and when they were finished, Jenny slowly got up and showered. Taking the time to carefully wash down there so no infection was caused; she dressed, repacked her bag, and called her mother. "Mum, do you mind coming and picking up our bridal clothes?"

"Of course not, love. I was planning to come at ten anyway. Give you two a chance to sleep in."

"Thanks, Mum." Jenny packed her gown and accessories, plus Spiros's suit into the suit bag she had brought. Ten minutes later, Sarah arrived.

"Thanks for coming." Jenny kissed her good morning and

motioned for Spiros to take their bags to the car, so she could have a moment alone with her mother. She briefly told her about last night and was reassured that the pain was normal and would subside in a day or two.

"You'll be fine, love," Sarah told her when she kissed her goodbye. "I'll see you when you get back." She carried the bag to her car. "Goodbye, Spiros. Take care of our Jenny."

"I will, Mrs Marsh." Spiros waved her off and waited for his wife.

Jenny finished checking the suite and pulled the door closed behind her. "Ready?"

"I am ready. Do you have everything?" He escorted her to their car and opened the door for her.

"I do." She kissed his cheek and gingerly eased into the front seat. It was uncomfortable, and she didn't know if she could manage the long drive to Sydney.

Spiros hopped in and started the car. "Ready for our honeymoon, my Jenny?"

Giggling softly, she said, "I know I'm yours now, Spiros, but you don't have to keep calling me, my Jenny. Now that we're married, I'm Jenny, your wife."

"My wife." He lifted her hand to his lips and kissed it. "My Jenny. My wife."

She laughed and they set off on their journey to Sydney.

*****

Even though they only had a week, they saw as much as they could, including some of Jenny's relatives who lived in the Sydney area, her two single uncles, and an aunt and uncle, who had come up for the wedding. Jenny took Spiros to all of the tourist attractions; they ate in many restaurants, sampled other culture's food, and only made love every second night to give Jenny time to get used to his size, and give the pain a chance to subside.

They drove home on Sunday to another surprise.

Now that they were married, they had to find a place to live, and had been discussing it the whole of the honeymoon, along with where they were going to stay when they got back, because they weren't sure they could stay with Jenny's parents, or Spiros's aunt and uncle.

As they pulled into the Marshes' driveway, the family came running out.

"Oh, you're back."

"How was it?"

"Did you have fun?"

"I did, I did, oh, I missed you girls." Jenny hugged her three younger sisters and saw her parents shaking Spiros's hand. "Mum, Dad." She hurried around the car and hugged them. "We seem to have a bit of a problem."

"And what's that, love?" Matthew asked.

"Well…" Jenny pulled her sapphire blue coat around her to keep the chilly late May winds out. "We don't have anywhere to stay."

At that point, Nikos and his family came bursting out of their house and over the fence to them. "Welcome back, welcome back. How was the honeymoon?" Nikos boomed, making Jenny blush.

"Uncle Nikos," Spiros murmured, flushing a bright red. "Do not be embarrassing. Jenny was just explaining that we do not have anywhere to stay now that we are home and married."

"Have you not told them?" Nikos asked Matthew.

"Didn't have the chance," Matthew replied, annoyed that his surprise was being taken over.

"Well, come, come, get in your car and follow all of us." Nikos waved at his son to get the car keys, and Jenny's parents urged them back into their car.

"What's going on?" Jenny asked, and tucked herself into their car.

"You'll see," her sisters called and climbed into the backseat of their parents' car.

Backing out, Spiros waited for the Marshes and his uncle before following them down the road and two neighbourhoods across. Jenny recognised the street they turned into as the one her two sisters lived on, and her brothers lived on the one behind. "Are we going to see the rest of the family?" Jenny murmured as they pulled up outside a small cream brick home three doors down from her sister. "Why are we stopping here?" They alighted and followed everyone up the drive and into the house. "*What* is going on?"

"Surprise!" everyone called.

Jenny saw her older sisters and brothers with their families standing in the lounge room of the house. *"What is going on?"*

"Welcome home, love." Sarah hugged her stunned daughter. "This is yours."

"What! What do you mean, it's ours?" Jenny glanced from excited face to excited face.

"We did for you what we did for your siblings," Matthew explained. "Along with Nikos, we set up the down payment on the house and it's in your name, so you'll have to pay the mortgage."

"And we added in a few decorations and some furniture," Nikos added. "We could not have you living in our spare room anymore."

"Oh…this is…oh…" Tears poured forth at the generosity. "Thank you, so much, everyone." Jenny moved from person to person, giving hugs and kisses. Once the champagne and ouzo were popped, they celebrated with an impromptu house warming and showed them both around.

The lounge room had a two-seater and two single chairs with a coffee table set up. Pictures were on the walls, and pretty blue curtains hung at the window. It adjoined the dining room with a six-person table set and wall buffet with hutch, and the kitchen was fully decked out for 1950s living.

There were three bedrooms; the master had a bed already set up, there were pictures and curtains, a dressing table for Jenny, and matching wardrobes and dressers.

"Hey, isn't that my wardrobe?" Jenny asked in surprise. "And my cupboard?"

"And the desk is set up in one of the other bedrooms for you to work or sew," Faye told her and smoothed out the pretty pink and blue bedspread. "We carted your furniture down here."

"And all of your clothes and accessories." Rebecca opened the twin wardrobes. "I gave you my wardrobe so you'd have a set, and my cupboard so you had both pieces matching."

"Oh, girls, thank you so much for all of this. It's wonderful." Jenny hugged them all and was led into the next two bedrooms to see curtains, coloured walls, single beds and wardrobes, with the desk being in the third room.

The bathroom was connected to the separate toilet, which was connected to the laundry at the back of the house.

They stepped outside onto the back porch and saw a huge yard with its shed and clothesline.

"Oh, everything is perfect," Jenny sobbed, unable to control her tears anymore. "It's all so perfect."

"And the fridge is full of food," Maria Stephanides said from the doorway. "Wasn't about to let our cousin and his new wife starve."

"Meat from *Stephanides Meats*, I take it?" Spiros grinned at his cousin.

"Of course." She grinned in return.

They walked back in and celebrated, telling everyone of the places they'd seen on their honeymoon and talking plans for the future.

*****

Since they still had a couple of days, it wasn't until Wednesday that Jenny and Spiros went back to work.

When Jenny walked into her workplace, she was pulled aside by the boss.

"Ah, Jenny, what are you doing here?" Miss Greyson asked nervously, smoothing out her tight grey pencil skirt and glancing around at the other girls.

"I'm coming back to work," Jenny said, removing her gloves and putting them in her handbag. "Is something wrong?"

"Jenny." Ms Greyson led her out of view of the other girls. With a slim feminine build, Jean Greyson was in her forties, had never married, but had worked since she was eighteen. With upswept brown hair, black-rimmed cat's eye-shaped reading glasses, and pointed features; she was chicly dressed for the times and the workplace in a soft grey cardigan to match her skirt, a crisp white shirt, and black kitten heels. "You know that once a lady is married she doesn't work. When you left we filled your position."

While Jenny knew that was how society supposedly worked, she also knew many a lady, single and married, like her mother, who still worked. "I was afraid that would happen," Jenny replied, looking back into the room. "And you still get to work because you're single, like my aunts. But my mother is married and still works as a nurse, so clearly, society is a little screwed up when it comes to what a woman's work actually is. You also waited until I was married and back from my honeymoon to tell me you'd fired me." Angry that her being married dictated her standing in society, Jenny asked about her wage and was told that the last week of work was it.

"So, I've had no wage for a week and a half. Nice." Jenny could barely contain her sarcasm and pulled her gloves from her bag. Even though she'd been taught to be ladylike at all times, now that she was a married woman she didn't feel the need to be. "Well, thank you for nothing, Miss Greyson. Good day." Jenny walked out the same way she'd walked in and set about finding work immediately. She went to see her father who suggested she help out his secretary with excess paperwork, and maybe ask the other council members if they needed extra help. She went to see her aunts who said they'd pay her to be a hair model and work in the salon a couple of afternoons a week, and she contacted her siblings to see if they needed an accountant, or typist, for a day, or two, a week. Being out of work wasn't a good thing, especially since they had a house to pay off and would more than likely be having a child in the next year.

Since the pain had subsided, sex had come every night and would continue except for when Jenny had her monthly cycle. Her mother had told her that would stop when she was pregnant, so to be conscious of the timing between each. Sex was enjoyable and she didn't want it to stop, even though it was still a little awkward because of Spiros's length.

But, until she was in labour, she needed to do something to help pay off their new home, and typing and accounting were it, although the idea of being a hair model did excite her.

She discussed it with Spiros that night over lamb casserole. "I just wish society wasn't so sexist," she told him, sitting down at the table. The idea was still so new, having a house with a table to sit at and a kitchen to cook in.

"But why do you not want to be a lady of leisure?" Spiros asked. "Even back home in Greece women do not work once married."

"Well, that may be so, but we have a house to pay off, and run, along with a car, so that means bills to pay and petrol to buy, and food for our fridge. We need all the money we can get to pay off as much as possible for when children come along. Maybe *then* I'll be a stay at home mother, but *until* then, we should work hard and save harder. I've worked since I was eighteen, as did my parents and my siblings. It's in the blood. Marsh blood."

"And you are now a Stephanopoulos," Spiros said. "And I will work hard to provide for my Jenny and our babies. That is what Stephanopouloses do."

"Aw." Jenny melted at his words and grasped his hand. "I get all the paperwork done on Monday. Once it's legal I will be Jenny Stephanopoulos. Your wife."

"You already are my wife, my Jenny." He kissed her hand and held it to his lips. "I cannot make you stay home, that is not your way. But promise me once the baby comes, you will be a mother, and not a worker."

"You clearly don't know how much work running a household *and* children is. Maybe you should give it a try," Jenny cheekily suggested.

"You are funny, my Jenny." Spiros went back to his casserole. "And a very good cook."

"I learned from the best," Jenny murmured and blew on her food to cool it down. Now, she just needed to get their life sorted.

*****

On Friday, she went to visit Effie. She'd been the best friend she could for the last few months, having *The Cherry Blossom* restaurant deliver one of her wedding meals to Effie in the hospital, along with the gifts for her guests. And she had all of the photos the photographer had taken, plus the photos everyone else had given her, to show Effie what she had missed out on.

Knocking on the door to the house, she heard a baby crying, but after a few moments, when no one answered, she called out. "Effie? It's Jenny. Are you there?"

Another minute of waiting, and finally a very rumpled, unshowered, unruly Effie answered the door wearing a vomit stained apron over her very plain and ugly dress. Her hair was a mess, and her pallor was sickly. Definitely *not* the Effie she used to know.

"Oh, Effie. Are you not well? Let me in and I'll help." Jenny moved through the door to see the house in disarray. Nappies were dumped everywhere, plates piled up in the sink, the smell of vomit and baby poo hung in the air. Even though it was winter, Jenny quickly flung open the windows and went to see the baby. "Hello, little one. How are you? I'm Aunt Jenny." She leaned over his bassinette, saw the dark hair and eyes peering back, and he stopped crying as the new stranger stared down at him. "I'm here to help your mummy."

Removing her coat and gloves, she set them over the back of a kitchen chair, rolled up her sleeves, and got to work. She soon had the dishes done, a load of laundry in the wash, and all the clean nappies neatly stacked in the nursery. "Now, how about a cup of tea?" She made a pot and poured two cups, taking them into the lounge room where Effie was curled up on the couch. "Oh, Effie, what's happened to you? Mum said she'd been around every couple of days, and your mother, aunts and cousins come too. Effie?" Gazing at her friend, she had no idea what would help her, so she got her bag and pulled the photo albums out. Settling beside her on the couch, Jenny flipped through the pages, talking about the wedding and reception, and all about the honeymoon. After half an hour, she gently shook her arm. "Why don't you have a nice shower? Wash your hair, and take your time. I'll look after the baby for a while. It will help you feel better." Getting nothing but a vacant stare from her friend, she led her into the bathroom and sat her down, then untangled Effie's hair and helped her into the shower.

At least Effie had enough wits about her to wash her hair and body, and then stood under the water.

Jenny helped her dry off, fetched a fresh dress, and dried and braided her hair. Getting Effie back on the couch with a blanket over her, Jenny cleaned up the lounge room, changed the bed for fresh linen, and reloaded the washing machine.

"There, all done." Dusting off her hands, Jenny hurried to close the windows and looked in on the baby, noticing the dirty clothes and nappy. She set about giving him a wash in the baby bath, and dressed him in a clean nappy, singlet, and onesie. He seemed content with all that was happening, and this new woman in his life that was taking care of him.

"What's his name?" Jenny already knew it was Alexandros, but she was trying to get Effie to talk.

She received silence in return.

Signing, Jenny knew she had to go, so placed the baby in his bassinette and tucked him in, cleared the cups, and made sure there was food in the fridge. "I need to go, but I'll give you my new number in case you need me, so call." She scribbled it down; along with her new address and name in the phone book next to the phone. "I put it under Jenny." Gazing at her friend's morose figure, she collected her things and kissed her on the cheek. "Please get better, Effie. Please snap out of it. You used to be so bubbly and alive, and now you're just…" Shaking her head sadly, Jenny sighed. "I'll see you next week, Effie." After checking on the baby one last time, she left.

December 1952

"Whew! It's going to be a hot one this Christmas." Jenny carefully bent down and picked up a stray piece of tinsel from the floor. Hanging it back on the tree, she swiped at a strand of loose hair and tucked it under the scarf holding it all out of her face. "I'm glad we put the awnings on the windows and managed to insulate the roof and walls. It's really helped keep the heat out, since we don't have much of a cooling system except for the fans." She settled next to Spiros on the two-seater couch in front of the fan. "It's going to be warm, and I think baby Stephanopoulos is already baking. He doesn't need to be overdone."

Smiling at Jenny's joke, Spiros laid his hand on her stomach. "Not long now. Only two months, and then baby Stephanopoulos will be here."

"It already seems like forever that I've been pregnant. I kind of want it over and done with already." Jenny removed his hand as it just added heat to her already hot body. "I think it will be a boy, so we better have a boy's name picked out."

"How do you know?" Spiros turned so he was facing her.

"Something about the way you carry a boy to a girl, or some such thing." Jenny dabbed at her sweaty forehead. "Between Mum, my sisters, my sisters-in-law, and all the women in town, they all say I'm having a boy."

"Good! He will have good strong Stephanopoulos genes." Spiros nodded his acceptance, glad that he'd been able to provide for Jenny, and now his future son and other children. He and his family, as well as the Marshes, had built a back deck onto the house, plus a covered area to the side of the yard, so the kids could play. They'd also covered up the driveway with a carport. Spiros wasn't lazy when it came to hard work, and he got in there with the best of them and used hammer and nails to add to the house, so his Jenny was comfortable.

"He'll also have good strong Marsh genes," Jenny told him. "He won't be all you."

Spiros chuckled. "Yes, I know, my Jenny. I am just proud to know that we are having a baby soon, and we are celebrating our first Christmas as husband and wife in our new home."

"Well…the home's not so new anymore." Jenny glanced around their house at the Christmas decorations. They had done up the second bedroom as a nursery and had plenty of hand-me-down baby clothes. Since boys grew so fast, Jenny's sisters and sisters-in-law had given her some things to get her going. And with everyone buying, or giving her items she needed, they only had to buy a pram and a cot, and make sure they were ones that could be used for future babies. "But we are celebrating as husband and wife, and speaking of which, have you seen Nicodemus lately? I was popping in on Effie every week, but as I get larger, I can only manage every month, or so. I don't think they're doing so well."

"Mmm, I have seen Nicodemus around," Spiros replied and linked his fingers with Jenny's. "But with other women."

"What! He's cheating on her?" Jenny was surprised and dismayed that Nicodemus could be so frivolous with Effie's emotions and leave his wife and baby home alone while he gallivanted around the countryside.

"Yes, unfortunately," Spiros murmured. "I saw him last week. I did not know the girl, so went up to him and asked why he was not home with his wife and baby. The young lady seemed very shocked. I do not think she knew. I think he had lied to her."

"Oh, that's just foul," Jenny retorted angrily. "How *dare he* do that to her! She doesn't deserve that. From what I could tell, and have been told, she's doing better, but still isn't back to the way she used to be. I don't think having a baby was a very pleasant experience for Effie. I think it has left her depressed."

"If Nicodemus has been cheating on her the whole time, it is no wonder." Spiros shook his head in dismay. "I cannot believe he could do that. I think back to Mykonos, before we came here. He had multiple jobs, could not keep one. I guess he cannot keep a family, either."

"Is he still in that job his in-laws found him back in June?"

"No, I do not think so. But he was, how you say, splashing the cash around when I saw him."

"So, he has money, but his wife and child sit at home getting nothing out of him. I'm glad her family are helping her." Jenny felt the baby kick. "She at least has them to help her because I sure as well haven't been able to the last few months. Ugh…baby's moving." She rubbed her belly and watched as Spiros placed his hand on top of hers. Her fingers linked with his. "I'm so glad you're not like Nicodemus. My father and brothers would have your guts for garters, and we'd have our marriage annulled, or get a divorce. Catholic, or not."

"Then I am glad I am not like Nicodemus," Spiros agreed with a nod of his head.

February 1953

They got through Christmas and New Year's on a heatwave and managed through January by having lots of cooling baths. Come February, Jenny was about to burst. And on February the thirteenth, she did. Or her water did, anyway.

"Argh," she screamed as the first sharp pain tore through her body while she stood in the kitchen. "Oh, my God, what's happening?" She grasped the sink edge and looked down at the floor to the bloody puddle between her legs. "What's happening? What's that? Oh my God, am I losing the baby?"

Her mother and two older sisters rushed from the dining table and around the counter. "That's the water the baby's been surrounded by. It means you've gone into labour, love. Let's get you cleaned up." Sarah led her to the bathroom and into a cold shower. Once out, she examined Jenny in the bedroom. "Barely dilated. It could be a while, so there's no need to get you to the hospital, yet."

"Yet?" Jenny panted. "What do you mean, yet? Am I not in labour?" Even though she had read the books, and had many a chat with her mother, sisters, and sisters-in-law, it was still a new undiscovered world with uncharted territory for Jenny.

"Just the beginning, Jenny." Sarah sat by her side. "All you can do is fill in the time until it's time to actually go to the hospital, and then the midwives and nurses will take care of most of it until the baby's ready to pop out, and then the doctor steps in and thinks he's saving the day, but really, you've done all the hard work and he's just pulling the baby out and taking the credit."

"Will I be in pain? Is it painful?" Jenny felt too weak to work up a panic just yet. "Couldn't've been if you had twelve of us."

"Well…there's also a little thing called contraception, which we have none of. So, if you want to be intimate with your husband, then you'll more than likely end up pregnant. I popped out twelve children, and yes, it's painful, and no, there are no drugs except for some gas. But that doesn't really help. It will hurt for ages after, and you may want to hold off a while on having sex again. Unless you want another baby so soon."

"Not if it's going to be like this," Jenny moaned. "It's awful. I'm so sweaty and sticky." She waved her hands to fan herself even though the bedroom fan was facing her and going on medium. "It's so hot. I'm so hot."

"I'll get you an ice water, help keep you cool." Sarah went to get it while Jenny contemplated ringing Spiros.

"How long will this last?" she asked when her mother came back. "The labour?"

"Could be hours. Could be days." Sarah laid a wet cloth on her daughter's forehead. "Why?"

"Just wondering if I should ring Spiros. I guess not." Sipping her drink, Jenny drifted off in the warmth of the bedroom and only awoke when Spiros came home.

"My Jenny." He rushed into the bedroom, and gathering her hands in his, kissed them.

"Spiros?" Jenny dreamily murmured. "I'm in labour."

"Your mother just told me and said it will be a while. Are you feeling all right?"

"Tired, hot, bulging. Can you get me another drink, please?"

"Of course, my love." He rushed out, but almost collided with Sarah.

"I thought she could do with another drink. You go and shower, cool yourself down, and I'll cool Jenny down," she told him.

"Thank you. I will not be long." He dashed off and was back in ten minutes by Jenny's side, holding her hand and cooling her down, and except for a light dinner of salad and meat, he never left her side until it was time to go to the hospital.

"Push, Jenny, I want you to push." Dr Salica was between Jenny's legs waiting for her baby to come out. He was the only paediatrician in Armidale, so birthed all the babies that came along.

Jenny clamped her jaw, blew out her cheeks, and growled. "Ooohhh." It was the fourth time she'd done it, after a twenty-hour labour, and she was over it.

"And…he's coming…one more push; he's crowning, push, Jenny, push."

Jenny pushed with all her might and felt the tiny human being slide out from between her legs. "Argh…" She collapsed back against the pillows, and her mother wiped her brow and held her hand.

"You did well, love," Sarah whispered.

"It's a boy," Dr Salica told them. "We'll just cut the cord and get him cleaned up, and then you can hold him."

After she was stitched up, Jenny was handed her baby. Dazed, and a bit confused after gas and being in pain for so long, she stared into the boy's eyes and saw they were as big and blue as hers. With a tuft of golden-brown hair the colour of hers, she knew, looking down into his chubby face, that he was going to look like her and not Spiros. Slowly, her lips curled into a smile, and the baby, noticing, tried curling his lips as well. Regardless of the pain she had experienced for the last day, it didn't measure up to the joy of holding her baby boy in her arms.

"See," her mother said. "It's worth it, isn't it?"

Nodding, Jenny's tears flowed over in jerky waves. "Y-yes," she stuttered. "Yes, it is. Look at him. He's got my hair and eyes."

"Jenny?" Spiros called softly from the doorway. Even though he'd been the manager of *Stephanides Meats* since January when the former manager had retired due to illness, Nikos had still given him the day off from work because of Jenny being in labour.

Their heads swivelled his way and Sarah waved him in. "Come. Come and meet your son."

Spiros robotically walked towards the bed, unsure of what to say, or do, but when he got to Jenny's side and saw the baby in her arms, he let out a gush of emotion. "Oh, Jenny, he is real. He is a person. He is a boy, and he is here, with us." His hands moved around both of them and gazed down into his son's bright blue eyes. "Just like my Jenny. Big blue eyes like your mama. Yes, you have. Big blue eyes like your mama. And her hair. Oh, he is definitely going to look like you when he grows up." His eyes turned from his newborn to his wife, damp with sweat and hard work. "Thank you, my Jenny, for giving me a son. For giving *us* a son." He kissed her cheek and saw her tired smile. "You must rest now. You have done so much." His heart was overflowing with love and happiness, but all he cared for was Jenny's wellbeing. "You must rest, Jenny. I will take the baby. Yes?"

"Yes," she murmured and handed the baby over to him. She watched with wonder as the expressions flew over his face; the love and happiness that overwhelmed him as he held his son close to his chest and stared into his eyes.

"Hello, my little one. My little Spiros junior," he whispered to his son.

"No, not Spiros junior." Jenny's voice came out tired and slow. "Carlos, Carlos Spiros Stephanopoulos." Resting her head against the pillow, she drifted off to sleep while Spiros nodded at the name she'd given their child.

February 1955

After abstaining from sex for over a year, Jenny was right back in the maternity ward of Armidale hospital giving birth to their second child two years later.

"Argh…" Jenny yelled through gritted teeth and pushed her second son out of her uterus. "Argh…" Collapsing against the pillows, she waited until she was cleaned up and her baby was wiped down and weighed. Considering contraception was not available, as the Catholic Church frowned heavily on it, and even though she hadn't wanted to, Jenny had pushed for abstinence. After Carlos, the pain had been almost unbearable, and even with all the words from her mother, sisters, and sisters-in-law about it getting better, Jenny hadn't wanted to be in the family way again so soon. The thought of having baby after baby scared her. She didn't want to have a hundred children like her family and many of her friends. Child after child. And while Spiros was not eager about abstaining and not making love to his Jenny, he understood that she was in pain and needed to take her time recovering. Besides, they had a baby to look after, and even he wasn't sure about having another one so soon, as Carlos was proving to be more than a handful.

Doctor Salica handed the baby to her. "Another boy, Jenny. I'd say this one looks like Spiros."

Holding the bundle of gurgling baby, Jenny stared down into the dark brown eyes. "He has Spiros's eyes and hair. Look at that tuft."

The little splotch of hair on the top of his head was as black as his father's. "You will *definitely* look like Spiros," Jenny whispered to her son.

"Jenny?"

She looked up to see her husband in the doorway holding Carlos who had not only celebrated his second birthday that day, but become a big brother as well. "Come and see your son, and Carlos can meet his brother."

Spiros walked over to the bed and peered down at his new son. "Oh, hello there, little one. You are finally here. Yes? Carlos." He looked at his squirming two-year-old and stood him on the bed next to Jenny. "Say hello to your baby brother. Remember we told you Mama was having a baby? Here he is. Your brand-new baby brother."

Carlos, ever the adventurous child full of boundless energy, took one look at his brother and shook his head. "No! I no wanna baby. I go home now."

A tired giggle came from Jenny. "You can go home soon, my baby. It's been a big day for you. You turned two and had a big birthday with everyone there. Received lots of presents, had a cake and became a big brother." She gently brushed his golden hair out of his big blue eyes. "Look at you, my little man. All grown up at two."

"I two." Carlos held up two fat fingers and bounced up and down. "I two, I two, I two."

Spiros caught him and swung him onto his hip. "And I am taking you back home, so just wait a minute." Turning to Jenny, he kissed her gently and rubbed his new son's cheek. "What are we calling this one?"

Looking down at the baby, Jenny said, "Tomas. Not Thomas, but Tomas. Tomas Giorgio Stephanopoulos."

"Oh…Jenny…" Spiros gasped softly. "Why…how…?" He looked at her in amazement.

"Why not?" she replied. "He looks like you, why not have your father's and grandfather's name as his middle name? Carlos has your name; Tomas has your father's."

"Oh…Jenny…" Tears welled in Spiros's eyes and he shook his

head sadly. "I…do not know what to say…thank you…"

"Of course." Jenny stared down at her brand-new baby boy before drifting off to sleep.

February 1957

While Jenny didn't know how many children they'd end up having, her second birth wasn't much better than her first, so abstinence played the part once more in keeping a check on when she got pregnant. And two years later, to the day, February the fourteenth, their third son was born after a four-hour labour.

"And push…"

"Argh…" Jenny pushed and out he came, slippery and long, just like an eel. "Ah…" She gasped and fell back against the bed. "I'm glad that's over. Only four hours this time, must be a record for me. At least we got to celebrate the boys' birthdays." They had managed to have a party for Carlos, who was four, and Tomas, who was two, before Jenny went into labour late in the afternoon.

"Yes, and didn't the boys love their cake." Sarah dabbed Jenny's face. "Fell right asleep just before you went into labour."

"Which is surprising, considering all the sugar in it. It normally makes Carlos haywire." Jenny winced as she was stitched up. "I'm glad that only happens every two years. Ah…" She shifted into a better position. "How is he?"

"See for yourself." The nurse handed him over and a gurgling baby boy with bright blue eyes and a shock of jet-black hair looked back.

"Hello there, my baby. Look at you all long and lithe. Slippery like an eel you were." Jenny pulled the blanket back to look at his squirmy body. "All long and skinny, you are. You're going to be tall when you're older. Yes, you are."

"My, what a combination," Sarah murmured, looking at her umpteenth grandchild. "Black hair, blue eyes, he's half you, half Spiros."

A smile lit up Jenny's face. "He is. I've got one, Spiros has one, and now we've got one combined. Best of everything."

"Jenny?" Spiros came through the door. "Your family are watching the boys. Have you had him already?"

"Yes. Come look. We were just talking about his looks. He has your hair and my eyes. He'll be a lethal combination when he's old enough to date. The girls will love him."

Spiros stood by his wife's bed and took photos of their son. "He is very good looking, long too. He will be tall, like me."

"Yes, that's what we said," Sarah took one last look at her grandson. "I'm going to visit Rebecca, and see how she and her daughter are doing."

"Okay, thanks, Mum." Jenny watched her mother leave then turned her attention back to her son. "It's funny to think that now I've had my third child, all of my siblings are now married and parents of their own. Rebecca had hers a few days ago, Faye and Barbara had theirs before Christmas, Ned's and Arthur's wives are due again next month. Philip's wife is due in July, and my older siblings have pretty much stopped. The young ones are taking over."

"Effie and Nicodemus have had their third baby, too," Spiros told her. "I saw Nicodemus when I came in. He is not happy about it." He stroked his son's cheek and received a gurgle.

"I doubt Effie is, either." While Jenny had kept in touch with Effie the last five years, it hadn't been the way it was before Spiros and his friends arrived. Jenny had no idea why Effie had not taken to being a wife and mother, but knew having another two children in the last five years was probably not the best decision. But then, there had been whispers over the last few years that her family had threatened Nicodemus that he must go back to his wife and child, or be sent back to Greece. That was how they were on to their third child. His philandering ways had caught up to him and he'd impregnated another two women, which he denied, of course. Unhappy in his marriage, there were rumours he'd been forcing Effie into sex to make up for not being able to plant himself where he wanted, and Effie's depression had worsened and gone back to how she was after their first son.

"I haven't seen Effie for quite some time," Jenny told Spiros. "I think he's going to be the death of her. When he was out with other women, she didn't care, she was better. Didn't have to deal with him, or see him. But when her family made him go back, it was probably the worst decision they made. They should have made him divorce her and sent him back to Greece."

"Yes, that probably would have been a better choice," Spiros murmured in thought. "I do not think he likes how his life has turned out."

"Isn't this what you all expected?" Jenny asked.

Spiros sighed at the memories of their boat trip. "Yes. We knew we would learn English and meet Australian girls. Marry one day and have children. I just do not think Nicodemus was ready for it so soon. I think it was the speed of what happened that was the problem." He looked down at his son and his lips turned up at the corners. "And what are we naming this one?"

Gazing down at her brand-new baby, Jenny smiled wearily. "Pedro Matthew Stephanopoulos."

"Ah…after your father."

"Yes. He gets one named after him as well."

November 1958

"Okay, well, everything sounds all right, Jenny," Doctor Martins told her. He was new in town and had replaced Doctor Salica who'd retired. "You can get dressed and go on home. I'll see you in January for your last check-up."

"Thank you, doctor." Jenny waited for him to leave the room before removing the white hospital gown and redressing in her yellow and white sundress. She was six months pregnant with her fourth child, having waited once more before having sex and getting pregnant, but since it was November 1958, she knew it would probably be her last. She wasn't prepared to keep pumping children out, and she loved sex with Spiros too much to risk continually getting pregnant, so she was more than prepared to go against her religion and use contraception.

Slipping into her white flats, Jenny grabbed her handbag and left the gown in the washing bin before leaving the room to see her frazzled mother trying to wrangle three boys. "Thanks for doing this. With Spiros at work, and Joanna and Harriet unable to look after them, there was no other way. Carlos, stop running around," she chastised the very energetic five-year-old. He hadn't started school yet, and being tired all the time, Jenny just couldn't keep up with him. At least he had his cousins down the road to run around with.

"Mama, I want to go," he whined, scrunching his legs together.

"Do you mean to the toilet, or home?" Jenny asked, quickly seeing if she had spare nappies and clothes in the baby bag.

"Both. I do wee."

Jenny's head swivelled around. "Wait until we… Carlos!" Sighing in frustration, she saw the puddle around his feet. "You just wet yourself."

"Yes, Mama. I do wee." Carlos gazed adoringly up at his mother, like a cherub who could do no wrong, while his mother frowned back. "We go home now?"

"Not until I get you cleaned up, mister. You just wet yourself." She smiled apologetically at the nurses who quickly came and cleaned it up. "I'm so sorry. He hasn't learned to tell me he needs to go to the toilet *before* he actually wets himself." Grabbing the nappy bag in one hand, and Carlos in the other, Jenny hurried him down the hall and into the ladies'. "How many times have I told you to tell me you need to go *before* you actually wet your pants?" She set the bag on the sink counter and pulled out a spare change of clothes, and a bag to wrap the wet items in. "You're not supposed to just wet yourself, Carlos." She pulled his shorts and underwear down, then removed his socks and shoes which were also wet.

"I do wee." He took off running around the room, waving his arms in the air. "I do wee, I do wee."

"Carlos Spiros Stephanopoulos get here now." Jenny pointed to the spot right in front of her, and when she used that tone; her boys did exactly what they were told.

With a quivering lip and blue eyes on the edge of overflowing with tears, Carlos reluctantly walked over to his angry mother with the frowning face and stood while she wiped him down and redressed him. He knew full well, that when his full name was used, he was in trouble. "I in trouble, Mama?" The tears overflowed and went sliding down his chubby cheeks.

Jenny looked him straight in the eye. "If you don't behave, you will be in *big* trouble. We have taught you how and when to go to the toilet, Carlos. And now you go and do this when I have my appointment. Why couldn't you be a good boy, today? I told you if you were good you could have an icy pole when we got home. But you won't be having one now. I'm *very* disappointed in you, Carlos." Jenny packed up the bag and looked down at a sobbing Carlos. Her heart went out to him, but then he only cried when he was in trouble and wasn't getting a reward. "Come along, Carlos. We're going home." Holding out her hand, she waited for him to take it.

Through waterlogged eyes, Carlos gazed up at his mother and slowly took her hand. He knew she loved him, covered him with hugs and kisses, but when he did the wrong thing, Mama got mad and didn't give him those hugs and kisses anymore.

They walked into the hallway and found Sarah with a quiet Tomas and Pedro. "We're going home now. No icy pole for Carlos, but if the other boys have been good, they'll get theirs."

Sarah looked down at a weeping Carlos. "Obviously not too happy with that."

"Well, he did the wrong thing. Come along, boys." She held her hand out to three-year-old Tomas who dutifully took his mama's hand and hurried along beside her. Sarah had an almost two-year-old Pedro in the stroller. Out in the car, Jenny buckled the boys up while Sarah put the bags and stroller in the boot, and then they headed off home.

"How was the appointment?" Sarah asked.

"Good. Said he'll see me in January for my last appointment." Jenny turned into her driveway and parked under the carport, glad they had the shade from the blistering Aussie summers, and cover from the cold and rainy winters.

"What's he like as a doctor? He's new, right?" Sarah asked as they alighted and gathered their things from the car.

"Yes, Doctor Salica retired, as you know, and Doctor Martins replaced him. Seems efficient enough." They got the boys inside and Carlos went to his room and closed the door.

"Can you get the boys their icy poles and then we'll put them down for their nap?" Jenny asked her mother and then opened Carlos's door. "What are you doing?" She saw him sitting on the floor between the bed and the window.

"Playing." His answer was as morose as his expression.

"Carlos." Jenny walked around the bed and sat on the side. "Do you understand why you're not getting an icy pole?"

"Because I was naughty an' wee myself," he mumbled, pulling apart a toy robot and trying to put it back together.

"That's right. And you only receive punishment when you've been naughty, so that you learn to be good instead." Jenny watched his face. It was still chubby, as was the rest of him, and his fat little fingers tried desperately to piece the toy together. "It doesn't mean we don't love you; we do, we're just trying to teach you the difference between right and wrong. Do you understand?"

Carlos looked up from his toy to see his mama gazing down at him. "Yes, Mama." He knew the difference. When he was bad, his mama looked at him like that. When he was good, he got smiles and hugs and kisses.

Unable to resist her baby, she ruffled his hair and bent down and kissed his cheek. "I love you, Carlos. Never forget that. And if you're a good boy for the rest of the afternoon, you can have your icy pole later. Okay?"

That brightened his day a little. "Okay, Mama. I be good boy."

"Good boy. If you feel like taking a nap, it's okay. It's quite warm today."

"Okay. Maybe later." Carlos went back to his toy.

Hating the fact she had to punish her children, Jenny left the room, with the door open, and put her son's urine-soaked clothes in a bucket in the laundry. Walking back into the lounge room, she saw the boys finishing their icy poles. "Taste good, my babies?" She took the sticks and wrappings and put them in the kitchen bin, then came back with a wet towel to wipe their mouths and hands. "You boys can play if you like." Pointing to the colourful cube brimming over with toys, she added, "Just don't be too noisy, okay?"

"Okay, Mama." Tomas ran over to the box and pulled it over on its side, so the toys would spill out and Pedro could get to them. "Here, Pedro, you play with this." He handed his brother a dual coloured sphere with cut out shapes and pulled it apart so the shaped blocks inside would fall out. "Put them in like this. I show you." He showed his baby brother how to match blocks to shapes and popped them in, repeating the gesture several times until Pedro got it, and then he moved on to a wooden pegboard with pegs that he hammered into the holes.

"Dat one…" Pedro pointed to a colourful plastic dog made of multiple pieces that came apart, so it could be put back together.

"Do you know how to do this one?" Tomas asked, and pulled it apart. "Like this, Pedro." He showed him how to put it back together.

"Funny how these two play so well, but Carlos just kinds of…" Sarah glanced towards the hallway to see if Carlos was listening.

"Steamrolls everything?" Jenny finished for her mother. "He *is* boisterous, I'll give him that." She leaned back in her seat and sighed. "He never seems to stop, always on the go." Watching her children, she glanced around their lounge room; they had updated the lounge suite in the last couple of years, added new decorations, and had a TV. With it only being a month and a half before Christmas, the tree was up and most of the presents were under it. Not that they bought much for the boys. They always got four presents each and that was it. One from their parents, one from their grandparents, one from Jenny's siblings, and one from the Stephanides family, and that was for Christmas and birthdays. Four presents each because there were so many grandchildren in the family now that money was stretched tight, and so many presents were handed down, or handed on if they were unused, or unwanted. But the boys never went without and never would, Jenny made sure of that. They had enough clothes to wear, and the cot, pram, and pusher had been used for all three boys and would be used for the next one as well, and when Jenny was finished having children, they would be handed on to someone else who needed them. That's not only how the Stephanopoulos family worked, but the community at large worked.

"Mmm…" Jenny rubbed her belly as the baby inside shifted. "This one's on the move." Even though she'd had three children, this felt different. This one *told her* it was different. "Mmm…" Changing positions, Jenny tried to get comfortable. "Oh, I think it's unhappy about missing out on an icy pole," she joked and then felt the baby settle down. "Okay…there we go."

"It could be shifting positions, somersaulting upside down ready to come out." Sarah watched the boys and saw Carlos sneak silently out of his room and hide in the hallway watching his brothers. "Hey," she whispered to Jenny, and when she had her attention, nodded in his direction.

Jenny saw him, and he saw her, running back into his room. "You can come out and play with your brothers, Carlos. You don't have to stay in your room."

It took only a moment before Carlos slowly walked back out and stood in the lounge room watching his brothers, *and* his mama.

"You can play with them, just be nice and behave yourself," Jenny told him.

Silently, he walked over to his brothers, sat down, and started playing with a toy.

"So…he *can* play nice?" Sarah murmured to her daughter.

"When he wants to," Jenny replied, feeling the baby move again.

Come afternoon, when the boys took their naps, so did Jenny, and Sarah stayed until Matthew came and picked her up. He arrived the same time as Spiros who had got a lift home from a co-worker, knowing Jenny had the appointment, so needed the car.

"Jenny and the boys are napping," Sarah told Spiros before she left.

He quietly thanked her and saw them off before wandering into the bedroom. Sitting beside his wife, his hand went to her stomach and he quietly smiled and kissed the tiny baby within.

"Mmm…" She awoke and straightened on the bed, so she could pull her meat scented husband into her arms.

"And how is baby number four?" he asked, wrapping his arms around her and resting his head near her stomach.

"Doctor says it's good."

"Hear that, little one. The doctor said you and your mama are good."

"Mmm…we are. Ready for dinner?" She responded to her husband's kisses and they lay that way until Carlos wandered in and disturbed them.

"Papa's home, Mama." He stood in the doorway rubbing his tired eyes.

"Yes, Carlos, Papa's home." Spiros left the bed and swung Carlos into his arms. "Was Carlos a good boy, today? Did he behave for Mama?"

Carlos looked away guiltily and clenched his hands together.

"Unfortunately, no. But I punished him and he behaved for the rest of the day." Jenny got to her feet, pain pinging in her lower back. "Ugh…" Her hand went to her back and rubbed it. "Baby's active."

"It is probably in need of food. How about I get the boys changed, and you can get tea ready," Spiros suggested.

"It's already done. Did it before taking my nap." Yawning, Jenny followed Spiros out of their room and went to set the table.

After Spiros had changed the boys, he hustled them out to the lounge room. "I want to take photos before we eat. The sun is perfect, quick before it disappears." He grabbed his camera from the side buffet in the dining area and ushered his family outside. "Stand on the porch and I will take the photo. Boys gather around your mama's legs, that is it. Aw, so cute." He backed up and looked through the viewfinder.

"The sun's in my eyes, Spiros, and it's hot, hurry up." Jenny made sure the boys were either in front of her, or to the side, and not hidden. "Can you see them?"

"Yes, yes, okay, look at me, hug your mama, and one, two, three." He took the shot of a laughing Jenny and the three boys gathered around her, and then took a couple more as they went inside. He set the boys at the table while Jenny gathered bowls for the lamb salad, serving it cold from the fridge.

They joked and laughed as they ate, and let the boys stay up a little later than usual to wear them out since it was Friday. Once they put them to bed, they listened to the radio, as they did every night, and danced to their favourite music. After a cooling shower, they turned off the lights and went to bed.

*****

Pain caused Jenny to wake in the middle of the night. Starting in her back, it ended up in her lower abdomen.

"Argh…" She doubled over in bed clutching her stomach. "Spiros… argh…"

Spiros flicked the bedside light on and rolled over. "Jenny? What is it? Are you in labour?"

"I don't know, I think something's wrong. I need to get to the hospital. Oh, my, God…" The pain gripped her and she screwed her face up against it.

"Yes, yes, the hospital." Spiros jumped out of bed and quickly dressed. "We cannot take the boys."

"Ring Joanna, or my mother, quickly." Jenny flung back the sheet and tried to roll over, but the pain was too intense.

"Oh, Jenny…" Spiros stopped short. "You are bleeding."

"What?" She managed to look over her shoulder at him. "I'm what?"

"You are bleeding, badly." He pushed the covers back further. "We need to get you to the hospital."

"Call my sister first, hurry," she growled through clenched teeth.

Spiros dashed out into the dining area and rang Joanna, and then ran outside to reverse the car, so he could get Jenny in easily. He ran inside, carefully lifted her into his arms and carried her out into the hall.

"Papa, what's wrong with Mama?" Carlos asked sleepily, standing in the doorway to his room. He'd awoken and heard sounds coming from his parents' room.

"Mama is not well, Carlos. I am taking her to the hospital. Go back to bed; Aunt Joanna is coming to look after you." Spiros hurried Jenny out to the car and into the front seat. "Your sister is coming. We will be there soon."

"Jenny, Spiros?" Joanna had thrown on her dressing gown and slippers and run three houses down the street.

"Look after the children." Spiros shut the door and ran around the car. "I have to get Jenny to the hospital." He jumped in and started the ignition while Jenny rolled the window down and grabbed her sister's hand

"Look after the kids and call Mum, tell her." Jenny weakly let go of her sister as they backed down the drive.

"I will, Jenny, I will. Don't worry about the boys." Joanna waved the car off and hurried inside where she found Carlos hovering in the front doorway. "Come back to bed, sweetie, Mama has to go to the hospital, and I have to make a call." After locking the door behind her, she ushered Carlos back to his bed and quickly made three calls. One to her parents, one to Rebecca who was a fully qualified nurse, and one to her husband, letting him know what had happened. Setting the receiver down, she realised the rest of the family would want to know, so started calling.

"Argh…" Jenny gripped her stomach. "What's happening?" Her screams mixed with sobs at the pain she was experiencing and the possibility of losing a child. *Not* something she wanted to do.

"We are almost there, Jenny." Spiros stepped on the gas and inched over the speed limit. If he was pulled over, he had a valid excuse.

"I don't want to lose this baby," she panted, both hands clutching her stomach. She was only six months and had had her appointment yesterday. What had possibly gone wrong within twenty-four hours?

"We are here, Jenny." Spiros sped into the emergency bay, madly honking the horn. Slamming to a stop, he turned off the car and ran around to pull her from the passenger side as nurses and doctors came rushing out. "Quickly, help her, she is bleeding." He laid Jenny on the bed and they rushed her inside and into a cubicle.

"What's happening? What's going on?" Jenny cried, seeing too many faces around her.

"We don't know, Jenny. We're going to have a look, just hold on." Doctor Britt examined her insides, pressing a hand against her stomach while nurses took her blood pressure and started a drip. "We're going to need a transfusion, so set up a bag of blood, she's lost a lot. And page Doctor Martins for me."

"Jenny." Sarah and Rebecca rushed into the cubicle.

"Mum." Jenny was openly weeping and close to hysteria. "I don't want to lose the baby." She weakly held out her hand for her mother to take.

"Oh, Jenny, my love. Everyone will do what they can, but sometimes, these things just happen." Sarah held Jenny's hand to her chest with one hand and gently stroked her daughter's hair with the other, saw how distraught Jenny was and her heart went out to her. She had seen women lose babies before, tragedies that still haunted her. "Sometimes things just happen, my love."

"I don't want to lose my baby," Jenny wailed. Her body jerked up and she screamed. "Mummy!" The wails and screams alternated as the doctor told her to push. She didn't want to, didn't want to lose her baby, but vaguely heard the doctor say the baby was crowning, and her mother and sister were by her side. Or at least that's what she thought was happening.

"Push," the doctor yelled from between her legs. "And again."

"No," Jenny screamed in a dazed pain. Everything sounded obstructed to her, as if underwater, or she had earmuffs on. Every sound, every decibel was muted, and she was almost deaf to it. Even her own screams.

"One last push." The doctor watched the excruciating pain on Jenny's face before his eyes flicked to the baby coming out of her body. Holding out his towel-covered hands, he caught the tiny body as it slipped into the world, silent and still. He wiped the baby's mouth, listened for a heartbeat, tried to resuscitate the tiny person he'd just helped bring into the world. All to no avail. There was no life within the tiny body. "I'm so sorry…" He didn't even realise the words had come from his own mouth. His eyes looked up at Jenny, her mother on one side, her sister on the other. The Marsh family were popular and well-liked in the community, and this was their first tragic loss they had experienced when it came to pregnancies and babies. "I'm so sorry."

Jenny didn't hear the words; she just gazed between her legs at the lifeless body of her baby. And then she noticed. "It's a girl…" Her lips quivered. "It's…a…girl…" The one thing she wanted most with every pregnancy was a daughter. "It's a girl," she screamed and kept screaming as Rebecca left her side to take the tiny human into her arms and take care of her.

The doctor came out of his stunned silence to see Jenny was bleeding uncontrollably. "Jenny, there seems to be a problem. We're going to have to stem the bleeding." He started dealing with the placenta and they frantically worked to stop the blood from flowing forth.

Weak from everything, Jenny collapsed back onto the bed, fading in and out.

Doctor Martins ran in, took one look at the mess, and ordered Jenny to the operating theatre. "There's no time, we need to stop the bleeding now." All hands reached for the bed and rolled it out of the room.

"Baby…" Jenny murmured, seeing a blurry vision of Spiros as they passed. "My baby…"

"Jenny, hold on, Jenny, my Jenny. Please hold on." Spiros, in a panic, watched his wife be taken away. He'd heard her animalistic screams, been frightened by them, but had not heard a baby, and no one was telling him what was happening.

"Spiros."

He turned to see Rebecca motion to him and followed her into the cubicle next to the one Jenny had been in. He saw what she was pointing to. His baby, in a crib, wrapped in a towel. "The…baby…?"

"Didn't make it." Rebecca's voice was soft, and she laid her hand on his arm. "I'm so sorry. The baby didn't make it. She's gone."

"She…?" His head slowly turned from his daughter to Rebecca, a heavy confused fog in his brain that emanated from his eyes.

"It's a girl, Spiros. You and Jenny had a daughter, but she didn't make it." Tears brimmed over and she let them fall freely. She had just watched her beautiful baby niece be born three months early and not make it. Her heart was broken.

"A girl…a baby girl…a daughter…" Spiros stared down at the tiny cherubic face with its rosebud lips and a black tuft of hair. "A girl…" It finally hit him. Hit him that Jenny had given birth to their baby and it had been, *was,* a girl. A daughter. "No…" He fell to his knees and sobbed, head in his hands, heart in his throat.

Sarah came back from emergency and saw Spiros on the floor. Her heart went out to him. "Jenny's been taken to surgery," she quietly told Rebecca. "They can't stop the bleeding."

"Oh, no," Rebecca murmured, seeing members of their family in the waiting area. "Joanna must have called them. You stay here."

"No." Sarah stopped her. "I'll go. You stay with Spiros and make sure nothing happens to that baby. We won't do anything until Jenny says so." With a heavy heart, she walked into the waiting room and told her husband and children what had happened. She then told them to go back home to their own children and she'd call them when Jenny was out of surgery. Matthew chose to stay, but their children went home.

*****

Come morning, Jenny woke. Her eyes blinked a few times, she turned her head to the right where her husband normally was, but found no bed, no window, no house. Breathing in sharply, she realised she wasn't in her bedroom at home, but the hospital, and all of last night came flooding back. "No, no, no." She clutched her stomach and winced. The pain was as bad as childbirth, which she remembered going through. "No," she screamed. "My baby, my baby."

Her parents and Rebecca came through the door, arms reaching out, consoling words coming from their mouths. Except for Spiros. He just silently climbed onto the bed beside her and held her while she screamed for their baby.

Doctor Martins walked in and managed to tell her what had happened. At first, they had no idea why she'd gone into labour, but with the removal of her uterus, they saw it was from a rupture of the umbilical cord. It had torn a hole in Jenny's uterus that couldn't be repaired, so they removed it. They had no idea why the baby had died. Jenny was healthy and ate well, but it was more than likely caused by a lack of oxygen, or blood. The only way to find out for sure was from an autopsy.

"No," Jenny screamed. "You are not cutting up my baby. I want to see her. I want to see her. Where is she? I want to hold my baby." She sobbed uncontrollably.

"I think for right now you need more rest and some food," Martins ordered. "You can see the baby later. You've had major surgery, Jenny, you need as much rest as you can get." He noticed the nurse standing by and took the syringe she held. "I'll give you something to relax."

"No. I don't want anything. I want my baby. Spiros." She clawed at her husband. "I want our baby, Spiros. I want our baby."

"I know you do, my love. But right now, you must rest. You have had surgery." Spiros held her as the effects of the injection kicked in. "You can see her later. You need to rest. You have had surgery. Shhhh, my love, shh, my Jenny." He held her tightly, rocking back and forth as she slipped into a light sleep. He hadn't been home. Hadn't changed clothes. Had sat sobbing in front of his daughter's crib all night as Jenny's parents came and went.

"We'll keep her sedated until tomorrow. It will give her body a chance to heal," Martins told them. "I know it's probably not ideal, but it's major surgery, and any frenetic movements could rupture the stitches."

"We know," Sarah murmured, watching her daughter and son-in-law. "We'll stay and watch over her."

"And in the meantime…" Martins glanced from one to the other. "What about the…" His voice caught on the word. "What about the baby?" He loathed the question, never wanted to ask it, but knew it was a part of his job requirement.

Spiros looked his way. "Until my Jenny has a chance to hold her and cry over her, you do nothing."

"We can't keep her up here, she will need to go to the morgue at least, to stop the—"

"We know!" Sarah coldly stopped him. "We will escort the baby down and make sure she is properly labelled. When Jenny's ready to say goodbye, she can. And *we* will decide what to do with her. *Not* you, and certainly *not* the hospital."

Nodding, Martins backed away. "Of course. When you're ready." He left the room and walked down the corridor into the doctor's lounge. Heaving a deep sigh, he bent over the sink and vomited. It was the first baby he'd lost since taking over at the Armidale hospital and he hoped to God it was the last.

"Spiros, we'll go and make sure the baby is taken care of," Sarah said and looked from his face to her daughter's. Even in sleep, Jenny was distraught.

"Thank you," he murmured. "I do not know what to do." Tears sprang to his eyes. "What do you do in times like this?"

"You rally around and help out," Matthew told him. "And that's what we're doing."

"Thank you." Spiros nodded and closed his eyes against the onslaught of pain and tears. Knowing he couldn't hold back any longer, he set them free.

*****

Later that day, Spiros went home to shower and change and see the boys. Joanna had packed them up and taken them to her house to stay, and he spent time with them until they fell asleep and he tucked them in. He left and went to see his family, telling them of the news. Nikos told him to take as much time off as he needed to be with his wife, and that he'd watch over the shop. Thanking his uncle, Spiros made his way back to Jenny's side and stayed with her the whole night.

*****

In the morning, when Jenny woke, with Spiros, her parents, and Rebecca by her side, she listened to everything Doctor Martins had to say. She'd had a hysterectomy due to the umbilical cord tearing away, and lost her daughter in the process.

Silent tears flowed down her face, making it red and swollen, but she managed to maintain her sanity by digging her nails into the bed covers and gripping them with clawed hands. Every single word out of his mouth were daggers in her ears, making them bleed with pain and anger. Pain at losing her only daughter, anger at never being able to have more children. This was what *God* had done to her and she *hated* him for it.

Once Martins had left, she gulped for air, trying to control the sobs threatening to explode out of her.

"Oh, Jenny," Sarah murmured. "Come. Rebecca and I will help get you cleaned up." They helped her into a wheelchair and into the bathroom, where, under the stream of hot water, she let her sobs free.

Not sure what to do, Spiros stood by the window looking out, arms wrapped around himself, trying to control his own tears.

"It's an unfortunate thing," Matthew murmured, standing by his son-in-law, hands in pockets, and a worried expression on his face. He feared for his daughter. "Very unfortunate."

When Jenny was ready, they settled her into bed, and Sarah and Rebecca went to get the baby. They brought her back and laid her in Jenny's arms, watching the barrage of emotions fly over her face.

Spiros quietly snapped photos. He'd brought the camera and spare film in case they were able to take pictures, and not wanting to interrupt his Jenny and her grieving, silently took the only photos they would ever have of their daughter upon her birth. Forever asleep in her mama's arms. Never to be a little sister, never to meet her big brothers, who would have loved and adored her.

"Alena," Jenny muttered between sobs.

"What's that, love?" Sarah laid a gentle hand on her daughter's arm.

"Alena." A hiccupping gasp. "That's the name I had if I had a baby girl. Alena."

Sarah glanced up at Matthew beside her. "That's a beautiful name, Jenny." Her husband slipped an arm around her waist and she held back her tears.

Jenny stared down at the tiny bundle in her arms. Her daughter. Her Alena. Gone before she'd even arrived. "Oh, my baby," she whispered, touching a gentle finger to her daughter's cheek. "My beautiful baby. My baby girl."

The baby remained silent, unmoving, cold to the touch.

"Why did you not stay? Why did you have to leave?" Jenny slid her finger through the little tuft of black hair. "You would've looked like Pedro, your brother." A sob left her. "A brother you will never meet, and who will never meet you. Neither will Tomas, or Carlos, your older brothers." She shuddered as more tears fell. "It's not fair."

Spiros climbed onto the bed and pulled his wife into his arms. "No, my Jenny. It is not fair. We did not deserve to lose our daughter. We did not deserve it." He held onto them both, holding them tighter, and they sobbed for the rest of the day.

*****

Three days later, Jenny was allowed out of the hospital in a wheelchair, and under the supervision of her mother and sister while everything took place. They had given their baby girl her first and only bath, and dressed her in a beautiful white ruffled satin gown and a matching bonnet. Jenny had bought the outfit years earlier, keeping it in her wardrobe for the day she had a baby girl. They had their daughter christened Alena Jennifer Stephanopoulos by both the Orthodox and Catholic Churches, and then, in a pure white baby coffin with pink satin lining and pillow, she was wrapped in a matching satin blanket and cremated at the local funeral home.

When it was over, it was back to the hospital where she finally saw her sons.

"Hello, my babies." Holding her arms out, she waited for Spiros to lift the boys onto the bed and into her arms. Smothering them in kisses, she held on tight. "How are you?"

"Good, Mama," Tomas said and patted her face. "Mama's been crying."

Through her sad smile, Jenny tried to keep the mood light. "It's because I've been unwell, and cooped up in here missing my babies." Tears threatened, but she smiled through them. "I had to have surgery, and I'm not quite ready to come home." The family had been talking, suggesting that Jenny take some time out to recuperate with family in Sydney. So far, she had refused because she had the boys to look after and needed to be taking care of her children. Because it wasn't as if she had anything else to do. No new baby to look after. No pregnancy to worry about.

"When Mama coming home?" Carlos asked, sitting dutifully beside his mama, cuddled up under her left arm.

"I don't know, sweetie." Jenny kissed his cheek. "I just don't know."

"Mama." Pedro stood up beside her, wrapped his arms around her neck and kissed her cheek. At almost two, he was starting to take after both of his brothers.

"Pedro," Jenny replied, smiling at her youngest. His big blue eyes and black hair set her heart pounding and tears prickling her eyes. "My baby." Her arms tightened around her boys and she breathed deeply to stop the tears. "So, what have you all been up to?" She listened to stories of playing with cousins and sleepovers.

"When we go home, Mama?" Carlos nestled against her. "I want to sleep in *my* bed in *my* room and play with *my* toys."

"Soon, sweetie." Jenny ruffled his hair and looked at her husband's solemn face. "Soon."

"Good, 'cause I don't want to miss out on Santa Claus and all the presents I'll be getting." Carlos casually crossed his legs and gazed expectantly at his mama.

"Christmas is quite some time away, Carlos." Jenny gulped back the lump in her throat. "It's many, many weeks away, yet."

"Naw, no fair," he whined, pouting his fat lips. "I want Christmas."

"Then you will have to wait, no whining, now," Jenny said sternly, realising that she wouldn't be able to cope with Christmas, let alone their birthdays in February. She was due in February. But this time, she wouldn't be having her fourth child. She wouldn't be having anything. Wouldn't be bringing home a new baby. Wouldn't be buying presents for a little girl come next Christmas. Wouldn't be buying pretty little dresses and shoes, or pretty bows and ribbons for her hair. Wouldn't be buying birthday presents, or watching her go to school, or graduate, or find a husband and have children herself. No. She wouldn't be doing any of that because it was never going to happen.

Spiros, noticing Jenny's expressions, called a stop to the boys. "Time to go to your aunt's now, boys. Mama needs her rest."

"Aw, do we have to?" Carlos whined, having missed his mama's hugs and kisses for nearly a week. "I don't want to."

"You have to, my baby." Jenny kissed his head. "I still need to rest." She kissed Tomas and Pedro and watched as Spiros took them out to their aunt and grandmother. Sighing from the pit of her still sore stomach, she knew she just couldn't. She just couldn't go home as if nothing had happened and get on with raising three boys.

Spiros came back in. "Your mother and sister are taking them home." He sat on the edge of the bed. "Jenny, what is wrong?"

She looked at him sharply. "Everything," she whispered fiercely, clawing at the sheets in a death grip. "Everything."

"Ah…my Jenny." Spiros grasped her hand and held it tight. "I…do not know what to do. I remember my mother went through this. It was not talked about, and we only found out from town gossips, but we Greeks do not talk about such things. I do not know what to say to make it better."

"You can't," she cried. "You just can't. No one can. I lost my baby girl; no one can make it better." The sobs racked her body. "I lost my baby girl."

"Oh, my Jenny." Spiros lay beside her, holding her while she sobbed on his chest. "I hate the fact I cannot help you. I do not know what to say, or what to do." He stroked her hair until the sobs subsided.

"I think Mum was right," Jenny finally said, her face was plastered against his shirt, soaked from her tears.

"About what, my Jenny?"

"That I should go away. Stay with my aunt and uncle in Sydney. I just don't know if I can deal with the boys right now. Not after surgery. I can't lift them, play with them, or do any housework. I need to heal from the inside, not just from the surgery, but from losing my child."

Kissing the top of her head, he said, "If that is what you feel is best, my Jenny, then you must do what is best for you and I will go along with it."

She lifted her head and looked into his tired brown eyes. "Will you look after the boys? My mum and sisters will help."

He frowned at her comment. "Yes, *of course,* I will. I am their papa. Do not worry about anything. I have worked it all out with Uncle Nikos. I will only work a few hours a day if I still want to, so we still have money coming in. I am sure your sisters will help out the rest of the time."

Nodding, Jenny sat up. "But don't work just for the sake of it. If you have to take time off, do that. I don't want the boys going without both parents until I get back."

"And when will you be back, my Jenny?" he asked gently.

Shaking her head, she said, "I just don't know."

*****

Three days later, after saying goodbye to the boys, Jenny, her mother and sister, went to Sydney on the train. They would settle Jenny in to her aunt and uncle's spare room, and then Sarah and Rebecca would come back the next day, leaving her to deal with her grief.

*****

"When is Mama coming home?" Carlos asked his father. They had seen their mama off at the train station with Grandma and Aunt Rebecca.

"When she is better, Carlos." Spiros drove home and pulled into the driveway. "Mama had surgery on her tummy. It is still sore, so she has to rest and see a special doctor in Sydney. She will be with *her* aunt and uncle." He looked over the back of the seat at his three boys. Carlos on the left, Pedro in the middle, Tomas on the right. Three sets of eyes, two like Jenny's, one like his, all stared back at him. "She will be home soon, my boys. Come, let me get you inside." He helped them inside where they played with their toys until their cousins came over after lunch, then they ran around the backyard until they wore themselves out and fell asleep on the lounge room floor.

After dinner, Spiros got them bathed and dressed for bed.

"When will Mama be home?" Carlos let out a huge yawn and fell back against his pillow.

"When she is better, my son." Spiros kissed his forehead and said goodnight. Turning off the main light, but leaving the night light on, he went next door to Pedro and Tomas's room. The plan had been to move Tomas into Carlos's room, so the baby would be in with Pedro. But that wouldn't be happening now.

"Time for bed, my sons." Spiros tucked them in and waited while they fell asleep. Turning off the light, he wandered aimlessly around the house. Stood at the back door listening to the trees blow in the breeze. Moved into the kitchen for a beer and left it half undrunk. Stood on the front porch seeing which neighbours were still up and what they were doing through their lounge, or bedroom, windows. Wandered into the lounge and retrieved the packet of photos he'd had developed.

Falling heavily onto the couch, he silently pulled out the photos and went through them. The pictures of Jenny in her yellow and white sundress with the boys around her legs. It seemed so long ago that he'd taken them. Had ushered them out to the porch to take the pictures. The next pictures were of Alena, asleep in her mother's arms, followed by pictures of her being christened, and then in her tiny coffin filled with pretty pink satin. Alena would not be buried. Jenny had insisted on not putting her daughter in the ground, wanting her baby with her always. She was cremated and kept in a pretty pink and blue urn that Jenny kept with her, never letting go, never leaving her behind. She'd even taken her to Sydney, so she was close by.

"Oh, my Jenny. I hope you can deal with this. I really do." Getting to his feet, he found himself in the hallway, checking on the boys, standing in their doorways, photos of his forever gone little girl in his hand. He looked from the boys to the photos and wept. Wept for them. Wept for Jenny. Wept for his little girl lost forever, and finally, wept for himself.

December 1958

Jenny came back to Armidale the week before Christmas. She'd been in Sydney for four weeks, recuperating, and sobbing her heart out all day and all night. Her aunt and uncle left her to it, thinking it best she got it out of her system before going home and back to the boys. She had a job to do in Armidale, and it was raising three sons and being a good wife.

Spiros and the boys picked her up in the afternoon. It was a hot summer's day and Jenny stepped down from the train in a blue cotton frock and white flats. She carried her bags with her.

"Jenny, my love. Over here, my Jenny." Spiros waved madly from near the conductor's office. He had Pedro in the pusher, and Carlos and Tomas on monkey straps. "Here, let me take your bags." He took them from her and set them down while she madly covered her sons in kisses.

"Oh, I have missed you, my babies. Mama missed you all so much." She kneeled down and put an arm each around Carlos and Tomas. "And how have you been? Have you been good for Papa, and Grandma and Grandpa?"

"Yes, Mama. I been good," Tomas chattered excitedly. "But Carlos hasn't."

Jenny glanced at her eldest, not surprised by Carlos being naughty, but surprised by Tomas telling on his brother. "Has Carlos been naughty?"

He had the decency to look ashamed, but said, "It was not me, Mama, it was Pedro."

"I no naughty." Pedro vehemently shook his head. "I good boy."

"I'm sure you have been. But it's hot, and you're probably in need of a nap, so let's get you all home. Come, boys." She pushed the stroller and locked them into the back of the car while Spiros loaded her bags into the boot. Once home, and in the cool, they had refreshing lemonade and put the boys down for their naps. Then, while Jenny unpacked her bags, she and Spiros had the time to talk.

"My Jenny, how are you?" Concern written all over his face, he reached for her hand, but she pulled away, preferring to hang her clothes.

"I'm fine. The doctor says that I'm healed enough to take on light duties, but to not pick the boys up, or anyone, or anything else. I'll have to wait another month, or so, which will come in handy since Carlos starts school in February." She avoided looking at him by removing Pedro's Christmas present and hiding it, and packing her clothes into the dresser drawer. "Obviously, we can't have more children. Definitely no more sex." She stopped and slowly closed the drawer. She loved sex with her husband, especially when they were in baby-making mode. But there would be no more of that, and no more baby-making. The pain attacked her heart, and even though she had spent the last four weeks crying all day and all night, she knew that she hadn't finished with the tears just yet.

"Jenny." Spiros stood behind her, his hands gently on her arms. "My Jenny. I am so sorry you went through this. It was not fair of God to do this."

"No," she muttered through clenched teeth. "But then I don't think God really cares anymore. I didn't go to church in Sydney. Don't particularly care if I go now I'm back. He took my little girl and I hate him." Turning from Spiros's grasp, she shut her empty case and opened her overnight beauty case. The first thing she saw was the velvet box containing the urn. Carefully lifting it out, she opened the box and removed the urn. She'd wanted something unbreakable. Not china, or glass, so she'd settled on a metal urn painted decoratively in pink and blue. Her two favourite colours for her favourite little girl. Her favourite child. Holding it to her chest, she lovingly kissed the top before placing it on her bedside cupboard. "He took her and we're never getting her back." She closed the box and put it into the bottom of the cupboard for safekeeping before closing the cupboard door.

Sighing, Spiros watched Jenny finish unpacking and put away her luggage. "Do you want to rest, my love?"

"No." Jenny walked out to the open plan living area, sat down at the phone table connected to the huge buffet with hutch cupboard opposite the dining table, and started ringing her family to tell them she was home.

*****

It was Christmas Day, and the boys were up early to tear into their presents. It didn't matter if they were still in urine-stained summer pjs and dirty nappies. They just wanted their goodies from under the tree.

Fourteen presents sat under there. Four for each son, and one each for Spiros and Jenny.

Ripping off the paper to his presents, Carlos liked what he saw. A new robot toy from his grandparents, books from his papa's family, clothes from his mama's family, and an action figure Superman from his mama and papa. "Yah!" He thrust his fat little fist holding Superman into the air. "I get Superman. Yah!" He ran around the room pretending he was flying.

"Calm down, Carlos, you'll step on your brother's toys and break something," Jenny told him. When he didn't stop her tone hardened. "Carlos! Sit down." She watched him stop and stare at her raised brow and then meekly come over and sit down with his presents.

Pedro and Tomas got similar presents, as it was easier to buy the boys pretty much the same things, but Carlos was having none of it.

"Pedro got my present," he wailed and pointed to the robot toy that his brother had opened. "I wanted that one. I wanted that one. Why didn't I get that one?"

"Carlos! Enough," Jenny snapped. "Be grateful for what you *did* get and don't complain about your brother's presents. You all got the same."

"No, I didn't." His tears poured down and he stomped his bare feet. "I wanted that one. I told you I wanted that one," he sobbed.

"No, you didn't, Carlos. You got the one you asked for, and you need to be grateful, otherwise, you will be punished for your tantrum. It's Christmas Day. Do you want me to take away all of your presents?" Jenny asked. She and Spiros were sitting in their sleepwear on the couch watching their children open their presents and Carlos throw a temper tantrum. She was really not in the mood for one of those, especially not on Christmas Day, and especially not since he'd been a good boy since she'd been home.

"But, Mama…" His sobs grew in decibels. "I told you I wanted that one." His face had turned red and he was itching to steal a toy. Picking up his brother's robot, with all eyes on him, especially Pedro's, he smashed the toy down on the floor and broke it.

Pedro watched, realised it was his toy Carlos had just broken, and burst into tears.

"Carlos, you vile little brat," Jenny yelled, making her sons jump. His tears stopped in shock. "How dare you break Pedro's toy. That cost money we don't have to throw around, and now he goes without because you had to be a selfish little brat and break it. Well, you know what?" She towered over her trembling son. "Now *you* don't get any of *your* presents, either. You can go without as punishment. You can go to bed without any tea, and you can play with the toys you already have because you don't get to have these for Christmas. Do you understand me?" It was cutting her to the core to see her son that way, but he had crossed the line.

"Y-y-yes…Ma…ma," he stuttered, his chubby little hands wrapped around each other in front of him, his pyjama top wet with his tears. When his mama wanted to scare him, she did. He stared from her angry face to Pedro's crying one, to his papa's upset one, and Tomas's wide-eyed shocked one. His lips quivered. He didn't want to go without his food, *or* his presents.

"Good. And *I'll* tell you when you can have them back. *Especially* the robot toy. You didn't want it, well, maybe I'll give it to one of your cousins instead, or some poor little boy who doesn't get presents. How about that?" She picked up his robot and waved it in front of him. "You didn't want it, so I'll give it to someone who does because *you* clearly don't deserve it. I come back home from being sick, and you can't even be a good boy for Christmas. After everything I've gone through, oh, *how could you,* Carlos." She promptly burst into tears and ran for her room, slamming the door behind her.

"Mama?" Tomas got to his feet and started after his precious mama. He hated seeing her upset, especially because of Carlos, and his tears started to fall.

"No, Tomas." Spiros kneeled on the floor and gently pulled him and a sobbing Carlos into his arms. He kissed them both. "It will be okay, Carlos. Do you know what you did wrong?" He got a teary nod in return. "Okay. How about I get you boys into the bath, hey? Get some fresh clothes on you, and I will probably need to change your beds as well. Let us go. Come, Pedro." He put all three crying boys into a big bubble bath and told them to behave while he quickly changed their beds. Sarah, and Jenny's sisters, had taught him how to use the washing machine, and he did a quick load while watching the boys through the open doorways connecting the bathroom to the toilet and laundry. When the boys were done, he dried and dressed them, and they helped him hang the washing out by handing him the pegs, then they all sat quietly in the lounge room reading the books the boys had received.

Lunch came and went with cold ham and salads since Jenny hadn't cooked the chickens, and finally, the boys went down for a nap. When they were asleep, Spiros called Sarah to let her know they wouldn't be coming due to Carlos being naughty and Jenny crying. Sarah told him they'd come over the next day. When the call was done, he checked on Jenny.

She rolled over and looked at him through swollen eyes. "That was horrible of me. I shouldn't have yelled at him."

"No...*but.*..he did break Pedro's toy and needed to be punished for his tantrum. I made sure to feed him extra at lunch, so he will not be hungry overnight since you said he was not getting any tea." He gently pushed the hair back from her face.

"Ugh." She covered her eyes. "I've never done that before. I feel awful. I've lain here all day crying about everything. Carlos, Alena, my surgery, my inability to ever have another child. Not being a wife to you."

"*Of course* you are a wife to me, my Jenny. You gave me three boys. A happy home. You make like wonderful." He leaned down and kissed her.

"But I can't be a wife to you anymore, Spiros. I can't have sex. I can't have children. I can't even lift the kids up, yet."

"And that is okay, Jenny. You still need to heal, and when you are ready to be intimate, you tell me, so I know. Okay?" He cupped her face and his thumb gently stroked her cheek. "The boys are down for a nap. We can have our showers now, and if you are hungry, we can eat something. We just had cold ham and salads."

"Oh, the chickens. I was meant to cook them." She groaned. "I forgot."

"And that is okay. We can have them tomorrow instead when your parents come. Would you like your present?"

"How about after we shower? I'm in need of a wash." Her grin was small, but some joy was coming back.

"Okay, let us go." Spiros led her to the bathroom and waited while she showered, holding the towel out for her and gently drying her off. She washed her face and towel-dried her hair while he showered, and then they dressed and sat in the lounge, so Jenny could eat and open her present.

"Oh, Spiros…" It was a narrow silver chain with crystals at intervals in bevelled settings. "It's beautiful, put it on me." She held her left hand out and he clasped it on her wrist. "The crystals are so pretty in pink and blue."

"Diamonds, my Jenny," he said proudly, glad that he could afford something so special for his wife.

She looked at him in horror. "Oh, Spiros, no. They must have cost a fortune, we can't afford—"

Spiros cut her off. "You know we can if we save up. And I saved up. Only the best for my Jenny." He kissed her hand and smiled.

"Kind of makes my present for you pale in comparison." She handed him a small box.

Spiros opened it and found a new watch. "Oh, Jenny, it is very nice. I did need a new one. You are the only one to buy me watches." He buckled it onto his wrist and showed it off. "I love it. Just what I needed."

"Good. I'm glad you like it. I wasn't sure which style to get you." She noticed Pedro peeking around the corner of the hallway wall. "Do you need a change, my baby?"

"Yes, Mama." His right foot casually rested on his left foot, and he clung to the edge of the wall, so he didn't fall over.

She moved to get up, but Spiros stopped her. "You rest. I will do it."

"I can get dessert instead. Think the boys will want some cake and ice cream?"

Spiros picked up Pedro and saw Tomas and Carlos come out of their rooms. "Oh, I think they will. I will get them cleaned up, and you get cake."

Jenny made up five bowls of Christmas cake with ice cream, decorated them with popcorn, lollies and chocolate Christmas biscuits, and set them on the table, waiting until Spiros brought the boys in. She held out her hand to Carlos. "Want some cake and ice cream?"

Carlos gazed up at her, wondering if she was still angry. But not seeing an angry expression, he shook his head. "You said I don't get any tea."

"You'll still go without later, but since this is afternoon tea, not normal tea, it doesn't count. You can still have this now. Do you want it?"

He reluctantly reached out and took a hold of her hand, and she led him to the table where she sat him on her lap.

"It's okay, my baby. Mama's not angry anymore." She ran her hand through his hair and kissed his cheek. "Here, Chrissy cake and ice cream with goodies on top." Jenny pulled the bowl towards him and whispered in his ear. "I love you, Carlos." She saw the soft grin spread over his lips as he picked up his spoon. Digging in to her dessert, they made small talk about the family coming around tomorrow.

July 1967

"Happy birthday, dear Papa, happy birthday to you. Hip, hip, hooray, hip, hip, hooray, hip, hip, hooray," Carlos, Tomas and Pedro sang to their father.

"Thank you, my sons," Spiros told his boys and gave them hugs and kisses.

"Another year older, Papa. You'll be as old as Grandpa soon," fourteen-year-old Carlos cheekily said. He came up to his father's nose, which only made him five foot five, but he'd been having growth spurts for a while and was nearly as tall as his mama.

"Is that so?" Spiros playfully cuffed him around the ear. "And so will you be, one day."

"Yeah, but not for a *really* long time," Carlos joked back. "You'll get there before me. Cut the cake already." He pointed at the chocolate and caramel concoction that his mother had made for his father's birthday, and couldn't wait to get his mouth around it. *Mama makes the best cakes,* he thought, salivating at the deliciousness that oozed out of the piece he was handed. "Thank you." Eyeballing the chocolate caramel sauce, he knew he had to wait until everyone else was served before eating. "Hurry up and serve."

"Patience, Carlos, it's your father's cake, he's dealing it out. Wait until everyone has a piece." Jenny passed a plate to Pedro who was beside her, and waited until Spiros put down the serving set. "Happy birthday, my darling."

"Thank you, my Jenny." Spiros's smile was ear to ear as he gazed adoringly at his beautiful wife. "Forty-two today. How did I get to be this old?"

"You! What about me!" Jenny exclaimed. "One year away from forty. We just celebrated our fifteenth wedding anniversary two months ago. We've been a couple for sixteen years, known each other for seventeen, almost, the milestones are racking up. Even the kids turned ten, twelve and fourteen. Pedro's finally in double digits." She tweaked Pedro's chin and he gave her a cheeky grin back.

He was finally a big boy at ten, and even though he only came up to his mama's chest, he still loved the hugs and kisses she gave him, and relished in the love she showered upon him. "I'm a big boy now."

"Hardly," Carlos scoffed and saw his mama's eyebrow rise. When that happened, you knew you were on the border of a telling off, and it was the warning that stopped you before you kept going. Backtracking, he added, "You won't be a big boy until you're a teenager. Even Tomas is still a year away from that." He looked at his brother for support, but Tomas's expression remained neutral, showing Carlos he wasn't getting involved.

Instead, Tomas shrugged and ignored his brother, knowing him well enough to not take sides. "I don't mind still not being a teenager."

Knowing he wasn't being backed up by anyone, Carlos glanced at each member of his family until his eyes lay on his mama who sat across from him. Her brow was back to normal position and he went back to eating his cake.

Jenny traded glances with Spiros and smiled. She knew her sons well, and while Carlos was turning out to look very much like her, he wasn't like her in manners and etiquette. But then, Jenny didn't know what it was like to be a fourteen-year-old boy and often consulted with her father and brothers about it. "*Of course* you're a big boy, Pedro; you're just not a teenager yet. Another three years to go. Tomas becomes one next year."

"Why do I have to wait so long, Mama?" Pedro swung his legs back and forth and put his face closer to the plate, so he could scoop the delicious caramel cream into his mouth.

"Because that's the way it is, my baby," she replied and scraped up the last of her cake. "It's another three years until you're a teenager."

They were interrupted by the phone ringing.

"I'll get it." Spiros wiped his mouth and got up to answer it. "Hello."

"Spiros, your uncle Nikos, has your mother rung, yet?" He didn't need to wish him a happy birthday, as he'd already done it earlier that day at the shop when he'd cracked open a bottle of ouzo to celebrate.

"No, I don't think so, why would she? Hang on." Spiros turned to Jenny. "Did any phone calls come today from Mykonos?"

"No, nothing." Shocked that they should be expecting something after all these years, Jenny watched her husband's face.

"No calls. Why? What's wrong?" he asked Nikos.

"Your mother, your sisters, your brothers, they've all called here today. Oh, Spiros… Your father…he's passed away." There had been no other way to say it, and it wasn't something Nikos could really ease into.

The wave of shock rolled over Spiros and he wasn't sure he'd heard correctly. "What?"

"Your father, Spiros, has died."

So many emotions flew past Spiros that he couldn't figure out which one he was actually feeling. He noticed heartache and sorrow, but wasn't sure what else there was. Silent, he slumped onto the phone table seat.

"Spiros, what is it?" Jenny moved to stand, but he waved her back and started speaking in Greek. "What happened?"

"From what I could gather, he had just come home from the shop with a side of meat and collapsed. The emergency people were called, but it was too late. He was gone. Your mother is in hysterics, so are your sisters. Your brothers flew in from Athens."

"*When* did it happen?" Spiros asked, his eyes focussed on the floor.

"Sometime yesterday afternoon, their time. They were dealing with it, but started making calls today to your mother's family. They got Melina and she told me when I got home. I've just rung them and spoken to your sister. I told them to ring you. She claimed to not have your number. I gave it to her. They haven't rung?"

"No, no calls," Spiros muttered, trying to figure out what it all meant.

"Then maybe you should call them. They're only morning, time-wise."

Sighing, Spiros looked at his family. He knew Tomas spoke Greek, he'd taught him himself, but Carlos and Pedro had never picked it up except for a few swear words and lines Uncle Nikos had taught them. He saw the worried expressions, especially on Jenny's face. "Would it even be worth ringing?" he went on in Greek.

"Spiros, no matter which way you cut it, you are not only the eldest son, but the eldest child. It's up to you. You must go home to see your mother and help deal with the funeral."

"I will be resented, unwelcome, unwanted, more than likely chased away. Why should I go?"

"For the reasons I just stated. Do you want to come over here? I can call your mother and you can talk to her. If she hangs up, I'll call back. If you call from your phone, they may hang up on you."

With the air in his body depleted, he bent until his arms rested on his legs. "I don't know, Uncle Nikos. Let me talk to Jenny and I'll let you know."

"Okay, just remember, we are ahead of them, time-wise. I'll wait for your call. I'm sorry you had to find this out on your birthday, Spiros."

"So am I, Uncle Nikos, so am I. I'll talk to you later." Setting the phone in its cradle, he ran his hands through his hair and stared at the floor.

"Spiros?" Jenny rose, unsure if she should go to her husband, or wait for him to come back to the table.

Lifting his head, a world-weary expression on his face, he said, "Have we finished celebrating? I have something to tell you."

"Ah…sure…I, I guess." Jenny quickly put the cake away and cleared the dishes. "Do you want more coffee?"

"Yes, please, and make it strong." He sat at the table and waited in silence for his wife to sit back down.

"Here." She set the strong Greek coffee in front of him, placed her hands on his shoulders reassuringly, and kissed his cheek. "What is it?

What's happened in Greece?"

He took her hand and kissed it. "Sit down, my love, and I'll tell you." Waiting for her to be seated, he remembered that the boys were on school holidays, and knew his uncle would give him time off work. But what would Jenny say?

"Well?" she asked an inkling snaking its way through her.

Having a sip of coffee, and taking a deep breath with closed eyes, he said, "My father has passed away."

"Oh, Spiros," Jenny murmured in shock, her hand going to his arm in comfort. "When?"

"Ah…yesterday, their time. It happened at home, after work. They couldn't save him. My brothers flew in from Athens, my sisters made phone calls to my mother's family because my father had none except for us." Another sip and the hot brew fled down his throat, burning as it went, but then it was what he needed on the cold winter's night.

"And they rang Nikos?" Jenny tried putting it together. "I've been home all day, there have been no calls from anyone."

"No, that's what I told Uncle Nikos. They all rang his place and Aunt Melina answered. She told him when he got home. He's made a couple of calls, even gave my sister my number, but no one's called. Uncle Nikos said I should. As the eldest, it's up to me."

"Yes, I guess it would be." Jenny nibbled her lip in thought. "Does this mean you want to finally go back?"

Spiros looked at his wife and saw Pedro beside her staring back with worried eyes. His eyes moved to his right and saw Carlos and Tomas with equally worried eyes. Sighing, he said, "I don't know. Uncle Nikos told me to come to his place and he'll call, to make sure I can talk to Mama in case my brothers, or sisters, answer and refuse me." His head slowly shook in mechanical motions. "Until I do that, I guess I don't know what we'll do."

"The boys have a week left of holidays; do you know when the funeral is?" Jenny's brain was churning over, thinking ahead to what clothes they would take to Mykonos and how'd she'd always wanted to see it. Just not for a funeral.

"No," he said with another head shake. "I guess I should find out."

"Go to your uncle's house, find out what's going on and make a decision," Jenny told him. "You need to know, and you know we'll be here when you get back."

Glancing at the clock on the wall opposite him, he saw it was only seven, so about twelve, lunchtime, in Mykonos.

"Go," Jenny urged. "We'll be here."

After draining his coffee, he kissed his wife and sons and drove to his uncle's house.

"Have you made a decision?" Nikos asked when he let him through the door.

"Not yet. That's why I'm here, to call and find out. Will you go to the funeral?"

"I could. He was my brother-in-law, and if you need backup," Nikos suggested with a shrug of his shoulders. "All of our kids are out of the home, so we could go with you."

A desolate sigh left Spiros's gut. "I guess we'd better find out then."

Nodding his assent, Nikos slapped Spiros on the shoulder and called Mykonos. His niece answered. "Phaedra, your Uncle Nikos. Put your mother on," he said in Greek.

Phaedra called her mother to the phone. "Uncle Nikos."

Katyana took the phone and wept. "Nikos, you are calling back. Oh, Nikos, what am I to do?"

"You should talk to your son, Spiros." Nikos winked at his nephew. "He is the eldest of the family. But you have your sons and daughters; it is time to deal with what has happened. When is the funeral? I am thinking of coming over for it." He listened for a few minutes. "In three days. Okay, and *have* you spoken to Spiros? He would want to be at his father's funeral. He would want to see you."

Katyana glanced over her shoulder at her children in the lounge room and lowered her voice. "I want to see him. I want to talk to him. I get his letters and read about my grandsons. I get your letters and read about him. But I am not sure Matthias would permit it."

"Katyana, do you not realise that I am your brother. Not only your *eldest* brother, but the head of the family. The head of *our* family, just as Spiros is the head of *your* family with Giorgio. He has a right to be there. His wife and sons have a right to meet you and pay their respects to a man they did not know, while Spiros has the right to pay his respects to his father and see his mother and family. He is entitled to be there, just as I am. He wants to talk to you, Katyana." He waved Spiros over. "But he is afraid he'll call and get one of his brothers, or sisters, and they'll hang up on him." Glancing at his nephew, he added, "He is here now if you wish to talk to him."

"He is there, with you?" she whispered, casting another glance over her shoulder. "Let me talk to him."

Nikos handed over the phone.

"Mama," Spiros said in Greek. "I'm so sorry Papa has passed away. I want to come home and see you. I want to bring Jenny and our boys. I wrote to you about them. I want them to meet you and see my homeland. I miss you, Mama. I always have and now..." Tears slid down his cheeks. "Papa's gone and he'll never meet my wife and sons."

Katyana tried to keep the conversation going as if she was still talking to Nikos. "Yes, yes, he has gone and I miss him, and all of you. I want you to come for the funeral, Nikos. *Can* you come?"

Spiros caught on to what she was doing. "Yes, Mama, I can. And I'll bring Jenny and the boys, and Uncle Nikos and Aunt Melina. We will all come."

"Thank you," she whispered, silent tears falling. "Thank you."

"*Of course* Mama. What day is the funeral?"

"Saturday, that is right. Three days from now."

"Okay, Mama. We'll be there. Who's staying with you?"

"Agathe is staying," Katyana told him, nodding her head towards her eldest daughter and glancing at other family members in her house. "We will have the service at the Orthodox Church, and then take Giorgio to the cemetery. He will be in the family crypt with his sister and mother."

"Okay..." Spiros murmured. "We'll be there in a day, or two, with Uncle Nikos and Aunt Melina. He'll be the one to call you, Mama, just in case someone else answers. I love you, and I'll see you soon. I'll put Uncle Nikos back on. Bye, Mama." He handed the phone to Nikos and wearily accepted a cup of coffee from his aunt. *Thank you,* he mouthed and drank the strong brew.

Nikos finally hung up. "We will need to book flights and get down to Sydney for them. And we will need accommodation because the hotels will be all booked out."

"Do you know anyone who could help?" Spiros asked. "Wouldn't that also mean my brothers and sisters can't find accommodation?"

"Maybe, unless they are staying with their families," Nikos replied. "Your sisters still live on Mykonos, but all of your brothers would have their in-laws to stay with. Mmm…" He scratched his chin in thought. "I have a friend who rents his house out for a couple of months over summer. I'll give him a call." He set to work making phone calls to Greece and booked plane flights for all of them. "Will Jenny mind?"

"Probably not." Spiros rose to leave. "She has probably packed our bags already." He arrived home to find she had started getting them ready.

"I had a long chat with the boys, and I'm getting our clothes prepared. The boys are packed, and I just need to finish ironing some of our things before packing them. I also rang Mum and Dad, and Joanna will watch the house while we're away, and collect the mail and milk." Jenny finished pressing a dress and slid it onto a hanger. "I take it we're leaving tomorrow?" She finally turned to her husband and saw how weary he was. "Did you get to speak to your mother?"

"I did." He slowly slumped onto the sofa. "She received my letters and can't wait to meet you and the boys. She wants to see me, can't wait for us to come. Uncle Nikos and Aunt Melina are coming with us to run interference with my siblings, and so he can see his sister." A sigh left him and he settled back, staring at nothing in particular as his eyes closed to half-mast. "I always wanted to take you to Mykonos one day, my Jenny. But I didn't think it would be for this."

She sat beside him and took his hand in both of hers. "I know. But you must have realised at some point that your parents would pass. Just like my parents will someday."

"Yes," he murmured; his eyes almost closed. "But not yet. I wanted to take you for our tenth anniversary, but the boys were still young and you were still recovering, so then I thought, we would go for our twentieth and make it a big holiday with the boys. They would be old enough to enjoy it more."

"We still can," she told him. "*Or*, we can take a bit of extra time now and see the sights. I know we're going for a funeral, but we could still take a look around, can't we? We can afford to, can't we?" She knew full well they could as she did their accounting, as well as the shop's books for Nikos.

"Yes." He finally looked at her and saw her smiling face. "Nikos has organised for us to stay at his friend's house. We have about two weeks, so we won't have to worry about that. And he's booked the plane tickets for tomorrow night. The funeral's on Saturday."

Jenny nodded. "I've asked Joanna to inform the school if we're not back in time for the boys to start again. I don't think the school will have a problem."

"I don't know how long we'll be gone for, Jenny. A week, maybe the two. I can't put a plan down. I just don't know what will happen once we get there. My father may have had a will, but he would've cut me out of it, so that may not be important, and I may not need to attend that." He shrugged. "I don't know how long we'll be gone."

"And that's okay," she said. "I guess it's just as well I got passports for the boys this year. I'd better get to packing our bags and see what the boys are up to." Leaving him sitting there in contemplation, she grabbed her dress, switched off the iron, and went to pack her bag. She knew it was summer in Mykonos, but packed a pair of slacks and a pretty blouse top to go with them, a few black dresses for funeral attire, and colourful dresses for the rest of the holiday. Slipping Alena's urn into its box, she packed it into her overnight case and finished packing her bags before starting on Spiros's. When she was done, she set them by their bedroom door and went to check on the boys who were about to fall asleep, but were still deciding what toys and books to take with them.

Jenny told them to leave most of it behind and just take the books they needed to read for school, a book for journaling in if they wanted to write about the trip, and a colouring book if they felt like something else to do. She gave their luggage the once over and placed the cases by their doors before seeing them off to bed. After hanging their travel outfits on their wardrobe doors, and placing their shoes aside, she collected her and Spiros's toiletries and packed them. Her make-up, hair accessories, and jewellery went into the overnight bag, and she was done.

"Oh, the cameras and passports." She hurried to collect them and the spare films for the cameras in case she couldn't get them in Mykonos, and tucked everything into her large tote bag that was currently all the rage. Making sure she had money to pay for their tickets on the train and plane, she ticked everything off her list and went to collect Spiros. "Time for bed. The boys are asleep, and we need to catch the train in the morning."

Wearily, realising he hadn't moved since he'd sat down, he gazed up at his wife. "Yes. We need to catch the train." He let her haul him to his feet and followed her into their bedroom, turning off the lights as they went.

*****

The next morning, Sarah and Matthew, and Nikos and Melina with Nikos junior arrived bright and early.

"Junior will take our car back home," Nikos explained. "Are we ready?"

Jenny gathered the boys and their luggage, and Spiros packed them into Matthew's car and his. Sarah would be driving their car back, while Jenny's sisters would tidy up and make sure the bed linen and clothes were washed and changed, or put away.

Jenny made one last check of everything. "Okay, we have our money, cameras, and passports. We just have to lock up."

They went on their way and arrived at the train station where Nikos paid for their tickets, to Jenny's surprise and dismay. She felt bad not paying her way, but Nikos insisted. Waving goodbye to her parents, she settled in for the long journey, and they arrived at the station in Sydney, where they were met by Jenny's aunt and uncle, and

Nikos's youngest son, Vasili, who'd been living and working in the city for the last ten years with his wife and five children. They spent a couple of hours catching up until it was time to head to the airport, and three hours later, they were on their way to Greece.

*****

They arrived in Athens close to sunset, Greece time, and with Nikos doing the talking, they were packed into two taxies and taken to the wharf. Mykonos didn't have an airport, so the only way to get there was by ferry.

Carrying their cases and bags on board, the family found a spot in the lounge area to leave their luggage and waited for the trip to commence. Once it did, the boys stood out on the deck watching as they sailed from the dock, and Jenny and Melina freshened up.

"Greece seems very…old," Jenny murmured to her husband as she sat beside him. She was nervous about everything. She'd been nervous about the plane flight, and now the ferry ride; not to mention she was going to be seeing Spiros's homeland and family. Being Australian, she hoped she and the boys were accepted.

"Well…it is, my love." Spiros chuckled despite the reason they were there. "As old as the gods. Didn't you like it?"

"Oh, I did, it's very charming. But we didn't get to see much of it, just what we saw from the plane, and then the taxi. I hope we can spend a couple of days there before we go home. Maybe?" Placing her hand over his, Jenny so desperately wanted this to go well for Spiros, but knew she didn't have much of a say in what happened with his family, and wouldn't be included in anything anyway. She just hoped to take the boys sightseeing as much as possible, so it wasn't a bad trip for them.

"Maybe we can. Show the boys where the Stephanopouloses are from, but the next few days will be…very…" He wasn't sure which words to use as so many just didn't seem right.

"Tiring," Jenny offered. "Exhausting, overwhelming, painful."

A small smile lit up Spiros's lips. "All of the above. Very emotional, very time-consuming. I don't want you and the boys to suffer for it. You and Aunt Melina can see the island together while Uncle Nikos and I deal with things if you like." He glanced from Jenny to his aunt. "You don't mind, do you?"

"No, not at all," Melina told him. "I'll play tour guide to Jenny and the boys."

"That's sweet, but if you're going to see your mother, shouldn't the boys and I come along?" Jenny had been told the odd story, or ten, of Spiros's family, and knew what they looked like as he'd brought a photo with him when he immigrated to Australia, and they'd received photos from Nikos that his sister had sent.

"Yes, you should. But I'm not sure the very first meeting would be good for the boys, or you," Spiros said. "Everyone will be there, and there could be issues."

"Such as?" Jenny asked.

"Such as, they may want to throw you out if you come with me to Mama's house."

"Are they that full of hatred?" Jenny was now starting to wonder how it would affect the boys emotionally. "You are the eldest, Spiros. Does that not mean anything here?"

"It does," Nikos boomed. He'd been watching the two of them converse and had to butt in. "Just as I am the eldest of *my* family, Spiros is the eldest of *his*, and we both have the right to be there. I take it your grandfather will be. Both of his children are gone now, along with his wife."

"Yes. I guess he'll be at the funeral and reception afterwards. I don't know if he'll be at the house. He may be staying somewhere else."

"So, when do you want to go there?" Jenny asked. "Tomorrow's Friday and the funeral's Saturday."

Sighing, Spiros considered his options. "I think I should go to the house tomorrow and find out what's happening. Talk to Mama, and make my position known."

"And what is that?" Nikos asked in interest.

Spiros looked him square in the eye. "That I'm the eldest and have every right to be at the funeral of my father."

*****

After a restless night, Spiros started the morning with a coffee on the balcony at sunrise. To see Mykonos again after seventeen years was mind-blowing, and he couldn't believe he was back. In fact, it felt as if he'd never even left.

"Hey." Jenny came to his side and took in the lightening of the sky, the rainbow of colours it showed off to early morning risers. "Wow, this is beautiful."

"It is, indeed, my love. And I'm so glad you finally get to see it, even if it is under dire circumstances."

She slid her hand across his back and around his waist, and resting her chin on his shoulder, breathed deeply. "It's so fresh here. And not as cold as Armidale."

"We are in summer, Jenny. It's a very busy month here on Mykonos. All of the tourists come for some sun; they drink at the beach bars and shop in the stores. I hope you and the boys don't have any trouble with other tourists."

"Why would we? We're tourists ourselves, so I don't think we will, and if Melina is playing tour guide, then she can get her Greek on and tell everyone to get out of our way."

Spiros chuckled. "I'm sure she will."

"What's the plan for today? Since the funeral is tomorrow, it probably won't be too polite if we just turn up at the funeral out of the blue. We should meet everyone. Your mother, at least."

"Ah…Jenny." He exhaled slowly. "I don't want to put you in that situation."

"But it's inevitable," Jenny told him. "It *has* to be done. And I'm a big girl. I may not speak a lot of Greek, though I can get by on certain phrases and sentences, so I'll be nervous if they can't speak English, but I'm sure Tomas will translate for us, since Carlos and Pedro don't know much, either."

"Yes, I'm sure he will." A small smile lit up Spiros's face and he took his wife into his arms. "But I'm also sure that not very nice things will be said, and since I and Uncle Nikos *do* understand it, it may make me very angry if they insult my wife and children. And since Tomas can understand it, I'm worried that it will hurt him."

"I know, and we can talk to him to prepare him. But no matter which way you want to dissect this, you need to see your family today, and we need to meet them today. Or tomorrow morning at the latest, but even that could cause issues."

"I know, I know." He kissed her cheek and sighed, marvelling at what a lucky man he was to have such an amazing and understanding woman for a wife. "I know."

They stood watching the sun rise and the day start on Mykonos, and the boys finally wandered out in their summer pjs and joined them.

"Ah…so pretty," Tomas enthused, leaning over the balcony railing, happy that he was getting to see his father's homeland, especially in summer. "Can we go exploring?" His excited face turned up to his parents.

"In a couple of days, my son. We have to meet the family today and go to your grandfather's funeral tomorrow. But after that, your mama and I will take you exploring. I'll show you all of the places I explored as a child, where I worked and played before moving to Australia and meeting your mama. But for now, let's get some breakfast into you, and get you into a shower and dressed for meeting your grandmother. We need to talk about it."

After a hearty breakfast, hot showers, and dressing respectfully in black, Spiros sat Jenny and the boys down to discuss his family and what might happen at his parents' house. "No matter what they say, my sons, don't take it to heart. They'll be saying it out of anger and spite. Don't listen to them, especially you, Tomas." He held his son's hand. "You understand Greek, and so you might hear things that aren't nice. Let it go in one ear and out the other. Don't take it to heart no matter what's said, or who says it. And you may need to translate for your mother and brothers. Okay?"

"Yes, Papa, I'll try." Tomas took his role very seriously. Even though he was the middle child, he had to help his mama and brothers with their Greek, and play tour guide and translator if the need be.

"Good." Spiros stood up and looked at his aunt and uncle. "Are we ready?"

"We are." Nikos nodded. "I rang earlier. Your mother will be there all day, as will your siblings, I'm sure. Are *you* ready?" He watched the emotions fly over his nephew's face.

The huge sigh Spiros let out deflated him. "No. It's been seventeen years. My father forbade anyone from being in contact with me, which is why I secretly sent Mama those letters."

"I know. Your father was a stubborn, angry man back then, and made everyone suffer just because you decided to spread your wings like the rest of us. That wasn't fair to any of you." Nikos shook his head apologetically. "I'm sorry, but let's see if we can start mending things now. Shall we?" He led them outside to the two cars they'd rented and set off for the Stephanopoulos residence. They parked a way down the street and alighted.

"I'll go first," Nikos told them in a low tone. "Melina can come with me, or stay with Jenny. Spiros, you come in next, and then Jenny and the boys." Everyone nodded and he set off.

"Wait," Spiros called softly and dug into his pocket for the front door key he'd left Mykonos with as a reminder of what he was leaving behind. "If someone lets you in, they'll shut the door behind you, but if you walk straight in, they'll not have time." He handed the key over. "Quietly, Uncle Nikos."

Nodding, Nikos quietly walked down the road with Melina, and Spiros, Jenny, and the boys slowly followed.

Spiros kept an eye out for any of his family and noted the line of cars down the street. He came to a stop outside, careful to not be seen from any window, and waved Jenny and the boys to stay back.

Jenny took note of her husband and stopped with the boys. She had dressed respectfully in a lightweight, long-sleeved, three-quarter length black dress buttoned up to the neck, with black gloves, shoes and handbag. She'd asked Melina about funeral attire and had packed accordingly. Her hair was swept back with black combs.

Keeping a hold on Pedro in front of her, she slid her right arm over his right shoulder and diagonally across his chest. He hung on to her arm with both hands. Tomas was to her left, and she had her arm around his shoulders, keeping her two babies close. Carlos was to her right. "Make sure your top buttons are done up, boys." She had allowed them to wear short-sleeved summer shirts with their black suits, but they had to be buttoned up and presentable.

Nikos quietly unlocked the door, pocketed the key, and swung the door open. "Katyana, I am here. Where are you?" He stepped into the small lounge room and looked at all of the people present.

"Nikos, oh Nikos, I am so glad you're here." Katyana moved to her brother's side and they hugged. "I am so glad you're here." They stood hugging and chatting in front of the fireplace with her children standing around watching.

Melina had walked in with her husband and was consoling Katyana for her loss, and wondering when the family was going to notice.

Katyana saw him over her sister-in-law's shoulder. She saw a woman and three boys behind him. "Spiros?" she asked in Greek.

Spiros calmly walked through the door and all heads swivelled to look. "Mama."

"Spiros," Matthias spat in shock and moved to shut the door on him. "Get out of here, you are not—"

Spiros slammed his hand flat on the door to stop it. "Not what?" he replied in Greek. "What are you going to say?" He sensed the anger and shock of his family, but knew the only way to deal with it was to stare his brother down. "Not what?" he repeated.

"You are not welcome here," Matthias retorted, glancing over his brother's shoulder at the woman and three boys.

Spiros lowered his voice. "Don't you *ever* tell me I am not welcome in *our* parents' home, because they are *our* parents. And as the eldest, I have *every* right to be here for *our* father's funeral." He pushed the door back and stepped aside. "Jenny," he called over his shoulder in English, "come and meet my mother."

Slowly, and unsurely, Jenny nudged the boys forward while still keeping her hands on Pedro and Tomas. They crossed the threshold, passed Spiros, and with their eyes taking in every face on the family, saw Nikos and Melina wave them over. They eagerly moved over to them with Pedro standing between Tomas and his mama with her arm around him.

Spiros closed the door and joined them, keeping a close eye on his siblings, which wasn't hard since the lounge room was quite small and enclosed. "Mama," he said and hugged and kissed an excited Katyana who couldn't stop chattering in Greek. "Mama…" He took his mother by both arms and stopped her to make the introductions in Greek. "Mama, this is my wife, Jenny."

Katyana stared wide-eyed at her three grandsons and daughter-in-law before putting her arms out to pull Jenny into a hug. She kissed both cheeks multiple times.

"Oh," Jenny was surprised by her ferociousness. "I am so, so sorry for your loss," she murmured sympathetically.

Spiros translated for his mother and went on. "And this is our eldest son, Carlos Spiros Stephanopoulos, who is fourteen years old." He rested his hand on Carlos's shoulder and shared a quick glance with Jenny. "Carlos," Spiros said in English. "This is your grandmother."

Carlos, nervous, even though he'd practised saying hello in Greek, couldn't remember how to say it, so said hello in English.

"Hello, Carlos, oh, my grandson, how big you are. You look just like your mama," Katyana said and laid her hands on his cheeks.

Spiros translated for his son. "She says hello, and that you look like your mother."

Carlos smiled and got a kiss on each cheek.

Spiros indicated to Tomas. "And Mama, this is Tomas Giorgio Stephanopoulos, our middle son. He's twelve and speaks fluent Greek."

"Oh, you have your grandfather's name, Tomas." Katyana grabbed his cheeks. "I am so glad you have come and that I get to meet you." She carried on in Greek, Tomas responded, and they conversed for a few moments while Spiros translated.

"And Grandma, this is my brother, Pedro Matthew Stephanopoulos," Tomas told her, taking over the introductions, he put his arm around his nervous younger brother. "The youngest at ten years of age." He then translated her words for Pedro who got kisses on both cheeks.

Katyana carried on, her hands and arms making gestures, and

Tomas translated for his mama and brothers.

"She's glad we're here, Papa has beautiful sons, healthy sons, a happy family. If only Giorgio could have seen them…"

Jenny smiled softly, well aware of the stares of her in-laws, and noticed Carlos inch closer and slip his arm around her waist. She still had Pedro under her left arm and Tomas was close, as were Nikos and Melina, but with seven sets of accusatory eyes glaring daggers at her, she was starting to feel like a germ under a microscope.

"Mama wants you to come into the dining room and sit, and we'll have refreshments," Spiros told his family and pointed to the room ahead of them.

"I'll go and make sure the others don't poison anything you eat, or drink," Melina murmured to Jenny. "You just never know."

"Oh, should I help?" Jenny asked, but was led by Nikos putting his arm around her and escorting her. "No need. Melina will make sure you all get something. Come."

They sat at the table, one that was much smaller than what Spiros had sat around as a child and adult, with Jenny and the boys on one side, his mother in her usual place at the end, and Spiros in his usual spot on his mother's right.

Conversations carried on in Greek between Katyana and her son, her and her grandson, and her and Nikos. One or the other translated for Jenny, Pedro and Carlos, and Melina came in with a tray of coffee for the adults, and iced water for the boys.

"Here we go." Melina handed them out and left a small bowl of loukoumi, a Greek confection similar to Turkish delight, on the table. "Is it all right for the boys to have this?" she asked Katyana.

"Of course, of course," Katyana replied in Greek. "Eat up, eat up." She gestured for the boys to try one, and Tomas told her they ate them at home.

"You eat Greek food?" Katyana asked him, looking at Jenny, not sure how, or why, a woman who was clearly not Greek would eat, let alone make, Greek food.

"Yes. Mama makes Papa's favourite foods, and Aunt Melina feeds us when we go to their place, and then we eat at the Greek Club once a month." Tomas had no problem telling his grandmother everything and launched into their whole life story in Greek with the others smiling and translating.

Spiros sharply glanced over his shoulder. His ears had picked up words he never wanted to hear again. "Mama," he interrupted in Greek. "Do you need the rest of the family here now? They're saying very unkind things."

"About you and your family?" Nikos asked, leaping out of his chair. "I will throw them out." He closed the dining room door behind him, leaving Jenny to look at her husband in surprise, and Spiros to shake his head for her to do nothing.

"Boys, girls, it's time you left for the day," Nikos told them as they gathered around. "Your mother wants time with her son and his family."

"Why is he here?" Costas spat, angry that Spiros had bothered coming back at all.

Nikos hardened. "Don't you dare take that tone of voice with me." He may have been in his sixties, but his girth and height outdid them all. Taking a threatening step towards his nephew, he went on. "Spiros has every right to be here to say goodbye to his father, and his family has every right to meet your mother. You will not cause problems for him." He shoved his meaty finger into Costas's chest. "Do you understand me? I am head of your mother's family, and Spiros is head of this one. *We* have every right to be here and you don't get a say. Do you understand that?"

Costas just glared at him with a hateful expression.

"What does he want?" Matthias asked. As second eldest, he expected to be in charge since their father had said he'd disown Spiros when he left.

"What does it matter to you?" Nikos asked him. "What does it matter to any of you?" He cast his gaze across them. "None of you boys have spent any quality time with your parents in the last decade, or so. I get your mother's letters, complaining she never sees her grandchildren *or* her children. You don't come near her. And the girls?" He looked at their downcast eyes. "How many of your husbands don't like you coming here? You live here on Mykonos, but how often do you see your mother?" He cast a disappointed eye over all of them. "You barely see your mother, and yet you criticise your brother for coming home. You denigrate his wife and children. Yes, I heard the words you used, and so did Spiros," he told his shocked nephews. "You should be ashamed, *your father* would be ashamed, and your mother would definitely be if she'd heard. Now, I suggest you all leave and stay gone until tomorrow. We will see you at the funeral. Go." He pointed at the door and watched angry expressions and furious glances exchanged among the boys.

Costas opened his mouth, but Nikos cut him off. "Don't! Just leave."

Knowing they wouldn't get anything else, and more than likely wouldn't be getting near their mother now, they left, filing out one by one, casting angry looks over their shoulders.

Nikos closed the door on them and sighed. They all knew it would be tough, especially from Spiros's siblings, but the words he and Spiros had heard about Jenny were totally uncalled for and something quite vile for a woman to be called. Even in Greece. He flung open the dining room door and got back to gossiping.

*****

After another restless night, they attended the funeral of Giorgio Stephanopoulos junior in the Orthodox Church.

Anyone who was anyone, or knew the Stephanopoulos family in some way, turned out to pay their respects, even if they only bought meat from him once a week. But all were shocked to see Spiros Stephanopoulos lead his mother down the aisle with a non-Greek woman and three boys following. Nikos and Melina came up the rear, shielding them from what could eventuate.

The whole town knew what had happened seventeen years ago. Spiros had left with his friends for Australia and promptly been disowned and disinherited by Giorgio. No one had spoken of him since, and one by one, the sons had left the shop and the island for Athens, other jobs, and lives.

Spiros settled his mother into the front pew and indicated for Jenny and the boys to sit beside him. Nikos and Melina sat behind them to protect them, and the rest of the family took their seats. Once the congregation got over their shock, they found their seats and the funeral service started.

After many people got up to talk about Giorgio, the priest led the family down the aisle with Giorgio's sons and sons-in-law, excluding Spiros, carrying the casket aloft their shoulders.

Spiros led his mother after them, with Jenny and the boys, and Nikos and Melina and their family members following closely behind. They walked after the casket as the priest led them to the cemetery where Giorgio was laid to rest with his mother and sister.

Spiros held his sobbing mother up as the family cast angry looks his way. He was stoic; it wasn't the time for anger and hatred, it was time to bury their father. Besides, he'd steeled himself for it, figured even his brothers-in-law would get in on it when it was none of their business. Once the crypt was closed, the crowd slowly dispersed, heading to the reception hall beside the church.

Jenny kept her boys close all the way, and knew she was being studied. She had the sense that she was being mocked, particularly by the silent expressions on their faces. She had kept her attire simple with a three-quarter black dress with long chiffon sleeves that was cinched at the waist and swished elegantly around her shapely calves. Her accessories consisted of black short gloves, shoes, handbag, sunglasses, and a small hat with netting over her face. Her hair was wrapped up into an elegant bun and her make-up was simple.

The boys wore black ties with their black suits, shirts and shoes. Carlos's hair glowed in the sun, just as Jenny's did, while Pedro and Tomas looked like everyone else. All three boys had brushed their hair back with side parts to look respectful.

They sat to the side of the reception hall, with Spiros and his mother. They watched while half the townspeople filed past to pay their respects to Katyana personally, kissing her cheek, her hand, crying with her, over her, glaring at Spiros, who eyed them back, looking down their noses at Jenny and her boys. Jenny simply raised her brow, narrowed her eyes and glared back, defying them to say, or do, anything.

"I've got a pretty good idea of who our cousins are," Carlos whispered to his brothers. "Anyone either side of our age, and hanging around our aunts and uncles."

"We could talk to them," Tomas, ever the optimistic, whispered back.

"We could try, but I don't think their parents would allow it." Carlos eyed their cousins, aunts and uncles.

Nikos and Melina made sure everyone had something to eat and drink, and sat with them in between mingling with the crowd. Melina passed on the gossip to Jenny. "The whole crowd is curious as to why Spiros is back, especially with a wife who is clearly not Greek, and neither is her eldest son. They think he's not Spiros's."

"What!" Jenny exploded, but quickly lowered her voice as the crowd turned to stare.

"What's wrong, Jenny?" Spiros spun around in his seat and leaned past Melina to talk to his wife.

"Tell him," Jenny urged her.

Melina cast a sly glance at the crowd. "Some don't think Carlos is yours as he doesn't look like you."

"What!" Spiros exploded in English and then calmed down. He sent a scathing look across the crowd. "I know who my son is, how dare they."

His mother asked him what was wrong, and he told her in Greek that the crowd were spreading rumours about Jenny and the boys.

Katyana was angry, spitting out Greek swear words to all who were gathered.

"Mama, enough, let's not give them any more of our energy. We are here for Papa."

Katyana calmed down and spoke to her son.

"Whoa!" Tomas's eyes had grown wide as he listened to his grandmother. "She was *angry*."

"What did she say?" Carlos asked, leaning closer to his brother.

"She berated everyone with some bad words Uncle Nikos taught us, and some I've never heard of." Tomas scanned the crowd to check their expressions. "They're not happy that she knows what they said."

"Because it was very clear that it was rude and disrespectful," Jenny murmured across Pedro who was beside her. Tomas was next, with Carlos at the end. "I don't want you to repeat, or remember, any of it. Forget you heard it."

"Yes, Mama." Tomas nodded dutifully, but kept an ear open for any conversations going on.

"Well," Carlos muttered, his anger growing. "Maybe we should make ourselves at home, and show them what Australians are." He glanced at their empty cups and then at the refreshment table. "How about we get something to drink?"

"Can we go to the toilet first?" Pedro asked under his breath. "I've got to wee."

Jenny heard her sons. "Make sure you go together. Tomas, you translate if necessary. Melina? Where are the toilets?"

"Off the main entrance," she said.

Jenny turned back to her boys. "Stay together, and don't neither of you leave without the other."

"Yes, Mama." They made their way to the bathroom, did what was needed, walked back into the room and over to the refreshment table where Tomas pointed out what was on the table, and politely asked the lady in Greek for three drinks.

The woman eyed the boys suspiciously, but poured them anyway.

Carlos stared back, making her nervous when he raised his brow the way his mother did. Oh, yes, he'd learned a thing, or two, from being in trouble, and had practised in the mirror for hours to perfect the brow lift. When they received their drinks, Tomas thanked her and they turned around to watch the crowd.

"Should we go over and introduce ourselves?" Pedro asked his brothers. But when they looked towards their father's family, they saw the children, who were glaring back at them just as curiously, were ushered away.

"That answers that," Carlos muttered. "Guess we're not allowed to mingle like the adults." He glanced over at his parents and saw them talking to an old man. "Who's that?"

"Spiros." Giorgio senior stood before his grandson. "How are you?"

Spiros stood and faced his grandfather. "I'm fine. And you? You look old."

A small grin crossed Giorgio's lips. "I am. So are you." His English wasn't perfect, but he spoke it well enough.

"Older, yes. Wiser, definitely."

Nodding, Giorgio looked down at Jenny. "And you must be the Australian that captured our Spiros's heart." He'd secretly been reading Katyana's letters when he visited them, not wanting his son to know.

"Yes." Jenny stood and offered her hand. "Jennifer Stephanopoulos. You're Spiros's grandfather?"

"Yes, yes I am." He shook her hands and held it between both of his for a moment. "It looks as if you've made our Spiros very happy and have given him three fine sons. Thank you for taking care of him."

Jenny softened and gazed into the dark brown eyes of an elderly man who could still walk upright and had a full head of hair. "You're very welcome. It's been my pleasure."

"Yes, yes." He let go of her and addressed Spiros. "Your father caused issues for all of us, and I've contributed to them for the sake of seeing my grandchildren and their children, and I have regretted it ever since. I am sorry, Spiros."

Spiros breathed in slowly, nodding, exhaling. "So am I, Grandfather."

"Well, I'm glad that you're happy and have found a good woman to love. Jenny," he nodded in her direction, "it was nice meeting you."

"Same to you, Giorgio," she murmured, watching as he conversed with Katyana for a few moments and then moved on. Watching as her husband turned to her and rested his hands on her upper arms. "Spiros, you can make up with him now. Surely you can."

"I'm afraid I can't, my love. My grandfather took my father's side and I understand, but I won't tolerate it anymore. I was disowned and he knows it. My father told me to never come back, that I would not be welcome."

"Your mother has welcomed you. That *has* to mean something?"

Jenny smiled softly and gently cupped his face. "Katyana still loves you," she murmured, so no one else heard. "She's glad you're here. Spend time with her, talk with her, tell her everything." She lovingly kissed her husband to show everyone they were a united front. "Let's show everyone where they can stick their rumours." Her infamous brow rose and her smile turned saccharine sweet.

Spiros laughed and kept on laughing. "Oh, my Jenny. I love you." He boldly kissed her and then watched as she went off with Melina to freshen up.

"Spiros, what were you saying?" Katyana asked, wondering why her son was laughing at his father's funeral.

"Oh, Mama." Spiros took her hand and kissed it. "I have the most incredible wife." He started telling her stories, making her laugh, making the other guests shake their heads in dismay, or anger, at the hilarity going on at a funeral reception.

The boys took their seats and listened to them while Tomas translated, and they watched as their mama came back with Aunt Melina and took her seat. Her head was held high and her eyebrow even higher.

Carlos grinned at her resilience and went back to people watching, his own brow held high as a battle cry and symbol for victory over the enemy who was denying him his Greek heritage.

After the service and reception, they went back to Katyana's home and talked until it was time to get the boys to bed. Katyana wanted to know if they were coming to church in the morning, and after deciding on a time to meet, Spiros and Jenny took the boys home for the night.

*****

The family spent the morning at church, and the rest of the day at Katyana's home telling more stories, looking at old pictures of Spiros as a child; watched as her other children came and went. They had been stared at in church and were stared at in Katyana's house. But not one of Spiros's siblings had brought their children or partners over to meet Jenny and the boys.

After another long day, and an early night, Spiros let them sleep in on Monday while he went for the reading of the will.

"You do not belong here, Spiros," Matthias told him. "Leave."

"I have a feeling I could still punch your lights out as I did when I was eighteen," Spiros replied as he walked past. "Care to find out?"

Nikos came up behind his nephews. "None of this rubbish. We are all deserving of being here." He sat on one side of his sister while Spiros sat on the other in the lawyer's office. The other siblings were present.

There wasn't much to the will. Giorgio's belongings went to his wife. These included the house and *Stephanopoulos Meats*, plus whatever money they had saved, and personal belongings they owned.

"But who takes over the house and shop?" Costas asked. "Mama cannot work in the shop, or take over the house by herself. Everything always goes to the eldest, except Spiros was disowned and disinherited." He was on his feet, angry that he'd heard nothing about it.

Spiros looked at his mother, unsure of why there had been no mention of it.

"Your father never made it legal," Aristotle Tarantino, the Stephanopoulos family lawyer, told them. He was actually Giorgio senior's lawyer, but since Giorgio junior had been the only heir left after his sister's death, and now his children had that role, he did the job.

"What?" Anatole also got to his feet. "What do you mean, he never made it legal? He never legally disowned and disinherited Spiros?"

Aristotle shook his head. "No, he did not, which means Spiros inherits the meat shop and the house automatically as the eldest." He looked to Spiros and his mother. "Do you have a problem with that, Katyana?"

"No, no," she cried. "I'd always hoped he'd never done it legally. Always hoped it would bring Spiros back." She grasped his hand and gazed into his eyes.

"Mama." He shook his head slowly, trying to clear the confusion. "I live in Australia with Jenny and the boys. We have a home, and the boys are in school, I manage Uncle Nikos's butcher shop."

Hearing those words, she let out a torrent of Greek. "If you run it there you can run it here. Why can't you come back? The boys could go to school here, Jenny could continue to be a housewife and join my women's clubs, and you could stay in the house with me while you get used to being back and look for a place of your own. Please do this, Spiros, please."

"Mama. It's not as easy packing up a family as it was packing me up. There's a lot to be considered." Spiros turned to the lawyer. "Are you absolutely sure?"

Aristotle nodded. "Absolutely. He did not legally disown you, so you inherit everything."

"Oh," Spiros sighed and looked at his uncle and mother. "I've got a lot of talking with Jenny to do."

*****

While they had been at the lawyer's, Jenny, the boys, and Melina had been walking around the main town of Chora, also known as Mykonos Town, which confused Jenny as to whether she was *on* Mykonos, or *in* Mykonos. They stopped in shops, ate delicacies from corner stores and street vendors, and stood looking at the windmills.

"Oh, they're so pretty," Jenny cooed. "We should get photos. Boys, go and stand in front of the windmill." Pulling her camera out of her bag, and checking to make sure there was enough film left before lining up the viewfinder, she lined up the boys and a couple of extra windmills into the shot before snapping it. "One more," she yelled, and the boys pulled silly faces. Laughing, she popped the camera away. "I wonder how Spiros is going. Should we meet them for lunch? Do we know where they'll be, or should we just go to Katyana's home?"

"Nikos told me they would call at two, so we should be home by then." Melina directed them down a white cobblestone street to more shops. "What time is it now?"

Jenny checked her watch. "Just on one. Do we have lunch?"

"Yes, let's." Melina led them to a restaurant where they grabbed a light meal of fish and salad done the Greek way, and then took the car back to their rental home, finding Spiros already there.

311

"What happened?" Jenny put her bag on the side table and rushed to her husband.

"Oh, my Jenny, so much." Spiros was sitting wearily on the sofa and told his aunt that Nikos was with his sister.

Melina nodded and had the feeling they needed to talk. "Boys, do you want to take a nap, or go out again? Let your parents speak."

"Um…" They looked at their mama for confirmation.

"You can go out, my babies. Just be back by five at the latest," she told them.

"I'll take them down to the beach and the waterfront." Melina collected the car keys and ushered the boys out the door.

Once it had closed, Jenny turned back to Spiros. "Right, what happened?"

"Oh…Jenny. A big surprise. A big, unexpected surprise that I just don't know what to do with." Spiros ran his hand through his hair and sighed. "It didn't go well."

"Oh, no. What happened? Oh, have you eaten? Do you need a drink, or a coffee, before you start?" She rose, but he pulled her back down.

"No, Jenny. I don't need anything except my wife." He pulled her into his arms and kissed her. The kissing didn't stop, even though Jenny tried to stop it to get back to the conversation, but Spiros didn't want to talk, he just wanted his wife. So, he swung her into his arms and carried her to their room where they made love in the glorious afternoon sun.

Sighing happily, Jenny laid her head on her husband's chest. "That hasn't happened in a while. What brought that on?"

"Everything," he murmured, thinking about all he had to tell her. "You wouldn't believe what happened today."

"Are you going to tell me?" She moved her head back, so she could look at his face. "What is it?"

"Not now. Let's leave it until tomorrow, so I can wrap my head around it and figure it all out."

"Okay." She frowned. "Are we seeing your mother tonight?"

"No. I told her we'd come tomorrow, or the day after. I want to show the boys around and have time to think about things. I need to make decisions, and talk to you, and she and Uncle Nikos need to deal with my siblings. They're not happy."

Jenny leaned up on her elbow and looked down at her husband. "Why am I getting the feeling I know what's happened?"

"Tomorrow, my love." Spiros ran his finger down her cheek, onto her neck, and down to her breast and nipple. "Today, I need my wife." He rolled her over and made love to her again.

*****

On Tuesday, Spiros took his family to Ornos for the day, and while the boys ran ahead exploring everything, Jenny and Spiros walked arm in arm behind them.

"You still haven't mentioned what happened at the reading of the will." Jenny kept her tone light. "Do you want to talk about it, yet?" They walked past a couple of restaurants and a few small stores.

"Maybe after lunch," Spiros replied just as lightly, seeing a little boutique that sold jewellery. "Let's go in here. You might like something. Boys…" He waited for them to come back before they entered.

"Oh, how pretty." Jenny removed her sunglasses and looked up at the crystal wind chimes hanging from the ceiling.

"Why are we in a jewellery shop?" Carlos asked, annoyed that it wasn't something cool like a book, or chocolate, shop.

"Because I want to buy your mother something," Spiros told him. "Don't make a fuss, or you won't get dessert after lunch."

Carlos grumbled his displeasure and poked a finger into a box of crystals, while Pedro and Tomas played with the small windmills on the shelf.

"Careful, boys," Jenny warned and noticed a lovely set of pink and blue crystal jewellery. It had been the only thing to really catch her eye, and she walked over to the cabinet to look at it. It was a pair of earrings with a set of three crystals. The stud was blue, with a larger pink, and a second, larger blue straight under it all in a row. It had a matching pendant on a silver necklace, a pretty chain bracelet with a row of matching crystals, and a ring completed the set. "So pretty."

"You do love pink and blue; don't you, my love." Spiros had seen her eyes light up as she looked at the jewellery.

"My favourite colours. Always have been. It would go with that diamond bracelet you bought me years ago." She looked for the store clerk and they inquired on the price for the whole set. "Mmm, a little out of our normal spend," Jenny murmured, gazing at the other jewellery to see if something else would do. "It's awfully pretty, though."

"Then you'll have it." Spiros waved the clerk over and ordered it to be wrapped up.

Shocked, Jenny spun around. "Oh, Spiros, no, I don't need—"

He cut her off and pulled out his wallet. "Anything for you, my Jenny." It was just as well he'd stopped at the bank and withdrawn spending money. "You know that. And we *can* afford it. You know *that*, too."

"Yes, I know we can afford nice things for Christmas and birthdays," she murmured close to his ear. "But this is neither." She accepted the parcel and thanked the clerk in Greek, surprising her.

They left the store and kept walking down the street where the boys took off ahead of them once more.

"What's going on?" She knew her husband, and knew after the reading of the will that something was brewing. Especially if he could spring a present like the jewellery set on her.

"Can I not buy my wife a nice piece of jewellery from my own country? My own island?" he asked. "We are here on holiday. I can afford to surprise my wife with something nice." He was still working up the courage to tell her, not sure how she would react, and he certainly didn't know if she'd want to go along with him and the plan. He'd been racking his brain for the last two days trying to come up with a way around it.

"We're technically not here on holiday, even though we've added that into the reason why, and yes, you are allowed to buy me something. But I just get the feeling there's a reason behind it." She glanced at her watch. "It's time for lunch. Anything in particular you want?" They kept walking.

"How about seafood? We eat so much lamb, chicken and beef, something else would be nice, and I happen to know of a nice seafood restaurant not far from here. It's on the waterfront, and we can watch the boats bob around in the current."

"Sounds lovely. Boys," Jenny called. "We're going to lunch. Come on." They hurried over to her and Pedro took her outstretched hand. Carlos took her other, and Tomas took his father's. Spiros led them down a couple of streets towards the water where they found the restaurant open for lunch.

"Here we go. I can't wait for some fresh fish." Spiros held out Jenny's chair and waited while she seated herself before taking his own chair.

They ordered and were served their drinks first, which the boys finished in seconds.

Jenny watched them and frowned. "You were supposed to keep that for the whole meal," she told them in an undertone, not sure what the price of anything was, and how it converted to Australian dollars. They looked guiltily at her.

"It's okay," Spiros told her, laying a gentle hand on her arm. "The boys have had an adventure. They're hot and thirsty, and we *can* afford food and drink." He waved the waiter back over and ordered another round for the boys.

Jenny's frown continued as she thought about what was happening, and why he suddenly had no problem handing out money left, right, and centre. While they were using this trip as a holiday, they couldn't exactly go wild with their spending.

They chatted about their adventures until their meals were served, and then ate in relative silence except for the odd murmured compliment about the food. Dessert and coffee came and went, and they were on their way along the waterfront, taking photos of the boys in front of boats, or on the rocks. They strolled along until they came to the beach and let the boys take their sandals off and run around barefoot. Spiros and Jenny sat in the shade to watch.

"Okay, it's time to spit it out." Jenny kept one eye on the boys and the other on Spiros.

Sighing, he knew it had to be told sometime. "The will was read yesterday."

"Yes, I know."

"Mama got it all, not that there was much to give her, just the house and the shop, and whatever was in their bank account…" He kept his gaze down, or on the boys, unable to look Jenny in the eye.

"And," she pushed. "Did it have to do with you being disinherited? Did your father do it after all? How did your siblings cope?"

"They were quite angry," Spiros told her. "Because Papa never legally disowned, or disinherited, me…" He left the sentence hanging, so she could take it in.

"Oh…" The shock slowly rained down. "Oh, that's wonderful. Isn't it? He didn't disown you because he still loved you, and knew that it was okay for you to spread your wings. That's wonderful." Jenny tugged on his arm. "Isn't it?"

"Yes, yes, I guess it is." Spiros nodded in agreement and finally looked at her. "It is, my Jenny. He didn't disown, or disinherit, me after all."

"I sense there's a but, though…" She gazed at his troubled expression and then heard Pedro scream, looking up to see Carlos holding some sort of crustacean over his brother's head. Pedro ran away and Carlos was nipped, so dropped the creature back into the water, but got a handful of water and threw it at Tomas, who started splashing back. "Don't get wet, boys. Leave it for another day when you can go swimming," she called and moved her focus back to Spiros when they waved at her. "What else?"

Another sigh. "That means, as the eldest, I inherit the meat shop, and upon Mama's death, the house." He couldn't look at her and stared forlornly at the sand instead.

"Okay…" she said slowly, trying to figure out what it meant. "Then sell the shop, or get someone to run it, so your mother will have an income. We have no idea when it will be her time. She could live another twenty, or thirty, years."

"But what if she doesn't, my love? What if Papa's death is the end of her? I know she doesn't go to see any doctors, and she's been ill off and on this last year, and was ill last year and the year before. I've missed out on my parents for seventeen years, Jenny. Now my father's gone and I'll never see him again. The boys will never meet him, and have only just met their grandmother. What if she died tomorrow?" He shook his head at the tragedy of life. "I've already lost Xenos and Nicodemus, and you've lost Effie, but you still have your parents and siblings. I only have my mother, and my siblings hate me for leaving. I just…" Breathing deeply, with tears in his eyes, he watched his sons frolic on the sands of his home island. Happy and healthy for the moment. They screamed and ran around in the water, splashed each other, built sandcastles and knocked them down. There were no beaches in Armidale, so the boys only got to see a beach once a year during school holidays when they holidayed on the Gold Coast, or in Sydney. Some of Jenny's eldest siblings had moved to the cities for work, and they would catch up. But what if the boys could be on a beach all year round?

"Please tell me you aren't thinking that," Jenny murmured, her eyes drifting shut. She'd been having her own thoughts about the family and what Spiros had said. She could see how happy the boys were on a beach in summer, and they could be there all summer long as she'd learned that Mykonos school holidays were in their summer, so the middle of the year, unlike Australia.

He turned his head to her. "Would it be so bad?"

"Yes!" Her eyes flew open and stared defiantly at him. "I wouldn't be near *any* of *my family*, or friends, and don't speak Greek fluently, or enough, to get by here. Plus, the boys would be taken away from their family and friends. They know no one here, just like I don't. You expect us to move here, and what, set up a house nearby? Live with your mother? What would we do with our house, our car, our belongings?" Jenny *did not* like where this was going, and expressed that in her body language by pulling her arm from Spiros's and sitting straighter.

"I know, my Jenny. I know it would be a big move. A move bigger than just me leaving for Australia seventeen years ago. I have all of you to think about. And that's what I've been doing since yesterday when I found out. *Thinking* about it. I just don't know what to do. I don't want the boys to miss out on their grandmother anymore. I don't want her to miss out on you *and* them. *I* don't want to miss out on her. I just…" A deep sigh came from his gut. "I don't know what to do."

"Would she move to Australia?" Jenny asked, already knowing what the answer would be.

"I doubt it." He grasped her hand and linked his fingers through hers. "I don't know whether to convince her to go, or to convince you to leave?"

"Oh, Spiros…" Jenny fretted. "Why did this have to come up? We came for a funeral and a holiday. Why did it turn into a conversation about moving? I didn't come here to move here. Regardless of how much I like it, or how much fun the boys are having here." She watched them fling sand at each other and laugh like maniacs.

"Yes, they're having fun; they don't get to spend enough time at a beach." Spiros watched his sons, noting how happy and carefree they were.

But that dull ache Jenny had inside made her know what the answer would be. Her brothers had moved interstate, or down to Sydney, and taken their families with them. That's what you did. When looking for a job to keep paying for your family, you moved, and the ever dutiful wife moved with you with no real say in the matter. But moving across the planet scared her. Her parents and sisters wouldn't be nearby in case something happened with the boys, or someone needed a babysitter in a hurry. Her sisters still lived down the road, or on the other side of town, and if anyone needed someone, or something, they were there for each other, but not if she was on Mykonos. And what would they do with the house and car? Rent them, sell them? What happened if they moved back in a couple of years? They would need to buy new ones if they sold up. But the boys would be older and possibly leaving home. Carlos was already fourteen; another four years and he'd be out of school and working, possibly living out of home. Tomas two years after that, and Pedro two years after that. What would happen once all of her boys turned eighteen and left home? Where would she be? What would she do? "I think we need to ask the boys if they'd like to live here. And I need to talk to my family, especially my parents. But tell me, why can't your siblings look after your mother?" Squeezing his hand, she looked him straight in the eye.

"I don't know," he replied. "My brothers all up and moved to Athens. I doubt they would want to move back."

"But *we're* expected to? Your mother could move to live with one of them."

"She was born and raised on Mykonos. Got married here, had all of us here. I don't even think my sisters come near her that often. So, if they don't come near her, why would they look after her?"

Sighing in frustration, Jenny mumbled, "Oh, Spiros. I just don't know. It's a big decision and affects *all* of us. Three of us can't speak Greek, and I've noticed not many speak English. How would we be received here? Did you *not* notice the looks we received at the funeral service and reception? *I* certainly did. And the gossipmongers were already talking about the boys, particularly Carlos because he looks like me. I just don't know if being here would be a mentally healthy environment for them."

"I know, my love. And I don't mean to make you upset." He kissed her hand and held it to his lips for a moment. "Can we just think about it, please?"

"I have to do a lot of conferring with my family and the boys first. You won't get an answer straight away. And what about the boys' schooling?"

"We would work it all out, my love," Spiros encouraged her. "Would it be so bad, us living here for a few years? At least until the boys are old enough to have their own lives. Another eight years and Pedro will be eighteen and the last to leave home."

"You don't know that. *I* don't know that. We have no idea how long our boys will stay with us, and I have no problem with them doing so until they get married and leave. Just like the Marshes did." Jenny sat a little higher, her back a little straighter. "While I understand you wanting to look after your mother and be the man of the family, and encourage that, I don't want it to come at the expense of your own. *Especially* the boys and what taking them away from their cousins and friends will do. They know no one here, only Tomas speaks Greek, and Carlos has already been singled out. That's not fair to him."

"I know, my love. I know. How about we enjoy the next few days, see Mykonos, sightsee, talk about it again in a few days, and I will try and figure out what to do?" He reached up and brushed her hair from her face. "We can talk to Uncle Nikos and Aunt Melina, maybe talk to the boys about whether they like it here, and gauge their reactions. Maybe?"

"Maybe…" Jenny knew, her gut knew, her brain knew, her heart knew. There were no maybes about it. They would be moving to Mykonos.

*****

After chatting with Nikos and Melina, taking the boys around the island and asking if they liked it and would want to live there, which Tomas seemed enthusiastic about, Pedro less so, and Carlos not at all, Jenny made a long-distance collect call to her parents to ask their advice, and at the end of all of it the answer came back to what her gut, heart and brain had already told her. They would be moving to Mykonos.

It was just a matter of how and when.

*****

Once Katyana learned of Spiros's idea, she begged him to move home and worked herself into a frenzy doing so. It took Spiros, Nikos, and Melina to calm her down, so they could all rationally talk about how it would work and how long they would stay for. She demanded they live with her and revealed to Spiros that, with having been ill, she wasn't sure how much longer she would be around for, so wanted to get to know her grandsons before she died. She'd missed fourteen years with them, her son's wedding, and missed Spiros for seventeen years of *his* life. She didn't want to miss any more.

When Spiros told her there would be no room for them and their belongings, she insisted on extending the house so the boys had rooms, and since it was summer, insisted on starting that as soon as possible.

"Mama, you can't afford to extend the house. I know how much money you have in the bank, and you can't afford extensions," Spiros told her. "Even if we pitched in, it wouldn't be enough."

"I can help out," Nikos said. "We could go thirds, or I could round up the family and help build it. You could save on labour. Who runs the construction companies around here?"

"Giorgio," Katyana mumbled, fiddling with her handkerchief. "I could ask him."

"No, Mama. He went along with Papa. I won't accept that." Spiros placed his hands on his hips and became defiant.

"Spiros, you are not accepting anything. This is still my house, in my name, until it goes to you upon my death, but in the meantime, if I want my son and his family to stay, they will need room." Katyana could be just as defiant as her son.

"Why did you not think of that when we had to sleep in the basement?" Spiros raised a brow. "My sons can too. There's enough room."

"No, no." Katyana shook her head. "We've had water issues in the basement, it needs to be cleaned out, but until it is, it's sealed off."

Spiros sighed his frustration. "Okay, the boys can't live in the basement. Then they can all sleep in with Jenny and me in the spare room."

"No, Spiros, let me do this, please," Katyana begged of her son. "Giorgio told me that if I ever needed anything to call and it would be provided for. Giorgio was his only son, his only child left after his sister, so I am now his only daughter-in-law, and our children his only grandchildren. He will take care of it, let me do this." She only came up to his shoulder, and her girth made her wider than him, but she was just as feisty.

With furrowed brows, Spiros knew he had no real need to hate his grandfather, but after receiving the cold reply of no when he'd written to invite him to Australia for their wedding, Spiros knew that his father had made things pretty clear where everyone stood. Have no contact with Spiros. The sigh left him on the exhale. "Okay, Mama. It's your house, and you can do what you want with it. But please make sure that the work is properly done and that I help with the layout. The boys will need a room each and can use the bathroom at the end of the hall. If it's possible, Jenny and I would like our own ensuite as you and Papa had."

Katyana nodded in excitement. "You help with the design; Giorgio will get everything done." Beaming with happiness, she called Giorgio and told him what she needed because her son was coming home.

Glad that he could make things better, he had a contractor and architect there the next day, and by the time Jenny and the boys were ready to go home, the plans had been approved by everyone, and the large area to the side of the house was ripped up.

Melina went home with Jenny and the boys while Nikos stayed behind with Spiros.

*****

Once home and in the arms of her family, Jenny burst into tears.

"I just don't know if I can do it. I feel so guilty taking them away from everything, especially all of you and their cousins."

The boys were playing with their cousins in the backyard as Jenny's sisters were all there with their children.

"There, there." Sarah held her and patted her back. "It's a choice we all have to make at some point. Do we stay where we are, or move for work, or so we're better off, and our children are better off? What would be so wrong with it?"

"I'd be there and all of you wouldn't. What happens if I need you and you can't come around to help out? Like all the times Tomas has been sick." Jenny sobbed on her mother's shoulder. "What do I do?"

"You grow up, Jennifer," Sarah stated so matter-of-factly that all of her daughters stopped what they were doing to stare at her.

"What?" Jenny wiped her face and stared into her mother's eyes; unsure she had heard correctly.

"Jenny," Sarah went on, holding her daughter by the arms. "You are a grown adult woman with three children. You're thirty-nine years old and have been married for fifteen years. You *will* cope, just as you have through all three children, just as you did through the death of your daughter and the inability to ever have children again. You will do there what you do here. Be the adult, the mother, the wife. You will take care of your husband and children, and make sure they don't go without."

"But his mother will be there. I probably won't even get a look in." Jenny blew her nose in the tissue her sister handed her.

"And that's okay," Sarah said. "It's her home until it's yours. But stand firm and don't back down. You're a Marsh!"

"And a Stephanopoulos," Jenny murmured, and gazed out the window to see her sons having fun with their cousins. "They won't have that anymore. The camaraderie of family. They'll only have each other. No one else."

"And you and Spiros," Matthew said, coming to stand by his daughter's side and looking out at his grandchildren. "Tell them it's an adventure."

"And how long do we go on this adventure for?" Jenny's miserable face turned to her father. "A year, two, ten? Twenty? The rest of our lives?"

"As long as you need to, love," he replied. "It's time for the boys to discover their Greek heritage, which isn't a bad thing. You have eight years until Pedro is eighteen, ten years until he's twenty, it's as long as he's been here in Armidale with us. And don't worry, we'll come and visit. Maybe have an excuse to get away from this cold winter air. It's summer over there, isn't it?"

"Yes, and lovely and warm." Jenny gazed out the window. She'd already made the decision, but was miserable about it, and felt so guilty taking the boys from their family. Even though she was right behind Spiros taking care of his mother, she just didn't know why Katyana wouldn't want to come to Australia and was instead making Jenny and the boys go there. Or was that *Spiros* making them go there?

Either way, it was just the beginning of what Jenny had to sacrifice.

August 1967

The boys went back to school for the month of August, so they had time to say goodbye to their friends and family, and Jenny had time to collect the reports for their new school. Being married to a Greek, she and the boys had no trouble with moving to the island, and they packed up their belongings ready for shipping. Not that they had much beyond their clothes and accessories, toys and books. Their favourite linen sets were packed, along with certain crockery and personal items, and the rest was given to family members. The furniture, prints, curtains, and other household items didn't worry Jenny as they would be staying with the house because they'd decided to rent it out for income. Joanna's husband was a real estate agent and helped get it ready and on the market. The house had a freshen up and was let out quickly. When moving day finally arrived, the small truck was loaded up with what was to be shipped over, and they took two cases each with their most valuable belongings.

Her parents and Melina travelled to Sydney with them, and they took taxies to the airport and stood chatting until it was time to board.

"Oh…I don't know if I can do this…" Jenny muttered to her family, fretting about her decision. "I just feel…sick to my stomach that we're leaving all of you."

"You can't see it that way, Jenny," Sarah consoled her. "You have every right to travel and live where you want, and if that's Greece for a few years, then it's not so bad. As your father said ages ago, see it as an adventure with the boys. They don't seem to be taking this as badly as you." She nodded at them standing by the window excitedly staring at the planes coming and going.

Jenny watched her boys. "Carlos isn't happy that we're going. He's fourteen, going through puberty, giving up the only house and bedroom he's known, his friends, his school, his family. He's worried he won't pick up Greek, and they won't speak English."

"Has he told you that?" Matthew asked, starting to understand why his daughter was so worried.

"Yes." Jenny turned back to them. "I found him crying a few times over different things. Taking his posters down, packing his toys and books. We've had quite a few conversations now. His cousins are like brothers, they're the same age in the same school. He won't have them to rely on, or play with, or hang around with. He's scared he's going to miss out on all of that, while Tomas wants to go. He's so excited he's like a puppy, running around and getting into everything. He was packed long before the rest of us, and told everyone at school we were leaving, whereas Pedro's both. He's excited and scared, but then, he's only ten. They're all so different and still only children."

"That's right; they're still children and will get to spend some time in their father's homeland with their grandmother. She deserves that time too, even if her husband didn't," Sarah said. "Everything will be okay, Jenny. We can holiday there once a year to see you and the boys. We can't be selfish. We've had you all these years, now it's Katyana's turn to know her daughter-in-law and grandsons."

Knowing, deep in her gut, that her mother was right, Jenny breathed in slowly and deeply to quell the nerves. It would only be for a few years until Pedro was out of school at least, and then they would start the process again of where to live. Stay in Mykonos, or come back home to Armidale. But really, it would all come down to what the boys wanted to do, and where they wanted to live as adults that would ultimately make the next choice of where they would live.

They heard the boarding announcement for their plane and bade her family a long and teary goodbye, with Jenny holding on tight and not wanting to let go until Tomas physically dragged her onto the plane. After putting their bags away, they buckled in for the long flight.

*****

At Athens airport, they were met by Spiros. "Oh, my Jenny, my boys." He hugged them fiercely, smothering them in kisses. "You're finally back. Finally here." He grasped Jenny by her face and kissed it all over. "I've missed you, my Jenny. So much."

"And I've missed you," she murmured against the onslaught of his lips.

"Ew, not in public, you two," Carlos grumbled unhappily and crossed his arms. He'd been listening to his small transistor radio and reading during the flight to keep his mind off the fact he was leaving his family and friends.

"Yes, stop this now." Jenny laughed and pulled herself away from Spiros. "How are we going to deal with *that* in your mother's house?" She watched him gather her two cases and lead the way to the taxi stand outside.

"We'll have to discuss that, but since we are at the opposite end of the house to Mama, she shouldn't hear." He loaded their cases into the car with help from the driver.

"And how is the building going? Is it done, yet?" Jenny asked before getting into the backseat, squashed in beside the boys.

"Yes, it is." Spiros shut the door and got into the front passenger side. "But we'll talk more on the ferry."

Driving through the city of Athens, they all oohed and aahed over the architecture and landscape in the late summer sun.

"We definitely need to spend time here, so the boys can see their heritage," Jenny told Spiros. "I'd like to look around at a more leisurely pace, too."

"Of course, my love. Maybe during the school holidays when they come up." Spiros glanced out the window and saw the ferry come into view. "But we need to get ready for the journey home."

That word stuck in her craw and she blanched. *Not really my home,* she thought. *Not sure if it ever will be. My home is in Armidale.*

Spiros paid the driver and they walked onto the ferry and settled into the lounge area with their luggage. Once underway, Spiros caught Jenny up on all that had happened, even Giorgio paying for the extension, which was fully finished, and telling him the history of the meat shop. Since he was taking over, Giorgio had thought it only fair to inform Spiros of how his father had received it in the first place, and as eldest heir next in line, what the family business actually was. Besides Giorgio, Spiros was the only one in the family to know, since his father was dead. "And now I'm telling you, so please keep it a secret."

Jenny's brows had risen at the start of the story and stayed that way throughout, and only now were slowly making their decent. "Wow! I…wow…" She glanced through the window at the boys out on the deck to make sure they hadn't overheard anything.

"I know. He felt I had to know. I told him I was disgusted and wanted nothing to do with the family business, and didn't want my children to ever know. At least while they're young. And regardless of the fact I'm next heir in line, I don't want it if that's what it's about. He could keep it."

"Will he be coming around to see Katyana? The boys?" Jenny inquired, worried of the impression he may have on her sons.

"I doubt it. He got the very distinct impression that if that's what the family business was, and Papa knew all about it, then I didn't want to know."

Sighing in dismay and shock, Jenny withdrew her hand from Spiros's and tried to clear her head. After breathing for a few moments to calm herself, she pulled the movie camera out of her bag. "It has a new film. I thought we could film the boys as we come into Mykonos. We need to lighten the mood after that story."

"Yes, very good idea, my love. Let's go outside and get the boys." They walked outside and waited until the island came into view and started filming. Tomas was so excited he was jumping up and down and pointing to his new home. Pedro just gripped the railing and stared, whereas Carlos was reserved, a half frown, half sneer, on his face, until Jenny kissed his cheek, slid an arm around his shoulders and pulled him in for a hug. He wrapped his arms around her and stayed there until they had to disembark.

Within the hour they arrived on the island and at Katyana's house where Spiros showed them around.

"Wow. What a change. And it was all done so quickly." Jenny deposited her cases in her new bedroom which had been painted a pale shade of blue, and had a new bed with pretty blue and pink linen. New blue curtains hung at the window, and the carpet had been replaced.

"We have a small ensuite and walk-in robe like the boys." Spiros led her to the small hallway where the boys' rooms were located and saw they had already picked which room they wanted. "Welcome home, boys. The bathroom is updated and refreshed, just for you." Each room had a double bed, colourful linen and curtains, a bookcase and desk, and a chest of drawers each, along with a narrow walk-in closet. "I hope you'll be happy here."

"From the look of it, they will be," Jenny murmured, watching Pedro jump up and down on his bed in his very own room. "Pedro, stop that."

He fell down and giggled. "My own room, Mama, with a big bed like you and Papa."

"I know." She smiled at his bright blue eyes and a happy grin. "Just don't jump on the bed; you'll break it," she chastised gently. They walked into the room facing the ocean and found Carlos standing at the window looking out at the view.

He turned his head to very seriously ask them, "Is it safe?"

"Is what safe?" Spiros asked.

"This room?" His frown was just as serious as his tone of voice. "Is the land under it steady and strong? Can it carry the weight of a new build?"

Spiros grinned at his son. "Planning on being an architect, or builder, are you? Yes, Carlos, it's fine. It was checked out and strengthened by professionals. The builders were professional, too."

Carlos nodded tersely. "Good, good. I don't want to fall through and die."

Jenny's brows rose in amusement. "I don't think your father would let that happen."

"Of course not," Spiros agreed. "Why don't you get unpacked and come out for a drink. It's almost teatime." He led Jenny out to the lounge room to find his mother home. "Mama, they've arrived."

Katyana exploded into happiness and rapid-fire Greek.

"Mama, Jenny doesn't understand," Spiros stopped her. "Show her what you've learned." Nodding encouragement, he waited.

"Jen-nee," Katyana said in stilted English and nodded her head while glancing from her son to her daughter-in-law. "It is so good to have you here. Welcome to your new home." She had been studying hard with the local English teachers, so she would have some idea of how to converse with her daughter-in-law and two of her grandsons.

Jenny was surprised and glanced at a smiling Spiros who told her his mother had been having lessons with the local teachers. "Oh, how wonderful," Jenny told her. "Thank you for inviting us to stay. Your English is very good after a month."

Katyana didn't quite catch all of what Jenny had said, and looked in bewilderment at her son to translate, which he did. She nodded happily and broke out in Greek.

Spiros waited a moment and then began translating as his mother grabbed Jenny in a big hug and kissed both cheeks. "She's happy that you'll join her women's clubs where she's been learning English, and you'll help teach her and the other women who want to learn." Spiros laid a hand on Jenny's shoulder. "I told her you taught me and I was a quick learner. She also wants to show you off to the whole town."

"You mean the town that treated you like a leper, and me and Carlos as outcasts?" Jenny muttered to him under her breath.

Spiros didn't know whether to grimace, or chuckle, so it came out half and half. Sliding an arm around his wife, he watched his mother hug and kiss the boys, who had come out of their rooms, and heard Tomas translate for them. He heard her say the same thing to them as she had said to Jenny, and watched her hustle them into the kitchen for Greek sweets.

Sighing, Jenny turned away from them and to her husband, an

unhappy expression on her face. "How long will we be here? Until Pedro is ready to leave home? And is my family going to be welcome? Where will they stay?"

Spiros gazed into his wife's sad eyes and saw fear and worry. "I don't know, my Jenny. But I'll make this as smooth and happy as possible. I promise."

"When will we go home?" she whispered, depression setting in.

Spiros's smile blazed across his lips. "We *are home*, my Jenny. We are home."

*****

As days turned into weeks, and weeks turned into months, months turned into years. And for Jenny, they weren't as horrible as she expected, but they weren't the best, either. Tomas and Pedro took to school and the beaches with gusto. Carlos was seen as an outcast, except by the girls at school who thought he was a golden-haired god. He decided to do things his way and make the most of it, just like his mother whom he watched closely and learned from.

Jenny taught Katyana and her friends English when the teachers couldn't, had joined the women's groups, been seen as an outcast and interloper, got to know her way around the streets of Chora and Mykonos, and knew which shops would serve her and which wouldn't. She did the accounts for the shop and home as she always did, and was the best wife and mother she could be in such trying circumstances. She learned recipes from her mother-in-law, had daily chats with afternoon tea and coffee, and taught Katyana some traditional Australian ways. Jenny also made sure she found a good female doctor to visit for whatever she needed, and had her parents, and a couple of sisters and their families, visit for her fortieth birthday and sixteenth wedding anniversary one year in. And while she still wasn't happy about living away from her family, she didn't *hate* Mykonos anymore, as Mykonos was never the issue.

Two years into her stay, everything changed.

June 1969

"What are you saying, doctor?" Jenny asked her physician to clarify.

"I'm saying, that Katyana has stage four cancer from years of ignoring doctor's visits, and she's quite ill from the flu that's been covering up the symptoms that have been left undiagnosed," Doctor Zenobios spoke to Jenny in English, and repeated in Greek for Katyana so she thoroughly understood.

"No, no, no," Katyana wailed, grasping Jenny's hand with one hand and waving the other around in hysterics. "No, no, no. I do not believe it." After two years of English lessons, her English wasn't fluent, but spoke it well enough to understand, although most times she burst back into Greek as it was simpler.

Jenny's heart was grasped by a very cold fist that squeezed. "Stage four?"

"Yes." The doctor looked from a shocked Jenny to a wailing Katyana. "It's quite advanced."

Jenny had spent six months convincing her mother-in-law to see a doctor after her flu-like symptoms had become worse over that time, and now, after tests and examinations, they'd been told this. "How…?" Jenny gulped in air and looked at the ceiling, trying to control her emotions. "How long?"

"Months, if that," Zenobios replied. "I'm sorry. I understand that older Greek women refuse to come to the doctor out of fear and embarrassment." She gazed sympathetically at them both. "So, I thank you for getting her here. But it's that fear and embarrassment that means they end up dying young, or when they don't need to, as is the case now. Katyana's only in her mid-sixties, she's had eight children, next to no health care, and next to no doctor visits."

"Do we know how long, exactly?" Jenny breathed and tried to pry her hand away from her mother-in-law's. But Katyana was hanging on for grim death.

"It's very advanced from what we can tell. You said she's lost weight, her appetite?"

"Yes, it's definitely been noticeable in the last six months. The weight loss, she was plump before, now…" Jenny's head turned to her left to see Katyana weeping. "She's lost a lot of weight. Has dark circles, coughs up blood, and coughs a lot."

"One of the symptoms," Zenobios murmured. "I can prescribe painkillers, maybe morphine in her last days, but I have no idea when they'll be."

Jenny's head nodded mechanically. "In the meantime, we have to keep it together and make preparations. Thank you, doctor." She rose, dragging Katyana to her feet, and having had enough of her wailing and histrionics, said firmly, "Katyana, stop it. Enough."

Katyana came to a shuddering halt and stared at Jenny, the only woman who'd been her rock for two years. "Yes, Jenny."

"Here's what we're going to do. This is our plan." Jenny held on to her tightly. "We will not tell the boys, only Spiros. We will not let them know anything is wrong until we have to. We will continue on with our lives, and make things as easy as we can for them until we can't anymore. Do you understand?" She gazed into her mother-in-law's eyes. "Do you understand?"

Katyana nodded. "Yes, Jenny. We will not tell the boys I am sick, just Spiros."

"Okay." Taking a deep breath, Jenny collected her bag, thanked the doctor, and took Katyana home where they called in the family lawyer to make plans, write a will, and get the preparations done.

When the boys came home they acted normally. And when Spiros came home they acted normally. But once the boys had gone to bed, they told Spiros who went white with shock and collapsed into a chair. After talking all night, the plan was set in motion. Unfortunately for all of them, there were only a few months left.

335

August 1969

In her final days, Katyana spent her time in bed telling the boys stories, chatting with her children and other grandchildren, who'd been called in, and making plans for Spiros and Jenny. "You are to have the house. Do whatever you want with it. Fix it up, make it bigger, repaint it, and keep the shop, it is yours, your legacy," she weakly told Spiros. "Your father's and now yours."

"Yes, Mama, we will." He watched her dazed expression and patted her hand.

She was worse, wasting away, weak, and they knew it wouldn't be long. She was so ill that she often mistook Tomas for her husband.

"Oh, Giorgio, you have come back," she cried when Tomas walked into the room. "You have come back to me."

Tomas, knowing his grandmother only had days, didn't mind if it made her happy. "Yes, Katyana, it is I, Giorgio." He went on to talk to her in Greek until she fell asleep, and then left with his father to let her rest.

"How is she?" Jenny asked when they walked into the kitchen. Carlos and Pedro were helping her with lunch, not wanting to be far from their mama.

"Asleep. Nearly gone." Spiros let out a deep sigh and leaned against the bench, feeling absolutely deflated. He took time off during the day to come home and help with his mother, spending only an hour in the morning and late afternoon working there. Although, most of the time, he just sat and thought about death, and what he was going to do without his mother.

"Why don't you take a break," Jenny suggested, pulling a sizzling lamb dish from the oven. "I'll keep yours warm until you get back."

"No, no, I'll stay here. But I'm not really hungry." He watched Tomas hug his mother and not let go.

At fourteen, Tomas was more mature than any of them, taking this all extremely well, and in stride. He also cried at night in bed when he thought no one heard. But they had, on many a night. Spiros glanced at his other sons.

Carlos was quiet and stoic, taking his cues from his mother, and Pedro's eyes darted around, taking it all in. He tried to be grown up and mature, like his brothers, but at twelve, he was still the youngest of the family and loved cuddling up under Jenny's arm when they sat on the couch and watched TV.

"You and the boys eat; I'm going outside for some air." He walked past them and onto the balcony attached to the back of the house, as the only door to it was in the kitchen. Breathing deeply, he knew the time would be soon. Two years ago he'd lost his father and come home. Now, he was losing his mother. At least he'd had the extra two years, and so had Jenny and the boys. They got to know her and spent two years with her, learning things, and being shown around Mykonos.

Mykonos.

He gazed across the sea and down to the town. The windmills, the ferry dock, the people bustling below. His island home. And now he had to prepare for another death. As though there hadn't been enough, already.

"Tomas, you ate in a hurry." Jenny was only halfway through her meal when he'd pushed his chair back.

"I want to go back to Grandma," he said and walked into the kitchen to put his plate in the sink, then headed into the bedroom and sensed it. "Grandma?" Climbing onto the bed beside her, he held her hand and pressed it to his cheek. "Grandma?"

"Giorgio," she murmured, her eyes opening a slit. "My Giorgio."

"I am here, Katyana," Tomas replied. "I am here. You rest now." He watched her eyes close and gently laid her hand on her chest, then rushed out to the others. "Mama, Papa, I think she's dying."

Jenny rushed in from the dining room, Spiros from outside.

"Stay with your bothers," Spiros ordered and rushed into his mother's room. "Mama." He sat beside her and studied her features.

Jenny closed the door and stood behind him. "Is she…?"

"Mama?" He felt for a pulse. "Weak, very weak. Mama?" Watching her chest barely rise, it took only a few minutes. "Oh…Mama…"

Jenny clutched her husband's shoulders, willing both of them to be strong.

Spiros leaned over and checked his mother's neck for a pulse. Not finding one, he shook his head and said, "She's gone."

"Oh…Spiros…I'm so sorry."

"So am I, my love. So am I." They stayed that way for a while until there was a knock at the door.

"Mama, I rang the doctor," Tomas softly called. "She's here."

Opening the door, Jenny swept Tomas into the lounge while the doctor did the exam.

"Is she gone?" Tomas asked from his mother's arms. He was as tall as her and almost as tall as Carlos.

"Yes, my baby, she's gone." Jenny held all three of her sons close and waited while Spiros and the doctor did what was needed. "Thank you for calling the doctor, Tomas. That was very smart and quick thinking of you."

"I knew I should when you closed the door," he mumbled against her shoulder. "I knew it was time."

"Yes, my baby, it was." Jenny watched the doctor come out and make a call for the ambulance, and Spiros come out and close the door behind him. She watched as the ambulance came and carried Katyana away to be checked into the morgue. And watched as the doctor left and Spiros closed the door on the world. Taking a deep breath, Jenny let it out slowly. "What's the next step?"

"Calling everyone, the lawyer, my siblings, Uncle Nikos, and all of her family." He wearily sat down on the couch, looking as if he'd aged fifty years in an hour.

"And, so, that's what we do," Jenny said. "I'll get to work."

Within a week, all of Katyana's family, and Jenny's parents had flown into Mykonos for her funeral. As with Giorgio's, she was buried in the family crypt with her husband, sister-in-law, and mother-in-law. After the reception when everyone left, life went on. As per her will, Spiros and Jenny received everything. Jenny aired out Katyana's room, removed the bed, and freshened up everything as per Katyana's instructions. She called in the priest to spiritually cleanse the room and house so that her and Giorgio's spirits were free to fly. The boys went back to school, Spiros went back to work, and Jenny's parents went back home. And now, Jenny finally had the freedom to do what she wanted, again, and that was raise her boys and look after her husband as *she* wanted, without the confines and constraints of the life she'd lived for two years. And once Pedro left school and turned eighteen, they could finally go home.

November 2018

"Didn't quite turn out that way, though…" Jenny came back to 2018. "And we all know what happened after that, so no point retelling *your* story. We've heard it a thousand times and lived it just as long." She watched the faces of her children, grandchildren and great-grandchildren, her siblings, their children, and their children and grandchildren. Everyone was quiet and watching her and Spiros.

At some point, Cabot had taken Jennifer from her arms and put her to bed, as Tony had with Antonio. Angie had Hunter asleep on her lap, and Viv had Valentina asleep on hers. Ava and Jaqueline had crawled onto their daddy's laps and fallen asleep. Izabella was being cuddled by her mama, and Christopher and Marais were asleep in their prams. Harper and Carys were the only ones still in front of Jenny, and they were falling asleep on each other.

"Naw, how cute, he called you Miss Jenny, and my Jenny," Angie murmured, smiling softly at her parents.

"Oh…" Cabot slowly rubbed his shocked face with both hands, trying to take it all in. "I have so many questions…like why didn't you call the great Carlos, Spiros junior…*that* would have been *hilarious.*" He scored a filthy look from his father.

"I have her full name," Alena muttered to no one in particular. "You never told me that."

"Mama, Alena died in November, and we got married in November, and you never said anything," Tomas said, tears in his eyes. "And why have we never seen those other photos? The ones of her christening and burial?"

"I hid them all away. Didn't want to see them, be reminded of what she looked like. Never looked at them again until Angie had Alena, and you all got to see the photo your father carried around. Had she lived she would have been sixty next week," Jenny told him, a small pang still pinching her heart. "Had she stayed in my tummy, she would have more than likely shared her birthday with you boys and been sixty in February. But she didn't." She stared at her sons, a grim smile on her lips.

"At least we know how come you managed to have us two years apart to the day," Pedro muttered, shaking his head at all he'd heard and the memories it dredged up. "I always wondered how you managed that without protection in the '50s."

"And we know why you never had any more children," Angie added. "You always said you couldn't have any more, but we never knew why."

"There was no need to tell you. It was my private business, and better left unspoken." She looked at Rebecca who'd been there the day of the birth. "Thank you for being there. Thank you for helping."

Rebecca nodded and wiped her tears away. "It was awful, and you're the only one in the Marsh family that went through it."

"Lucky me," Jenny said without a trace of sarcasm. "We've gone through a lot of things over the years."

"And we found out from my mother that my father probably didn't disown me because he always hoped I'd come back and take over. He was actually kind of envious that he hadn't had the same willpower to stand up to his own father, so he could see the world. But by taking the shop, he thought he had in his own way. I'm not sure if he was wrong," Spiros told them.

"And I still have all of the jewellery you've bought me over the years." Jenny reached out and took Spiros's hand in hers. "They were simple pieces then, not like the big clunky pieces my granddaughters have worn these last decades." She cast a glance at Alena who had a huge thick gold triangle in one ear, and a square in the other. The earrings reached her shoulders and constantly tangled in her hair.

Alena blushed and shrugged a shoulder, knocking the earring which she had to adjust. "They're not *that* bad, Grandma."

Jenny's brow rose. "Are you sure about that?" Studying her two eldest granddaughters, she added, "And I kept all of my dresses for my daughter, if I had one, but I didn't, so I kept them for future grandkids, and you've used them for *Haus of Stefan* inspiration. Old school, isn't that what you kids call that style?"

Diana and Alena chuckled. "Try *vintage*, Grandma," Diana said. "And I love every single one of them. So do our customers."

Danté had been thinking the story through and picked up on the small details. "Is that why there are all those photos of our fathers and uncles outside the windmill year after year, Grandma? You took the original in 1967 and then make them recreate it year after year. How many are there now, fifty, or something? With all three of them standing outside the windmill pulling stupid faces."

Jenny chuckled along with the family. The pictures had all been put into one album and chronicled for fifty-two years. "Over one hundred as I take two every year, as I do with you kids, for the fun of it. One of them smiling and one of them being silly. Memories for when we're gone." Her gaze moved among the faces in the crowd and landed on Carlos who sat with his arms on his legs, hands clenched, as he looked at the floor. "Carlos? Say what you need to."

"I have a question." He lifted his head and looked at her. "Why the hell did we never come back to Armidale after Grandma died? We were only there for two years; we could have come back to our home, our life, *our grandparents* who were still alive. Our aunts and uncles, friends and school, *our cousins.*" He shot to his feet and waved an irritated hand at all of the cousins sitting behind him. "We could have come back to *our family, our life.* Why did we never come back? Why did *you* never bring us back?" His finger pointed accusingly at his mother.

"Carlos," Tomas muttered, his heart torn after hearing the whole story and reliving his grandmother's death.

"No, Tomas." Carlos spun around to face him. "Did *you* ever ask?

Did y*ou* ever know? What about you, Pedro?" he said to his younger brother. "Did either of you ever ask why we never came back?" He turned back to his mother and father. "Why? After those two years… why didn't we?"

Jenny softened. "Because everybody made choices, Carlos. Your grandparents chose to disown your father. *He* chose to sail to Australia. *I* chose to marry him. And *we* chose to move to Mykonos. No, I didn't like it; I *hated* it, leaving my family behind, and taking you three away from that. But once I moved you boys across the world, I didn't want to do it again until you'd finished your schooling and were adults. By then, you loved the place and had jobs you loved, so we stayed. We stayed until we didn't and went to live in New York for nearly four years, and then when Tomas…" She gazed lovingly at her son. "*He* chose to go home to Mykonos and not here, and *we* made that choice *for him*. And then you and Pedro made the choice to move back there as well. And *we, all of us adults,* made the choice to make what we could out of it. Every person made a choice based on someone else's choice all the way down the line, Carlos. You would not have the life you've lived if we hadn't made *that* choice. If I'd brought you back you wouldn't be with Viv, Pedro with Angie, Tomas with Roger, you'd have married nice Australian girls, and not have the kids you have, you wouldn't be living where you do, flying around the world when you want, having the careers you have. Your life would be *so* different if I'd brought you back to Armidale. *We* wouldn't have all of this." She waved a hand at all of her family. "*This* wouldn't exist. *I* made the choice to stay until you were adults and had spent time getting to know the other half of your heritage and finishing your education. The choices that came next were on the three of *you*."

Carlos sighed and roughly ran his hands through his hair, ruffling it about in frustration. A guttural growl left his throat. "Doesn't mean I like it, *or* agree with it." He barged through the crowd of stunned onlookers and out the door.

Viv, Pedro and Tomas rose to follow.

"No!" Jenny told them sharply, surprising them. "Leave him for a few minutes and then I'll go." She watched them sit back down and noticed Carys and Harper. "Someone had better come and get the girls before they fall over."

Diana and Alena rushed over and picked up their daughters, but Alena kneeled by her grandmother's knees. "Why didn't you tell me?"

"I never told anyone, except that her name was Alena." Jenny watched tears fall down her cheeks and Harper cling to her mother in a drowsy state. "Your parents came up with the idea of giving you my name as your middle name. And because, at the time, I thought her first name would be burden enough. I didn't want to make it worse. But now that you're an adult, I think it's a great honour being named for your aunt. Just as Jennifer's named in honour of me. It's not a burden anymore, Alena. It's an honour. Especially since I've always believed you were her." She wiped her granddaughter's cheeks. "No crying now, Harper's asleep, so let's not wake her."

"Okay," Alena whispered and got to her feet, then leaned down and kissed Jenny's cheek. "I love you, Grandma."

"I love you too, my baby."

"Whatever happened to your friends?" Angie asked, rocking back and forth to keep Hunter asleep. "Effie, Nicodemus and Xenos. And Nikos and Melina?"

"Uncle Nikos died in the early '80s," Spiros told her. "Aunt Melina in the late '80s. All of my cousins moved away and moved on, and most have now passed."

"And Effie and Nicodemus passed away in the late '60s. She ended up having another child and leaving with Nicodemus when he got a job on a cattle station up in north Queensland," Jenny informed them. "They were living in a caravan, when one day, it blew up and killed all six of them. It was found out later that a gas leak had been set off, specifically, the hosing had been cut, and it looked as if she was about to start cooking."

Jenny glanced at Spiros. "Personally, I think Effie cut the hose and lit the match. She never got used to her life as a wife and mother, and Nicodemus never treated her well. Now we call it post-partum, or straight up depression. I think she had it the whole time and chose to commit suicide and homicide instead. That was her way out, and she took him with her for all he'd done to her. Sometimes…" Her voice broke. "Sometimes, I've wondered…if she'd had the abortion, or given the child up for adoption, that she might still be alive today," Jenny muttered more to herself than everyone else. "I felt so guilty over her death for years. We all knew she was depressed, but no matter how much we tried, we just couldn't help her."

"Oh, Jenny, please don't beat yourself up over it," Rebecca told her softly. "Just as you made yours, Effie made her own choices."

"Doesn't make me feel any better when I could have helped her," Jenny said morosely.

"Oh…how sad," Diana murmured, the pain of death a burden too heavy to bear, and not one she wanted to think about in her family. "And Xenos?"

"He found himself a wife in 1960 after moving to Sydney to work in construction," Spiros said. A soft smile lit up his lips, and then faltered. "He died in an accident on the site, leaving his pregnant wife so heartbroken that she went into early labour, and not only lost the baby, but her own life." A tear trickled down his cheek. "Even Christos and Yannis died in the '70s in accidents after moving to Athens."

"Jesus Christ," Antonio muttered and ran his hands over his face. "So much death."

"And all of my siblings, except for my youngest sister, are gone, along with their partners and some of their children," Spiros finished.

"And all of my older siblings are gone, along with their partners and some of their children," Jenny added, noting who was left. Philip, Rebecca, Faye and Barbara had all lost their partners, but still lived near each other in Armidale and saw each other every day.

"And all of our friends," Viv murmured, looking at Cabot and Antonio and being reminded of long lost friends Cabot Conroy and the DeLucas.

"And all of my family," Angie said. "Except for the odd sibling that kept popping up out of the bloody blue." All of the family grinned at that and remembered what it was like for Angie learning about her second brother whom Jenny considered an honorary member of their family.

"How *are* Alfonso and his family?" Jenny asked. "Didn't they just have another baby?"

"Yes. He's fine, so's his wife. Henry's five now, Bonnie's two and a half, and the baby's two months old," Angie replied half-heartedly. In all the years since finding out about Alfonso, she'd never really grown close to him, just conversed every now and then and on special occasions. And she'd refused to look for any other potential siblings, fearing lawsuits and a loss of money which she still felt she'd earned the right to keep, which Alfonso often jokingly threatened to do to stir his big sister up.

"And all of the in-laws." Tomas looked into Roger's face, knowing that his own parents had really been the only ones that Roger had ever had.

"So much loss, so much pain, so much to do…" Jenny muttered and managed to get to her feet. "I need to go and talk to Carlos. Boys, help your father. Everyone, take a break and freshen up. Cabot, come with me. We're going to see your father and sort this out."

She held out her hand to him and he took it, helping her out of the room and into the main entrance hall. "Mmm, so much smaller in my day." Looking around, she found her son outside on the front steps. "And don't make any jokes about that," she warned Cabot, who grinned in return. They walked out onto the steps. "I remember that day sixty-six years ago. Your father and I walked out those doors and stood here while Nikos presented us with our car." Breathing deeply, she remembered long-ago times as if they were yesterday, and waited for Carlos to wearily get to his feet and sullenly stand in front of her with his hands in his pockets just as he had as a teenager. "Now, what's this really about?"

Signing, Carlos slowly shook his head. "Everything."

"Then start at the beginning and don't leave anything out."

He recalled all of the planning they had done that year, getting ready for Jenny's death, and then their own when they eventuated. Death. Death destroys everything.

"Well, not quite." Jenny leaned on her cane. "I'm ninety, Carlos. Your father's ninety-three, in a wheelchair half the time and in need of help on a daily basis. *We're old,*" she stressed. "It was time to pass on the baton to you and your brothers, so you can take over the running of the business, and I can live the next however many years I have in relative peace."

"Ha!" Cabot exclaimed and cocked a brow in amusement. "In this family?"

Jenny laughed softly. "I know. There's not much of that. But this family wouldn't exist the way it does if it wasn't for the choice to stay after Katyana died. Your schooling was important and I wanted you to finish it in one place. By the time you had, you were working in the meat shop earning a wage, and at eighteen, well, we all know what *you* started doing," she told Carlos.

That got a grin out of Carlos. "Yeah, I know. And I did grow to love Mykonos after a while. I was just a typical resentful brat who got angry that his life had been disrupted by his parents' choice—"

"Sounds like someone else I know." Jenny glanced at Cabot who pretended not to have heard and was looking up at the sky and whistling softly.

Carlos's grin grew at the comment and then sobered. "I wanted to go home, but, as we have all learned from you, home isn't about a house, or a country, it's where the family is, and I've looked up to you my entire life, Mama." He sighed and swallowed hard. "I always took my lead from you. I learned how to do the eyebrow rise at fourteen. I followed your choices and decisions where family and business were concerned. And yes, when we went home for Tomas, I knew that's where we belonged."

"Not here in Armidale?" Jenny's curiosity was piqued.

He breathed deeply and shook his head. "No. Strangely. I've learned, since returning to Mykonos, that Armidale wasn't home by that point, and probably hadn't been since we left it in 1967."

"So…why the question? Why the anger?" she asked.

"As Tomas said earlier with Danté, death," he replied. "We've lost *so* many. You and Papa have lost *so* many. The three of us, and Roger, Viv, and Angie have lost *so* many. It's like everyone keeps dying on us, but we're still here. Why?" He shrugged and gazed up at the stars, hoping they'd give him the answer. "Why?"

"Because we were meant for something great," she said. "As simple as that. Our parents had us, and we came together and had the three of you, and you all got your partners and brought eight children into the world."

"Are we *really* still counting Simon as Tomas's son?" Carlos asked dubiously.

"Once Tomas legally adopts him, most definitely. But we already have these last eleven years." Jenny gently poked his chest. "Makes him the oldest grandchild."

"Baha!" burst out of Cabot and he hid his laughter behind both hands while his gaze flicked back and forth between his unamused father and very amused grandmother.

Jenny laughed with him and gazed affectionately at her son. "You always did hate being outdone by that. Tomas beat you to being a grandfather."

"Yeah, yeah." Carlos ran a hand through his knotty hair, making it even kinkier, and stared out at the busy Armidale night. "What happened to our house? And the car?"

"Barbara got the car. She and her husband needed one, so they bought it. We rented the house out for years until the noughties, I think, when rezoning meant a new redevelopment. The council bought us out and it was knocked down along with my siblings' old houses. You did see it the times we came back, though, and we've shown the kids."

"And most of the family have moved away," Carlos went on. "Our cousins all live in Queensland, or the central coast."

"It's only my brother and sisters who live here with a couple of grandkids and their families. The warmer climate doesn't appeal to them, so they live near each other on the same street."

"And Great-Grandma and Grandpa's old house?" Cabot asked. "And Grandpa's Greek relatives?"

"Both houses are gone. Remember we came and cleared out my parents' home when they died, you saw them then. The family voted, and all but *I* decided to sell regardless of all the memories we had.

That's where Spiros and I met. It held memories for us."

"I remember the two of you standing on the driveway pointing at all the spots you kissed," Carlos teased his mother. "You and Papa *got it on*."

"Silly." She giggled like a young woman in love and then the melancholy set in. "I guess we did. So many memories were there because that's all that remains. The houses are gone, so we can't go back and sit on the porch, or stand in the drive and reminisce, and remember back to when we'd kiss across the fence."

"Ooohhh, saucy, Grandma," Cabot joked.

"We *were* back in the day, so don't joke," Jenny said. "That was as saucy as you got outside marriage unless you had sex and got into trouble. Back in the day…" So much had changed, so much had gone, and while she didn't know how long she had left, she knew she had to teach her family all they needed to know for future generations. "Time marches on, Carlos. People come, and people go, just as we will one day. Your father and I before everyone else."

"Unless Cabot decides to get in first," Carlos muttered, shoving his hands back into his pockets and looking away.

"And now we come to *that* problem. Again!" Jenny noticed Cabot's hurt expression. "Spit it out, Carlos."

Another sigh left his gut. "It's just…all the estate planning we've done this year has brought it all back again. *All of it.* Alena, Tomas, all our friends, and what we went through with them, I *never* wanted to go through that again." He looked over his left shoulder at his son. "But you just had to *fuck* that up, didn't you? Everything we'd taught you, drummed into your skulls, *all* of your skulls, and Cabot still had to go and do what Cabot wanted to do." His brows furrowed deeply and he turned to face his son. "We nearly lost you, Cabot. Do you *really* understand, or comprehend, that?" Watching his son's face redden, he went on. "*We lost Tomas. Actually lost him. He was dead. He died.* So many friends died from fucking HIV and AIDS and we *never* wanted our kids to deal with that. *Ever.*" Tears poured forth and he wiped his face with both hands. "Argh! We *never* wanted to deal with that again. But you had to go and put yourself at risk and *contract it.* And then you try and kill yourself." He shook his head at his son's shame-filled face. "You tried to kill yourself, Cabot, and *that killed me* to the core. *And* your mother." He extended his arm and pointed at the reception hall as if pointing at Viv. "She was hurt so badly that she blamed herself for you trying to kill yourself. That it was *all our fault.*" Carlos gasped in air. "And it took Xanthe to convince us we'd done nothing wrong. That it was all down to you. *Every choice you made was down to you.*" Pacing back and forth, he glanced up at the night sky. "My son tried to kill himself because he contracted HIV. My other son, his twin, tried desperately to find him and stop him from doing it. That *scared* Antonio, *and* scarred him for life." He stared into Cabot's waterlogged face. "You scared us so badly, Cabot. We nearly lost you because you made an idiotic decision. And quite frankly," another head shake, "I've never fully gotten over it. *Losing my son.* That's a scar that never heals."

"You didn't lose me," Cabot sobbed and wiped his face with both hands, the identical action to Carlos.

"No. But I still could, couldn't I? If something happens and you get ill and your meds don't work anymore… Or you get another disease and the HIV turns into AIDS. I can still lose you, Cabot, and that fucking sucks." Carlos grabbed his son by the back of the head and pulled him into his arms. "I love you. I don't want to lose you because your HIV develops into AIDS."

"I love you, too, Papa," Cabot mumbled against his father's shoulder, his arms wrapped tightly around him. "And I don't want AIDS, either. I never did. But I'm safe, I take my meds every day, and watch my health the way Dan and Derek taught me. Tony and I both do."

Jenny watched them cry in each other's arms and wiped her cheeks and sniffed. Bringing the conversation back to its origins, she went on. "It had to happen, Carlos. Me handing the reins over to you, Pedro, and Tomas. Training the kids to take over your old roles in the business. It had to happen."

"I know, Mama. I just don't want you to die." Carlos pulled her into the hug and pressed his lips to her temple.

"I know, my baby. But just like Armidale, things change. And while I like coming here every couple of years to remember what was, and how your father and I started our home, our home has mostly been Mykonos. Especially after 1981."

"Yeah, it has." He kissed her cheek. "And it always will be now."

"Just be sure to bring the grandchildren back and tell them this is where their great-grandma and grandpa met and married, and where you were all born."

Carlos laughed and stroked her hair. "We will."

Cabot nodded enthusiastically and gave a crying hiccup. "Absolutely. Jennifer will know exactly who she's named after and where she's from."

"Good." Jenny nodded her assent. "Because, believe it, or not, she'll probably turn out just like you, and you turned out just like your father, who turned out just like his mama," she told them. "Although, now that I've told my and your father's story, there's definitely a stubborn Greek streak in both of you."

"I did happen to notice that Spiros junior was exactly like his father," Cabot said slyly through hiccupping breaths, noting his father's disdain at the name. "Took off for God knows where, doing God knows what, with God knows who at such a young age."

Jenny had snorted and burst out laughing at the name, remembering back to when Spiros had called Carlos that in the hospital.

"And that's exactly where you get it from, little boy." Carlos cuffed his ear. "You're just like me. *And I am not,* Spiros junior."

"Probably why you've never really got along," Jenny murmured thoughtfully. "Too much alike."

"Xanthe said that once, many a year ago in therapy." Cabot thought back. "That the two of you are like two peas in a pod and I'm the third, but I feel like I'm being pushed out. That's what she suggested my issue was."

"Oh, you had bigger issues than that, kid," Carlos told him. "*Much* bigger."

"Yeah, yeah, but I came good." Cabot put his hands up in surrender. "I'm a devoted husband, father, and uncle, and even though you may not believe it, a devoted brother, cousin, son and grandson." He put his best smile on, hoping to impress them.

"Yeah, yeah, so *you* say. I can still argue that Antonio's the better son." Carlos raised a brow.

Cabot pointed to it and grinned. "Just like Grandma."

"I should think so. I learned from the best." Carlos matched his grin and wrapped his mother in a hug.

"I think it's time to go in." Jenny motioned for them to move and they made their way back into the hall to find everyone milling around, taking photos, or videos, talking, laughing, and being a family.

"Ugh, I can't get Christopher to stop crying," Dom said to Davina. "Maybe he's got gas." He saw Cabot laugh at him and scowled.

"Not so easy, is it?" Cabot grinned.

"Now you're using Cabot's excuse from before, *real* original." Danté held out his arms. "Give 'im here." He took his nephew into his hands, much to Dom's surprise, and holding him up so he could look into his nephew's eyes, he said, "Stop crying at once, Christopher Spiros Stephanopoulos. You've been fed, watered and degassed, as well as changed, there's no need to cry, you're a Stephanopoulos, so no more."

Christopher stopped crying, staring in apprehension at the man holding him.

"What the hell…?" Dom muttered, staring at his brother in shock. And he wasn't the only one, as Danté never wanted to help out with his nephews, nieces, *or* cousins, and refused to change nappies, feed them, or look after them.

Danté spied his grandmother still standing with Carlos and Cabot. "Have you lot learned *nothing* from Grandma after all these years? Geez!" He noticed the twinkle in her eyes and beaming smile.

"Oh, well done, Danté." A stunned Cabot applauded and everyone else chimed in. "Well done. I'll have to hire you as a babysitter if you can do that for Jennifer."

"Pft! You couldn't afford me." Danté handed his nephew back to his still stunned brother and looked him in the eye. "Neither could you, so don't bother asking."

Dom huffed and shook his head. "Well…I'll…bugger!"

Carlos helped his mother back to her seat and kissed her cheek. He did the same with his father and then went into Viv's arms.

"Everything okay?" Viv asked, hugging her husband tight.

"We're fine," he replied, breathing in her scent.

Jenny sat watching her family while they turned to watch her. "I don't know whether this will be the last time we come here," she told her siblings as they crowded round. "At least Spiros and I. I have a feeling it will be, which is why we'll be staying through to probably May next year. One last birthday, one last anniversary with however many of you are still alive and kicking. But I know it won't be the last time my children come here. It's their birthplace, after all, and I hope that they continue to bring the grandkids here to see where their Australian side came from. The Marsh side. And…" She glanced at her grandchildren. "That you all bring your children and grandchildren here to show *them* where *their* history came from, for future generations to learn. And while I don't want to toot my own horn, maybe some sort of statue, or really huge monument that you'll dedicate to me, maybe a hall of fame, lots of photos, lots of videos of who we are and where we're from…" The twinkle in her eye gave her away.

"Grandma…" Cabot pulled a face. "Do you really want all that?"

"If it makes you remember me and your grandfather and where you come from, then absolutely," she said. "You're Marsh Stephanopouloses. It's in the blood for future generations to remember us by."

"Okay," Cabot agreed. "We'll let our children and grandchildren know about Spenny and where they came from." He tried to keep a straight face while waiting for her reply.

"Who and what?" Jenny asked, perplexed by the name.

"Spenny," Cabot explained. "Your celebrity couple name. Spiros and Jenny, Spenny." He looked over his shoulder at his grinning cousins and siblings. They'd made the names up years ago for fun, but never mentioned it. "Just like the great Carlos and Vivian are Carvian." He pointed to his confused parents and moved on to his laughing aunt and uncles. "Uncle Pedro and Aunt Angelina are Pangelina, or Pangie, whichever one you want to use. And Uncle T and Roger are Tomoger."

"Oh, goodness, what *do* kids come up with these days?" Jenny shook her head at the silliness.

"We'll do whatever it takes, Grandma," Diana said, getting back on topic and looking to her siblings and cousins for confirmation. "Whatever it takes."

"And we'll do what *we* can, Jenny. You're the eldest of all of us now," Barbara said.

"And we'll make sure our kids know who their relatives all are," Chris added, hiding a grin. "And who their cousins are. Except for Carlos, coz he's a yobbo as we all know."

Carlos reached over the back of his seat and cuffed Chris around the ear, but Chris retaliated and got Carlos in a headlock, pretending to punch him, making everyone laugh.

"That's good to know, my babies." Jenny glanced at her sisters and thought some things through. "You know, I never understood why Mum told me what she did. Told me that I needed to grow up and be an adult at thirty-nine. That being an adult meant making decisions and doing what was needed. I thought I already was, but I understood it later, come the '70s, especially after '77 with everything that happened. But I always vowed to never do what my parents did."

She gazed across her family. "My parents made us leave and never kept us close. But I didn't want to do that. I wanted my babies close, and kept you close while still giving you the freedom to do what you wanted, and you always came home and stayed. I raised you to love, honour, defend, and support each other, and that's what you've done. I did what my parents didn't. I kept you close while letting you fly, and look at all the careers you've got, the lives you live; *none of that* would be possible without the way Spiros and I raised you. Without the money to fund it, or without the drive that you got from us, none of that would have happened."

Her lips turned into a teary smile. "I love you all, my babies, and I am so glad you stuck around to share your journeys through this life with not only each other, but your father and me. If it's one thing I've learned, it's that home is where the family is, and I am *always* with my family. That's what Mum taught me. That I am the head of *my family*, just as my siblings are the heads of theirs. That's why Armidale hasn't been home in a long time. Even though it's where your father and I met and fell in love, married and had our children. *Our home is our family*, not a house, not a town, not a country. *Our family.* So remember that, always. And now," she grasped Spiros's hand and smiled, "I say we dance. Help your father and me up for our nightly dance." It was a tradition they'd continued to this day and would continue until their last.

Tomas, Carlos and Pedro helped their father out of his wheelchair and onto the dance floor with their mother, so he could dance with his Jenny.

"I love you, Spiros. Look at what we've made," Jenny whispered in his ear and looked over his shoulder at all of her family who watched them with loving smiles on their faces.

"Something wonderful and magical, my Jenny," he murmured back, gazing into her still bright blue eyes. "Something wonderful and magical."

About the Author

L.J. has been writing since 2006, when her first of many novels, *The Road To Vegas,* was born. In 2016 she created the *Porn Star Brothers* series about three sizzlingly hot Australian born Greek Island raised brothers who became the hottest porn stars in '70s America.

L.J. lives in Australia, loves '80s music, disaster movies, and collecting Jackie Collins books as Jackie is her inspiration and mentor.

L.J. Diva is the adult pen name for author Tiara King. You can find more about Tiara on her website; follow her on social media, or visit her publishing house, Royal Star Publishing.

 Socials

tiaraking.com.au/ljdiva

royalstarpublishing.com.au

Sign up for *Tiara's* Newsletter...

Make sure you're always in the know and never miss free exclusives, the latest news, book updates, and so much more with newsletters from...

tiaraking.com.au

Have you read these?

The Porn Star Brothers Series

Porn Star Brothers
Forever
Love Never Dies
Stefan: The New Generation
DeLuca
Spiros & Jenny
And Always

The Illicit Things Series

Her
Him
Madam X

A Novel Investigations Series

Designs in Crime
A Killer Plot
Murder on the Set
A Novel Investigation (omnibus)

Or these?

NOVELS

Burning Desires
Anything for You
Falling for London
The Road To Vegas
Hollywood Dreams
The Billionaire's Dirty Little Secret

SHORT STORIES

The Body
The Perfect Plot
The Star of Your Own Crime Scene